Fluidization behavior and liquid injection in
three-dimensional prismatic spouted beds

Fluidization behavior and liquid injection in three-dimensional prismatic spouted beds

Vom Promotionsausschuss der
Technischen Universität Hamburg

zur Erlangung des akademischen Grades

Doktor-Ingenieur (Dr.-Ing.)

genehmigte Dissertation

von

Swantje Pietsch

aus

Bremerhaven

2019

Gutachter:

1. Prof. Dr.-Ing. habil. Dr. h.c. Stefan Heinrich

2. Prof. Dr. ir. J.A.M. Kuipers

3. Prof. Dr.-Ing. Frank Kleine Jäger

Tag der mündlichen Prüfung:
20.12.2018

Bibliografische Information der Deutschen Nationalbibliothek
Die Deutsche Nationalbibliothek verzeichnet diese Publikation in der Deutschen
Nationalbibliographie; detaillierte bibliographische Daten sind im Internet über
http://dnb.d-nb.de abrufbar.
1. Aufl. - Göttingen: Cuvillier, 2019
   Zugl.: (TU) Hamburg, Univ., Diss., 2019

© CUVILLIER VERLAG, Göttingen 2019
   Nonnenstieg 8, 37075 Göttingen
   Telefon: 0551-54724-0
   Telefax: 0551-54724-21
   www.cuvillier.de

   ISBN 978-3-7369-9949-7
   eISBN 978-3-7369-8949-8

Preface

Die vorliegende Arbeit entstand während meiner vierjährigen Tätigkeit als Doktorandin am Institut für Feststoffverfahrenstechnik und Partikeltechnologie der Technischen Universität Hamburg.

An erster Stelle möchte ich mich bei meinem Doktorvater, Herrn Prof. Dr.-Ing. habil. Dr. h.c. Stefan Heinrich, dem Leiter des Instituts, für seine andauernde Unterstützung und Förderung bedanken. Durch ihn habe ich nicht nur viel über Feststoffverfahrenstechnik gelernt und in fachlichen Diskussionen neue Denkansätze zu meinem Forschungsthema bekommen, sondern auch die Möglichkeit erhalten, meine Ergebnisse auf internationalen Fachtagungen zu präsentieren und zu diskutieren. Seine Begeisterung für Partikeltechnologie und sein Enthusiasmus waren eine besondere Motivation für mich.

Ein großer Dank geht zu meinen Projektbetreuern bei der BASF, Herrn Prof. Dr. Frank Kleine Jäger und Herrn Dr. Michael Schönherr, für die zahlreichen fachlichen Diskussionen und Anregungen und die Fokussierung meiner Arbeit auf die industrielle Relevanz. Ich bedanke mich für die Forschungsaufenthalte und die Gestaltung des Feierabends bei Besuchen bei der BASF in Ludwigshafen.

Herrn Prof. Dr. Kleine Jäger danke ich ebenso wie Herrn Prof. Dr. ir. J.A.M. Kuipers, Leiter der Multiscale Modelling of Multiphase Flows Forschungsgruppe an der Technischen Universität Eindhoven, für die Übernahme der Zweitgutachten und dem damit verbundenen Aufwand.

Großer Dank gebührt meinen Kolleginnen und Kollegen am Institut für Feststoffverfahrenstechnik und Partikeltechnologie für die zahlreichen fachlichen Diskussionen, die Unterstützung und die tolle Arbeitsatmosphäre am Institut, die mich gerne zur Arbeit kommen lassen. Ein besonderer Dank gilt hier meiner langjährigen Bürokollegin und Freundin Jana Kammerhofer für die vielen witzigen Momente und Erlebnisse.

Ich bedanke mich bei Herrn Dr. Ernst-Ulrich Hartge für viele fachliche und praktische Ratschläge zu Versuchsaufbauten und die Übernahme von administrativen Aufgaben. Für ihr Engagement bei Umbauten oder Reparaturen der Versuchsanlagen bedanke ich mich bei dem technischen Personal des Instituts, Frank Rimoschat und Heiko Rohde.

Ein großer Dank geht an die vielen Studierenden, die in Form von Bachelor-, Projekt- oder Masterarbeiten oder als studentische Hilfskräfte zum Erfolg dieser Arbeit beigetragen haben. Hier möchte ich ganz besonders Paul Kieckhefen danken, der einen wesentlichen Beitrag im Bereich der Simulation geleistet hat.

Bei der Firma BASF SE möchte ich mich für die großzügige Finanzierung des Projektes bedanken.

Widmen möchte ich diese Arbeit meinen Eltern, Petra Sommer-Pietsch und Bernd Pietsch. Sie haben mich geprägt, mich immer unterstützt und ich weiß, dass ich mich immer auf sie verlassen kann. Dafür danke ich ihnen von Herzen.

Besonders bedanken möchte ich mich bei meinem Lebensgefährten Jan Braune. Seine andauernde Unterstützung, Fürsorge und unermüdliche Geduld mit mir sind für mich das größte Geschenk.

Abstract

The spouted bed technology was developed in 1954 by Mathur and Gishler (1955) when they failed in drying wheat granules in fluidized beds. In comparison to classical fluidized beds, which were developed 32 years before as gasifier by Fritz Winkler (Basu and Fraser, 1991), the flow pattern in a spouted bed is more structured. High gas velocities in the center of the process chamber cause a fountain-like spouting of the particles with a downwards movement along the walls. The technology has shown great applicability for particles which are difficult to handle in fluidized beds, as e.g. very small or very big or cohesive ones. For this reason, it has attracted interest for continuous operation in industry as e.g. by the industry partner of this research project, the BASF SE in Ludwigshafen, Germany.

Different apparatus configurations of spouted beds are nowadays available. In this thesis, prismatic spouted beds of different size were investigated as they have shown advantages in terms of up-scaling and process handling. The laboratory apparatus, named *ProCell*® *5*, was investigated in its original version and as transparent replica made of plexiglass, which allows for visual observation of flow patterns. By means of pressure drop fluctuations and high-speed camera recording, the stability was quantified in dependence on the particle bed mass, its composition, the gas volume flow rate and draft plates installed in the process chamber. All investigations were performed with spherical Gedart B particles. These were chosen as model systems due to the similar size to active agent particles used by the project partner BASF. In addition to experiments regarding spouting stability, the liquid injection for coating purposes was investigated and quantified among others by digital image analysis and optical coherence tomography (OCT). Both flow pattern and liquid injection were investigated using coupled CFD (*Computational Fluid Dynamics*) and DEM (*Discrete Element Method*) simulations. The models, parameters and the applied coarse-graining algorithm for handling high numbers of particles are described in detail in this work.

In addition to the characterization of the laboratory apparatus, a pilot scale prismatic spouted bed (*ProCell*® *25*) was operated in continuous operation. The main aim was the measurement of the residence time distribution (RTD) and the minimization of back-mixing between the different stages in the process chamber. For the determination of the RTD the tracer impulse method was used, whereby a new tracer production method by coating of bed particles with a magnetizable paint was developed. Different opening geometries in the plates, which separate the four chambers, were tested and validated regarding their influence on the particle transport and back-mixing.

Contents

Symbols

Latin symbols

a	projected area	$\mathrm{m^2}$
B	brightness	-
Bo	Bodenstein number	-
c	concentration	$\mathrm{kg\,kg^{-1}},\ \mathrm{kg\,m^{-3}}$
c	specific heat	$\mathrm{J\,kg^{-1}\,K^{-1}}$
C	dimensionless concentration	-
Co	Courant number	-
d	diameter	m
d_i	distance measure	m
D	dispersion/diffusion coefficient	$\mathrm{m^2\,s^{-1}}$
e	coefficient of restitution	-
e	error	$\%$
E, I, P	images	-
$E(t)$	exit age distribution	$\mathrm{s^{-1}}$
f	factor	-
F	frame	-
F_i	force i	N
$F(t)$	sum distribution of residence time	-
$\mathcal{F}$	Fourier transform	Pa
g	gravitational acceleration	$\mathrm{m\,s^{-2}}$
h	enthalpy	$\mathrm{J\,kg^{-1}}$
h	height	m
H	bed height	m
i	point	-
I	image	-
I_i	inertia tensor	$\mathrm{kg\,m^2\,rad^{-1}}$
j	y-intercept	-

J	empirical correction factor	-
J_{HS}	cost function	-
k	kinetic energy of turbulence	$\mathrm{m^2\,s^{-2}}$
K	kernel	-
K_{pf}	momentum exchange coefficient	-
L	length	m
m	mass	kg
M	torque	$\mathrm{N\,m}$
$\dot{m}$	mass flow rate	$\mathrm{kg\,s^{-1}}$
MV	measurement variance	-
$\dot{n}$	molar flow rate	$\mathrm{mol\,s^{-1}}$
n	number	-
N	number	-
Nu	Nusselt number	-
p	pressure	Pa
P	circumference of the particle projection	m
PV	process variance	-
q	density distribution	$-,\ \mathrm{m^{-1}}$
Q	sum distribution	-
$\dot{Q}$	maximum heat flux for evaporation	$\mathrm{W\,m^{-2}}$
r	radius	m
R	correlation coefficient matrix	-
$\mathcal{R}$	recurrence matrix	-
Re	Reynolds number	-
R_{pf}	momentum exchange between particles and fluid	$\mathrm{kg\,s\,m^{-3}}$
s	layer thickness	m
s	total deformation	m
S	surface area	$\mathrm{m^2}$
S,T	set of particle positions	-
$\mathcal{S}$	sphericity	-
SP	sphere	-
t	time	s
t	treshold	-
u	uniformity	-
u	velocity	$\mathrm{m\,s^{-1}}$
$\vec{u}$	particle displacement field	-
U	dimensionless velocity	-
v	velocity	$\mathrm{m\,s^{-1}}$

V	volume	m^3
$\dot{V}$	volume flow rate	$\mathrm{m}^3\,\mathrm{s}^{-1}$
w	width	m
w_c	cohesive energy per contact area	$\mathrm{J}\,\mathrm{m}^{-2}$
x	position on x-axis	m
X	dimensionless length	-
$x(t)$	input signal	-
$X(t_i)$	state at time point i	-
y	position on y-axis	m
$y(t)$	output signal	-
Y	Young's modulus	$\mathrm{N}\,\mathrm{m}^{-2}$
z	position on z-axis	m
Z	dimensionless length	-

Greek symbols

α	volume fraction	-
α_c	coating fraction	-
β	form parameter	-
γ	damping parameter	-
δ	coarse-graining scaling factor	-
ε	porosity	-
ε	rate of dissipation of turbulence energy	$\mathrm{J}\,\mathrm{kg}^{-1}\,\mathrm{s}^{-1}$
ζ	scale parameter	-
η	dynamic viscosity	$\mathrm{Pa}\,\mathrm{s}$
θ	dimensionless time	-
κ	spring constant	-
λ	coupling constant	-
λ	thermal conductivity	$\mathrm{W}\,\mathrm{m}^{-1}\,\mathrm{K}^{-1}$
μ_c	mean of coating fraction	-
μ_s	static friction coefficient	-
ν	Poisson ratio	-
ν_t	Eddy viscosity	$\mathrm{m}^2\,\mathrm{s}^{-1}$
ξ	Boolean state variable	-
ϖ	generalized cohesive energy per unit contact area	$\mathrm{N}\,\mathrm{m}^{-1}$
ρ	density	$\mathrm{kg}\,\mathrm{m}^{-3}$
σ	normal stress	Pa

σ^2	variance	Pa
σ_c	standard deviation of coating fraction	-
τ	shear stress	Pa
τ	hydrodynamic residence time	s
φ	friction angle	degrees
χ	fraction of coating suspension deposited on particles	-
ω_k	rotational velocity	$\mathrm{rad\,s^{-1}}$
ω	specific rate of dissipation	-

Indices

0	initial
aux	auxiliary
ax	axial
ctr	center
c	coating
cnt	count
cor	correction
col	column
CSTR	continuous stirred tank reactor
cyl	cylindrical
d	drag
disp	dispersion
drop	droplet
e	edge point
eff	effective
el	elastic
em	empirical
f	fluid
fluc	fluctuation
G	Gaussian
i	ongoing number
imp	impact
in	inner
j	ongoing number
k	ongoing number
l	ongoing number

l	liquid
lam	laminar
liq	liquid
mf	minimum fluidization
min	minimum
ms	minimum spouting
n	normal
p	particle
pos	position
post	post-processing
pre	preshearing
proj	projected
R	reactor
recu	recurrence
ref	reference
res	restitution
s	solid
sat	saturation
sh	shear
sp	square pixel
st	static
t	tangential
t	tresholded
turb	turbulent
T	tracer
v	vapor
w	wall
wb	wet bulb
x	x-direction
y	y-direction
z	z-direction

Abbreviations

CHT	circular Hough transform
CFD	Computational Fluid Dynamics
COR	coefficient of restitution
DEM	Discrete Element Method

FFT	fast Fourier transform
GUI	graphical user interface
KTGF	kinetic theory of granular flow
PIV	particle image velocimetry
PSD	power spectrum distribution
PTV	particle tracking velocimetry
ROI	region of interest
RTD	residence time distribution
SPE	Institute of Solids Process Engineering and Particle Technology
SST	shear stress transport
TFM	two-fluid model
TUHH	Hamburg University of Technology

1

Introduction

1.1 Spouted bed technology

Particles, which are difficult to handle in fluidized beds due to their size or surface properties, can be fluidized in spouted beds. The term *spouted bed* has been introduced by Mathur and Gishler in 1954 (Ernest and Mathur, 1957) to describe a type of dense-phase solids operation by which they could dry moist wheat particles which had caused slugging during fluidized bed operation. The spouting can be obtained with a gas or a liquid, whereby the fluidization quality with a liquid is reported as low (Mathur and Epstein, 1974). Therefore, spouting is mostly investigated with gas media and the research of this thesis is focused on the gas-solid process.

1.1.1 General process description

In contrast to fluidized beds the gas enters the process chamber via a slit or a narrow circular inlet instead of a distributor plate over the whole cross-sectional area. The smaller cross-section of the gas inlet causes high gas velocities that accelerate particles, which gives the typical spout pattern. Due to the increasing cross-sectional area with height and the decreasing gas velocity, the upward particle transport is decelerated and the particles fall from the mushroom-shaped fountain zone at the highest point of the spout along the apparatus walls back into the ground area, which is called annulus zone. From these zones with dense particle packing, the particles move again into the gas inlet area and the circulation cycle repeats. The flow pattern is more directed and less random than in fluidized beds as shown in figure 1.1, which results in improved heat, mass and momentum transfer. Because of the high gas velocities in the spout region and the resulting vigorous particle circulation, higher temperatures than in analogous

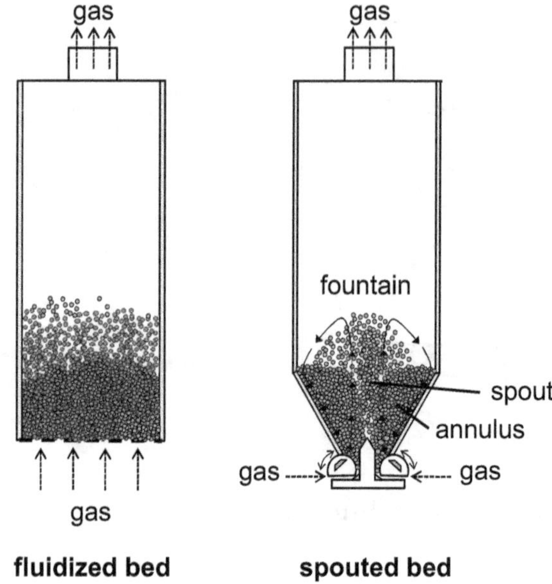

FIGURE 1.1: Comparison of flow patterns in a fluidized (left) and a spouted bed (right) apparatus.

fluidized bed operation can be used and the risk of single spots with high temperatures is reduced (Epstein and Grace, 2011). This is advantageous for drying purposes as well as for processing of temperature-sensitive material as e.g. enzymes, which usually must not exceed temperatures higher than 60 °C in order to avoid denaturing (Toole and Toole, 2008).

Since its invention different types of spouted beds have been developed, which are categorized as axisymmetric, asymmetric or slot-rectangular. The three-dimensional apparatus investigated in this thesis can be assigned to the category of slot-rectangular spouted beds and is often termed as prismatic. The apparatus geometry has been investigated intensively by Gryczka (2009) and Salikov (2017) in a pseudo two-dimensional variant in order to reduce the computational effort. The gas inlet in the present prismatic apparatus is realized by two parallel slits whose heights are adjustable by two rotatable, flattened cylinders (Mörl et al., 2001). By temporary decreasing the slit height, the gas velocity is increased which allows loosening of blockages without a stopping of the process. Besides the geometry of the apparatus, the flow pattern in a spouted bed and its stability depend on the gas velocity, the particle bed height and the properties of the bed and wall material. For a given geometry and particle type, a regime map can be obtained indicating the different spout regimes and their transitions. The spout regime is then dependent on the gas velocity: At low gas velocities, the particle bed remains static, which is termed as the fixed bed region. With increasing gas velocity, bubbles are formed that ascend to the bed surface. The regime of stable spouting is reached at the so-called minimum spouting velocity (u_{ms}). Here, the typical spouted bed flow pattern with its three zones, namely spout, fountain and annulus zone, can be observed. By further increasing the gas velocity the spout shows instabilities, which can be seen by lateral deflections and by variations in the bed expansion height. Mathur and Gishler (1955) created regime maps by plotting the bed depth against the superficial air velocity for example for Ottawa sand fluidized in a spouted bed column with a diameter of 152 mm. Salikov et al. (2015b) obtained a regime map for a pseudo two-dimensional prismatic spouted bed apparatus made of polycarbonate with 1.8 mm γ-Al2O3 particles. In their proposed dimensionless depiction the particle Reynolds number in the inlet slits is plotted against the ratio between the height of the gas inlet slit h and the static bed height H_{st}. The spouting stability was experimentally characterized and quantified by Salikov et al. (2015b) via observations with a high-speed camera and by fast Fourier transform (FFT) of pressure drop fluctuations measured with a high frequency pressure detector. Also Freitas et al. (2004), Chen et al. (2008), Piskova and Mörl (2008), Gryczka et al. (2009) and others used a Fourier transform of the bed pressure drop for analysis of the spouting stability in rectangular spouted beds. The power spectra obtained by Freitas et al. (2004) show a well-defined dominant frequency between 5 and 7.5 Hz as an attribute of the dense stable spouting in a slot-rectangular bed with a single vertical gas inlet. Gryczka et al. (2009) found a similar dominant frequency as a characteristic value of stable spouting in the prismatic spouted bed with two adjustable gas inlets (about 6 Hz). A frequency of around 6 Hz for the same prismatic apparatus was confirmed by Salikov et al. (2015b). Salikov et al. (2015b) could increase the range of stable spouting by inserting two parallel plates into the process chamber. They found that the area above the middle profile and the interface between the spout and the annulus zone are characterized by oscillations and spout deflections, which can be reduced by the plates. Luo et al. (2004) found the installation of draft plates in their investigated slot-rectangular spouted bed to result in an unstable "conveying-moving bed" after a bubbling and slugging regime. The installation of additional stabilizers in spouted beds has also been reported for other geometric types. Altzibar et al. (2008) reported a reduced fountain height and a higher drying efficiency with a conical spouted bed equipped with a draft tube. They found the minimum spouting velocity, the peak pressure drop and the operating pressure drop to be influenced by the geometric factors of the tube (Altzibar et al., 2009).

At high gas velocities, Salikov et al. (2015b) ascertained a second stable spouting regime with lower particle void fractions, namely the dilute or jet spouting, which had not been reported before. They recommended the dilute spouting regime for low to intermediate bed masses in large apparatuses due to the increased risk of particle elutriation and defined it promising for the stable spouting of very fine particles. Brandt et al. (2013) and Wolff et al. (2014) made use of the dilute spouting in a prismatic process chamber with a very large free-board zone for the granulation of µm-sized ceramic particles with a thermoplastic polymer in order to produce homogeneous composites with ultrahigh packing density. Similarly, Eichner et al. (2017) conducted spray coating in the dilute spouting regime of a specially designed prismatic apparatus with a large relaxation zone to achieve uniformly polymer coated µm-sized copper particles.

In fluidized beds the bed pressure drop increases linearly with the gas velocity during the fixed bed state until the minimum fluidization velocity u_{mf} is reached and fluidization is initialized. During fluidization of the bed, the pressure drop is constant and independent of the gas velocity. In case of a spouted bed, the pressure drop-gas velocity behavior is different. Again, the bed pressure drop is linearly increasing but after that a bed pressure drop peak occurs which is caused by first bubbles bursting the bed surface. Afterwards the bed pressure drop is drastically decreasing to a point at which spouting begins (u_{ms}). During stable spouting the bed pressure drop is almost constant but decreases when reaching the instable spouting regime.

Geldart (1973) classified particles according to their properties and the resulting fluidization behavior into four different classes from A to D. Group A particles have a particle size between 20 and 100 µm and a density below 1400 $\mathrm{kg\,m^{-3}}$. Beds consisting of this material expand considerably before bubbling occurs. Geldart group B includes particles in a size range between 40 and 500 µm with a density between 400 and 1400 $\mathrm{kg\,m^{-3}}$ and shows bubbling at the minimum fluidization velocity. Group C particles are small and cohesive powders with a particle size between 20 and 30 µm and are difficult to fluidize. Particles categorized into group D are large and/or dense particle powders which require high gas volume flow rates for fluidization. In this thesis, microcrystalline cellulose particles and alumina (γ-Al2O3) particles were investigated, both in a particle diameter range of around 500 µm with densities of about 1300 $\mathrm{kg\,m^{-3}}$ and thereby classified as Geldart B particles. For the alumina particles, additional studies were performed with particles of 1.8 mm and 3.0 mm size.

In contrast to fluidized beds no universal equations for the calculation of the maximum bed pressure drop or the minimum spouting velocity exist but a lot of correlations for different geometries are available, which differ in the particle range or bed geometry that they are valid for or in the properties that they take into account. Due to their quite broad range of bed geometries and particle properties the correlations by Olazar et al. (1992) for conical and cylindrical columns, respectively, are recommended for the estimation of the maximum pressure drop if the pressure drop at stable spouting is known [16]. For slot-rectangular spouted beds e.g. Rocha et al. (1995) and Mitev (1979) obtained correlations for the maximum bed pressure drop, where the column diameters in the equation of Rocha et al. (1995) are the equivalent diameters calculated from the rectangular area of the process chamber. The more general correlation of Mitev (1979) contains an empirical correction factor J, which depends on the geometry of the apparatus and the properties of the particle bed:

$$\Delta p = J g \rho_{\mathrm{s}} H_{\mathrm{st}} (1 - \varepsilon_{\mathrm{mf}})$$
$$\text{with} \quad J = 1.2 \quad \text{for} \quad H_{\mathrm{st}} < 180 \text{ mm} \quad \text{and} \tag{1.1}$$
$$J = 0.72 \cdot 10^{1.26 \cdot H_{\mathrm{st}}} \quad \text{for} \quad H_{\mathrm{st}} > 180 \text{ mm},$$

with the gravitational constant g and the porosity ε. For fluidized beds this correction factor is equal to 1. The minimum spouting velocity for cone-base cylindrical columns with a diameter smaller than 0.5 m is usually calculated by the equation obtained by Mathur and Gishler (1955):

$$u_{\mathrm{ms,cyl}} = \frac{d_{\mathrm{p}}}{d_{\mathrm{col}}} \left(\frac{d_{\mathrm{col,in}}}{d_{\mathrm{col}}} \right)^{\frac{1}{3}} \sqrt{\frac{2 g H (\rho_{\mathrm{s}} - \rho_{\mathrm{f}})}{\rho_{\mathrm{f}}}}, \tag{1.2}$$

where d_{p} is the particle diameter, d_{col} is the diameter of the column, $d_{\mathrm{col,in}}$ is the inner diameter of the column, H is the bed height and ρ_{f} the density of the fluid. For the dimensions of the investigated prismatic *ProCell* apparatuses and the used particle sizes, no correlation for the calculation of the minimum spouting velocity is known in literature. In addition, most of the known correlations for conical and cylindrical vessels were developed for column diameters of 61 cm or even smaller with reported problems in fitting the experimental results for higher diameters (Mathur and Epstein, 1974).

Since its original invention for drying purposes, spouted bed technology has been adapted for a wide field of applications. Most of them include an additional phase, namely a liquid phase, for agglomeration, granulation or spray coating (see figure 1.2). During agglomeration several core particles are connected by a liquid binder, whereas in spray granulation particle growth is obtained by solidification of liquid droplets around single core particles. The principle of spray coating is similar to granulation but much smaller layer thicknesses are desired. Particle coating is widely used in various industries, as e.g. for food, detergents and fertilizer processing or in pharmaceutical applications. The main challenge is the formation of a homogeneous layer without cracks and voids in order to protect the core material from the environment or to protect the environment from an unwanted release of the core material. Often, the coating is applied on active substances like pharmaceutical ingredients or enzymes, which should be released under and only under defined conditions as a certain pH value in the gastro-intestinal system or on agricultural fields. Besides the homogeneous distribution on the scale of one single

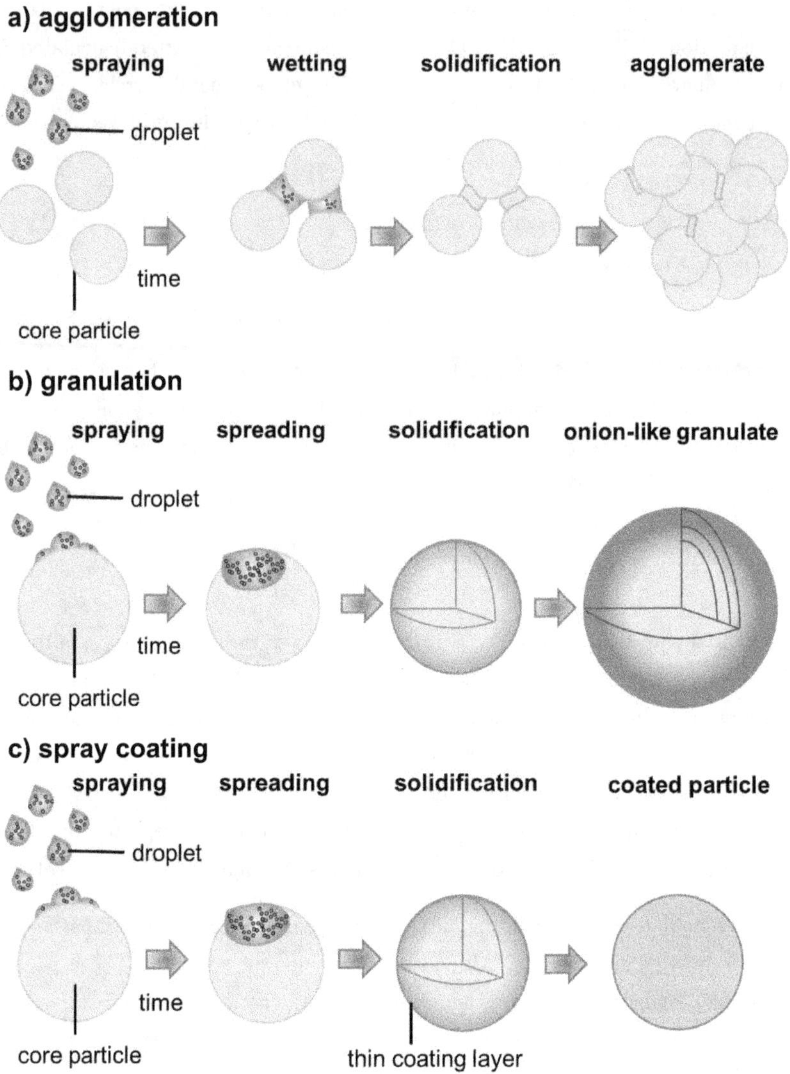

FIGURE 1.2: Principle of particle growth due to a) agglomeration, b) granulation and c) spray coating.

particle, the homogeneous coating of the entire particle bed in one production charge is a criterion of quality. Due to the high importance of the coating quality for product value, its measurement has been investigated with different tools within the last years. The methods can be differentiated into in-line, on-line, at-line and off-line procedures, whereby the in-line measurement is preferred as it allows a fast investigation without an interruption of the process (Knop and Kleinebudde, 2013). Classical measurement techniques are based on an external, non-real-time analysis: A representative sample is taken from the process at given time points and measured externally by e.g. electron microscopy or particle size analysis or by analysis of the time-dependent dissolution behavior. For example van Kampen et al. (2015) analyzed the coating quality of sodium chloride particles coated with maltodextrin in a fluidized bed process by measuring the dissolution rate of the core material. Klukkert et al. (2016) applied multispectral UV imaging to measure the tablet film coating quality of tablets produced in a pan coater. They could detect cracks on the surface and differentiate between homogeneous and inhomogeneous coatings. In general, the sampling has the disadvantage of a process disturbance due to the interception of particles by a sampling device. Additionally, human labor is needed and the analyzed particles have to be discarded, which increases waste and decreases process efficiency. Different in-line measurement techniques, as e.g. Raman or near-infrared (NIR) spectroscopy and their application in the field of particle technology have been described in literature within the last years. Romero-Torres et al. (2006) used Raman spectroscopy to quantify the coating layer thickness during pan coating of tablets with methylcellulose, polyethylene glycol and a blue fluorescent dye. By application of partial least squares calibration algorithm they were able to measure the layer thickness in an interval between 50 to 151 µm, which refers to the range of a linear relationship between the fluorescent layer thickness and the Raman spectral data. For measurement of smaller layer thicknesses a more detailed calibration work would be necessary as proposed by the authors. Recently, Barimani and Kleinebudde (2018) used Raman spectroscopy to measure the end points in coating processes with colored tablets. They used six differently colored coatings with pigments and/or dyes, whereby again some of them caused fluorescence and thereby interfering with the Raman signal. Similar to the work of Romero-Torres et al. (2006) different calibration methods were tested, whereby the partial least square algorithm led to the best model performance parameters. This algorithm was able to predict the endpoints of all coating experiments until a total coating time of 50 min, which was related to coating thicknesses between 21 and 38 µm. Lee et al. (2011) investigated a fluidized bed process for coating of pharmaceutical pellets, where they measured the layer thickness with NIR spectroscopy. They used external methods, namely confocal laser scanning microscopy (CLSM) and laser diffraction particle size analysis (LD-PSA), for the NIR calibration model. Layer thicknesses between 0 and 90 µm were detected. Even though deviations of CLSM and LD-PSA measurements occurred in the interval between 30 and 60 µm, both calibration models were found to have correlations with R^2 values exceeding 0.995. When an appropriate number of spectra was taken for averaging, the accuracy of the thickness prediction of NIR with the calibration models was greater than 99 %. Gendre et al. (2011) showed that real-time NIR measurements can be performed on non-finished drug products to predict the dissolution properties of the cured coated tablets, which is important in terms of quality criteria of sustained release coated particles. The study was performed with three different calibration models. Cahyadi et al. (2010) compared different non-destructive methods, X-ray fluorescence (XRF) as well as Raman and NIR spectroscopy, to quantify the thickness of tablet (6 µm size) coatings. For model calibration they used data from cut cross-section analysis with stereomicroscope. XRF was shown to be a useful method to quantify the amount of coating applied onto the tablet but errors in thickness measurements occurred. Both NIR and Raman spectroscopy were able to predict the non-linearity of coating thickness but only Raman was found to be capable of differentiating tablets coated under different conditions. May et al. (2011) introduced the terahertz pulsed imaging (MPI) measurement as a non-intrusive in-line measurement technique for coating thickness determination. By means of a waveform processing and analysis algorithm in Matlab, the data stream from the coating sensor was analyzed in real-time. The results from in-line measurements agreed well with off-line MPI data and with weight gain measurements. Nevertheless, the measurement time was with 9 min for one single particle time consuming and direct measurements of coating thickness were only possible with a minimum layer thickness of 40 µm. Recently, the application of optical coherence tomography (OCT) for coating layer measurement has been introduced. The method has been widely used for medical imaging but also other application fields were reported before (Stifter, 2007). For example the tomography method was used as quality control tool for paper characterization (Fabritius et al., 2006), silicon integrated circuits (Serrels et al., 2010) or fiber composites (Stifter et al., 2008). For tracking coating processes, it has been first introduced by Koller et al. (2011). Since then, the method has been successfully applied to coating processes in fluidized beds (Markl et al., 2015b), pan coaters (Markl et al., 2015a, 2014) or drum spray coaters (Markl et al., 2014). Optical coherence tomography is an interferometric approach, which makes use of the coherence properties of light in order to obtain depth profiles of investigated semi-transparent and turbid materials in a contactless and non-destructive way (Fercher, 2010, Wojtkowski, 2010). The generated cross-section images are obtained by measuring the magnitude and the time delay of light, which is reflected back from the sample. By using core particles and coating suspensions with different refractive indices, the layer thickness is accessible. It is also possible to characterize multilayer structures, whereby a minimum thickness of 10 µm is necessary as this is the resolution limitation. The algorithm in the work of Koller et al. (2011) has been implemented in the in-line OCT measurement unit used by Markl et al. (2015a,b). The system was kindly borrowed by this research group of Prof. Khinast from the Research Center Pharmaceutical Engineering (Graz, Austria) for experimental investigations on the applicability of the method for the regarded laboratory spouted bed.

1.1.2 Continuous operation

As all gas-solid processes, spouted beds can be performed in batch or continuous operation, whereby throughputs between 20 $kg\,h^{-1}$ and 10000 $kg\,h^{-1}$ are common (Glatt Ingenieurtechnik GmbH, 2006). In batch operation, the material is fed into the chamber before the process is started and is collected after the process has been stopped. Batch processes are mainly used for research, whereas in industry continuous operation with high productivity is preferred for efficiency. Continuous spouted beds are often of prismatic geometry configuration, whereby the scale-up from smaller scale is performed by increasing the depth of the apparatus. Pilot scale plants often consist of several stages, which are serially connected. With this configuration, different unit operations as e.g. granulation, coating and drying can be realized afterwards in one process. The series connection of unit operations in one plant requires a certain residence time of the particles in every single stage to ensure that for example the coating layer is of required thickness or drying is sufficient. Additionally, back-mixing has to be avoided as e.g. already coated particles should not return into the granulation zone but enter the drying area. In order to measure and adjust the movement of particles through continuous gas-solid processes, the knowledge of their residence time distribution (RTD) is of great importance. The residence time is defined as the time that a particle needs to get from the inlet of the apparatus to its outlet. For a general description of residence time behavior, ideal and real reactors are distinguished (Levenspiel, 1999). In case of ideal reactors, two defined border cases exist, the ideal stirred tank reactor and the ideal plug flow reactor (see figure 1.3). In ideal stirred tank reactors, a perfect micro-mixing is assumed resulting in a homogeneous concentration independent of the location in the apparatus at every time. In continuous operation, every particle has the same residence time in the reactor. Ideal plug flow reactors are based on the continuous flow of a flat profile, which results in concentrations that are depending on the location but independent of the time. Again, every particle needs the same time from inlet to outlet.

The behavior of particles in real reactors deviates from perfect micro-mixing and from perfect velocity profiles, which is caused by different flow velocities of fluids, dead zones and bypasses. As a consequence thereof, particles need different times to pass the process chamber. For quantification of the residence time behavior, exit age distributions are used. It is assumed that the flow is stationary and incompressible (ρ_f = const.), the transport at the in- and outlet is caused by forced convection and that the boundary condition closed-closed according to Danckwerts (1953) is valid. This condition means that a particle, which has entered the plant, is not able to leave it through the inlet again and that a particle that has left the reactor through the outlet cannot enter it again. For mathematical description of residence time behavior, the fraction of particles

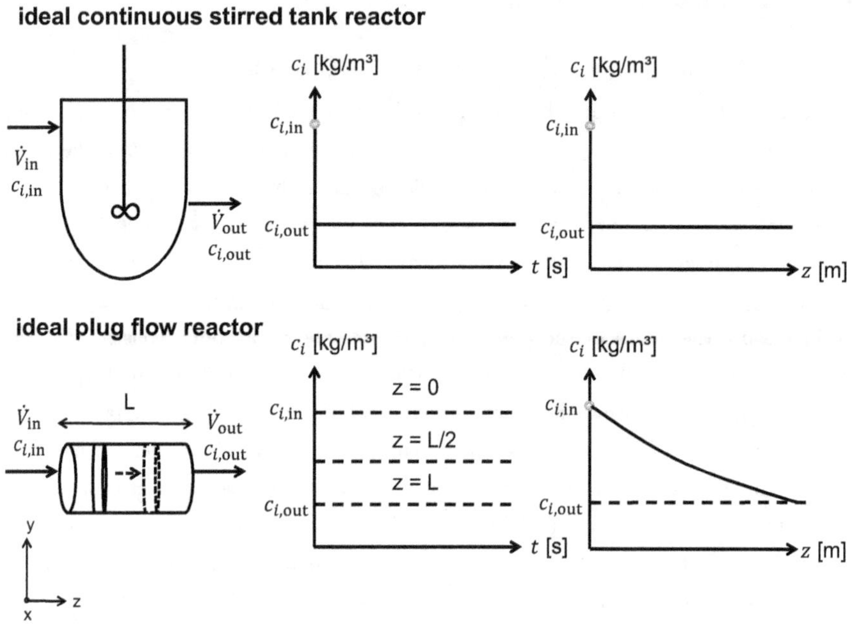

ideal continuous stirred tank reactor

ideal plug flow reactor

FIGURE 1.3: Time- and location-dependent concentration profiles of ideal reactors; top: ideal continuous stirred tank reactor (CSTR), bottom: ideal plug flow reactor.

leaving the reactor in time interval Δt is plotted against the time t, which results in the exit age distribution $E(t)$ with the unit s^{-1}. The dimensionless value $F(t)$, defined as $F(t) = \int_0^t E(t)\,dt$, gives the fraction of particles with a residence time less than t in the reactor, whereby after an infinitely long period all particles have left the apparatus:

$$F(t) = \int_0^t E(t)\,dt, \tag{1.3}$$

$$\int_0^{t_i} E(t)\,dt < 1; \qquad \int_0^{\infty} E(t)\,dt = 1. \tag{1.4}$$

The first moment μ_1 of the exit age distribution gives the mean residence time $\bar{t}$ of particles in the reactor:

$$\mu_1 = \bar{t} = \int_0^{\infty} t^1 E(t)\,dt. \tag{1.5}$$

If the density does not change and no dead volumes or bypasses occur, the mean residence time is equal to the hydrodynamic residence time τ that is calculated from the reactor volume V_R and the particle volume flow rate $\dot{V}_p$:

$$\tau = \frac{V_R}{\dot{V}_p}. \tag{1.6}$$

Due to variations in bed mass and particle throughput, the dimensionless residence time θ is often used for comparability, which is defined as the ratio of residence time and mean residence time:

$$\theta = \frac{t}{\bar{t}}. \tag{1.7}$$

The dimensionless time definition results then in dimensionless expressions for the density and the sum distribution of the residence time as shown in equations 1.8 and 1.9:

$$E(\theta) = \bar{t} \cdot E(t), \tag{1.8}$$

$$F(\theta) = F(t). \tag{1.9}$$

Besides the first moment of the exit age distribution from equation 1.5, which gives information about its position, the zeroth and second moment are used for characterization. The zeroth moment μ_0 is equal to the area under the curve and, analogous to equation 1.4, it has to be equal to 1:

$$\mu_0 = \int_0^\infty t^0 E(t)\,\mathrm{d}t = \int_0^\infty E(t)\,\mathrm{d}t = 1. \tag{1.10}$$

With the first (1.5) and second moment (1.11), the empirical variance σ^2, which gives the broadness of the distribution, can be calculated:

$$\mu_2 = \int_0^\infty t^2 E(t)\,\mathrm{d}t, \tag{1.11}$$

$$\sigma^2 = \int_0^\infty (t - \bar{t})^2 E(t)\,\mathrm{d}t = \mu_2 - \mu_1^2. \tag{1.12}$$

For experimental determination of the residence time distribution, usually tracer substances are used. The tracer is injected with the continuous flow at the inlet of the apparatus and its concentration $c(t)$ or a proportional signal $S(t)$, as e.g. the pH value, electric conductivity or fluorescence, is measured at the outlet:

$$E(t) = \frac{\dot{m}(t)}{m_0} = \frac{\dot{V} \cdot c(t)}{\int_0^\infty \dot{V} \cdot c(t)\,\mathrm{d}t} = \frac{c(t)}{\int_0^\infty c(t)\,\mathrm{d}t} = \frac{S(t)}{\int_0^\infty S(t)\,\mathrm{d}t}. \tag{1.13}$$

Generally, the experiments are based on the measurement of the system response to an applied disturbance by the tracer injection at the inlet. The injection can be conducted as impulse or step or periodically or stochastically. In this thesis, the impulse method is used, where the tracer is injected in a very small time interval Δt. In ideal case, this is a Dirac impulse defined as follows:

$$\int_{-\infty}^\infty \delta(t)\,\mathrm{d}t = 1. \tag{1.14}$$

In practice, the time interval Δt should be smaller than one percent of the mean residence time $\bar{t}$ (Baerns, 2013). Additional requirements for the tracer are the same chemical and physical properties (e.g. density) as the feed material. Furthermore, the tracer has to be inert, must not adsorb in the process chamber, it has to be detectable in small amounts and completely miscible with the feed material (Salami, 1968).

Experimental determination of residence times in gas-solid processes with different types of tracers has been performed for several decades, whereby most of the described methods in literature have been applied to horizontal fluidized beds. The methods include various stimulus response studies, radioactive, chemically doped and different sized tracer particles. Hull and von Rosenberg (1960) used radioactive Zr / Nb-95 adsorbed on a catalyst as tracer particles to determine the residence time distribution in a pilot scale fluid catalytic cracking process. Satija and Zucker (1986) measured the residence time in a 3.05 m × 0.305 m vibro-fluidized bed dryer with baffles. They used tracer particles coated with a dye, dissolved them after passing the fluidized bed and measured the dye concentration with a colorimeter at 500 nm. The group found the vibration amplitude to be the most important influence factor on the residence time. At high vibration amplitudes lower residence times were measured, which was explained by the bed height gradient along the length of the dryer. The height variation could be decreased by reducing the weir spacing from 61 to 30.5 cm. Nilsson and Wimmerstedt (1988) measured the residence time distribution for sand particles of three different sizes and for apatite granules in a horizontal fluidized bed with a length of 2.1 m. For sand experiments they used potassium sulfate crystals of the same particle size as tracer. The tracer concentration was determined by adding a certain quantity of taken sample to a defined volume of water and measuring the conductivity of the solution. For the experiments with apatite they colored some of the particles with yellow dye and determined the concentration of these tracer particles at the outlet by collecting and counting them. They performed about 60 experiments with varying bed flow velocity, particle size, superficial gas velocity and bed height. Their measured residence time distribution matched those predicted by the dispersed plug flow model, with the dispersion coefficient increased with increasing bed height, gas velocity and bed flow velocity and with decreasing particle size. Jacob (2010) used two types of phosphates with different pH behavior as tracer particles. He analyzed the pH value of the samples collected at the outlet and could determine the tracer concentration by means of calibration data. Idakiev and Mörl (2013) used γ-Al2O3 particles coated with iron powder as tracer material for measuring the residence time distribution in two continuous fluidized bed apparatuses. The type of tracer allowed a fast and easy separation by a magnet. Nevertheless, the iron coated particles were not proved regarding their applicability as tracer particles and the shown scanning electron microscope pictures suggest that the coating layer has a high risk of abrasion as the layer is not homogeneously distributed over the surface. No information about the tracer production is provided in the publication but it is assumed that the homogeneous distribution of the iron particle slurry on a bed of particles is difficult due to the required permanent mixing in the suspension. Idakiev and Mörl (2013) found the installation of weirs, their number and geometry as well as the air volume flow rate to influence the mean residence time. In another study Bachmann et al. (2016) derived a dimensionless correlation for predicting the Bodenstein number (Bo), which is a measure for the axial dispersion in horizontal fluidized beds. They found the correlation to match well own experimental data and data from literature. Nevertheless, for all used data, the exit age distribution was similar to that of a stirred tank reactor with a small delay at the beginning resulting automatically in a high coefficient of determination with the derived correlation.

Several mathematical models for the description of residence time distributions have been developed as e.g. the tank in series model, the segregation model or the dispersion model. The tank in series model was developed by MacMullin and Weber (1935). For the description of the distribution with this simple model, only the number of equally sized reactors and the mean residence time are required. In the theory of the axial dispersion model it is assumed that in a real plug flow reactor the flow of an ideal plug flow reactor is superimposed by axial dispersion, which can be described by Fick's first law. Bachmann and Tsotsas (2015) measured the residence time distribution in a horizontal fluidized bed with four chambers and tested three different models in order to determine the dispersion coefficients of different process conditions. They found the dispersion model to be again a better fit than the application of the method of moments or the tanks in series approach. The authors measured the residence time distribution experimentally by manually counting colored tracer particles in the sample. As this is labor-intensive work, the used tracer amount was small resulting in a low resolution of the data.

1.2 Numerical simulations

With simulations additional information on the microscale of the process that is not available in experiments is accessible and the number of often time-consuming experiments is reduced. Different simulation approaches with associated advantages and disadvantages are used for numerical investigation of gas-solid processes. They differ in the resolution and the treatment of the phases (continuum or discretized). The coupled CFD-DEM simulations, often termed as Euler-Lagrange method, is the state of the art for modeling of spouted beds (Rong et al., 2010, Salikov et al., 2012, 2015a, Yang et al., 2014). In this approach *Computational Fluid Dynamics* (CFD) describes the fluid phase by solving the Navier-Stokes equations. The solution of the equations can be performed by different discretization approaches. Concerning a spatial discretization the finite-difference method, finite-volume-method or finite-element method are often applied. In this thesis, the finite volume method is used to solve the Navier-Stokes equations. It discretizes the Navier-Stokes equations by dividing the physical space into a number of arbitrary polyhedral control volumes (Jasak, 1996, Versteeg and Malalasekera, 2007). The second tool of the CFD-DEM approach is the *Discrete Element Method* (DEM) for determination of the motion and forces of particles that makes use of Newton's equations. The tracking of each individual particle and its contact forces is an important advantage of DEM compared to pure CFD simulations (Euler-Euler or two-fluid model, e.g. (Duarte et al., 2009, Ozarkar et al., 2015, Sinclair and Jackson, 1989, Versteeg and Malalasekera, 2007)), because the bed dynamics can be analyzed on the scale of the single particles and important values, which can be hardly accessed in experiment as e.g. collision velocities or particle rotation, can directly be determined. When applying pure CFD simulations to a pseudo two-dimensional prismatic spouted bed, deviations from experiments in bed expansion height and solid fraction were reported (Gryczka et al., 2009). The CFD-DEM method however can be a powerful tool for design of tailor-made spouted beds for specific applications (Salikov et al., 2012). In recent years plenty of work has been done in the area of CFD-DEM simulations of fluidized beds or spouted beds or combinations of both (Bao et al., 2013, Fries et al., 2013, Heinrich et al., 2015, Liu et al., 2015). Nevertheless, most of the work was focused on axisymmetric spouted beds (e.g. Rong et al. (2010), Yang et al. (2014)) or on those with very small depth (pseudo two-dimensional) (e.g. Salikov et al. (2015a)) in order to reduce the computational effort.

When investigating applications as e.g. granulation or coating processes, an additional phase comes into play: the liquid phase in the form of droplets. In case of full CFD-DEM simulations, the droplets are simulated as an additional Lagrangian phase. When resolving the contacts of each and every droplet with particles or the wall and taking into account the heat and mass transfer, the simulation time and data generation is huge and difficult to manage. Different approaches for approximation have been described in literature. Goldschmidt et al. (2003) presented a DEM model with simple closures to describe the particle-droplet coalescence and agglomeration in a fluidized bed for spray granulation. They modeled particle contacts with a hard sphere model and assumed agglomeration every time a collision between wet spots on particle surfaces occurs. When colliding with a droplet the particle surface is partially wetted with a film of constant thickness, which is shrinking with time in order to account for the drying of the used binder. The model was extended by Link et al. (2007) for a spout-fluidized bed. Fries et al. (2011) conducted CFD-DEM simulations of different fluidized bed configurations used for spray granulation. They investigated the homogeneity of the liquid distribution by analysis of the residence time behavior in a biconical spray zone. They found the geometry of the Wurster coater to have the most homogeneous wetting behavior due to the directed flow regime. Recently, Sutkar et al. (2016) investigated a pseudo two-dimensional spout fluidized bed with liquid injection. The group implemented heat and mass transfer equations in their numerical model. In the approach, mass, volume and momentum are transferred from one droplet to the particle in case of a collision of both. It was assumed that droplets form a uniform layer around the whole particle after collision. They verified their simulations by analytical solutions and by comparison of experimental data obtained by visual analysis and by infrared thermography with the data from simulations.

1.3 Objective and strategy

Nowadays, almost 2,000 publications concerning "spouted beds" are available in the peer-reviewed literature database *Scopus* (Elsevier B.V., 2018). Nevertheless, former investigations were mostly focused on conical or cylindrical columns or on prismatic chambers with a small depth (pseudo two-dimensional) as they allow a faster process simulation due to the decreased number of particles. The aim of this PhD thesis was to investigate a three-dimensional prismatic spouted bed as the influence of the third dimension had been observed in previous studies but has not been investigated in detail before. Due to the good heat, mass and momentum transfer, the spouted bed is well known for processes with liquid injection. Thus, besides the characterization of the flow pattern, the applicability of the plant for coating purposes was investigated. As the regarded laboratory *ProCell® 5* apparatus only contains a small observation window in the front, a transparent replica made of polycarbonate was used to investigate the spouting behavior along the depth of the process chamber. Besides visual observations of the flow pattern with a high-speed camera, pressure drop measurements and particle tracking velocimetry (PTV) were used for quantification. In the experiments with liquid injection, the coating progress was tracked with high-speed camera and analyzed with digital image analysis, which gave qualitative results about the coating progress. In order to quantify the coating homogeneity and progress, a recently developed method for in-line measurement of coating layer thicknesses was first applied in a spouted bed.

The experimental investigations supplied macroscopic information about the flow behavior and the coating process. Nevertheless, no information on the microscale was accessible. Thus, for a better understanding of the flow behavior and of the particle-droplet interactions, simulations of the spouted bed process were performed in this thesis. Related to the improvement of computational power, the modeling of gas-solid processes has become more and more important within the last years. Most of the previous numerical investigations of spouted bed processes were based on Euler-Euler simulations, which handle the particles as continuum phase or considered pseudo two-dimensional models in order to decrease the computational effort. In this thesis, the three-dimensional apparatus was modeled and simulations were performed with CFD and DEM in order to describe the particle behavior and flow pattern in detail. With the improved numerical model the influence of the spouting stability on the liquid injection was investigated. By injection of droplets into the spouted bed, the progress of coating was calculated and the resulting coating homogeneity was compared for different process conditions.

In addition to the laboratory spouted bed, experiments on pilot plant scale in continuous operation were performed. To make the leap from laboratory trials to industrial applications, scale-up effects and the transition from batch to continuous operation have to be investigated. The *ProCell*® *25* pilot scale spouted bed plant consists of four chambers with each containing a two-fluid nozzle. This allows the combination of different unit operations (e.g. granulation, coating, drying) in one apparatus, which is advantageous in terms of high throughput and efficiency. For characterization of the flow pattern, a novel tracer method for the measurement of residence times was developed, which allows fast and reproducible measurements without waste of tracer material and without time-consuming tracer separation. To reduce back-mixing in the apparatus, plates with different opening geometries were inserted to physically separate the chambers. Dispersion coefficients for different process conditions were accessible for quantification and comparison by means of discontinuous back-mixing experiments.

1.4   Outline of the thesis

This thesis contains both experimental and numerical investigations. In chapter 2, the investigated apparatuses are described. Furthermore, different experimental setups for measuring the particle properties necessary for calculations and for calibration of the numerical model are presented. Additionally, the developed method for measuring the residence time in the pilot scale plant in continuous operation is described and the procedure for production of the tracer particles is specified.

Chapter 3 is focused on the numerical part of the thesis. In the first section, the used particles are characterized with the methods introduced in chapter 2. The obtained particle properties and characteristics were subsequently used in the numerical models, which are introduced in chapter 3. Details of the coupling between CFD and DEM are discussed and the most important mathematical correlations are introduced. The used coarse-graining approach, by which several particles are represented as parcels in order to decrease the computational effort, is presented in detail. The injection of droplets was realized in a post-processing step after the resource-intensive CFD-DEM simulations. The algorithm and its assumptions are also given in chapter 3. At the end of this chapter the results of an alternative simulation approach, the rCFD (*recurrence Computational Fluid Dynamics*) method, are presented after a short introduction of the underlying mathematical correlations.

Chapter 4 is dedicated to investigation of coating progress and flow patterns using digital image analysis. With particle tracking velocimetry (PTV) the velocities of single particles can be measured and with brightness analysis the color change of single particles during a coating process can be tracked. Both methods are described in detail.

In chapter 5 a detailed study of the experimental behavior of the laboratory spouted bed *ProCell®5* is given. In order to validate the numerical model, pressure fluctuations were measured and analyzed in frequency space using the Fourier transform in both experiments and simulations. Different drag models and turbulence models were tested regarding their representation of experimental behavior and a mesh independence study was performed. Several process configurations were investigated experimentally and numerically with the optimal models and quantified regarding their spouting stability. The stability could be increased by inserting two parallel draft plates into the process chamber, whose influence is shown in detail in the regarded chapter 5.

In the next part, chapter 6, the liquid injection for coating purposes is discussed. By running several simulations, the influence of the spouting stability on the coating homogeneity was quantified via the surface coverage of the particles and linked to the circulation frequency of the particles. Due to the high computational effort, only seconds of the process could be simulated by coupling CFD and DEM. To obtain information about a complete coating process, which takes several minutes, simulations with the rCFD approach were performed in order to check whether tendencies from the first few seconds are valid for a longer period as well. Besides the numerical analysis, experiments are presented in which digital image analysis and optical coherence tomography (OCT) were used for measuring in-situ the coating homogeneity and the layer thickness.

Chapter 7 examines a bigger scale and is focused on the pilot scale plant *ProCell®25* and its continuous operation. The residence time measurements for different transfer geometries between the four chambers are given and interpreted. By means of discontinuous operation it is shown which configuration is the best for the reduction of back-mixing.

Finally, in chapter 8 the main results of this thesis are summarized.

2

Experimental methods

2.1 Introduction

In this chapter the measurement methods and experimental setups required for determination of particle properties are shown in the first section 2.2. This includes particle size analysis, properties determining the collision behavior and experiments for characterizing the flow behavior. As the spouted bed apparatus is the central part of this research project, its operation principle and the applied configurations are described in detail for both, the laboratory plants and the pilot scale plant in section 2.3. After that, in section 2.4, the focus is set on the continuous operation and the developed tracer method. Additionally, definitions of the residence time distribution and its characteristic values are presented. The last section 2.5 is dedicated to methods applicable for measurement and validation of the coating layer thickness, its distribution and its quality. The in-line measurement system of optical coherence tomography (OCT) is presented as well as conventional off-line methods. Besides the OCT method, digital image analysis was applied for in-situ measurement of the coating quality. This approach is covered separately in chapter 4.

2.2 Particle characterization

In order to characterize the used material and to investigate the influence of the coating layer, the size, the apparent particle density and the envelope density of the particles were measured. For the DEM calculations, particularly the contact model, further detailed information on the mechanical material properties is required. Therefore, the restitution coefficient, the Young's modulus and the friction coefficient were determined in experimental setups that are also described in the following.

2.2.1 Particle size and size distribution

The knowledge of the particles' shape and their size distribution is of great importance regarding the assumptions made during simulations as e.g. an ideal spherical shape or a monodisperse system. Additionally, the size analysis allows the comparison of coated and uncoated particles and gives information about unwanted agglomeration or shape changes. Off-line size analysis with the *CamSizer XT* (Retsch Technology, 2018) was applied, which is based on an optical particle evaluation.

The measurement area is lighted by two strobe lights. As shown in figure 2.1 two cameras with different resolution (basic camera and zoom camera) are installed and track the shadow projection of passing particles, whereby bigger particles are recognized by the camera with lower resolution (basic camera) and small particles by the camera with higher resolution (zoom camera). The *CamSizer XT* can be used with different devices that transport the particles into the measurement area. For the investigations in this thesis, the free-fall device was used because the particles were free-flowing and not sticking. The free-fall channel vibrates with a certain intensity, which transports particles into the measurement zone. If cohesive particles, as e.g. small powders, are used, another channel with an additional supply of compressed air can be applied in order to avoid agglomeration or clustering of the small particles. Besides the size distribution, information about the shape, particularly the sphericity $\mathcal{S}$, is tracked. The sphericity is defined according to DIN ISO 9276-6 (DIN German Institute for Standardization, 2012):

$$\mathcal{S} = \frac{4\pi a}{P^2},\tag{2.1}$$

with a as the projected area of the particle and P as the measured circumference of the particle projection. For an ideal sphere the sphericity is 1 and for all other geometries it is below 1.

2.2.2 Apparent particle density

A helium pycnometer was used for measuring the apparent solids density ρ_s according to DIN EN ISO 2811-1 (DIN German Institute for Standardization, 2016a). The apparent density includes the volume of the solids phase plus closed pores within the particle. A gas pycnometer consists of two chambers of known volume. One chamber is filled with the particle sample and the fixed volume of the second chamber remains constant as reference volume. Additionally, valves for injecting the pressurized helium and a pressure transducer are installed. When helium is added to the system by opening the

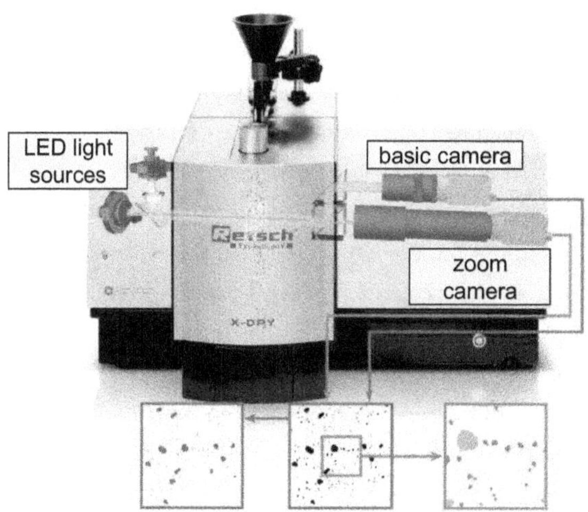

FIGURE 2.1: Measuring principle of *CamSizer XT* (according to Retsch Technology, Germany).

inlet valve, the resulting equilibrium pressures are used in conjunction with the ideal gas law to determine the apparent particle density ρ_s:

$$\rho_s = \frac{m_{\text{sample}}}{V_{\text{sample}}} = \frac{m_{\text{sample}}}{V_{\text{cell}} - \frac{V_{\text{ref}}}{\frac{p_1}{p_2} - 1}}, \tag{2.2}$$

with the mass of the sample m_{sample}, its volume V_{sample}, the known volume of the empty sample chamber V_{cell}, the volume of the reference chamber V_{ref} and the equilibrium pressures p_1 and p_2.

2.2.3 Envelope density

The envelope density ρ_p, in this thesis also named particle density, is needed as input parameter for simulations. It includes the external volume of a particle with the open and closed pores referring to DIN EN ISO 18847 (DIN German Institute for Standardization, 2016b). For spherical and monodisperse particle systems the envelope density can be calculated by the ratio of the mass of one single particle m_p to its volume V_p:

$$\rho_p = \frac{m_p}{V_p} = \frac{m_p}{\frac{\pi}{6} d_p^3}. \tag{2.3}$$

2.2.4   Restitution coefficient

The restitution coefficient is a measure of the energy dissipation during a collision of two contact partners and therefore an important parameter for the DEM calculations. When a particle collides with another particle or a wall, the contact partners compress and exchange their kinetic energy into internal stresses due to deformation during the impact. The reaction force resulting from the impact deforms the particle, which causes contact displacement or an overlap of the contact partners. In the following restitution phase, the elastic contribution of the impact energy, that has been adsorbed during compression, is released and accelerates the partners away from each other. The square root of the ratio of the elastic energy during restitution $E_{\mathrm{kin,res}}$ to the initial kinetic energy $E_{\mathrm{kin,imp}}$ is defined as the coefficient of restitution e. The equation can be simplified by the expression via the relative velocities v_{rel} of the contact partners 1 and 2. If only the coefficient in normal direction e_n is considered, it can be calculated as

$$e_n = \sqrt{\frac{E_{\mathrm{kin,res}}}{E_{\mathrm{kin,imp}}}} = \frac{|v_{\mathrm{rel},n,\mathrm{res}}|}{|v_{\mathrm{rel},n,\mathrm{imp}}|} = \frac{|v_{\mathrm{rel},n,\mathrm{res}} - v_{2,n,\mathrm{res}}|}{|v_{1,n,\mathrm{imp}} - v_{2,n,\mathrm{imp}}|}. \tag{2.4}$$

For the measurement of the normal restitution coefficient of the used particles a free-fall tester was used as outlined in Figure 2.2, which had been intensively investigated before (Buck et al., 2017, Crüger et al., 2016a,b). The particle is held by a vacuum tweezer at a defined height. The particle falls down onto the target plate after being released. The impact of the particle and the plate is tracked by a high-speed camera that is directly connected with a computer system. Image analysis with Matlab allows the determination of the impact and rebound velocities of the particle. As the plate is fixed, it does not have a velocity and the relative velocity in equation 2.4 is simplified to the velocity of the particle v_{p}. The restitution coefficient is material dependent and therefore only valid for the regarded particle and wall material. It was found by Crüger et al. (2016b) that for glass spheres with mean diameters of 0.91 and 1.74 mm the dry restitution coefficient is nearly independent of the velocity.

2.2.5   Young's modulus

The Young's modulus Y of the particles is determined from the force-displacement curves obtained by single particle compression tests with the device *Texture Analyser* (Stable Micro Systems Ltd, United Kingdom). The particle is placed between two plates. By downwards movement of the upper punch with a defined velocity u, the particle is compressed and the force-displacement curve is monitored until its breakage (figure 2.3). The distance between the two plates is defined as initial diameter of the particle.

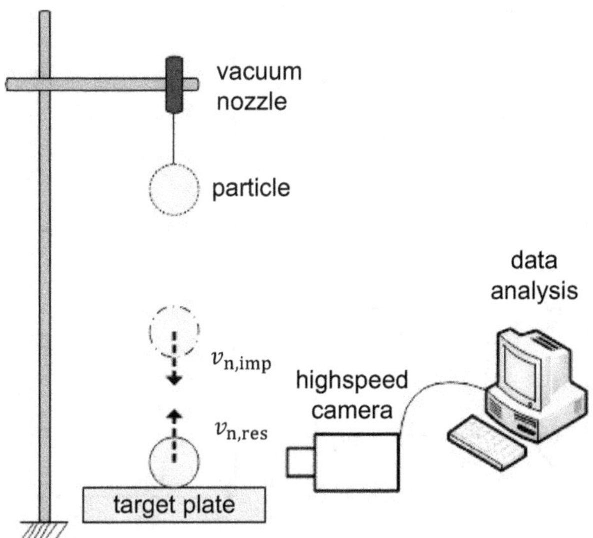

FIGURE 2.2: Experimental setup for the measurement of the normal restitution coefficient e_n.

In preliminary experiments, different load velocities were investigated with the present particle types (Antonyuk, 2006), whereby no influence of the collision velocity was found. The compression tests presented in this thesis were made at a velocity of $0.04\ \mathrm{mm\,s^{-1}}$. According to Hertz (1882) the nonlinear relation between the elastic contact force F_{el} and the total deformation of both contact partners s can be calculated as:

$$F_{\mathrm{el}} = \frac{2}{3}Y^*\sqrt{r^*s^3},\tag{2.5}$$

with the mean Young's modulus Y^* and the mean radius of both partners r^*. In case of a particle-wall contact, the radius of the plate r_{w} is infinite and can therefore be neglected:

$$r^* = \left(\frac{1}{r_1} + \frac{1}{r_{\mathrm{w}}}\right)^{-1} \overset{r_{\mathrm{w}} \to \infty}{\approx} r_1.\tag{2.6}$$

Then equation 2.5 can be simplified to

$$F_{\mathrm{el}} = \frac{2}{3}Y^*\sqrt{\frac{d_1}{2}s^3}.\tag{2.7}$$

By plotting the force-displacement curve with $6 \cdot \dfrac{F}{d^{\frac{1}{2}}}$ on the coordinate and $s^{\frac{3}{2}}$ on the abscissa, the mean Young's modulus Y^* can be determined as the slope of the curve in the elastic area. With this mean value and the assumption of a stiff wall ($Y_2 \gg Y_1$), the particle's Young's modulus can be calculated according to equation 2.8:

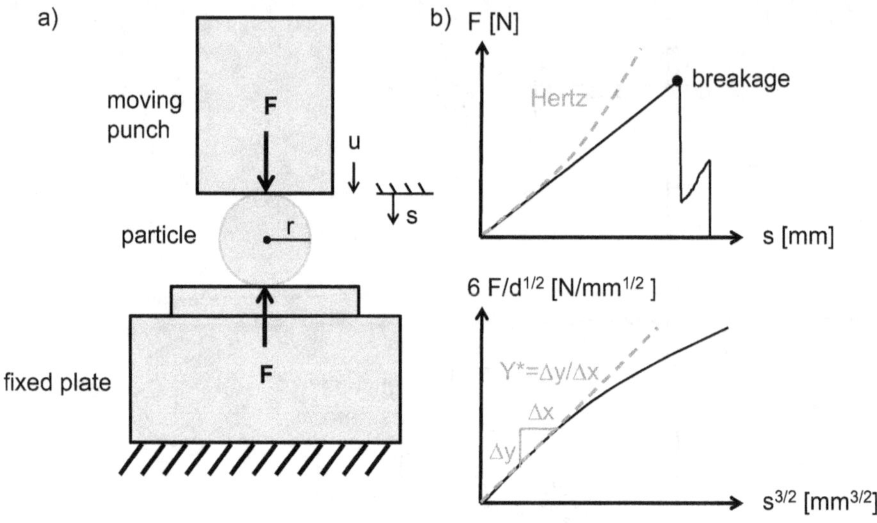

FIGURE 2.3: a) Measurement principle of the *Texture Analyser* (Stable Micro Systems Ltd, United Kingdom) and b) data analysis for calculation of the particle's Young's modulus Y.

$$Y^* = 2 \left(\frac{1-\nu_1^2}{Y_1} + \frac{1-\nu_2^2}{Y_2} \right)^{-1} \approx \frac{2}{1-\nu_1^2} Y_1. \tag{2.8}$$

2.2.6   Friction coefficient

The knowledge of flow properties is important in order to describe the flowability of solids and to evaluate their fluidizability. In order to determine flow properties, as e.g. the coefficient of friction, shear testers are used. In this thesis the ring shear tester *RST-XS.s* (Dr.-Ing. Dietmar Schulze Schüttgutmesstechnik, Germany) was applied, whose basic principle is shortly described here. The reader is referred to the book of Schulze (2008) for a detailed description of the flow behavior of solids and the measurement techniques.

When measuring the flowability with a shear tester, one obtains the yield limit of a consolidated bulk solid, which is also called yield locus. The shear test consists of two steps: The first step is the consolidation of the bulk solid, which is called preshearing, and in the second step the *shear* or the *shear to failure*, the points on the yield limit, are measured. For preshearing, the bulk is loaded in vertical direction by a defined normal stress $\sigma = \sigma_{\mathrm{pre}}$. Shear stress is induced by shifting the bottom ring and the lid laterally against each other. At the beginning of the shear, the shear stress often increases linear with time, which indicates that the bulk solid has deformed elastically. By a further increase of the shear stress, the slope of the curve becomes flatter indicating plastic deformation. Finally, at τ_{pre}, the shear stress remains constant even though the specimen is sheared further and the stationary flow regime is reached. The pair of values of σ_{pre} and τ_{pre} is plotted in a Mohr diagram. After the preshear procedure the shear deformation is reversed until the shear stress reaches zero. For the second step, the shear step, the normal stress σ_{sh} is reduced to a value smaller than that for preshearing ($\sigma_{\mathrm{sh}} < \sigma_{\mathrm{pre}}$). The consolidated material is again sheared and will start to flow, when a sufficient large shear stress is reached. Then the particles move against each other, which results in a decrease in bulk density, whereby the shear stress decreases. The maximum shear stress characterizes incipient flow and the corresponding pair of values gives one point of the yield locus in the Mohr diagram as shown in figure 2.4. The measurement procedure is repeated under variation of the normal stress to obtain the yield locus, while the identical normal stress for preshearing σ_{pre} is used. The yield locus is defined as follows:

$$\tau = \tan \varphi_i \cdot \sigma + \tau_c = \tan \varphi_i \cdot (\sigma + \sigma_z). \tag{2.9}$$

From the *shear stress-normal stress* diagram the internal friction coefficient μ_{st}, which is needed as input parameter for DEM, can be calculated as shown in Figure 2.4. The coefficient is defined as follows:

$$\mu_{\mathrm{st}} = \tan \varphi_i. \tag{2.10}$$

The shear cell allows the determination of the wall friction coefficient $\mu_{\mathrm{st,p-w}}$ by positioning a plate made of the wall material at the shear plane at the top of the bottom ring.

2.2.7 Minimum fluidization velocity

Even though the fluidization behavior in spouted beds differs from that in a fluidized bed and no universal or to the investigated prismatic spouted bed applicable correlation for the determination of the minimum spouting velocity exists, it can be approximated by an experimental setup with a fluidized bed (figure 2.5a). The minimum fluidization velocity u_{mf} in a fluidized bed is reached at that velocity at which the bed pressure drop remains constant after it has been linearly increasing during the fixed bed state in case of laminar flow ($Re < 2300$) (figure 2.5b). A laboratory fluidized bed made of plexiglass was used for measurement of the minimum fluidization velocity in this thesis.

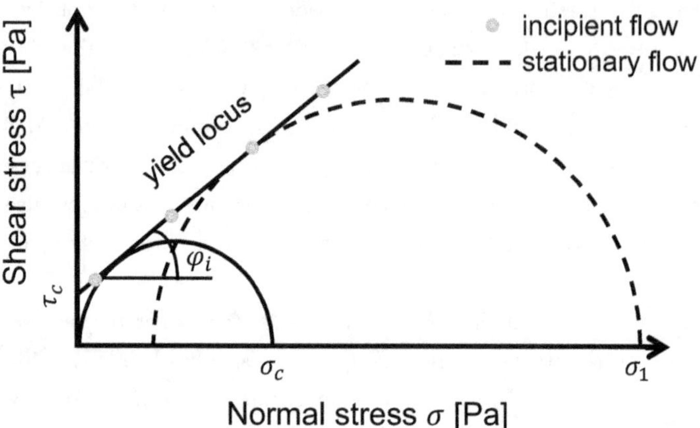

FIGURE 2.4: Exemplary yield locus plot (Mohr diagram).

The column with a diameter of 10 cm was filled with the bed material. The fixed bed should be fluidized and the gas flow should be interrupted as quickly as possible to ensure a uniform mixing of the bed. After that, measurements should be conducted with decreasing gas volume flow rates at at least five different gas velocities. The gas velocity is controlled via the gas volume flow rate.

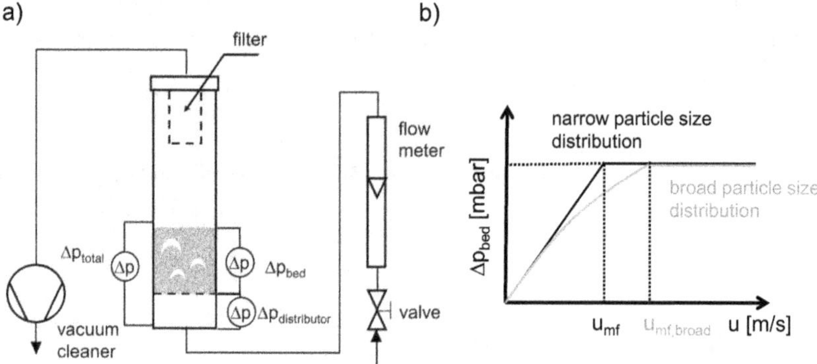

FIGURE 2.5: a) Experimental setup of measurement of minimum fluidization velocity in a column with a diameter of 10 cm at the Institute of Solids Process Engineering and Particles Technology, TUHH and b) dependence of the bed pressure drop on the fluidization velocity in a fluidized bed.

2.3 Spouted bed apparatuses

The investigated apparatuses have in common the three-dimensional prismatic geometry with a prismatic angle of 60°. The two commercial plants *ProCell® 5* and *ProCell® 25* are produced by Glatt GmbH (Germany). Both apparatuses differ in depth and length but also in their operating mode as the smaller one is mostly used for batch processes and the bigger one for continuous operation.

2.3.1   Laboratory spouted bed

According to the application and the bed material used, the *ProCell LabSystem* of company Glatt can be operated with different inserts: the *ProCell® 5* spouted bed insert, the *GF® 3* fluidized bed insert and an additional Wurster insert for the fluidized bed chamber (Jacob, 2009). In this research project the spouted bed configuration, termed as *ProCell® 5*, was investigated, which is shown with its geometry and an installed two-fluid nozzle in figure 2.6. The three-dimensional process chamber has a width of 250 mm and a depth of 200 mm. Typical batch sizes in this project were in the range from 1.0 to 2.0 kg bed material.

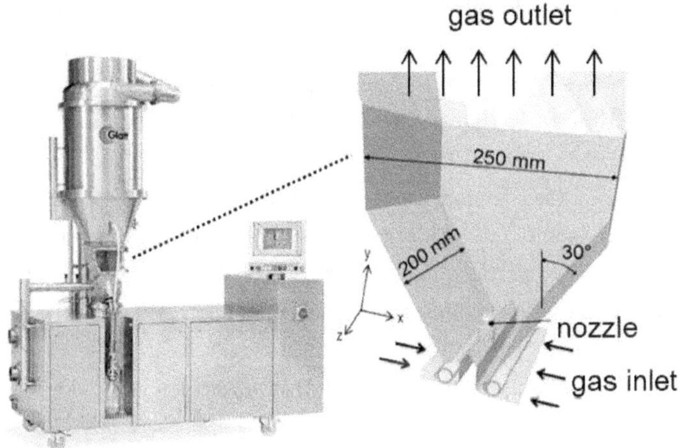

FIGURE 2.6: Laboratory spouted bed *ProCell® 5* (Glatt, Germany) with the geometry of the original process chamber.

The flowsheet of the plant is shown in figure 2.8. The entire process is controlled by a SPS system (Siemens, Germany), whereby all recorded process parameters are stored on a hard drive. The air coming from the environment is sucked through the apparatus by an exhaust fan. Before entering the process chamber, the air passes an electric heater. The air enters the process chamber through two adjustable horizontal slits with a maximum height h of 3.5 mm (see figure 2.7). By moving the rotatable cylinders, the inlet pressure drop and with that the gas velocity can be adjusted by reducing or increasing the height of the slits. In this thesis, all experiments were performed at a maximum slit height of 3.5 mm. Only in case of observed plugging, the velocity was temporarily increased

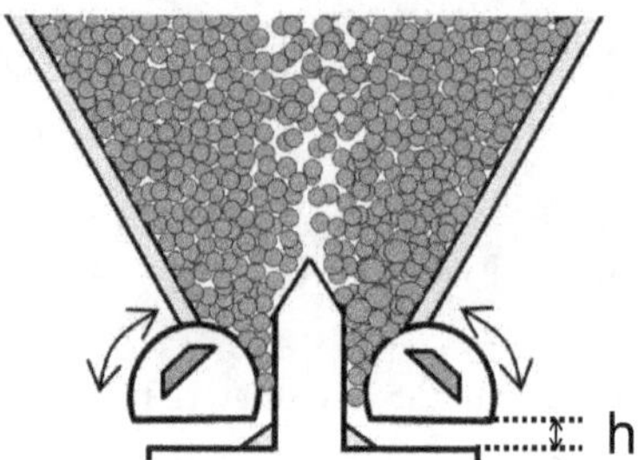

FIGURE 2.7: Movable cylinders for adjustment of the slit height h and thereby the
particle flow velocity.

in order to loose the blockage. In the expansion chamber above the process chamber
the gas velocity is reduced due to the increased cross-sectional area. The outlet air is
filtered by nine bag filters before leaving the plant. The plant is equipped with four
temperature sensors and four pressure sensors. The first temperature sensor TIRC2
is located directly behind the electric heater and protects the cartridge. The sensor
TIRC1 is located below the process chamber. The temperature in the process chamber
is measured by sensor TIR3 and for recording the temperature of the exhaust gas the
sensor TIR4 is installed. With pressure sensor DPIR1 the pressure drop of the inlet area
is measured and the sensor DPIR2 measures the pressure drop over the particle bed.
The pressure drop of the bag filters is measured with DPIRC1. It is possible to clean the
filters by pressing compressed air through the filters in defined time intervals. During
this cleaning procedure particle fine material is pushed back from the filters into the
process chamber. As this would result in agglomeration of the dust to the wet particles
in the chamber, it must not be used during coating processes. The integrated zigzag
sifter is applied during continuous spray granulation processes, when the product needs
to be separated from the fine material. As the increase in mass during coating is low
and the process is investigated in batch operation, the sifter was not used during the
described experiments. The specifications of the components and sensors of the whole
plant are given in the appendix.

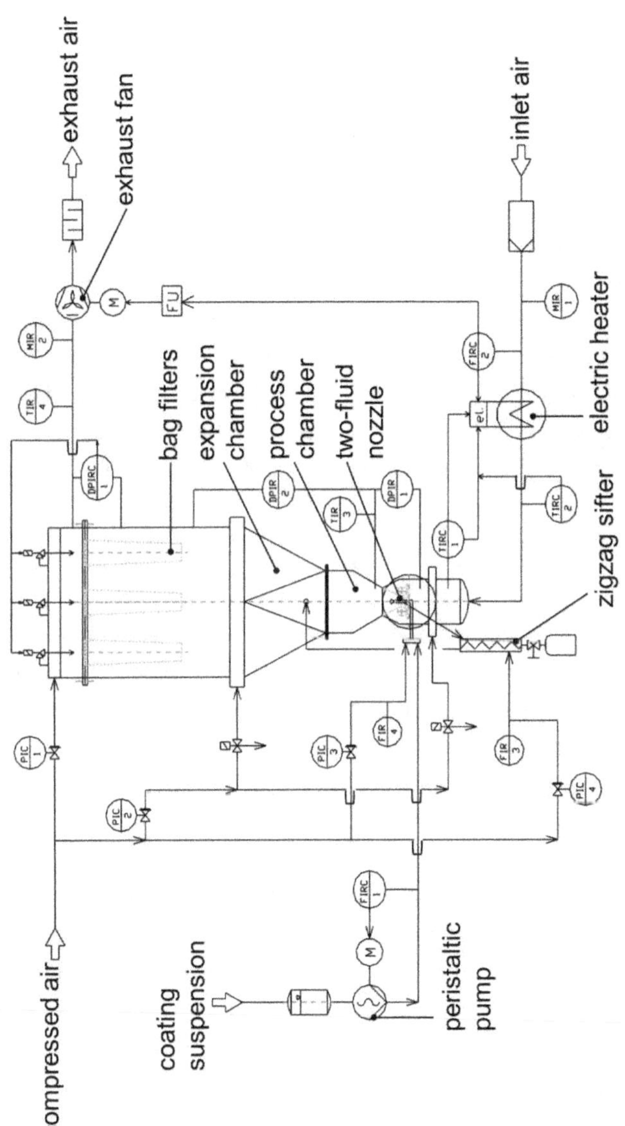

FIGURE 2.8: Flowsheet of the Glatt *ProCell*® *5* plant at the Institute of Solids Process Engineering and Particle Technology, TUHH.

2.3.1.1   Liquid injection

Besides experiments concerning the gas-solid flow behavior, the liquid injection for the coating process was investigated. The coating suspension was pumped via a peristaltic pump and atomized by the two-fluid nozzle *970-S4* (Schlick, Germany) in bottom-spray configuration. The use of hot plates allowed the preheating of the coating suspension, which could additionally be stirred in order to avoid demixing.

2.3.1.2   Sampling procedure

In order to monitor the coating process, samples were taken during the process via a sealed port in the process chamber, which is positioned 140 mm above the gas inlet. As the amount of coating suspension sprayed on the particles during the coating process is low, the change in the spouting behavior from uncoated to coated material is also low as shown in the measurements of the particle size distribution and density. Therefore, the process is still assumed as homogeneously fluidized and the taken samples are assumed as representative for the entire particle bed at the defined time point.

2.3.2   Laboratory transparent replica

As the observation window in the *ProCell®5* apparatus is small and only two-dimensional, a transparent replica (wall material *Europlex®*, Evonik, Germany) of the spouted bed process chamber was installed to visually observe the particle flow pattern. Analogous to the commercial apparatus, air is sucked through the apparatus by an exhaust fan (*SKG 420-2V*, Elmo Ritschle, Germany) that is controlled by a frequency converter. The particle motion was recorded by a high-speed video camera (*NX-S2*, Imaging Solutions GmbH, Germany) at a frequency of 100 fps. The pressure drop was measured with a high-speed differential pressure detector (*PD-23/8666.1*, Keller, Germany) in the freeboard zone above the particle bed. The sampling frequency in the experiments was with 400 Hz much higher than typical pressure oscillations in spouted beds. The gas inlet slits were fully opened for the duration of the experiment and only closed by moving the rotatable cylinders in order to loose temporary plugging. A flow chart of the experimental setup is shown in figure 2.9.

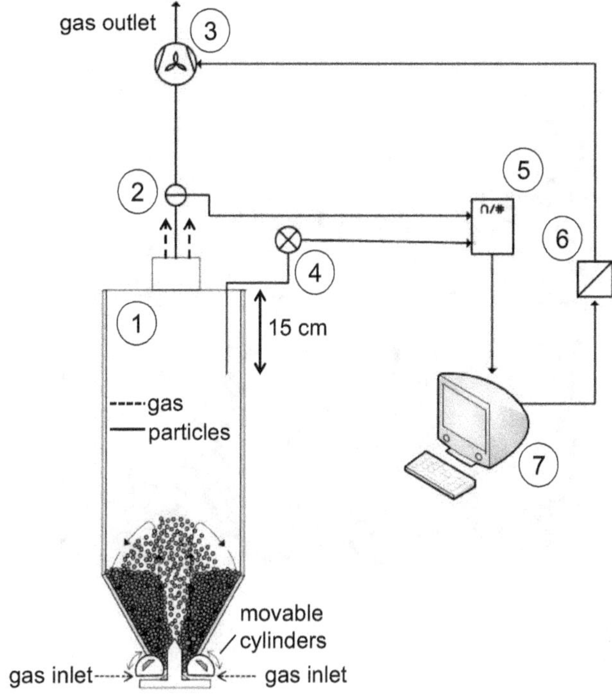

FIGURE 2.9: Flow chart of the experimental setup of the laboratory transparent replica:
1) apparatus, 2) anemometer, 3) fan, 4) high speed pressure detector, 5) analogue-to-
digital converter, 6) frequency converter, 7) computer.

2.3.3 Pilot scale spouted bed

The investigated continuous spouted bed *ProCell*® *25* (figure 2.10) consists of four
stages, whose gas volume flow rates and the gas temperatures can be adjusted individually. In the original configuration supplied by company Glatt the chambers are
not separated from each other. In every chamber a two-fluid nozzle is installed in bottom spray configuration. To conduct continuously operated granulation processes, a
grinding-classification circuit is installed as shown in the flowsheet of the whole plant
in figure 2.11. For the dry RTD measurements presented in this thesis the grinding-
classification circuit was not used and no liquid was injected. Nevertheless, in order to
prevent particles falling into the nozzle tip, nozzle air was used. For continuous operation of the plant, particles are inserted via a rotary valve that is connected with the
chamber via a tube at the right hand side above the bed (figure 2.12). The particles are
transported along the bed by the fluidization gas and leave the chamber on the left hand
side slight above the gas inlet slits through another rotary valve. For the measurement
of the residence time distribution of the particles in the process chamber, a novel tracer

FIGURE 2.10: Photo of the spouted bed *ProCell® 25* (Glatt, Germany) at the Institute of Solids Process Engineering and Particle Technology, TUHH.

method with magnetizable particles was developed as described in the next section 2.4.1. In order to compare different configurations of the chamber and to reduce back-mixing, plates with different transfer geometries were installed between the four chambers of the horizontal spouted bed. Experiments without separation plates were performed as a reference.

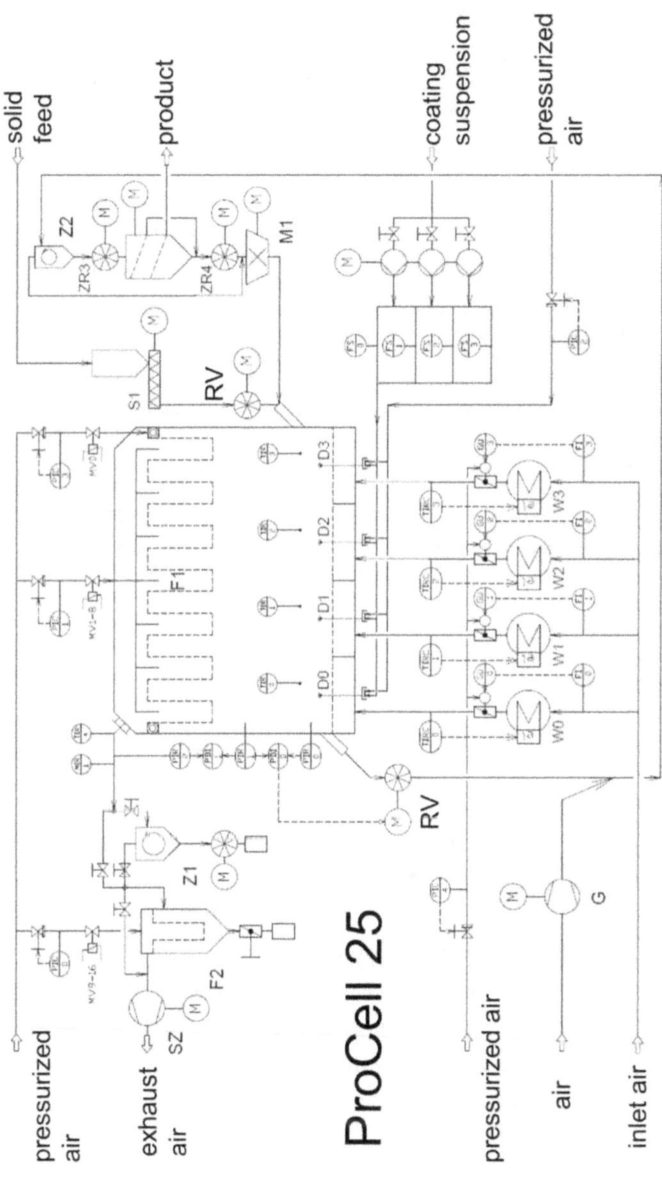

FIGURE 2.11: Flowsheet of the Glatt *ProCell® 25* plant at the Institute of Solids Process Engineering and Particle Technology, TUHH.

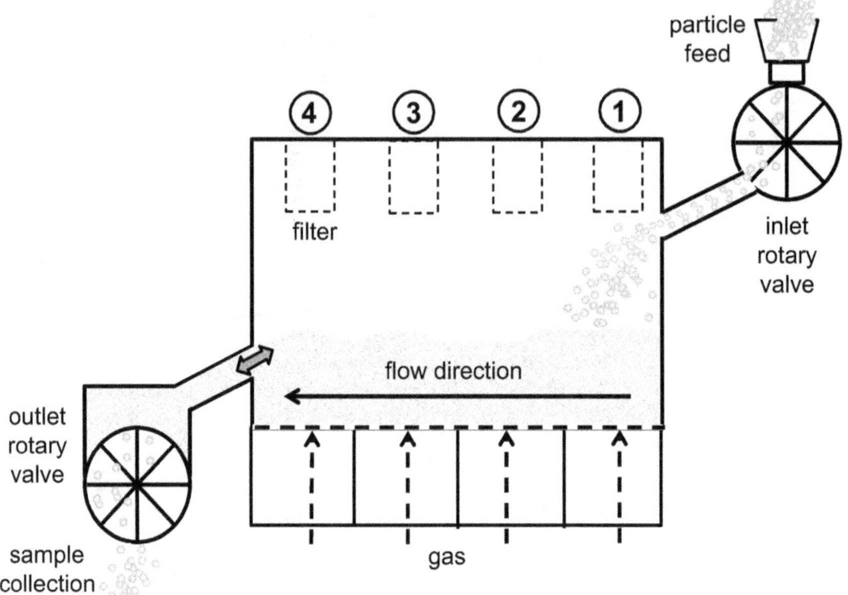

FIGURE 2.12: Schematic draw of pilot scale continuous spouted bed *ProCell® 25* (Glatt, Germany).

2.4   Residence time measurements

2.4.1   Tracer production

A marker substance (tracer) is used to track the particle flow through the horizontal spouted bed and to measure the residence time distribution. For the production of the tracer particles, the bed material for RTD measurements, *Cellets® 500*, was coated with the commercially available paint *Magneto® Grundfarbe* (Alpina, Germany), which is commonly used as primer for production of a magnet board on walls. The paint is a synthetic resin dispersion with water and fillers. It has a silver grey color and is completely mixable in water. The boiling point is at 100 °C and the paint has a density of 2400 kg m^{-3} at 20 °C. The elements sodium, aluminum, sulfuric and zirconium as well as the magnetizable metals titanium and iron were detected by the central laboratory of the TUHH via X-ray fluorescence analysis.

Tracer production was performed in *ProCell® 5* laboratory spouted bed in a batch coating process with a two-fluid nozzle (*970-S4*, Schlick, Germany) with a tip diameter of 1 mm installed in bottom-spray configuration. 1 kg of *Cellets® 500* particles was used as bed material. The gas volume flow rate was adjusted to 125 m^3 h^{-1}. The temperature in the chamber was set to 40 °C. The coating suspension was injected via a peristaltic pump at a flow rate of 5 g min^{-1}. Due to the high viscosity of the paint, it was diluted with 10 vol.-% water. The dispersion was preheated to 35 °C to further decrease the viscosity. Samples were taken at different times during the process and analyzed regarding their changes in properties and their magnetizability. Minimum coating amount was defined as the minimum mass of coating agent per kg particles, which is necessary to ensure that all particles of the batch adhere to a magnetic rod.

2.4.2 RTD experiments

All RTD experiments were performed with a bed mass of 10 kg *Cellets*® *500* in the spouted bed and additional 3 kg in the process volume of the outlet rotary valve. A gas volume flow rate of 125 m^3 h^{-1} was adjusted in every chamber. The particle flow rate at the inlet and the outlet was adjusted to 1 kg min^{-1}. Extensive calibration work was done before the experiments to ensure the applicability of the feeding and outflow method. It was proved that no abrasion of the paint occurs during passing the rotary valves and that the particles stay free of damage. Each experiment was started when steady state conditions were reached meaning a constant inflow and outflow of 1 kg min^{-1}. At a certain time point, defined as $t = 0$, the inflow at this very minute consisted of 500 g tracer and 500 g uncoated particles. Tracer injection was performed as fast as possible in order to obtain a short impulse. The outflow of each following minute was collected and used as one sample point for residence time distribution determination. The tracer particles were separated by a magnetic rod (*MTN 25/200 N* Sollau s.r.o., Czech Republic) and the weight in each sample was measured.

2.4.3 Analysis of the RTD measurements

The residence time distribution $E(t)$ (Danckwerts, 1953) is calculated from the amount of tracer in a sample i in relation to the total mass of tracer injected $m_{\mathrm{T,total}}$:

$$E(t_i) = \frac{\dot{m}_{\mathrm{T},i}}{m_{\mathrm{T,total}}}. \tag{2.11}$$

By means of the continuous mass flow rate of particles and the particle bed, the hydrodynamic or technical residence time τ can be calculated according to equation 1.6. In practical applications the residence time is distributed meaning that tracer particles are slower or faster than the hydrodynamic residence time. Not all tracer particles leave the process within the experimental operation time, meaning that the requirement of equation 1.10 cannot be reached as not all injected tracer particles are collected within the regarded time interval:

$$\int_0^{t_{\text{end}}} E(t)\,\mathrm{d}t < 1. \tag{2.12}$$

In order to solve this problem, extrapolation schemes can be applied. In this thesis, the extrapolation is performed with the 2-parameter Weibull distribution, which is defined as follows:

$$E_{\text{Weibull}}(t) = \zeta\beta(\zeta t)^{\beta-1}e^{-\zeta t^{\beta}}\,for \quad t > 0. \tag{2.13}$$

ζ is the scale parameter and β is the form parameter, with $\zeta > 0$ and $\beta > 0$. For $\beta = 1$ the Weibull distribution resolves to the exponential function. In order to fit the two parameters ζ and β to the experimental values, a Weibull mesh is constructed by a double logarithmic application:

$$\ln(-\ln(1 - (F(t)))) = \beta\ln(\zeta) + \beta\ln(t). \tag{2.14}$$

The parameter β is equal to the slope of the line when plotting the left side of the equation against $\ln(t)$. The second parameter ζ is obtained with the y-intercept j as:

$$\zeta = e^{j/\beta}. \tag{2.15}$$

2.4.4 Residence time models

As mentioned in section 1.1.2, the behavior of real reactors differs from the two ideal systems continuous stirred tank reactor (CSTR) with a homogeneous mixing at any location and plug flow reactor with its time-independent concentration at a certain location. Therefore, different models are used to characterize the real reactor systems. In this thesis, the cascade model and the dispersion or diffusion model are used to describe the residence time behavior and the mixing pattern in the horizontal spouted bed.

2.4.4.1 Tanks-in-series model

With the tanks-in-series (cascade) model, it is assumed that a real system can be described by a series connection of several connected stirred tank reactors with each of them ideally mixed and of the same size (figure 2.13). Additionally, no back-mixing between the reactors is possible. By means of the series connection, the input signal of the reactor i is equal to the output signal of the reactor $i - 1$. In general, the output signal $y(t)$ is connected to the input signal $x(t)$ by the convolution integral:

$$y(t) = \int_{-\infty}^{\infty} x(t - t')E(t)dt. \tag{2.16}$$

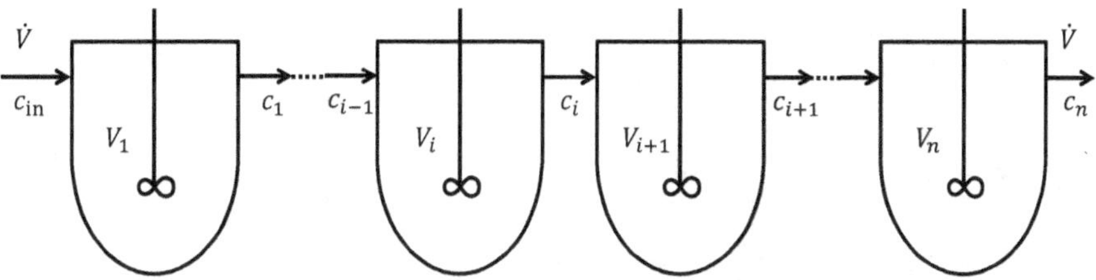

FIGURE 2.13: Cascade consisting of N ideal stirred tank reactors.

The residence time distribution $E(t)$ of a stirred tank reactor with a tracer injection as Dirac impulse is calculated by:

$$E(t)_{\text{CSTR}} = \frac{1}{\tau} \cdot e^{-\frac{t}{\tau}}. \tag{2.17}$$

If the output signal is convoluted with the residence time distribution of the second CSTR in case of a cascade, the total residence time distribution can be calculated according to equation 2.18 under the assumption that the reactors have an equal hydrodynamic residence time $\tau_1 = \tau_2 = \tau_i$:

$$E(t) = \frac{1}{\tau_i}\frac{t}{\tau_i}e^{-\frac{t}{\tau}}. \tag{2.18}$$

With the dimensionless time $\theta = \frac{t}{\tau}$ the residence time distribution function of a cascade with N reactors can be calculated to:

$$E(\theta) = \frac{N(N \cdot \theta)^{N-1}}{(N-1)!}e^{-N\theta}. \tag{2.19}$$

The hydrodynamic residence time can be determined as the product of the reactor number and the residence time of one single reactor:

$$\tau = N \cdot \tau_i. \tag{2.20}$$

The plot of the residence time distribution as a function of time gets more and more narrow with increasing number of reactors. For an infinite number, the residence time behavior approximates a plug flow reactor and can be detected as a δ impulse in the plot as shown in figure 2.14.

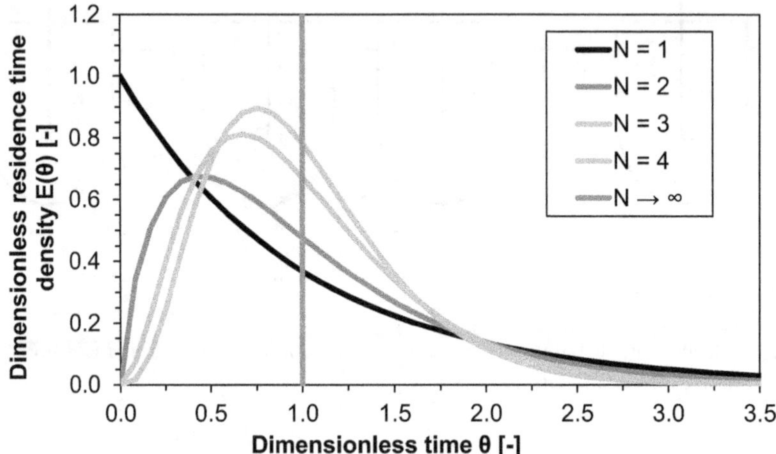

FIGURE 2.14: Plot of the dimensionless residence time distribution as a function of the dimensionless time for different numbers N of connected stirred tank reactors.

2.4.4.2   Axial dispersion model

The axial dispersion model is based on a plug flow reactor with ideal mixing in radial direction and superimposed axial dispersion of the material (Li et al., 2017). The dispersion is due to two different phenomena: 1. molecular diffusion for compensation of concentration differences and 2. deviations from ideal plug flow behavior caused by vortices and turbulent velocity variations (see figure 2.15). Both phenomena are linearly dependent on the concentration gradient and thereby the dispersion can be described analogous to the diffusion in Fick's first law (Atkins and de Paula, 2011):

$$\dot{n}_{\text{disp}} = -A \cdot D_{ax}\frac{dc}{dx},\tag{2.21}$$

with the axial dispersion coefficient D_{ax}, the dispersion flow rate $\dot{n}_{\text{disp}}$ and the concentration c. By means of the material balance after the impulse feeding of tracer material, the following expression is obtained, which is also known as the 1D Fokker–Planck equation (Risken, 1996):

$$\frac{\partial c_{\text{T}}}{\partial t} = D_{ax} \cdot \frac{\partial^2 c_{\text{T}}}{\partial x^2} - u_p \cdot \frac{\partial c_{\text{T}}}{\partial x},\tag{2.22}$$

with the tracer concentration c_{T} and the particle flow velocity u_p. For quantification of the ratio between convective and dispersive particle transport, the dimensionless Bodenstein number Bo can be used, which is equal to the product of particle velocity (u_p) and apparatus length (L_{bed}) divided by the dispersion coefficient (D_{ax}):

$$Bo = \frac{u_{\text{p}} \cdot L_{\text{bed}}}{D_{ax}}.\tag{2.23}$$

By using the Bodenstein number, the dimensionless time $\theta = \frac{t}{\tau}$ and a dimensionless length $X = \frac{x}{L_{\text{bed}}}$, a dimensionless dispersion model is obtained:

$$\frac{\partial c_{\text{T}}}{\partial \theta} = \frac{1}{Bo} \cdot \frac{\partial^2 c_{\text{T}}}{\partial X^2} - \frac{\partial c_{\text{T}}}{\partial X}. \tag{2.24}$$

In case of $Bo \to \infty$, the particle flow corresponds to an ideal plug flow reactor without axial mixing and a dispersion coefficient around zero. In the residence time distribution a narrow peak occurs. For ideal mixing and a dispersion coefficient tending to infinity, the distribution is broader and flatter as shown in figure 2.16. For an open-open system with continuity of flux at the boundaries, there is an analytical way to solve the dimensionless dispersion-convection-equation. In case of a closed-closed system, meaning that no entered particles can leave the apparatus via the inlet again and that no particles that have left the apparatus via the outlet can enter it again, there is no analytical solution available. Instead, the equation has to be solved numerically, which has been done e.g. by Bachmann et al. (2016), who proposed a new dimensionless correlation for prediction of the Bodenstein number by using data from their own experiments and from experiments of literature. Alternatively, the Bodenstein number can be calculated implicitly with the variance related to the dimensionless residence time, which is defined as:

$$\sigma_\theta^2 = \frac{\sigma^2}{\tau^2}. \tag{2.25}$$

For a closed-closed system, the Bodenstein number has a discontinuity at $X = 0$ and $X = 1$, as no backflow is allowed. Under this assumption, the Bodenstein number can be calculated with equation 2.26:

$$\sigma_\theta^2 = \frac{2}{Bo} - \frac{2}{Bo^2}(1 - e^{-Bo}). \tag{2.26}$$

2.4.4.3 Diffusion model

In the field of fluidized beds the application of Fick's second law is also common for description of the horizontal mixing. The diffusion coefficient is in this thesis termed as dispersion coefficient D_{ax}, which then includes again the molecular diffusion and the mixing due to flow behavior and is more suitable than the term "diffusion" when handling solids:

$$\frac{\partial c}{\partial t} = D_{ax}\frac{\partial c^2}{\partial x^2}. \tag{2.27}$$

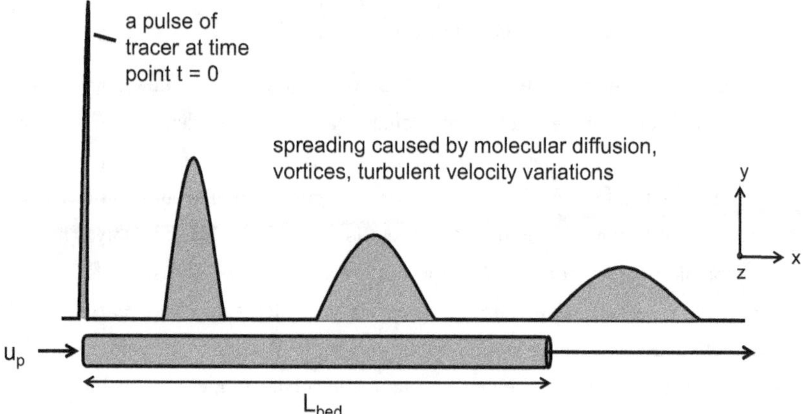

FIGURE 2.15: Spreading of tracer due to superimposed axial dispersion in a plug flow reactor according to the axial dispersion model.

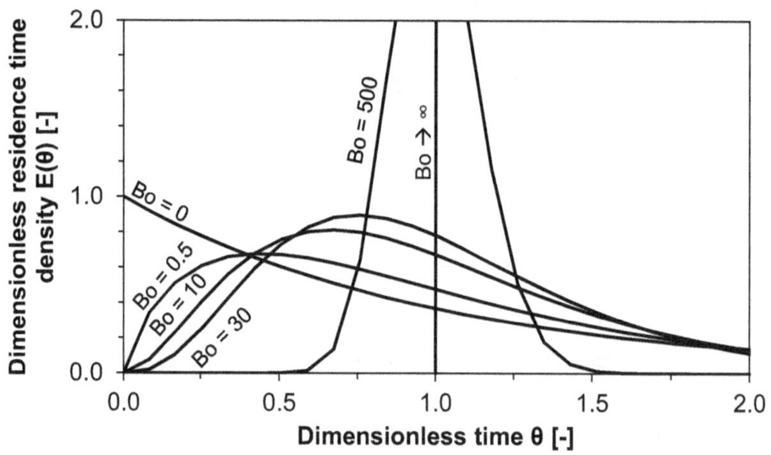

FIGURE 2.16: Dimensionless residence time density function for different Bodenstein numbers.

For applicability of the model, the boundary condition closed-closed has to be satisfied meaning that no particle transport through the in- or outlet is possible:

$$t = 0, 0 \leq x \leq L_1; \quad c = 1, \tag{2.28}$$

$$t = 0, L_1 \leq x \leq L_{\text{bed}}; \quad c = 0, \tag{2.29}$$

$$x = 0, x = L; \quad \frac{\partial c}{\partial x} = 0. \tag{2.30}$$

For the mentioned initial and boundary conditions, one obtains the following analytical dependence of the concentration on the dispersion coefficient:

$$c(x,t) = \frac{1}{2} + \frac{2}{\pi} \sum_{n=1}^{\infty} \frac{1}{n} \sin(\frac{n\pi}{2}) \cos(\frac{n\pi x}{L}) e^{-\frac{n^2\pi^2}{L^2} D_{ax} t}. \tag{2.31}$$

By fitting of equation 2.31 to experimental data with the sum of least squares method, the dispersion coefficient can be determined and used for quantification of different process conditions. In case of a continuous process, a small dispersion coefficient is desired in order to force the directed flow of particles by convection.

2.5 Analysis of coated particles

In order to evaluate the coating quality or even for quantification of coating layer thickness, different methods have been applied. For quality analysis, digital image analysis has been applied, which will be introduced in chapter 4 in detail. For the measurement of the coating layer thickness, the application of an optical in-situ method, namely optical coherence tomography (OCT), has been examined. Additionally, the coated particles were investigated externally with microscopic techniques for validation purposes.

2.5.1 Optical coherence tomography (OCT)

Optical coherence tomography is an interferometric method that makes use of the coherence properties of light in order to measure depth profiles of investigated semitransparent and turbid materials in a contactless and non-destructive way (Fercher, 2010, Wojtkowski, 2010). The generated cross-section images are obtained by measuring the magnitude and the time delay of light, which is reflected back from the sample. Different refractive indices of different materials affect the back reflection, which allows the investigation of multilayer structures with a spatial resolution of 10 µm. Optical coherence tomography has been widely applied for medical imaging but was also reported for a lot of other applications (Stifter, 2007), such as for quality control tool for paper characterization (Fabritius et al., 2006), silicon integrated circuits (Serrels et al., 2010) or fiber composites (Stifter et al., 2008). Additionally, several studies regarding the investigation of coating quality have been reported for measurements in fluidized beds (Markl et al., 2015b), pan coaters (Markl et al., 2015a, 2014) or drum spray coaters (Koller et al., 2011). Refractive index changes on both the air/coating and the coating/-particle interface occur due to the different refractive indices of the different materials. The depth of the coating layer is measured by comparing the time delays of single scattered photons to a reference light. A sketch of the measurement principle is shown in figure 2.17. For a detailed description of the OCT method, the reader is referred to the work of Markl et al. (2014).

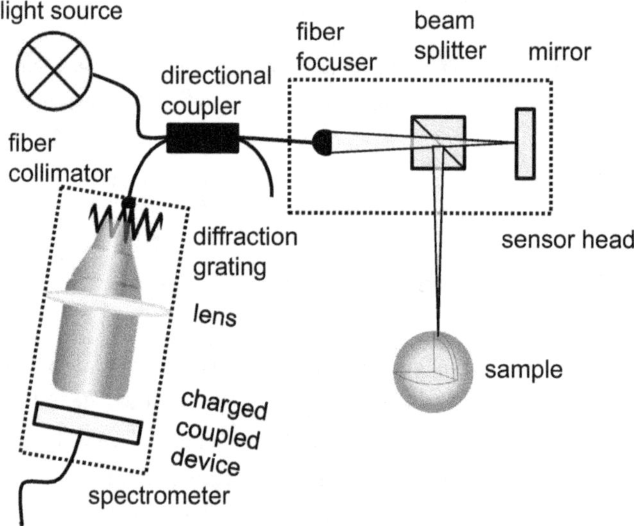

FIGURE 2.17: Sketch of the measurement principle of the optical coherence tomography method according to Markl et al. (2014).

The experimental setup including the spouted bed apparatus, the OCT system and the data processing unit is schematically shown in figure 2.18. The OCT sensor head was positioned on a metal stage in front of the observation window of the *ProCell*® 5 apparatus. The observation window is made of borosilicate glass with a thickness of 1.6 cm. In order to measure the refractive index correctly, the same glass was installed in the sensor head. Different positions of the OCT sensor in the area of the observation window were tested. A central position of the sensor head was found to track the highest number of particles during the process. The sensor head was connected via an optical fiber with the data analysis unit. The in-line measurements were carried out at different defined time points during the process with a minimum record time of 10 min and a

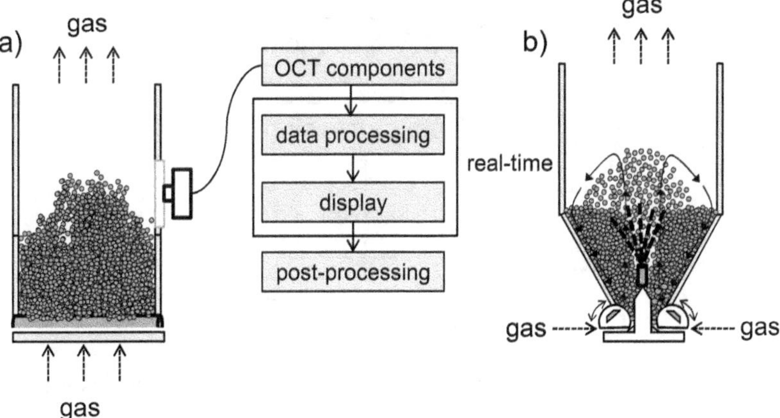

FIGURE 2.18: Experimental setup of in-line optical coherence tomography measurement in the laboratory spouted bed *ProCell®5* in a) side and b) front view. The sensor is positioned in front of the observation window made of borosilicate glass.

frequency of roughly 30 fps. The acquired measurements were displayed in real-time on the computer unit. The in-line measurement algorithm detects the coating layers, marks them by an ellipse and measures the layer thickness in its center. All images where a layer thickness is measured are stored as *positives*. Besides the positives, the raw data acquired in an interval of 1 s were stored allowing a later analysis with different settings. The stored images were further post-processed to validate the analysis algorithm. Particle samples were extracted at different time points during the experiment in order to perform off-line analyses for validation.

Besides the in-line measurement, off-line OCT measurements were performed for validation. Off-line measurements were conducted with the same OCT system and a rotary plate. A representative sample was placed on the plate and the rotation was started. The OCT sensor head was positioned few centimeters above the moving particles as shown in figure 2.19. Again, the images and the measurement of coating layer thickness were shown in real-time on the screen. The measured values were compared with the in-line data acquired at the corresponding time points.

2.5.2   Particle size analysis

To validate the measured layer thicknesses, off-line particle sizes were measured with the *CamSizer XT* as already described in section 2.2.1. The layer thickness was estimated as the difference between the mean particle diameter $d_{50,3}$ of the raw material and that of the coated particles. Besides the particle size, the mean sphericity $\mathcal{S}$ of the particle samples was measured.

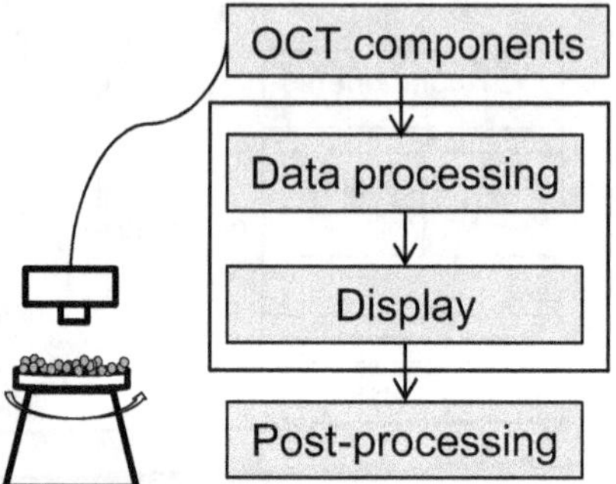

FIGURE 2.19: Experimental setup of off-line OCT analysis by applying a particle sample onto a rotary plate.

2.5.3 Theoretical growth model

Besides, the experimental determination of the coating layer thickness in the batch experiment, it was estimated by a theoretical growth model analogous to the calculations in the work of Markl et al. (2015b). As input parameters, the properties of the core material (Cellets®500 particles) and the coating suspension are needed. Under the assumption of an ideal spherical shape of the core particles, the mass of the core particle m_{core} can be determined via:

$$m_{\mathrm{core}} = \frac{4}{3}\pi r_{\mathrm{core}}{}^3 \rho_{\mathrm{core}}, \tag{2.32}$$

with r_{core} the radius of the core particle and ρ_{core} its solid density. The time-dependent particle mass $m_{\mathrm{p}}(t)$ can be calculated according to equation 2.33:

$$m_{\mathrm{p}}(t) = \frac{4}{3}\pi r_{\mathrm{core}}{}^3 \rho_{\mathrm{core}}\Big(1 + \frac{\dot{m}_{\mathrm{c}} \cdot x}{m_{\mathrm{p},0}^{\mathrm{bed}}} \cdot t\Big), \tag{2.33}$$

with mass flow of the coating suspension $\dot{m}_{\mathrm{c}}$, its solid content x and the mass of the initial particle bed $m_{\mathrm{p},0}^{\mathrm{bed}}$. Under the assumption of a spherical shape of the coated particles the mass of one particle is equal to that of the core particle plus the mass of the produced coating layer (Mörl et al., 2007):

$$m_{\mathrm{p}}(t) = \frac{4}{3}\pi r_{\mathrm{core}}{}^3 \rho_{\mathrm{core}} + \frac{4}{3}\pi (r_{\mathrm{p}}(t)^3 - r_{\mathrm{core}}^3)\rho_{\mathrm{c}}, \tag{2.34}$$

where ρ_{c} is the density of the solidified coating layer and r_{p} is the time-dependent size of the particle. Due to the small particles and the even smaller coating layer, the mass of one particle is not known. In order to calculate the layer thickness s_{c}, the coating and the particle mass are set into a ratio:

$$\frac{m_{\text{c}}}{m_{\text{core}}} = \frac{3s_{\text{c}}(t)}{r_{\text{core}}^3}\left(r_{\text{core}}^2 + s_{\text{c}}(t)r_{\text{core}} + \frac{1}{3}s_{\text{c}}(t)^2\right)\frac{\rho_{\text{c}}}{\rho_{\text{core}}} = \frac{m_{\text{feed,c}}}{m_{\text{bed,0}}}. \tag{2.35}$$

The ratio of the coating mass and the mass of one core particle is equal to the ratio of the total coating mass injected $m_{\text{feed,c}}$ and the initial particle bed mass $m_{\text{bed,0}}$. In the presented experiment, the suspension is sprayed in bottom-spray configuration and therefore in direct current with the particles. It can be assumed that a certain amount of droplets is sprayed against the apparatus walls or to the filters, which is indicated by the increasing contamination of the observation window with increasing process time. Therefore, the suspension mass deposited on the particle bed is reduced (Andersson et al., 2000), which is modeled by a fraction χ that is assumed to be constant in one batch. Under the assumption that the suspension is equally distributed on the whole particle bed, the distributed coating suspension can be calculated via the time and the spray rate $\dot{m}_{\text{c}}$ and the solids content x:

$$\chi\frac{m_{\text{feed,c}}(t) \cdot x}{m_{\text{bed,0}}} = \chi\frac{\dot{m}_{\text{c}} \cdot x \cdot t}{m_{\text{bed,0}}}. \tag{2.36}$$

By combination of equations 2.35 and 2.36 and under the assumption that no agglomeration, breakage or attrition occurs, the time dependent coating thickness is ascertainable:

$$s_{\text{c}}(t) = r_{\text{core}}\left(\left(\chi\frac{\dot{m}_{\text{c}} \cdot x \cdot t}{m_{\text{bed,0}}}\frac{\rho_{\text{core}}}{\rho_{\text{c}}} + 1\right)^{\frac{1}{3}} - 1\right). \tag{2.37}$$

2.5.4 Light microscope

For microscopic analysis of the coated samples, the light microscope *BX51* from company Olympus (Germany) was used. The device enables magnifications between 50 and 1000 x. In order to estimate the particle size enlargement due to the coating layer and to investigate its quality, the single particles were abraded in order to analyze the inner particle's cross-sectional area. A detailed description of the surface quality, as e.g. roughness, was not possible as the microscope does not supply a depth of focus, which means that only one depth can be focused.

2.5.5 X-ray microtomography

In order to measure the layer thickness of the particles and its homogeneity at the end of the coating process, they were analyzed with X-ray microtomography (μ-CT). The principle uses X-rays to create cross-sections of the analyzed object (figure 2.20). As the method is repeated at different heights in several slides, the object can be recreated as 3D-model. The method has been widely applied in medicine but is also used for biomedical investigations, food, fossils or particle characterization. The used model μCT *35* (Scanco medical, Switzerland) works with a small-angle-cone-beam. The slice thickness can be varied between 3.5 and 70 µm with a nominal resolution in the same range.

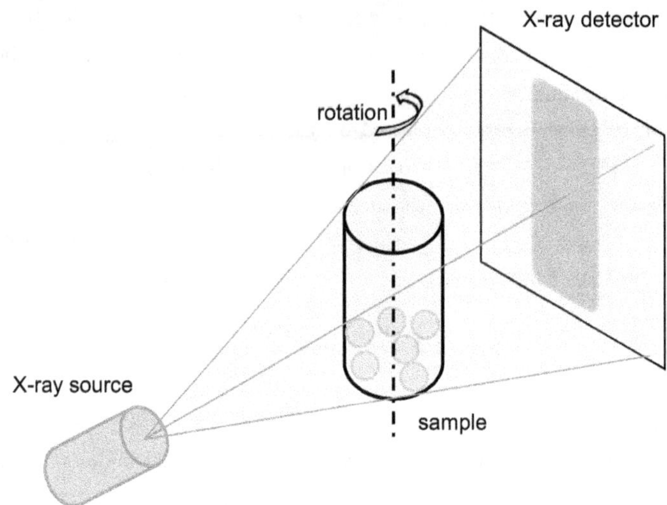

FIGURE 2.20: Sketch of the measurement principle of X-ray microtomography.

3

Fundamentals of numerical simulations

3.1 Introduction

The coupling of *Computational Fluid Dynamics* (CFD) and *Discrete Element Method* (DEM) is the state of the art in the numerical investigation of gas-solid processes. Experiments on laboratory or pilot plant scale offer often only limited information concerning the particle behavior as the size of the observation windows is small and the central part of the process chamber is not accessible. Additionally, most measurement methods are intrusive and disturb the flow behavior. Non-intrusive methods are often expensive and again limited to provide information in only two dimensions. In contrast, simulations present a powerful tool for studying the influence of process parameters on the performance and stability of the fluidization behavior. The simulations require a detailed characterization of the particles. This is presented in section 3.2 according to the experimental setups described in chapter 2. Coupling of CFD and DEM, termed as Euler-Lagrange simulations in contrast to pure CFD Euler-Euler simulations, gives information on the scale of single particles as each and every particle is tracked and involved in the calculation of forces and velocities. The approach resolves the contact between particles through contact laws, as described by Cundall and Strack (1979). The calculation of the particles' behavior is based on solving Newton's equations of motion, whereas the fluid phase is described by solving the volume-averaged Navier-Stokes equations. The underlying equations and the coupling of both tools are described in section 3.3. Due to the increasing computational power it is nowadays possible to conduct simulations with 10^6 particles on a common desktop computer and with access to clusters even 10^9 particles can be calculated. As the number of particles in most industrial applications and also on pilot plant scale is much higher, coarse-graining approaches are applied. In this thesis, particle coarsening is performed by which several particles are clustered as parcels as described in section 3.3.1. To validate the numerical data, the Fourier transforms of the pressure drop signals measured in experiments and simulations were compared. The basic principle is described in section 3.5.1.

The investigated coating process includes the injection of droplets into the gas-solid phase, thus an additional phase needs to be included. As the liquid loading during the regarded coating process is low, the injection of droplets was performed after the CFD-DEM simulations in a post-processing step. The implementation is described in detail in section 3.4. With the help of a statistical approach, the surface coverage of particles with liquid was calculated and compared for different process configurations. As the surface coverage of the particles is highly dependent on the residence time of particles in the spray zone and on the spouting stability, the residence time and circulation frequencies were calculated from the numerical data as described in subsection 3.5.2. In the last subchapter of this simulation part, a short introduction into the *recurrence Computational Fluid Dynamics* (rCFD) procedure is given. The rCFD method is an important tool regarding the simulation of industrial processes and laboratory processes during long term operation. It is based on a statistical approach and utilizes recurrent fields for predicting following time steps.

3.2   Particle properties

In this section the experimental results regarding the material characterization are presented. The target product, which shall be coated in future industrial scale, is a temperature-sensitive material, which must not exceed temperatures above $50°C$ in order to avoid loss of functionality. For handling the sensitive material the spouted bed apparatus has been chosen as its structured flow pattern contains fewer hot spots or inhomogeneities than fluidized beds. As the target material is hazardous and needs to be handled in special laboratories, model particles were used, namely microcrystalline cellulose (*Cellets*®) and γ-Al2O3 particles with a similar particle size range as the industrially relevant system. Both the cellulose and the ceramic particle types are highly spherical, have a white color and narrow particle size distribution. The alumina particles have a higher porosity allowing liquid suction into the pores, which comes along with a high possible moisture content without a collapse of the fluidized bed. In contrast, the cellulose particles are less porous and highly electrostatic, which makes them sticking to apparatus parts and walls. In order to prevent sticking, antistatic spray (*TOOLCRAFT*

887243) was applied to transport and dosage equipment and the apparatus made of polycarbonate.

Both material types were used for experiments regarding stability analysis. For coating investigations, the cellulose particles were chosen in order to neglect the influence of liquid migration into pores. All presented simulations were performed with γ-Al2O3 particles of 0.6 mm size. For experimental investigations also particles with a size of 1.8 mm and 3.0 mm were used.

Particle size and size distribution

The particle size sum distribution Q_3 of *Cellets*®500 determined with *CamSizerXT* is shown in Figure 3.1. The particle diameter range is between 0.42 and 0.96 mm with a

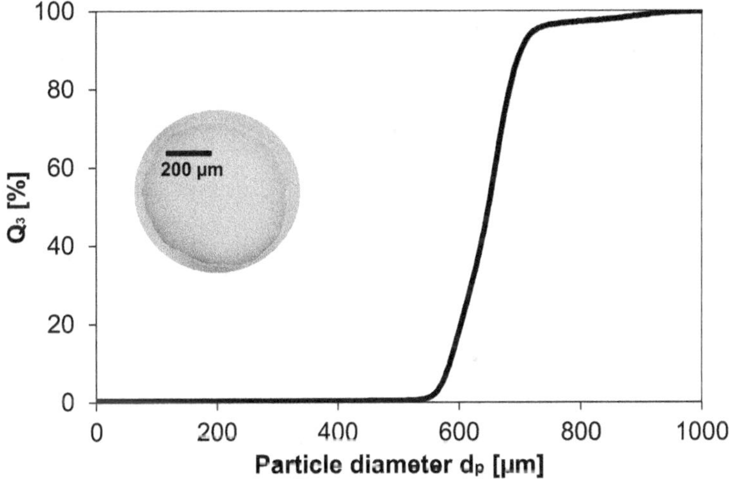

FIGURE 3.1: Cumulative particle mass size distribution Q_3 of *Cellets*®500 particles and exemplary light microscope image of a single particle.

mean diameter of $d_{50,3} = 0.57$ mm. The sphericity was determined to 0.95. Analogous, the size distribution of the small γ-Al2O3 particles is given in figure 3.2. The distribution is narrower compared to *Cellets*®500 and ranges from 0.48 to 0.69 mm with a mean diameter $d_{50,3} = 0.656$ mm. Again, the particles are with a mean sphericity of 0.96 almost ideal spherical. Additionally, the distributions of the 1.8 mm and 3.0 mm sized γ-Al2O3 particles are shown in figure 3.3. Again, high sphericities of 0.966 and 0.986, respectively were measured. The mean diameter $d_{50,3}$ is with 1.78 mm almost identical to the producer value of 1.8 mm for the middle size fraction but its smaller than the

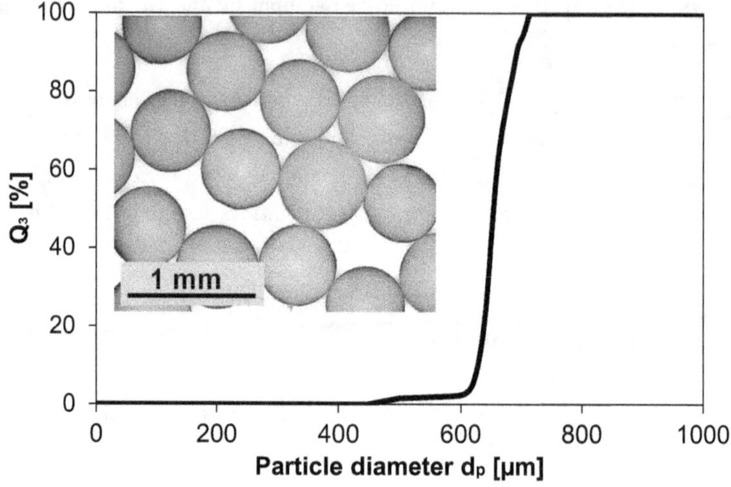

FIGURE 3.2: Cumulative particle mass size distribution Q_3 of small γ-Al2O3 particles (quoted size of 0.6 mm) and light microscope image of particles.

mentioned 3 mm for the biggest fraction, where the mean diameter was determined to $d_{50,3} = 2.67$ mm.

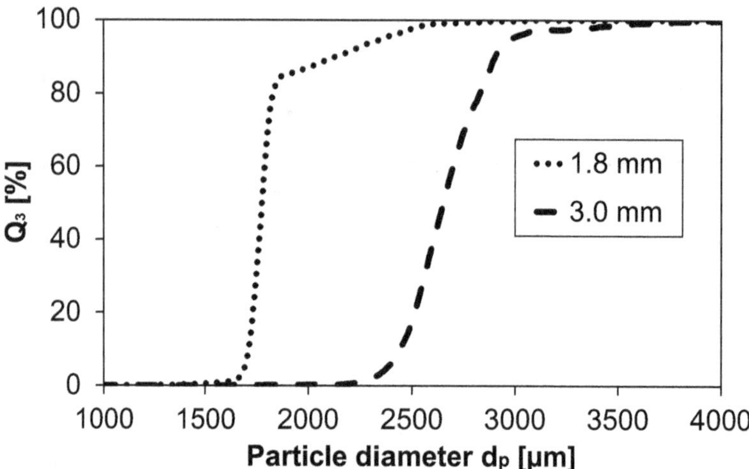

FIGURE 3.3: Cumulative particle mass size distribution Q_3 of medium sized γ-Al2O3 particles (quoted size of 1.8 mm) and of big γ-Al2O3 particles (quoted size of 3.0 mm).

Apparent particle density

The solid density was measured with helium pycnometer as described in subsection 2.2.2. Besides the raw material of $Cellets^{®}500$ and γ-Al2O3 the particles coated with the magentizable paint were analyzed in order to evaluate their applicability as tracer material. The measured values are shown in table 3.1.

TABLE 3.1: Apparent particle densities determined with helium pycnometer.

Material	Apparent particle density [$\mathrm{kg\,m^{-3}}$]
$Cellets^{®}500$	1481
γ-Al2O3 0.656 mm	3095
γ-Al2O3 1.8 mm	3240
γ-Al2O3 3.0 mm	3385
Magnetizable $Cellets^{®}500$	1600
Magnetizable γ-Al2O3 1.8 mm	3104

It can be seen from table 3.1 that the densities of $Cellets^{®}500$ and γ-Al2O3 with a size of 0.656 mm differ a lot even though the particles are of the same size. This is due to the fact that the alumina particles are highly porous allowing the helium to get into the pores, whereas the $Cellets^{®}500$ particles contain almost no open pores. The measurements of the coated particles have been performed with those samples with the minimum necessary coating layer thickness to make them adhere to the magnetic rod. The variation of the particle density of the coated particles from uncoated material is in both cases smaller than 10 %. Therefore, it is concluded that the variation in fluidization behavior is small, which makes the particles regarding their density be applicable as tracer material.

Envelope density

For simulations, the particle density is needed. Therefore, it was calculated for the γ-Al2O3 particles with a size of 0.656 mm by taking 50 representative particles. The weight of the sample was measured, which allowed the determination of the weight of one single particle. By assuming an ideal spherical shape, the true density was calculated by dividing the weight of one single particle by its volume determined with the Sauter mean diameter of the particle type. The true density of the γ-Al2O3 particles ($d_{50,3} = 0.656\mathrm{mm}$) was determined to 1328 $\mathrm{kg\,m^{-3}}$.

Restitution coefficient

The restitution coefficient was measured for the particle type used in simulations: γ-Al2O3 particles with a mean size of 0.656 mm. The coefficient for the collision of a particle with a wall made of steel, $e_{\mathrm{p-w}}$, was determined to 0.73 ± 0.087 and the mean value was used. A direct measurement of the restitution coefficient of two colliding particles was not possible with the described experimental setup. As the observable collision behavior is similar to the collision with a wall, it was set to $e_{\mathrm{p-p}} = 0.72$.

Young's modulus

Analogous to the coefficient of restitution, the Young's modulus is necessary for performing CFD-DEM simulations and was therefore determined for the γ-Al2O3 particles with 0.656 mm in size as this was the material used in the simulations. The Young's modulus was determined by measuring the force-displacement curve for 13 representative particles. As described in section 2.2.5 the mean Young's modulus Y_{p}^{*} can be calculated from the slope of the curve. This is exemplarily shown for the first measurement in figure 3.4. An overview of all measured data is given in table 3.2. With a Poisson ratio ν of 0.3 the averaged particles' Young's modulus was determined to 3.06×10^{9} Pa. According to literature data for steel, a value of 2.5×10^{9} Pa was chosen for the walls' Young's modulus Y_{w}.

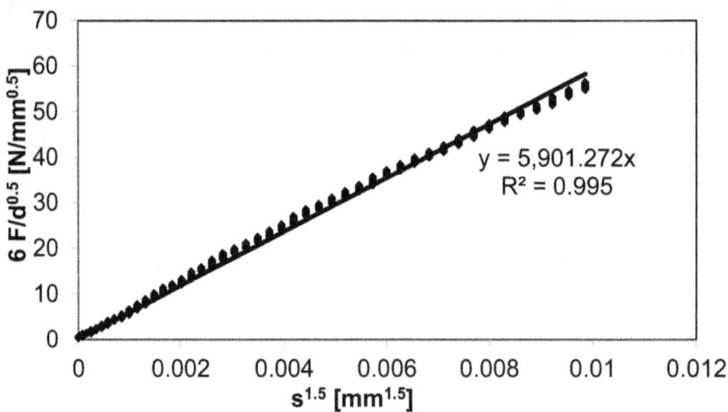

FIGURE 3.4: Exemplary force-displacement curve obtained during compression of representative γ-Al2O3 particles (0.656 mm).

TABLE 3.2: Measured mean Young's moduli Y_{p}^{*} and resulting particle Young's moduli Y_p by assuming a Poisson ratio ν of 0.3; γ-Al2O3 particles (0.656 mm).

Measurement no.	Y_{p}^{*} [N mm^{-2}]	Y_{p} [N m^{-2}]
1	5901.27	2.69×10^9
2	5648.92	2.57×10^9
3	4177.91	1.90×10^9
4	5980.08	2.72×10^9
5	5753.68	2.62×10^9
6	7763.14	3.53×10^9
7	7644.61	3.48×10^9
8	8839.61	4.02×10^9
9	7728.29	3.52×10^9
10	6701.20	3.05×10^9
11	7947.69	3.62×10^9
12	7649.67	3.48×10^9
13	5650.22	2.57×10^9

Friction coefficient

The friction coefficient was measured with a Schulze ring shear tester *RST-XS.s* as described in section 2.2.6. The internal friction coefficient between the particles was determined to 0.65. For the coefficient between the γ-Al2O3 particles of 0.656 mm size and the wall a value of 0.16 was measured. Nevertheless, in the CFD-DEM simulations the values were set to 0.06 and 0.05, respectively, which showed higher physical consistence with the experimental data as the rolling friction was not taken into account.

Minimum fluidization velocity

The minimum fluidization velocity was determined experimentally with a plexiglass fluidized bed column as described in section 2.2.7. For the γ-Al2O3 a velocity of 0.16 m s^{-1} was determined. The bulk density ρ_{bulk} was measured by filling and weighing a container of known volume to 764.8 kg m^{-3}.

3.3 CFD-DEM coupling procedure

In this thesis, all CFD-DEM simulations were performed with the open source software *CFDEMcoupling*® (Goniva et al., 2012), which couples the CFD tool *OpenFOAM*® (Weller et al., 1998) with the DEM software *LIGGGHTS*© (Hager et al., 2014, Kloss et al., 2012). For visualization purposes the software *ParaView* was used. The simulations were focused on the laboratory plant *ProCell® 5* as the spouting stability and the process of droplet depositions has to be understood in detail before a larger scale can be investigated. The geometry of the process chamber, shown in figure 2.6, was drawn in CAD software *SolidWorks* and the simulation mesh was generated with the hexahedral cut-cell based *OpenFOAM®* meshing tool *snappyHexMesh*. For the fine inlet geometry a cell size of 3.125 mm ($1.7 \cdot d_{\mathrm{p}}$) was chosen. The process chamber area above the inlet had a cell size of 6.25 mm ($3.5 \cdot d_{\mathrm{p}}$) and above a height of 0.5 m a mesh size of 12.5 mm ($7 \cdot d_{\mathrm{p}}$) was used as the particle void fraction is usually low in this upper part of the apparatus. In total, the simulation mesh contained around 700,000 cells of mostly hexahedral type.

The gas phase dynamics in presence of an additional granular phase were solved by applying the PISO algorithm in OpenFOAM to the incompressible Navier-Stokes equations:

$$\frac{\partial \alpha_{\mathrm{f}}}{\partial t} + \nabla \cdot (\alpha_{\mathrm{f}} u_{\mathrm{f}}) = 0, \tag{3.1}$$

$$\frac{\partial (\alpha_{\mathrm{f}} u_{\mathrm{f}})}{\partial t} + \nabla \cdot (\alpha_{\mathrm{f}} u_{\mathrm{f}} u_{\mathrm{f}}) = -\frac{\alpha_{\mathrm{f}}}{\rho_{\mathrm{f}}} \nabla p + \alpha_{\mathrm{f}} g - \frac{1}{\rho_{\mathrm{f}}} R_{\mathrm{pf}} + \nabla \cdot \left(\frac{\alpha_{\mathrm{f}}}{\rho_{\mathrm{f}}} \tau \right), \tag{3.2}$$

where p is the pressure, g is the gravitational constant, α_{f} is the volume fraction of the fluid, u_{f} is its velocity and ρ_{f} its density. The stress tensor τ can be calculated via $\tau = \mu_{\mathrm{f}} \nabla u_{\mathrm{f}}$, where μ_{f} is the dynamic viscosity of the fluid. The term R_{pf} represents the momentum exchange between the fluid and the granular phase and is for numerical reasons split-up into an implicit and an explicit term using the averaged particle velocity u_{p} in the regarded cell:

$$R_{\mathrm{pf}} = K_{\mathrm{pf}}(u_{\mathrm{f}} - \langle u_{\mathrm{p}} \rangle). \tag{3.3}$$

The momentum exchange coefficient K_{pf} contains the drag forces F_{d} that are acting in the regarded cell volume V_{cell}:

$$K_{\mathrm{pf}} = \frac{\alpha_{\mathrm{f}} \cdot \left| \sum_i F_{\mathrm{d},i} \right|}{V_{\mathrm{cell}} |u_{\mathrm{f}} - \langle u_{\mathrm{p}} \rangle|}. \tag{3.4}$$

Different drag models are available for calculating K_{pf}. Most of these models are of empirical or half-empirical nature. In this thesis, the following drag models were tested and the obtained flow regimes were compared among each other and to experimental results: Gidaspow, Di Felice, Koch and Hill and the drag model by Beetstra. The widely used drag model by Gidaspow et al. (1991) is a combination of the Ergun equation (Ergun and Orning, 1949) applicable for description of pressure drop through porous media and Wen and Yu equation (Wen and Yu, 1966), which is valid when viscous forces dominate the flow and internal forces are negligible and was derived using experimental data from

Richardson and Zaki (1997). Depending on the volume fraction of the fluid, the drag model switches between both correlations, whereby the Ergun equation is used to model the drag equation at lower fluid void fractions ($\alpha_f \leq 0.8$) and Wen and Yu correlation is used in case of a dispersed phase ($\alpha_f > 0.8$) (Lundberg and Halvorsen, 2008). The drag model by Di Felice (1994) has been developed by extending the sinking velocity model for a single particle. Both models from Koch and Hill (2001) and Beetstra et al. (2007) have been derived from highly resolved Lattice Boltzmann simulations. Beetstra et al. (2007) recommended using their drag model for dense beds of particles with solid fractions exceeding 0.5. The expressions for calculation of the momentum exchange coefficient for the different drag models are given in table 3.3.

TABLE 3.3: Drag models proposed for particulate flows.

Drag model	Expression
Gidaspow et al. (1991)	

$$\alpha_f \leq 0.8 \rightarrow K_{pf} = 150\frac{(1-\alpha_f)^2 \nu_f \rho_f}{\alpha_f d_p^2} + 1.75\frac{(1-\alpha_f)|u_f - u_p|\rho_f}{d_p} \qquad (3.5)$$

$$\alpha_f > 0.8 \rightarrow K_{pf} = \frac{3}{4}C_d \frac{\alpha_f(1-\alpha_f)|u_f - u_p|\rho_f}{d_p}\alpha_f^{-2.65} \qquad (3.6)$$

$$C_d = \frac{24}{\alpha_f Re_p}[1 + 0.15(\alpha_f Re_p)^{0.687}] \qquad (3.7)$$

$$Re = \frac{|u_f - u_p|}{\nu_f}d_p \qquad (3.8)$$

Di Felice (1994)

$$K_{pt} = \frac{3}{4}C_d \frac{(1-\alpha_f)\rho_f \alpha_f}{d_p}|u_f - u_p|f(\alpha_f) \qquad (3.9)$$

$$f(\alpha_f) = \alpha_f^{-\chi} \qquad (3.10)$$

$$\chi = 3.7 - 0.65e^{-\frac{1.5 - \log(\alpha_f Re_p)^2}{2}} \qquad (3.11)$$

Koch and Hill
(2001)

$$K_{\mathrm{pf}} = \frac{18\nu_{\mathrm{f}}\rho_{\mathrm{f}}\alpha_{\mathrm{f}}^2(1-\alpha_{\mathrm{f}})}{d_{\mathrm{p}}^2}\left(f_1(\alpha_{\mathrm{f}}) + \frac{1}{2}f_2(\alpha_{\mathrm{f}})Re_{\mathrm{p}}\right) \tag{3.12}$$

$$\alpha_{\mathrm{f}} > 0.4 \rightarrow$$

$$f_1(\alpha_{\mathrm{f}}) = \frac{1 + 3\sqrt{\frac{(1-\alpha_{\mathrm{f}})}{2}} + \frac{135}{64}(1-\alpha_{\mathrm{f}})\ln(1-\alpha_v) + 16.14(1-\alpha_{\mathrm{f}})}{1 + 0.681(1-\alpha_{\mathrm{f}}) - 8.48(1-\alpha_{\mathrm{f}})^2 + 8.16(1-\alpha_{\mathrm{f}})^3} \tag{3.13}$$

$$\alpha_{\mathrm{f}} < 0.4 \rightarrow f_1(\alpha_{\mathrm{f}}) = \frac{10(1-\alpha_{\mathrm{f}})}{\alpha_{\mathrm{f}}^3} \tag{3.14}$$

$$f_2(\alpha_{\mathrm{f}}) = 0.0637 + 0.212(1-\alpha_{\mathrm{f}}) + \frac{0.0232}{\alpha_{\mathrm{f}}^5} \tag{3.15}$$

Beetstra et al.
(2007)

$$K_{\mathrm{pf}} = \frac{18\nu_{\mathrm{f}}\rho_{\mathrm{f}}\alpha_{\mathrm{f}}(1-\alpha_{\mathrm{f}})}{d_{\mathrm{p}}^2}f(\alpha_{\mathrm{f}}) \tag{3.16}$$

$$f(\alpha_{\mathrm{f}}) = \frac{10(1-\alpha_{\mathrm{f}})}{\alpha_{\mathrm{f}}^2} + \alpha_{\mathrm{f}}^2(1 + 1.5\sqrt{(1-\alpha_{\mathrm{f}})})$$

$$+ \frac{0.413Re_{\mathrm{p}}}{24\alpha_{\mathrm{f}}^2}\left[\frac{\alpha_{\mathrm{f}}^{-1} + 3\alpha_{\mathrm{f}}(1-\alpha_{\mathrm{f}}) + 8.4(Re_{\mathrm{p}}^{-0.343})}{1 + 10^{3(1-\alpha_{\mathrm{f}})}Re_{\mathrm{p}}^{-\left(1+4\frac{(1-\alpha_{\mathrm{f}})}{2}\right)}}\right] \tag{3.17}$$

Besides the variation of the drag model, the influence of the used turbulence model was investigated. The following models were examined: k-ω and k-ε turbulence model and the laminar model. The k-ω and k-ε turbulence models belong to the two-equation-models for turbulence modeling and are the most prominent ones of this category. The basic idea of the k-ε model is the derivation of equations of momentum balance for the fluctuations in all directions and the following conversion into a dependence on the kinetic energy of turbulence k (Launder and Sharma, 1974). A transport equation is formulated for k, which allows the consideration of turbulence production and dissipation. The turbulence dissipation is considered by an additional differential equation that is connected to the eddy viscosity ν_t:

$$\nu_t = C_\mu \frac{k^2}{\varepsilon}. \tag{3.18}$$

k and ε are scalar-valued vector fields for which boundary conditions have to be defined that are dependent on the geometry and the flow values at the boarder of the system. Besides the standard k-ε model deviations are known, as e.g. the realizable k-ε model

(Shih et al., 1995). This model contains a feasibility condition, which ensures that also in case of high tensions, no negative normal stresses occur. This results in an improved prediction for rotating and riving jets.

By means of the k-ω model, systems with dominant wall effects and flows with low Reynolds numbers can be predicted more accurately, whereby the specific dissipation ω is taken into account:

$$\nu_t = \frac{k}{\omega}. \tag{3.19}$$

Nevertheless, problems have been reported in the prediction of free flows and systems with high pressure gradients. Therefore, variations have been developed as e.g. the k-ω-SST (*shear stress transport*)-model, which uses the original k-ω model in the region near the walls and a k-ε model in the freeboard zone (Andersson et al., 2011).

For the simulation of particle collisions a soft sphere model (Cundall and Strack, 1979) based on correlations of Hertz (1882) was applied.

3.3.1 Coarse-graining approach

With today's computational power and access to high performance clusters, lab-scale processes can be simulated in a reasonable time. However, industrial processes with millions and billions of particles still require coarse-graining methods (Lu et al., 2016, Radl et al., 2011). In general, two different approaches can be distinguished: grid coarsening and particle coarsening (Ozel et al., 2016). Latter was used for the simulations presented in this thesis. By performing particle coarsening, computational parcels, whose diameter is by a certain scaling factor δ bigger than the diameter of the original particle, are tracked instead of the primary particles, which then results in a reduced number of particles N_p that need to be simulated:

$$\delta = \frac{d_\mathrm{p,scaled}}{d_\mathrm{p}}, \tag{3.20}$$

$$N_\mathrm{p} \propto \frac{1}{\delta^3}. \tag{3.21}$$

In this PhD thesis, the coarse-graining approach according to Bierwisch et al. (2009) was used, which is based on a dimensional analysis of contact laws regarding the conservation of the macroscopic coefficient of restitution and stress state by conserving relative particle/parcel overlap in binary contacts. This approach depends on material properties of the primary particles. To perform the scaling in a physically realistic way and to keep force and velocity information, the energy density and evolution of energy have to be kept as in the original system. In order to preserve the density of the gravitational force, the void fraction field α_f and the solid density ρ_s are kept constant:

$$\alpha_f = \alpha_f', \tag{3.22}$$

$$\rho_s = \rho_s', \tag{3.23}$$

whereby the inverted comma denotes the quantities of the scaled system. To keep the energy dissipation per volume and time constant, the restitution coefficient e is also not scaled:

$$e = e'. \tag{3.24}$$

The number of collisions in space and time scales with $\frac{1}{\delta^3}$ and the effective mass m_{eff} with δ^3, whereby the effective mass is calculated by the mass of two collision partners i and j:

$$m_{\text{eff}} = \frac{m_i m_j}{m_i + m_j}. \tag{3.25}$$

In order to preserve the energy dissipation rates, a dimensional analysis gives three dimensionless numbers $\Pi_{1,2,3}$, which as well as a reference velocity u_0 have to be kept constant during coarse graining:

$$\Pi_1 = \frac{\varpi}{r_{\text{p,eff}} \tilde{Y}}, \tag{3.26}$$

$$\Pi_2 = \frac{\gamma_e m}{r_{\text{p,eff}} \sqrt{\rho_s \tilde{Y}}}, \tag{3.27}$$

$$\Pi_3 = \frac{\kappa_t}{r_{\text{p,eff}} \tilde{Y}}, \tag{3.28}$$

$$u_0 = \sqrt{\frac{\tilde{Y}}{\rho_s}}, \tag{3.29}$$

where ϖ is a generalized cohesive energy per unit contact area, $r_{\text{p,eff}}$ is an effective particle radius (3.30), $\tilde{Y}$ is calculated by the Young's modulus Y and Poisson ratio ν (3.31), γ_{em} is an empirical damping parameter and κ_t is a tangential spring constant.

$$r_{\text{p,eff}} = \frac{r_{\text{p},i} \cdot r_{\text{p},j}}{r_{\text{p},i} + r_{\text{p},j}}, \tag{3.30}$$

$$\tilde{Y} = \frac{Y}{(1 - \nu)^2}. \tag{3.31}$$

It is worth to mention that the mass-specific particle drag force in the scaled system is calculated based on the original diameter of a single particle as it would otherwise overestimate the drag in an unrealistic manner. In the presented simulations, a scaling factor of 4 was chosen. Higher scaling factors are severely restricted by the fine details of the inlet geometry and its influence on the particle packing structure as well as the grid, which has to be fine enough to capture the spout jet. Further particle coarsening would require the grid to be coarsened as well, as the applicability of drag laws is questionable for grid sizes smaller than the particle diameters.

3.3.2 Simulation parameters

The results from particle characterization experiments of the γ-Al2O3 particles (0.656 mm) presented in section 3.2 were used as simulation input parameters. All particle and fluid properties are summarized in table 3.4. As an implicit solver was used, the CFD time step of $\Delta t_{\mathrm{CFD}} = 5 \cdot 10^{-5}$ yielded regardless of Courant-Numbers of $Co = max \frac{u_f \Delta t_{\mathrm{CFD}}}{\Delta x} < 3$ stable simulations. The Co number exceeded the commonly used restriction of $Co < 1$ due to the small cell sizes around the nozzle. Nevertheless, evidently higher numbers can be used (Andersson et al., 2011), which was assayed for the regarded simulations in preinvestigations.

3.4 Liquid injection

As mentioned before, the liquid injection was performed during post-processing by replaying the particle flow fields. Though the liquid injection comes along with changes in viscous, surface tension, capillary, contact and drag forces (Antonyuk et al., 2009), their change and the building of liquid bridges were not taken into account here due to the low liquid injection rate and the very small coating layers. In addition, the droplet deposition efficiency was assumed to be 100 % because of the small liquid injection rates. When using higher rates, as for example in spray granulation processes, the deposition efficiency needs to be taken into account, as e.g. modeled by Li et al. (2011).

For the droplet injection, the mesh around the nozzle was calibrated based on the spray pattern determined in experiments, in which a dye was used for visualization: A piece of tulle was fixed in the process chamber at a defined height. The fluidization gas was turned on without any particles in the bed. Diluted methylene blue dye was injected at a pump rate of 5 g min^{-1} for around 20 s. After that time, the process was stopped and the tulle with the blue color was pressed on a white sheet of paper. The procedure was repeated at different heights as schematically shown in figure 3.5.

By means of the different spray pattern prints, the height-dependent area of liquid injection was determined as shown in figure 3.6. The droplet injection was simulated as

TABLE 3.4: Fluid and particle properties and simulation parameters for CFD-DEM simulations of spouted bed process in *ProCell®5* aparatus with γ-Al2O3 particles.

Parameter/Setting	Symbol	Value	Unit
CFD time step	Δt_{CFD}	$5 \cdot 10^{-5}$	s
DEM time step	Δt_{DEM}	$2.5 \cdot 10^{-7}$	s
Liquid injection	Δt_{post}	10^{-4}	s
Particle diameter	d_{p}	656	µm
Scaling factor	δ	4	-
Particle density	ρ_{p}	1328	$\mathrm{kg\,m^{-3}}$
Fluid density	ρ_{f}	1.225	$\mathrm{kg\,m^{-3}}$
Fluid dynamic viscosity	μ_{f}	$1.7894 \cdot 10^{-5}$	$\mathrm{kg\,m^{-1}\,s}$
Young's modulus particles	Y_{p}	3.06	GPa
Young's modulus wall	Y_{w}	2.5	GPa
Poisson ratio particles	ν_{p}	0.3	-
Poisson ratio wall	ν_{w}	0.3	-
Restitution coefficient *p-p*	$e_{\mathrm{p-p}}$	0.72	-
Restitution coefficient *p-p*	$e_{\mathrm{p-p}}$	0.73	-
Static friction coefficient *p-p*	$\mu_{\mathrm{st,p-p}}$	0.06	-
Static friction coefficient *p-w*	$\mu_{\mathrm{st,p-w}}$	0.05	-
Slit height	h_{slit}	3.5	mm
Droplet diameter	d_{drop}	40	µm
Field sampling frequency	f_{sample}	10^2	Hz
Liquid droplet injection rate	f_{liq}	$2.5 \cdot 10^6$	Hz
Liquid mass rate	$\dot{m}_{\mathrm{liq}}$	5	$\mathrm{g\,min^{-1}}$

follows: The post-processing-solver, which is a combination of the *sprayFoam*-solver and the *cfdemPostproc*-post-processing tool, loads the velocity fields and particle positions. A Lagrangian droplet phase is allowed to evolve in the loaded velocity fields. Droplets were injected with a frequency of $2.5 \cdot 10^6$ droplets/s at the nozzle inlet patch with a mass flow rate of 5 g/min. A particle-droplet capturing efficiency of 100 % was assumed, whereby an area of the particle equal to the droplets diameter ($d_{\mathrm{drop}} = 40$ µm) is covered with the coating agent. The heat transfer coefficient for the heat transfer between the gas and the particles/droplets was evaluated using the empirical correlation of Gnielinski (1978) for the transfer coefficients of single spheres:

$$Nu = 2 + \sqrt{Nu_{\mathrm{lam}}^2 + Nu_{\mathrm{turb}}^2}, \tag{3.32}$$

with

$$Nu_{\mathrm{lam}} = 0.664 Re^{0.5} Pr^{0.33}, \tag{3.33}$$

$$Nu_{\mathrm{turb}} = \frac{0.037 Re^{0.8} Pr}{1 + 2.443 Re^{-0.1}(Pr^{0.667} - 1)}. \tag{3.34}$$

With consideration of the coarse-graining approach, the maximum heat flux for evaporation $\dot{Q}$ was calculated via

$$\dot{Q} = Nu\ \pi d_{\mathrm{parcel}} \alpha^3 \lambda (T_{\mathrm{air}} - T_{\mathrm{wb}}), \tag{3.35}$$

with Nusselt number Nu, thermal conductivity λ, temperature of the air T_{air} and wet bulb temperature as the temperature of water deposited on the particles T_{wb}. The air temperature was set to 323.15 K and the temperature of the water on the particles was calculated iteratively with the saturation vapor and adiabatic conditions. The calculation approach is given in the appendix C. In the time loop of the solver, droplet cloud evolution was alternated with deposition steps, in which contact detection was performed and droplets were captured by the particles. A statistical approach by Kariuki et al. (2013), expressed by equation 3.36, was used to determine the surface coverage distribution of the liquid on the particles in the bed:

$$\frac{S_{\mathrm{p,covered}}}{S_{\mathrm{p}}} = 1 - \left(1 - \frac{a_{\mathrm{drop,proj}}}{S_{\mathrm{particle}}}\right)^{\frac{m_{\mathrm{liq}}}{m_{\mathrm{drop}}}}, \tag{3.36}$$

with m_{liq} the mass of captured liquid, S_{p} the surface area of particles, $a_{\mathrm{drop,proj}}$ the projected area of a droplet and m_{drop} the mass of a droplet.

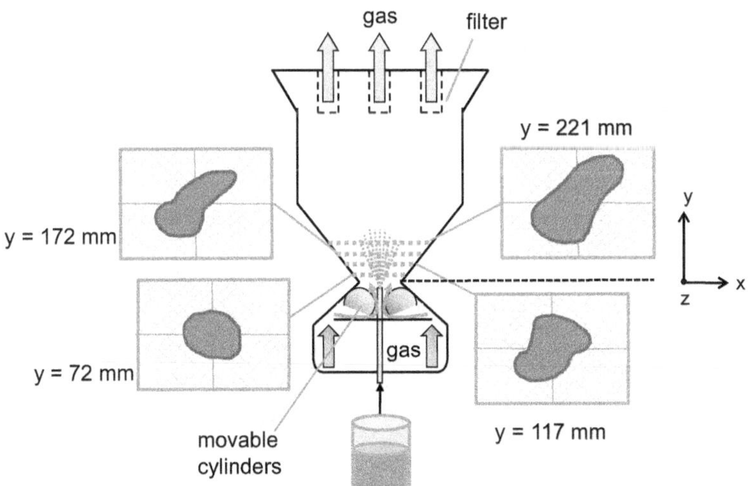

FIGURE 3.5: Calibration of nozzle mesh by stepwise experimental determination of the spray pattern at different distances from the nozzle tip.

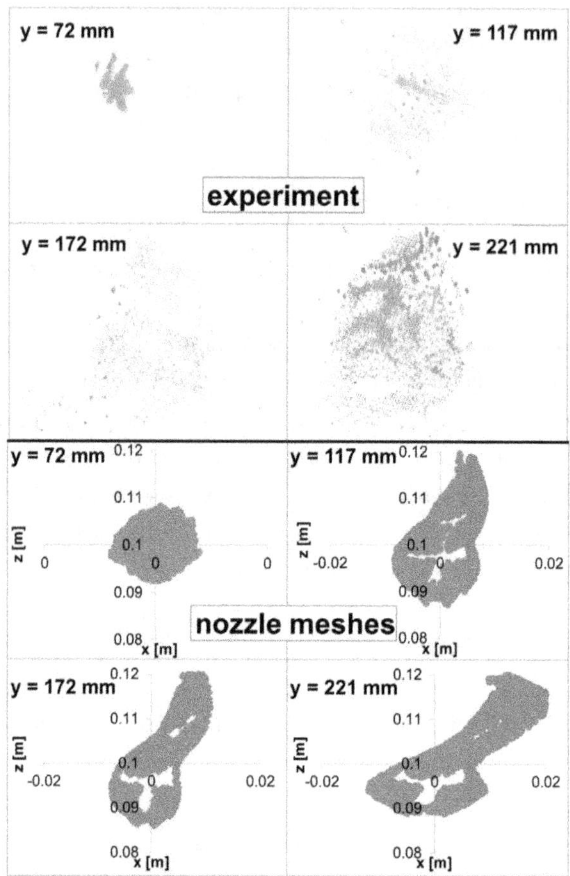

FIGURE 3.6: Experimentally determined spray pattern of the two-fluid nozzle (*970-S4*, Schlick, Germany) at different heights and respective constructed nozzle meshes.

3.5　Process quantification

With coupled CFD and DEM simulations, process information on the scale of single particles can be obtained. In order to compare different configurations quantitatively, the Fourier transform of the measured pressure drop time series as well as circulation frequencies from DEM calculations were used. The Fourier transform allows not only the evaluation of the spouting stability but also acts as quantity for validation procedure to experimental data.

3.5.1 Fourier transform

Gas pressure fluctuations were measured in experiments and simulations. Experiments were operated in under-pressure mode and the pressure drop was measured in the free-board zone above the bed. Simulations were performed with the boundary conditions of a defined inlet velocity and atmospheric pressure at the outlet. Thus, the pressure drop was averaged over the inlet with a sampling frequency of 1 kHz. The Fourier transform of the signals decomposes the original function into sinusoids of different frequencies with their respective amplitudes. A narrow single peak in the power spectrum distribution PSD indicates homogeneous pressure fluctuations and therefore stable spouting. In case of irregular spouting, the pressure fluctuations are irregular, which results in a broad peak distribution in the power plot. In this thesis, the Fourier transform $\mathcal{F}$ of the time dependent pressure signal $p(t)$ was conducted in Python package $numpy$, whereby it is defined as follows (Link, 2006) :

$$\mathcal{F}p(t)(\omega_k) = \frac{1}{N_{\text{datapoints}}} \sum_{m=0}^{N_{\text{datapoints}}-1} p(t_m)e^{-\frac{2\pi mk}{N_{\text{datapoints}}}i}, \tag{3.37}$$

where $N_{\text{datapoints}}$ is the number of sampling points and ω_k is the angular frequency. The power spectrum distribution PSD is calculated according to equation 3.38. From the distribution the main frequency of the pressure drop fluctuations can be determined.

$$PSDp(t)(\omega) = ||\mathcal{F}p(t)(\omega)||^2. \tag{3.38}$$

3.5.2 Circulation frequencies

As described in subsection 1.1.1 the flow pattern in a spouted bed can be divided into three different regions: spout, fountain and annulus region. The zones differ in particle velocities and flow directions as well as in void fractions. In order to classify those regions in the simulations, granular properties are considered as those properties are directly calculated by $LIGGGHTS^{®}$ in each time step. For classification, a Boolean state variable is defined for each particle i for the spout region $\xi_{i,\text{spout}}$ as most interesting zone regarding coating processes as it contains the nozzle and is the zone of most of the particle-droplet interactions. The spout region is characterized by particles reaching velocities up to $10\ \mathrm{m\,s^{-1}}$ in the positive height, whereas particle movement in the other zones is mostly in negative direction. Therefore, all particles having a vertical velocity $u_{\text{py},i}$ greater than or equal to a threshold velocity u_{spout} were chosen to be in the spout region:

$$\xi_{i,\mathrm{spout}} = \begin{cases} 1 & u_{\mathrm{py},i} \geq u_{\mathrm{spout}} \\ 0 & \text{otherwise} \end{cases}. \tag{3.39}$$

The threshold velocity was determined by particle tracking velocimetry (PTV) as will be described in chapter 4. The assignment of particles to the spout zone allows the calculation of the circulation frequency in the regarded system. By an additional evaluation of the vertical velocities, the time and intensity of particle-droplet interaction can be estimated.

3.6 Recurrence CFD (rCFD)

Though the application of coarse-graining approaches allows the investigation of pilot plant scale apparatuses at least for several seconds in acceptable times, the simulation of industrial scale apparatuses with much more particles or of the whole process length remains a challenge. The recently developed *recurrence Computational Fluid Dynamics* (rCFD) method (Lichtenegger et al., 2017, Lichtenegger and Pirker, 2016) addresses the problem for pseudo-periodic processes by extrapolating globally recurring patterns in a physically meaningful way and describing the transport and interaction of passive scalars by Lagrangian tracers. As the regular flow pattern in spouted beds contains a lot of periodicity, they represent an excellent application field for rCFD. The method is based on tools from recurrence statistics, namely recurrence plots and signal reconstruction.

3.6.1 Recurrence analysis

According to whether the state $X(t_i)$ is depending on the previous state $X(t_{i-1})$, a deterministic system can be categorized as either ordered or unordered. Ordered systems are characterized by completely predictable time evolutions. Given a time series of an ordered system, a function can be fitted to extrapolate the series without loss of accuracy. Eckmann et al. (1987) proposed recurrence plots to visualize patterns inherent in chaotic signals and systems. The non-tresholded, normalized recurrence matrix is defined as follows:

$$\mathcal{R}(t_i, t_j) = 1 - \frac{\|\mathbf{X}(t_i) - \mathbf{X}(t_j)\|}{\max_{k,l}(\|\mathbf{X}(t_k) - \mathbf{X}(t_l)\|)}. \tag{3.40}$$

The denominator is used for normalization, whereby those states are used that give the maximum value for $\|\ \|$. Values between 0 and 1 occur in the matrix, with 1 along the diagonal. Values of 0 or close to 0 indicate the lowest degree of similarity between the referenced states, while a value of 1 is connected to identical states. Almost all fluid-mechanical systems show transient behavior as for example the occurence of vortex shedding, turbulence, heat transfer and chemical reactions. Nevertheless, the behavior is often found to be deterministic chaotic as described by van den Bleek and Schouten (1993) for fluidized beds and e.g. Salikov et al. (2015b) for spouted beds. The occurence of recurrence patterns in the systems makes them being a good application for recurrence CFD.

3.6.2 Simulations with rCFD

Before performing rCFD simulations, the system needs to be simulated in detail with CFD-DEM for a sufficient time interval. The length of this sampling period is impor-tant as only the mixing patterns present during this period can be reproduced in rCFD. In general, a longer interval of sampling increases the confidence in the results but at the same time increases the memory required. On the other hand, systems with highly disparate time scales of overall system behavior would require a lot of memory which makes them not suitable for rCFD simulations. Due to the weak causal relationship between temporally distant states, a time-series $\mathbf{X}(t_i)$ can be time-extrapolated by join-ing sequences from the sampled time series. The recurrence plot, as described with the matrix in equation 3.40, provides information about the similarity of two states $\mathbf{X}(t_i)$ and $\mathbf{X}(t_j)$. The extrapolation scheme works as follows:

1. Calculate recurrence plot and divide recurrence plot into two halves.

2. Choose starting point $\mathbf{X}(t_i^{\mathrm{recu}})$, $t_{\mathrm{start}}^{\mathrm{recu}} \leq t_i^{\mathrm{recu}} \leq t_{\mathrm{start}}^{\mathrm{recu}}$ from sampled signal.

3. Append consecutive sequence $\{\mathbf{X}(t_i^{\mathrm{recu}}), \mathbf{X}(t_{i+1}^{\mathrm{recu}}), ..., \mathbf{X}(t_{i+n}^{\mathrm{recu}})\}$ of random length n (or until end of current half is reached) to extrapolated signal.

4. Search opposite half of recurrence plot $\mathcal{R}\{t_{i+n}, t_j\}$ for a maximum value of t_j.

5. Define $t_j := t_i$, go to 3.

The process of searching for a recurrent state in step 4 is referred to as *recurrence jump*. There are two approaches available for the rCFD method, the Eulerian and the Lagrangian. In the Eulerian method, the quantities can be transported in any phase by solving the Eulerian transport equation, whereas in the Lagrangian method, which was used for the simulation presented in this thesis, the quantities are transported by Lagrangian tracers. Thus, the volume fraction fields and velocities in Lagrangian approach can be calculated via equations 3.41 and 3.42:

$$\alpha(x) = V_\mathrm{T} \sum_{i \in \mathrm{T}} g(||x - x_i||), \tag{3.41}$$

$$u(x) = \frac{\sum_{i \in \mathrm{T}} q(||x - x_i||)u_i}{\sum_{i \in \mathrm{T}} q(||x - x_i||)}, \tag{3.42}$$

where V_T is the volume of a Lagrangian fluid element/tracer and $q(x)$ is a density distribution function. The equation of motion of a single tracer i is given by:

$$\dot{x} = u_i^\mathrm{recu} + u_\mathrm{fluc}, \tag{3.43}$$

where u_i^recu is the velocity derived from the recurrence velocity field and u_fluc is the fluctuation velocity that is introduced to reproduce void fractions. The origin and calculation of the fluctuations is described in detail by Lichtenegger and Pirker (2016).

4

Digital image analysis

4.1 Introduction

The following chapter is dedicated to applying digital image analysis for particulate flows. The analysis of image data acquired by high-speed camera recording allows on the one hand the measurement of flow velocities and directions. The approach, namely particle tracking velocimetry (PTV), is described in section 4.2. The next section 4.3 is based on a similar method and detects single particles in the first step but the analysis is further extended by extracting brightness properties on the scale of pixels, which are then used to investigate the coating quality.

4.2 Particle tracking velocimetry (PTV)

In order to measure the particles' dynamics in experiments and for comparison with numerical data, the particle flow velocity fields are of high interest. Common approaches to analyze the velocity field in gas-solid applications are the installation of probes or image techniques (Werther, 1999). Olazar et al. (1998) used an optical fiber probe for measuring particle velocities in conical spouted beds. They found the stagnant bed height and the particle size to have a strong influence on the velocity profile in the spout. He et al. (1994) also used a fiber optic probe to measure the voidage profiles in the spout, fountain and annulus zone of spouted beds. A disadvantage of the insertion of probes into the process chamber is the resulting disturbance of the flow profile, whose influence cannot be determined. Therefore, digital image analysis methods, such as particle image velocimetry (PIV) or particle tracking velocimetry (PTV), have been developed for measuring the flow profiles without an interruption of the system itself. Liu et al. (2008) measured the velocities and fluctuations of granular solids in a two-dimensional spouted bed. van Buijtenen et al. (2011) used PIV for validation of their discrete particle model for simulation of multiple-spout fluidized beds. PIV is an image based approach, which determines the particle velocities based on the correlation between subsequent image frames. With this approach it is not possible to track the trajectories of individual particles but the overall flow field is calculated based on the whole image. The advantage of PTV on the other hand is the tracking of each individual particle, which is also possible with DEM simulations and is therefore the means of choice in this thesis. The method allows the direct measurement of particle trajectories in the apparatus without an interruption of the process. For the presented investigations, the laboratory plexiglass replica of the spouted bed apparatus *ProCell® 5* was used. A high-speed camera was positioned in front of the process chamber in order to record the flow pattern. Afterwards, individual particles were captured and detected from the image frames. With the knowledge of the experimental setup, the instantaneous particle velocities were calculated by their displacement over time.

4.2.1 Particle detection

Before the particles can be tracked, they have to be detected and separated from the background. In this context, the quality of the images is very important. The image material needs to fulfill two criteria: 1. The resolution of the whole image must be high enough to resolve individual particles and the resolution of one single particle must be high enough to distinguish it from e.g. scratches or dirt on the apparatus' window. 2. The frame rate of the images must be high enough to allow the reconstruction of the particle trajectories. In some methods the particle displacement between two images must not exceed one particle diameter (Hagemeier et al., 2015b). With particle diameters not larger than 1 mm and velocties up to 10 m s^{-1}, the frame rate needs to be in the order of

$$f = \frac{10\text{m s}^{-1}}{1 \text{ mm}} = 10 \text{ kHz} \tag{4.1}$$

to track fast particles, which gives the need for the use of a high-speed camera. In this work the high-speed camera *IDT NX4 S2* (IS - Imaging Solutions GmbH, Germany) equipped with a 50 mm f/2.8 macro lens (SIGMA CORPORATION, Japan) was used.

Different algorithms for particle segmentation are available, which have been tested in this thesis on synthetically generated images: (i) correlation with image pattern, (ii) correlation with synthetic pattern, (iii) Hough transform and (iv) blob detection.

4.2.1.1 Correlation with manual pattern selection

The pattern matching algorithm (i) is provided by *OpenCV* (Itseez, 2017). A sample pattern is slid through the image and a distance metric is evaluated for each sliding position. The metric is chosen empirically using the fast normalized cross correlation (Yoo and Han, 2009), which yields the following formula for the correlation coefficient of two images I and P:

$$R(x,y) = \frac{\sum_{u,v} \left(\bar{P}(u,v) \cdot \bar{I}(x+u,y+v) \right)}{\sqrt{\sum_{u,v} \bar{P}(u,v)^2 \cdot \sum_{u,v} \bar{I}(x+u,y+v)^2}}, \tag{4.2}$$

with u as a position in x-direction and v as a position in y-direction of the pattern. The notation $\bar{M}(x,y)$ denotes the distance of M to the mean of the matrix M in a region of the size of the pattern $[w \times h]$ and can be calculated as follows:

$$\bar{M}(x,y) = M(x,y) - \frac{1}{w \cdot h} \sum_{u=0}^{w} \sum_{v=0}^{h} M(x+u,y+v). \tag{4.3}$$

The pattern matching yields a matrix R with elements from the interval $[0,1]$. A value of 1 indicates a perfect match of the image and the pattern at that position. The pattern can be selected in two different ways: manual or automatic. In case of the manual pattern selection, a cut from a video frame is selected via a graphical user interface (GUI) as shown in figure 4.2 a, whereby the size and position of the region of interest (ROI) can be adjusted. The manual pattern selection is expected to perform well for homogeneous particle properties making a visual detection easy for the user. Nevertheless, the manual selection requires an additional check by the user resulting in a slow and inconvenient analysis. Thus, an automatic particle pattern synthesis was developed.

4.2.1.2 Correlation with automatic pattern selection

This algorithm takes into account the general appearance of the particles that are considered in the regarded spouted bed process, i.e. soft specular lighting, circular shape and constant diameter. The lighting effects on the particle were modeled using a two-dimensional Gaussian function with adjustable parameters a and b depending on the lighting conditions:

$$f_{\mathrm{G}}(x,y) = a \cdot \exp\left(-\frac{(x-x_{\mathrm{c}})^2 + (y-y_{\mathrm{c}})^2}{2b^2}\right), \tag{4.4}$$

with $\vec{x}_{\mathrm{ctr}} = [x_{\mathrm{ctr}}, y_{\mathrm{ctr}}]$ the center of the synthesized particle. To simulate the roundness of the particles, the Gaussian function is applied if and only if

$$||\vec{x} - \vec{x}_{\mathrm{ctr}}|| < r_{\mathrm{p}}. \tag{4.5}$$

The remaining space in the square-shape ROI is filled with white uncorrelated noise to have no impact on the pattern matching algorithm. The result of a synthetically generated particle pattern is shown in figure 4.1.

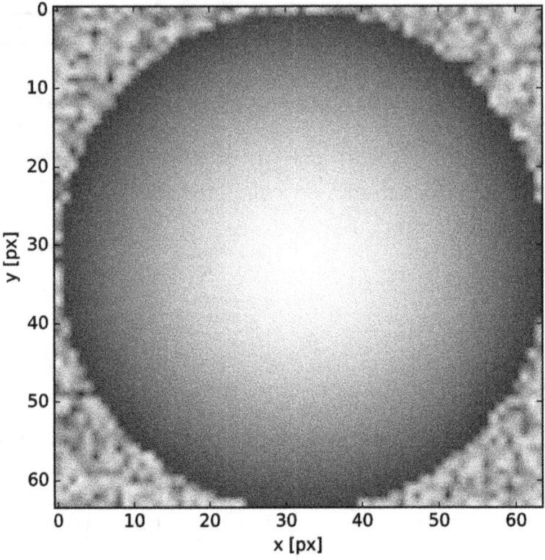

FIGURE 4.1: A synthetically generated particle pattern with $d_{\mathrm{p}} = 64$ px.

To determine the final positions of the particles in the image space, two post-processing steps are necessary. Generally, it is assumed that the local maxima of R coincide with the positions of the particles. However, the straightforward application of a maximum search algorithm resulted in many mistakes with false particle detection. Thus, before finding the local maxima of R peaks with correlations lower than a threshold value t are removed using a filter:

$$R_{\mathrm{t}}(x, y) = \begin{Bmatrix} R(x, y) & \text{if} & R(x, y) > t \\ 0 & & \text{else} \end{Bmatrix}. \tag{4.6}$$

Hagemeier et al. (2015a) used a threshold value of $t = 0.6$, however good results were achieved with a threshold of $t = 0.8$ for the images acquired with the used high-speed camera. The threshold was chosen empirically by minimizing the particle count error (see equation 4.8) and depends mostly on the visual homogeneity of the particles in the image. Finally, a particle is marked as detected on every peak of the resulting thresholded matrix R_t. The resulting particle position estimation can be reviewed in figure 4.2.

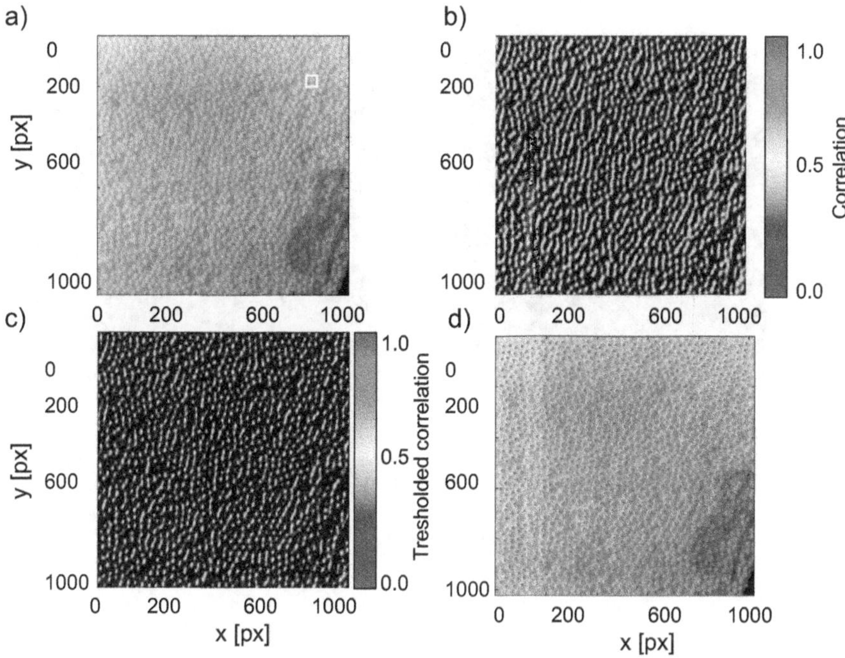

FIGURE 4.2: Steps to detect particle positions in an image: a) selection of the reference particle (manual pattern selection); b) correlation of the image with the selected reference particle; c) result of the correlation after applying a threshold of $t = 0.8$; d) locations of the maxima of the thresholded correlation indicating the positions of the particles.

4.2.1.3 Circular Hough transform

Besides the correlation approaches, the circular Hough transform (CHT) approach has been tested (Gonzalez and Woods, 2007, Pedersen, 2007) in this thesis. The approach has been designed to detect imperfect circular shapes in edge images and is based on a voting scheme. The approach makes use of the fact that a circle with the radius r can be parameterized in the following way:

$$(x - a)^2 + (y - b)^2 = r^2.$$

(4.7)

The voting takes place in a discretized version of the parameter space $A = span\{a, b, r\}$ called the *accumulator*, where each edge point p_e from the image votes for all combinations of a, b and r that yield a circle containing the edge point p_e. The points in the parameter space corresponding to the accumulator's maxima are considered as the best fitting circles as shown in figure 4.3.

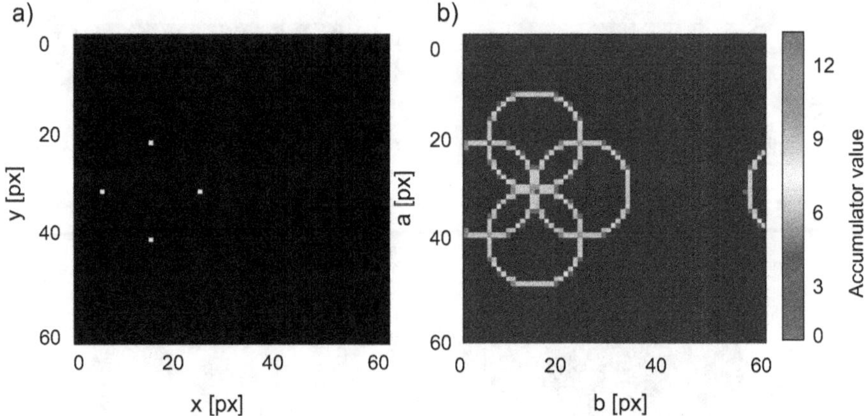

FIGURE 4.3: Visualization of particle detection with circular Hough transform approach: a) Binary image with four points. b) Values in the Hough accumulator for $r=10$ px. The maximum is at $a=32$ px and $b=15$ px, which is the center of the circle that includes all four points.

4.2.1.4 Blob detection

The fourth particle detection approach tested in this thesis is the blob detection technique that aims to find regions with similar properties as color or brightness in an image. The word *blob* stands for a binary large object, which is an object that consists of connected pixels in a binary image. Therefore, in a first step, the video frame is converted to a binary image, where the edges of the particles are detected. This is done by means of the edge detection using Gaussian blur and the Laplacian operator on the image. Gaussian blur is obtained by blurring an image by a Gaussian function. This image processing algorithm is used to reduce image noise and detail. By means of the Laplace operator the edges of the particles are detected. In the resulting binary image, the connected black regions can then be detected by a four-connectivity algorithm as implemented in *OpenCV* (Itseez, 2017). By means of that the white outlined objects are detectable.

4.2.1.5 Verification

For verification of the detection algorithms, realistic test images were generated in the open source 3D rendering software *Blender* with known particle positions. These test images were produced based on data from CFD-DEM simulations in order to get realistic distributions of particles positions. A comparison of an image frame of particle positions obtained by *Blender* via the simulation data and an image frame captured during experiments is shown in figure 4.4. Obviously, the synthetically generated image is sharper and has a higher contrast than the image from experiment. In addition, in the real image imperfections from scratches on the plexiglass apparatus wall are detectable, which do not appear in the synthetically generated images. Nevertheless, the synthetic images do appear realistic and can be used for validation purposes.

a)										b)

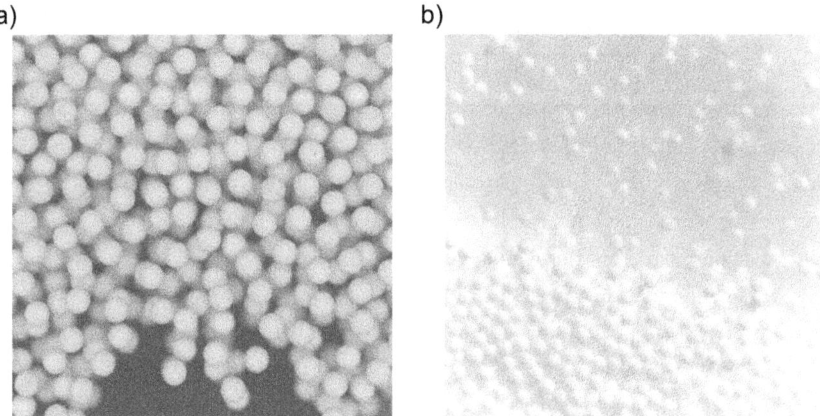

FIGURE 4.4: Comparison of synthetically generated image with particle positions and image captured from experiment: a) Image frame rendered using *Blender* with d_p=1 mm. b) Image frame captured in experiments using the high-speed camera with d_p=0.6 mm.

To quantify the correctness of the algorithms, two statistical error measures are defined: the particle count error e_cnt and the mean position error $\bar{e}_\mathrm{pos}$. The particle count error is defined as the ratio between the number of particles that are visible in an image and those that have been detected by the algorithm. Negative values indicate a fewer number of detected particles and positive values indicate an excess:

$$e_\mathrm{cnt} = \frac{N_\mathrm{detected}}{N_\mathrm{visible}} - 1. \tag{4.8}$$

The mean position error is the average distance of the detected particles j to their nearest visible particle i and gives information about the accuracy of the detected particle positions. The higher the value, the worse is the accuracy of the detection method:

$$\bar{e}_\mathrm{pos} = \frac{1}{N_\mathrm{detected}} \sum_{j=1}^{N_\mathrm{detected}} \min_i ||p_\mathrm{detected,j} - p_\mathrm{visible,i}||. \tag{4.9}$$

The evaluation of the error measures is given in table 4.1. It can be seen that both Hough transform and blob detection detect more particles than visible in the image, whereby the correlation detection algorithms only detect little less particles than visible.

TABLE 4.1: Error measures of particle detection on synthetically generated images with ground truth data.

Method	e_{cnt} [%]	$\bar{e}_{\mathrm{pos}}$ [px]
Correlation (image pattern)	−6.75	15.9
Correlation (synthetic pattern)	−13.9	17.2
Hough Transform	68.2	16.7
Blob Detection	51.4	18.1

False positive counts of particle detection are considered worse than false negatives, because it is possible to apply PTV with particle detection that omits many particles, while a tracking of non-existing particles will have a negative effect on the accuracy of the tracking algorithms. A comparison of the two pattern matching algorithms shows a little smaller error for the manual pattern selection. Thus, this method was used for particle detection in this thesis though it requires more time due to the necessary selection by the user.

4.2.2 Particle tracking

As the particle detection has been performed, algorithms are needed to work on subsequent sets of particle positions to determine their velocities. The following notation is used: S denotes the set of particle positions in the $n-1$-th frame and T denotes the same in the n-th frame. The number of particles detected in frame S is denoted M. Different PTV algorithms have been tested for their applicability on the spouted bed apparatus as e.g. the correspondence problem and the variational framework. The algorithm of the correspondence problem tries to find the optimal matching between each single particle in S to a single particle in T. It has been found that the variational iterative PTV approach shows highest tracking reliability, lowest mean particle velocity error and at the same time the lowest computation time. Therefore, only this approach is presented in detail. In contrast to the correspondence approach, the variational approach does not try to find the correspondence between different frames but the ansatz is similar to determining the optical flow in an image. Thus, the optical flow as the foundation of the approach is first described in subsection 4.2.1.1 followed by its application to PTV in subsection 4.2.2.2.

4.2.2.1 Optical flow

Optical flow is the distribution of apparent velocities of movement in an intensity image (Gibson, 1950). Under the assumption that the brightness level of one individual particle does not change over time, it is possible to determine the optical flow pattern by matching each pixel in a frame to its corresponding pixel in the next frame. A method for calculating the optical flow in an image sequence was proposed by Horn and Schunck (1981). The method is based on the assumption of smoothness of the spatio-temporal intensity gradients in the images. Optical flow is determined by assuming that the brightness of a particular point in the image E is constant:

$$\frac{\mathrm{d}E}{\mathrm{d}t} = 0. \tag{4.10}$$

Because the point is moving through the image over time, the partial derivatives of its motion have to be considered (Horn and Schunck, 1981):

$$\frac{\partial E}{\partial x}\frac{dx}{dt} + \frac{\partial E}{\partial y}\frac{dy}{dt} + \frac{\partial E}{\partial t} = 0. \tag{4.11}$$

Let $\frac{dx}{dt} = u_x$ and $\frac{dy}{dt} = u_y$ and denote partial derivatives $\frac{\partial E}{\partial \gamma} = E_\gamma$, then equation 4.11 becomes

$$E_x u_x + E_y u_y + E_t = 0. \tag{4.12}$$

If each point in the image could move independently of each other, any arbitrary constellation of point matching would be possible and a reconstruction of the trajectories cannot be calculated. In order to enable the calculation, it is assumed that adjacent points move in a similar way. This can for example be obtained with the assumption that the difference between the velocity of any point and the average velocity of its neighboring points is limited. For this purpose a cost function J_{HS} is created:

$$J_{\mathrm{HS}}(u_x, u_y) = \alpha^2[(\bar{u}_x - u_x)^2 + (\bar{u}_y - u_y)^2] + [u_x E_x + u_y E_y + E_t]^2, \tag{4.13}$$

with $\bar{u}_x$ and $\bar{u}_y$ the average neighborhood velocities, which can be calculated by applying a weighted average of the velocities of the surrounding pixels. In order to find the optical flow, i.e. u_x and u_y, the minimum of the cost function needs to be found. To find the minimum of J_{HS} its derivatives with respect to u_x and u_y must vanish:

$$\frac{\mathrm{d}}{\mathrm{d}u_x} J_{\mathrm{HS}} \overset{!}{=} 0 \wedge \frac{\mathrm{d}}{\mathrm{d}u_y} J_{\mathrm{HS}} \overset{!}{=} 0. \tag{4.14}$$

In a first step, the values of E_x, E_y, E_t and $\bar{u}_x$, $\bar{u}_y$ need to be found. For their approximation different convolution kernels can be used. Convolution is a common tool for working with image data numerically. The method combines each pixel of an image with its neighboring pixels using a linear combination that is defined by a convolution kernel K. Given an image M, the convolution of the image and a kernel of size $m \times n$ yields

$$[M * K](x, y) = \sum_{i=0}^{m} \sum_{j=0}^{n} M(x + i - a_i, y + j - a_j) K(i, j), \qquad (4.15)$$

where a_i and a_j are the location of the center of the kernel K in x and y direction, respectively.

Analogous, different convolution kernels for the approximation of the values of E_x, E_y, E_t and $\bar{u}_x$, $\bar{u}_y$ can be used:

$$K_x = \frac{1}{4} \begin{bmatrix} -1 & 1 \\ -1 & 1 \end{bmatrix}, K_y = \frac{1}{4} \begin{bmatrix} -1 & -1 \\ 1 & 1 \end{bmatrix}. \qquad (4.16)$$

With these convolution kernels the spatial derivatives can be calculated by applying them to the first frame I^n and the next frame I^{n+1}:

$$\begin{aligned} E_x &= I^n * K_x + I^{n+1} * K_x, \\ E_y &= I^n * K_y + I^{n+1} * K_y. \end{aligned} \qquad (4.17)$$

The temporal derivatives must have the same size as the spatial derivatives, which is why the kernel K_t is applied in equation 4.18 before taking the differences in equation 4.19.

$$K_t = \frac{1}{4} \begin{bmatrix} 1 & 1 \\ 1 & 1 \end{bmatrix}, \qquad (4.18)$$

$$E_t = I^n * K_t - I^{n+1} * K_t. \qquad (4.19)$$

The average velocities $\bar{u}_x$ and $\bar{u}_y$ are approximated by using a 3×3 smoothing kernel on the raw displacements:

$$\bar{u}_x = u_x * \frac{1}{12} \begin{bmatrix} 1 & 2 & 1 \\ 2 & 0 & 2 \\ 1 & 2 & 1 \end{bmatrix}. \qquad (4.20)$$

The derivatives of equation 4.13 with respect to u_x can be calculated by setting equations 4.21 and 4.22 to zero, which results in an equation system of the size twice the image dimension.

$$\frac{dJ_{HS}}{du_x} = 2\alpha^2(\bar{u}_x - u_x) + 2(\bar{u}_x E_x + \bar{u}_y E_y + E_t) E_x, \qquad (4.21)$$

$$\frac{dJ_{HS}}{du_y} = 2\alpha^2(\bar{u}_y - u_y) + 2(\bar{u}_x E_x + \bar{u}_y E_y + E_t) E_y. \qquad (4.22)$$

The equation system can be solved with the help of a standard matrix-inversion approach, as e.g. the Gauss-Jordan approach. As the size of the matrix discourages this approach, an iterative method by Horn and Schunck (1981) is chosen, which results with the iterative step k in the following values for u_x and u_y:

$$d^k = \frac{\bar{u}_x^k E_x + \bar{u}_y^k E_y + E_t}{\alpha^2 + E_x^2 + E_y^2},$$

(4.23)

$$u_x^{k+1} = \bar{u}_x^k - E_x d^k,$$

(4.24)

$$u_y^{k+1} = \bar{u}_y^k - E_y d^k.$$

(4.25)

These equations can be iterated until convergence is obtained.

4.2.2.2　Variational particle tracking velocimetry

The application of variational methods to the particle tracking problem was first proposed by Ruhnau et al. (2005) and Ruhnau (2006). Analogous to the classical optical flow problem, the task of variational PTV is to find a particle displacement field $\vec{u}(x, y)$ that most closely represents the instantaneous velocity field of the particles in the frame. For this purpose the distance measure $d_T(\vec{s})$ is defined as

$$d_T(\vec{s}) = \min\{||T_i - s||_2\}, i = 1, 2, ..., M.$$

(4.26)

Then the optimization problem that attracts each particle from $i = 1$ to M of frame S to its nearest neighbor in frame T can be defined as

$$J_1(\vec{u}) = \sum_{i=1}^{M} [d_T(\vec{S}_i + \vec{u}_i)]^2.$$

(4.27)

The term in equation 4.27 vanishes for all $\vec{u}$, which match any particle in S to any other particle in T. In order to represent the correct flow field similar to the approach of Horn and Schunck (1981), a global regularization term that enforces an additional constraint upon the flow field is established. One possible way to do this, is to penalize the summed magnitude of the gradient of $\vec{u}$:

$$J_2(\vec{u}) = \int_{\Omega} \langle \nabla \vec{u}(s), \nabla \vec{u}(s) \rangle \mathrm{d}s,$$

(4.28)

with the convex hull Ω (subset of an affine space that is closed under convex combinations (Hazewinkel, 1995)) of the area, which contains all points $\vec{S} + \vec{u}$. The terms in equations 4.27 and 4.28 can be joined to an overall cost function $J(\vec{u})$ with a coupling constant λ:

$$J(\vec{u}) = J_1(\vec{u}) + \lambda J_2(\vec{u}). \tag{4.29}$$

The optical displacement field is then found by minimizing this cost function to:

$$\arg \min_u J(\vec{u}). \tag{4.30}$$

In 4.30 $\arg \min_u$ refers to the inputs of u, at which the function output is as small as possible.

4.2.2.3   Iterative minimization

Cohen (1996) showed that variational problems consisting of a local deformation term and a global regularization term - equations 4.27 and 4.28, respectively - can be formulated as a multi-step iterative minimization using an auxiliary variable. Because the term in equation 4.27 is non-convex, the splitting is necessary. Applying Cohen's approach to the term and introducing the auxiliary variable $\vec{u}_{\mathrm{aux}}$ yields:

$$J_{\mathrm{aux}}(\vec{u}, \vec{u}_{\mathrm{aux}}) = \frac{1}{2} \sum_{i=1}^{M} [(1-\alpha)[d_{S+\vec{u}}(S + \vec{u}_{\mathrm{aux},i})]^2 + \alpha[d_{\mathrm{T}}(S + \vec{u}_{\mathrm{aux},i})]^2] + \lambda J_2(\vec{u}). \tag{4.31}$$

The minimization of equation 4.31 is equivalent to subsequently minimizing two split terms (Cohen, 1996):

$$E_I(\vec{u}_{\mathrm{aux}}) = \frac{1}{2} \sum_{i=1}^{M} [(1-\alpha)[d_{S+\vec{u}}(S + \vec{u}_{\mathrm{aux},i})]^2 + \alpha[d_{\mathrm{T}}(S + \vec{u}_{\mathrm{aux},i})]^2], \tag{4.32}$$

$$E_{II}(\vec{u}) = \frac{1}{2} \sum_{i=1}^{M} [d_{S+\vec{u}}(S + \vec{u}_{\mathrm{aux},i})]^2 + \lambda \int_{\Omega} \langle \nabla \vec{u}(s), \nabla \vec{u}(s) \rangle ds. \tag{4.33}$$

The term in equation 4.32 represents a local deformation of the flow field towards the respective nearest neighbors of each particle, as described before. To minimize this term iteratively, an update step can be designed. This method yields a value for $\vec{u}_{\mathrm{aux}}$ that reduces the values for $d_{S+\vec{u}}(S + \vec{u}_{\mathrm{aux},i})$ and $d_{\mathrm{T}}(S + \vec{u}_{\mathrm{aux},i})$ simultaneously. When iterating, it converges to the nearest neighbor solution closest to the initial $\vec{u}_{\mathrm{aux}}$. For the determination of $\vec{u}$ in equation 4.33 a smoothing of the gradients of $\vec{u}$ is needed similar to the approach shown in equation 4.20. Due to the inhomogeneous distribution of the particles, the smoothing step cannot be performed using matrix convolution. Instead, a distance based averaging approach has been applied in this thesis, which averages the displacement field $\vec{u}$ in the n nearest neighbors of each particle, using the distance of each particle pair as an inverse weight. The listings of the attraction step towards the minimization of E_I and the global regularization step towards minimizing E_{II} are given in the appendix D. It can be shown empirically, that the combination of both steps converges towards the minimum of equation 4.31, even if only iterated for a short time, i.e. 30 iterations.

4.2.2.4   Application to spouted bed apparatus

The presented particle tracking velocimetry algorithm was used to determine the threshold velocity used for allocation of particles to the spout zone and thereby calculating the circulation frequencies as described in section 3.5.2. Exemplary, the resulting data is shown here for a gas volume flow rate of 120 $\mathrm{m}^3\,\mathrm{h}^{-1}$. The velocities were measured 3 cm above the middle profile. From the plot shown in figure 4.5 a threshold velocity of 0.37 $\mathrm{m\,s}^{-1}$ is set for these conditions. For 70 $\mathrm{m}^3\,\mathrm{h}^{-1}$ a threshold velocity of 0.28 $\mathrm{m\,s}^{-1}$ was determined and for 100 $\mathrm{m}^3\,\mathrm{h}^{-1}$ it was found to be 0.32 $\mathrm{m\,s}^{-1}$. Every particle having a positive velocity equal to or higher than the respective value was allocated to the spout zone.

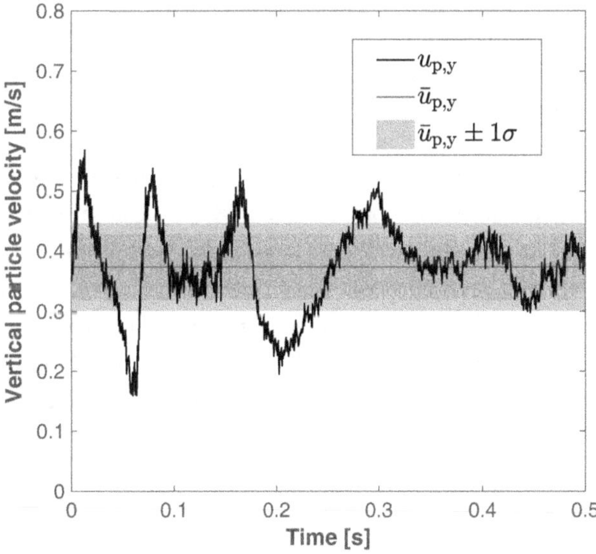

FIGURE 4.5: Recording of spout velocities and averaging of those for an exemplary gas volume flow rate of 120 $\mathrm{m}^3\,\mathrm{h}^{-1}$.

4.3 Quantification of coating quality

For quantification of coating quality with digital image analysis, the individual particles were detected with the particle tracking algorithm as described in section 4.2. As the coating process is slow, the correlation based method still works if the particles' brightness changes over time. After detection all particles are segmented and analyzed individually. This allows the detection of even small scratches or uncoated spots instead of just gaining information about the mean coating quality. After segmentation images are normalized to reduce effects introduced by external lighting conditions. Lighting fall-off along the spheres is compensated using a mask $M_{i,j}$ that can be multiplied with the particle fovea. The mask is pre-initialized to be a circular cut out of the particle size d_p:

$$M_{i,j} = \begin{cases} 0 & \text{if} \quad ||[i - \frac{d_\mathrm{p}}{2}, j - \frac{d_\mathrm{p}}{2}]|| > \frac{d_\mathrm{p}}{2} \\ 1, & \text{else} \end{cases}. \tag{4.34}$$

Then, a Gaussian lighting model of the spherical particles can be fitted to the mask to compensate lighting fall-off:

$$M_{i,j}^\mathrm{G} = M_{i,j} \cdot \left(a \cdot e^{\frac{-r_\mathrm{p}^2}{2c^2}} \right)^{-1}. \tag{4.35}$$

Equation 4.35 resembles the inverse of the lighting model used in the synthetic particle detector from equation 4.4, with parameters a, r_p and c selected appropriately.

After the particles are detected and normalized, each particle image is analyzed for its respective coating fraction. As the coating layer thickness is not accessible via image analysis, the coating layer is evaluated regarding the darkness of the particles and its distribution. The relationship between particle coating thickness and particle color, i.e. brightness, is assumed to be a linear interpolation from the lightest particle color meaning 0 % relative coating and the darkest color meaning 100 % relative coating. For each pixel of the normalized particle image, its brightness is clamped to an interval $B_\mathrm{p} \in [0, 1]$ according to equation 4.36. Let B_p' be the brightness of the normalized pixel, then

$$B_\mathrm{p} = \frac{B_\mathrm{p}' - B_{max}}{B_{\max} - B_{\min}}, \tag{4.36}$$

if $B_\mathrm{p}' \in [B_{\min}, B_{\max}]$, otherwise the pixel is discarded. This has the effect, that specularity on the particles is not misclassified as uncoated area. The values for $B_{\min}$ and $B_{\max}$ can be configured and were inferred by evaluating histograms of particles with low and high coatings, respectively. The values of B_p are then quantized into k bins of equal size. To determine the value of α_c, a threshold of the relative coating has to be fixed, which classifies particles into coated and uncoated ones. This means that all particles with

$B_\mathrm{p} \leq B_\mathrm{p}^{\mathrm{cutoff}}$ are considered as coated. The cutoff value needs to be set with respect to the target coating result, e.g. the complete covering of the particles meaning that no pixels of the core material brightness should be detectable. The correlation between layer thickness and brightness has to be determined, e.g. by electron microscopy and the brightness of the target layer thickness is then set as cutoff value. The thicker the required coating thickness, the darker is the target particle and therefore the $B_\mathrm{p}^{\mathrm{cutoff}}$ needs to be set to lower values.

As the particles are spherical and the evaluated pixels show the projection of a sphere into a circle in the image plane, area normalization needs to be performed. Pixels near the boarder of the circle correspond to a larger area of the sphere, which is visualized in the error distribution in figure 4.6.

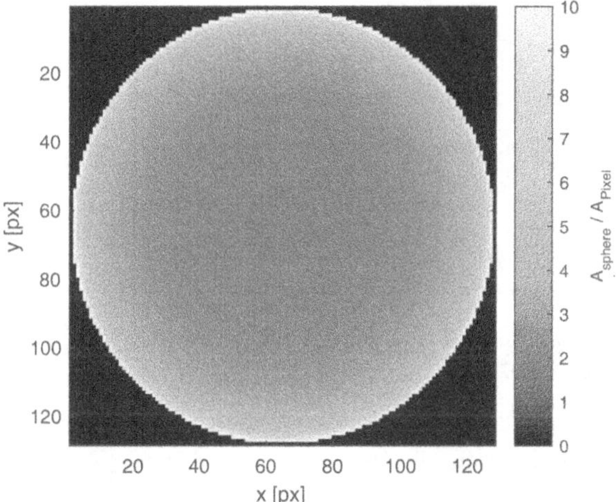

FIGURE 4.6: The ratio of the area of the sphere in the projection plane versus the area of the pixel is increasing the closer the pixel is to the boarder of the sphere. Pixels that are only partially on the sphere are excluded from the evaluation.

To calculate the ratio between the pixel area and the area of the surface of the sphere under the pixel, first the projection of the sphere onto the image plane has to be reversed. For simplicity it is assumed that this projection is a parallel projection along the z-axis. The corresponding point i_sp on the sphere from the point i_image can be found by intersecting the ray $\vec{i}$ with the sphere SP:

$$\vec{i}(t) = [x, y, a]^T + t \cdot [0, 0, 1]^T. \tag{4.37}$$

Without loss of generality, let $a = 0$, then equation 4.37 becomes

$$\vec{i}(t) = [x, y, t]^T. \tag{4.38}$$

SP can be defined as

$$SP : R = ||\vec{x} - \vec{x_{\text{ctr}}}||, \tag{4.39}$$

and again without loss of generality, $\vec{x_{\text{ctr}}} = [0, 0, 0]^T$ and $R = 1$. The intersection of the ray and the sphere yields

$$\vec{i} = [x, y, \pm\sqrt{1 - (x^2 + y^2)}]^T. \tag{4.40}$$

The image of the sphere has a finite resolution. The side length of each square pixel is d_{sp}, the area of a pixel is $S_{\text{pixel}} = d_{\text{sp}}^2$. Therefore, the coordinates $\vec{p_{ij}}$ of each corner of the pixel at x and y are

$$\vec{p_{11}} = [x - \frac{d_{\text{sp}}}{2}, \quad y - \frac{d_{\text{sp}}}{2}, 0], \tag{4.41}$$

$$\vec{p_{12}} = [x - \frac{d_{\text{sp}}}{2}, \quad y + \frac{d_{\text{sp}}}{2}, 0], \tag{4.42}$$

$$\vec{p_{21}} = [x + \frac{d_{\text{sp}}}{2}, \quad y - \frac{d_{\text{sp}}}{2}, 0], \tag{4.43}$$

$$\vec{p_{22}} = [x + \frac{d_{\text{sp}}}{2}, \quad y + \frac{d_{\text{sp}}}{2}, 0]. \tag{4.44}$$

These points can be transformed back onto the sphere using equation 4.38. The resulting points on the sphere are the border points of the sphere section that has the corresponding area A_{sphere}. For simplicity, the corresponding area is calculated by approximating the area of the spherical section with a polygon spanned by $\vec{p_{ij}}$. The area of the polygon can be calculated as following:

$$S_{\text{sp}} \approx ||(\vec{p_{11}} - \vec{p_{12}}) \times (\vec{p_{21}} - \vec{p_{11}})|| + ||(\vec{p_{22}} - \vec{p_{12}}) \times (\vec{p_{22}} - \vec{p_{21}})||, \tag{4.45}$$

where $\times$ denotes the vector cross product. The correction factor f_{cor} between the area of the pixel and the area of the sphere is simply the ratio between the two:

$$f_{\text{cor}} = \frac{S_{\text{sp}}}{S_{\text{pixel}}}. \tag{4.46}$$

After normalizing with regard to brightness and covered area, the coating fraction α_{c} can be calculated by evaluating all particles in the image and adding up the ratio of the coated area of the particle A_{coated} compared to the total particle surface area A_{p}.

$$\alpha_{\text{c}} = \frac{A_{\text{coated}}}{A_{\text{p}}}, \tag{4.47}$$

which for spherical particles becomes

$$\alpha_c = \frac{A_{\text{coated}}}{\pi d_p^2}. \tag{4.48}$$

Besides the complete coating of all particles, it is beneficial, if all particles in the apparatus have similar levels of coating. Therefore, not only the overall coating fraction but also the uniformity of the coating u_c is analyzed. It is defined as the coefficient of variation of the particles' coating fraction:

$$u_c = \frac{\sigma_c}{\mu_c}, \tag{4.49}$$

where μ_c denotes the mean of the coating fraction and σ_c denotes its standard deviation. Even though normalization is performed, the algorithm is limited to almost the same experimental setup and camera settings every time as the lighting needs to be identical for comparison reasons and qualitative statements.

5

Characterization of laboratory spouted bed

5.1 Introduction

This chapter presents the results that have been obtained by experimental and numerical investigations on the *ProCell*® *5* apparatus. The experiments were performed with both the laboratory plant from company Glatt and with the transparent replica made of polycarbonate, which allows a more detailed investigation of the flow pattern as well as high frequency pressure measurements. This chapter is organized as follows: In section 5.2 experimental investigations regarding the spouting stability of the *ProCell*® *5* apparatus for both γ-Al2O3 particles with a size of 656 µm and *Cellets*® *500* are presented. Afterwards, special emphasis is placed on the numerical analysis of the process. Studies regarding the mesh independence, simulation conditions and used models (turbulence and drag models) are presented. Then, in subchapter 5.4, the results from simulations under optimized conditions are shown and compared with experimental data. In section 5.5 the influence of draft plates on the spout pattern is evaluated using numerical and experimental data. The optimized configuration of the plates was designed using simulations with the aim of a homogeneous spouting behavior.

5.2 Experimental determination of spouting stability

In a first step, the regimes of stable and instable spouting were experimentally determined by analysis of pressure drop signals and by visual observation of the spout pattern and bed expansion height. By means of Fourier transform of the pressure drop signal and the resulting power plot, the stability was evaluated as a single narrow peak refers to stable spouting and a broad peak distribution indicates instable spouting. A spouting analysis with finding of stability dependencies has been performed by Gryczka et al. (2009) and Salikov et al. (2015a) for pseudo two-dimensional apparatuses. In this thesis, it was found that spout deflections or variations in bed expansion height also occur in the third dimension indicating that it needs to be taken into account.

The spouting stability was investigated for both γ-Al2O3 and *Cellets® 500* particles with a particle bed mass of 1 kg. In both cases the dependence on the gas volume flow rate was quantified, whereby the flow rate was increased in intervals of 10 $m^3\,h^{-1}$. Additionally, γ-Al2O3 particles with 1.8 mm and 3.0 mm were mixed with the smaller ones in different concentrations in order to evaluate the influence of a binary or ternary mixture. For the *Cellets® 500* particles, which were later used for coating, the bed filling and thereby the static bed height were varied as well in order to get a regime map indicating the range of stable and instable spouting.

5.2.1   Experiments with γ-Al2O3 particles

Experiments with γ-Al2O3 particles were performed with a monodisperse system with particles of 656 µm size and with binary and ternary systems, where additional fractions of 1.8 and 3.0 mm size were added.

5.2.1.1   Monodisperse system

Experiments with varying gas volume flow rates (20 - 170 $m^3\,h^{-1}$) at a constant bed mass of 1 kg with 656 µm sized particles were performed. Up to a gas flow rate of 30 $m^3\,h^{-1}$ the bed remained completely static and the measured pressure drop fluctuations were irregular with low amplitudes. With increasing gas velocity small cavities were observed, which turned into bubbles that ascended to the bed surface. The minimum spouting velocity u_{ms}, which corresponds to the point of initial spouting, was determined at a gas volume flow rate of 40 $m^3\,h^{-1}$. Stable spouting occurred at gas flow rates between 40 and 70 $m^3\,h^{-1}$. The corresponding pressure drop signals show regular fluctuations, which result in single peaks in the power plots. From the power plot of a gas volume flow rate of 50 $m^3\,h^{-1}$ a main frequency of about 5 Hz can be determined. The power plot and the corresponding snapshots, obtained by high-speed camera observation, are shown in figure 5.1.

Further increase of the gas velocity results in irregular bed expansion heights and spout deflections. This inhomogeneity is also visible in the irregular pressure drop fluctuations

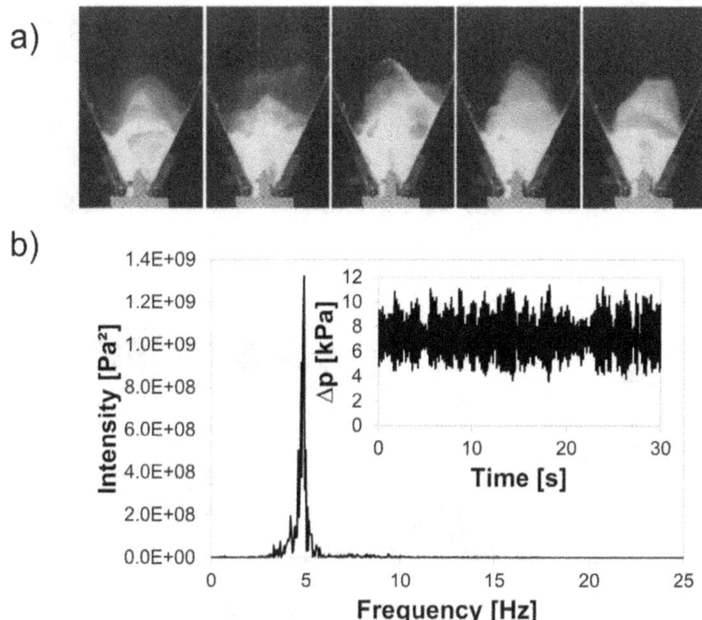

FIGURE 5.1: a) Snapshots obtained from experiment with 1 kg γ-Al2O3 particles (656 µm) at a gas volume flow rate of 50 $m^3\,h^{-1}$ (stable regime) in time interval of 0.1 s and b) corresponding FFT power plot with measured pressure drop fluctuations.

and the broad peak distribution in the power plot indicating the instable regime. Exemplarily, the spout pattern at a gas volume flow rate of 100 $m^3\,h^{-1}$ is shown in figure 5.2.

In former investigations of spouted bed processes a second stable regime (dilute spouting) after the instable regime was described (Salikov et al., 2015b). This could not be investigated in the regarded experiments as a gas volume flow rate above 170 $m^3\,h^{-1}$ could not be adjusted due to particle elutriation.

In the final analysis, a dependency of the spouting stability on the gas volume flow rate for the given bed material and spouted bed apparatus was obtained by plotting the amplitude expressed as standard deviation of the pressure drop fluctuations against the gas volume flow rate. The transition from bubbling to stable regime and from stable to instable regime can be detected by a sudden increase in the standard deviation. During stable spouting, the amplitude is almost constant as shown in figure 5.3.

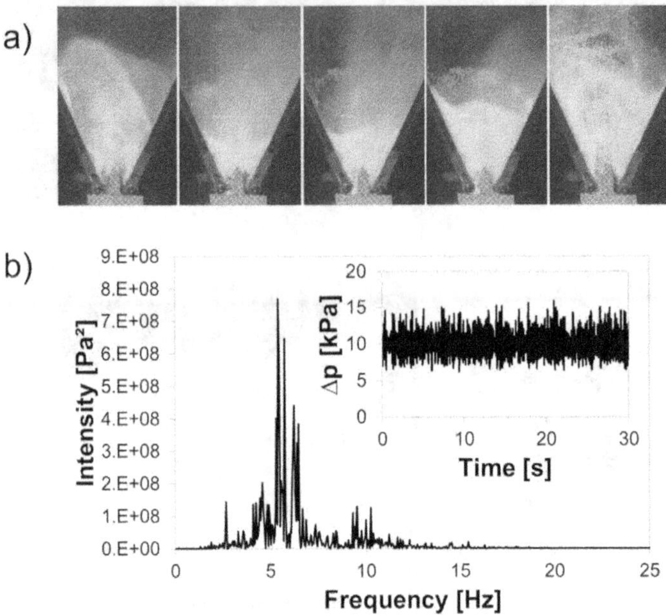

FIGURE 5.2: a) Snapshots obtained from experiment with 1 kg γ-Al2O3 particles (656 µm) at a gas volume flow rate of 100 m^3 h^{-1} (instable regime) in time interval of 0.1 s and b) corresponding FFT power plot with measured pressure drop fluctuations.

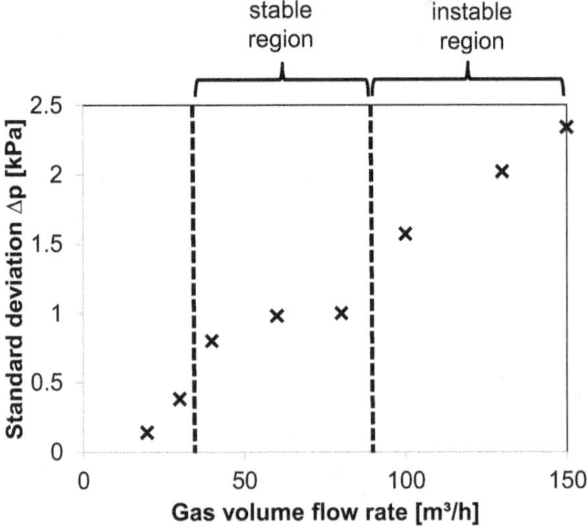

FIGURE 5.3: The standard deviation of the pressure drop time series as function of the gas volume flow rate for a bed mass of 1 kg γ-Al2O3 particles (656 µm) indicating the transition between bubbling, stable and instable spouting.

5.2.1.2 Binary system

In order to determine the influence of a binary mixture of particle sizes, experiments were performed with 656 µm and 3.0 mm sized γ-Al$_2$O$_3$ particles. For this combination of particles three different mixtures were used in addition to the measurement of the pure fractions as shown in table 5.1. In order to visually observe the flow pattern, the small particles (656 µm) were colored in yellow, whereas the big ones (3.0 mm) stayed uncolored. By means of visual observation and high frequency pressure measurements the stability range of each mixture was determined. The resulting gas volume flow rates of stable spouting and the range of the interval are given in table 5.2.

TABLE 5.1: Experimental design for investigation of the influence of binary systems on the spouting stability in *ProCell*® 5 apparatus made of polycarbonate.

Experiment No.	0.6 mm [wt.-%]	3.0 mm [wt.-%]
1	0	100
2	25	75
3	50	50
4	75	25
5	100	0

From table 5.2 it can be seen that the size of the interval of stable spouting is determined by the small particle fraction. The stable range is more similar to that of the small particle fraction than to that of the bigger particles. Nevertheless, a small increase of the stable range of the small particles can be obtained by adding particles having its stable regime at higher gas volume flow rates. On the other hand, the stability range of the big particles is markedly reduced and shifted to smaller gas volume flow rates even at a mass concentration of 25 wt.-% of the small particles. Additionally, segregation was observed during experiments with binary mixtures. Bigger particles accumulated in the spout region of the apparatus, whereas smaller ones were primarily visible in the annulus zone.

5.2.1.3 Ternary system

As typical industrial processes include even more than two different particle sizes the third particle size of 1.8 mm (according to manufacturers' data) was added which was colored in red. The conditions listed in table 5.3 were tested, which resulted in the stability ranges given in table 5.4.

In case of the equivalent mixture of the three fractions, no stable spouting regime was observed. This indicates that a dominant phase is required for obtaining a homogeneous

TABLE 5.2: Experimental determined stability ranges for binary mixtures of different compositions.

Composition (656 µm [wt.-%], 3.0 mm [wt.-%])	Stable range [m³ h⁻¹]	Interval size of stable spouting [m³ h⁻¹]
0, 100	100 - 170	70
25, 75	70 - 110	40
50, 50	50 - 80	30
75, 25	40 - 90	50
100, 0	40 - 80	40

spouting. From the three other cases it is concluded that the gas volume flow rates of the stable regime are higher the bigger the particles of the dominant phase are. On the other hand, the big interval of stable spouting that was measured for the 3.0 mm sized particles, is decreased by adding the other two fractions. It can be summarized that the stability range and the corresponding gas volume flow rates of small particles can be increased by adding bigger particles but the range and the flow rates from big particles are decreased by adding smaller particles. Similar to the binary mixtures, segregation was observed, which is exemplarily shown in figure 5.4. The accumulation of big particles in the spray zone could be critical when performing granulation experiments with a wide range of particle sizes as a further increase of only the big particles might result in a bed collapse.

TABLE 5.3: Experimental design for investigation of the influence of ternary systems on the spouting stability in *ProCell®5* apparatus made of polycarbonate.

Experiment No.	0.6 mm [wt.-%]	1.8 mm [wt.-%]	3.0 mm [wt.-%]
1	33.3	33.3	33.3
2	60	20	20
3	20	60	20
4	20	20	60

TABLE 5.4: Experimental determined stability ranges for the different combinations of ternary mixtures.

Experiment No.	Stable range [m³ h⁻¹]	Interval size of stable spouting [m³ h⁻¹]
1	-	-
2	30 - 90	60
3	50 - 100	50
4	60 - 110	50

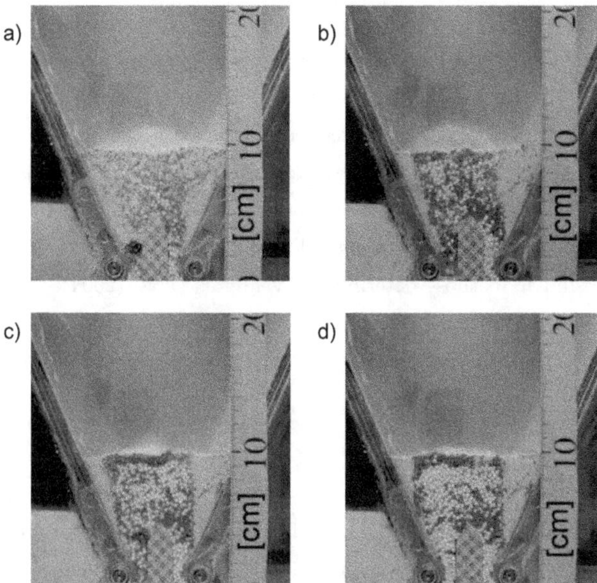

FIGURE 5.4: Segregation effects observed during experiment with a ternary mixture of γ-Al2O3 particles; 1 kg; 20 wt.-% 656 µm, 20 wt.-% 1.8 mm, 60 wt.-% 3.0 mm; gas volume flow rate: 50 $m^3\,h^{-1}$. The time interval between images is 30 s.

5.2.2 Experiments with *Cellets® 500* particles

Analogous to the results with the γ-Al2O3-particles, the dependency of the spouting stability on the gas volume flow rate was determined for *Cellets® 500* particles with, in the first step, a constant bed mass of 1 kg.

5.2.2.1 Constant bed mass of 1 kg

Up to a gas flow rate of about 30 $m^3\,h^{-1}$ the bed remained again completely static. The corresponding pressure fluctuations are irregular with low amplitudes resulting in a broad distribution in the power plot with low intensities. With increasing gas velocity, small cavities were observed above the gas inlet region. At a gas flow rate of about 30 $m^3\,h^{-1}$ first bubbles were formed above the gas inlet, which ascended through the bed to the surface. Up to a flow rate of 50 $m^3\,h^{-1}$ the number of bubbles and their intensities increased. Visual observations showed intermittent blocking of one of the gas inlet slits, which could be unblocked by slightly increasing the gas velocity. Plugging of the slits occurred randomly and was non-reproducible.

At gas flow rates between 50 and 70 $m^3\,h^{-1}$, stable spouting with its typical well-differentiated regions of spout, fountain and annulus was observed as shown in figure 5.5

for a gas volume flow rate of 50 $m^3 h^{-1}$. The pressure drop signal and the corresponding power plot of the flow rates belonging to the stable regime are also shown in figure 5.5. The pressure drop fluctuations are regular, which results in a narrow frequency distribution with a slim peak at the main frequency. The main frequency of the pressure fluctuations slightly increases from 4.5 to 6 Hz and also the intensities depend on the gas volume flow rate. The gas volume flow rate of 50 $m^3 h^{-1}$ is the point of initial spouting and corresponds to the minimum spouting velocity u_{ms}. The main frequencies in the stable regime are similar to those determined by Freitas et al. (2004), Gryczka et al. (2009) and Salikov et al. (2015a). Within the stable regime, the system is less chaotic than in the previous regimes. Nevertheless, irregularities in the depth were observed. The fountain was not constant in height over the depth of the bed but showed two spouts with lower bed expansion in between. With increasing gas volume flow rate, slight lateral spout deflections became apparent.

At gas flow rates exceeding 70 $m^3 h^{-1}$, the lateral deflections became more prominent and random changes in the bed expansion height were observed as can be seen in figure 5.6. Additionally, isolated ejections occurred, which resulted in elutriation of bed material. The pressure signals and FFT plots concur with the visual observations. Exemplarily, the plots for gas volume flow rates of 80, 110 and 140 $m^3 h^{-1}$ are also shown in figure 5.6. The fluctuations show high variations in amplitude and frequencies, which result in additional peaks with smaller amplitude around the main frequency in the power spectrum distributions. The main frequency increases with higher gas volume flow rates, whereby the amplitudes of the additional peaks increase. Starting at a gas flow rate of 150 $m^3 h^{-1}$, the variations in pressure drop amplitudes continue to increase, resulting in a power plot where no main frequency can be identified anymore. The distribution is broader than before and is slightly shifted to the right with increasing flow rate up to 170 $m^3 h^{-1}$ as can be seen in figure 5.7. At the same time, the peak at a frequency around 2.5 Hz appears and increases in the interval between 150 and 170 $m^3 h^{-1}$. With increasing gas flow rate within the instable region, the intensities decrease, which indicates the initialization of another stable region, the dilute spouting. This spouting regime could not be reached because of high particle elutriation at gas flow rates exceeding 170 $m^3 h^{-1}$.

5.2.2.2 Varying bed mass

In order to obtain a regime map for the given spouted bed apparatus and the *Cellets® 500* particles, the described experiments were repeated for bed masses of 1.25, 1.5, 1.75 and 2 kg. Again, the amplitude of the pressure drop fluctuations together with the visual observations and the power plots, as explained previously, were used to identify the borders

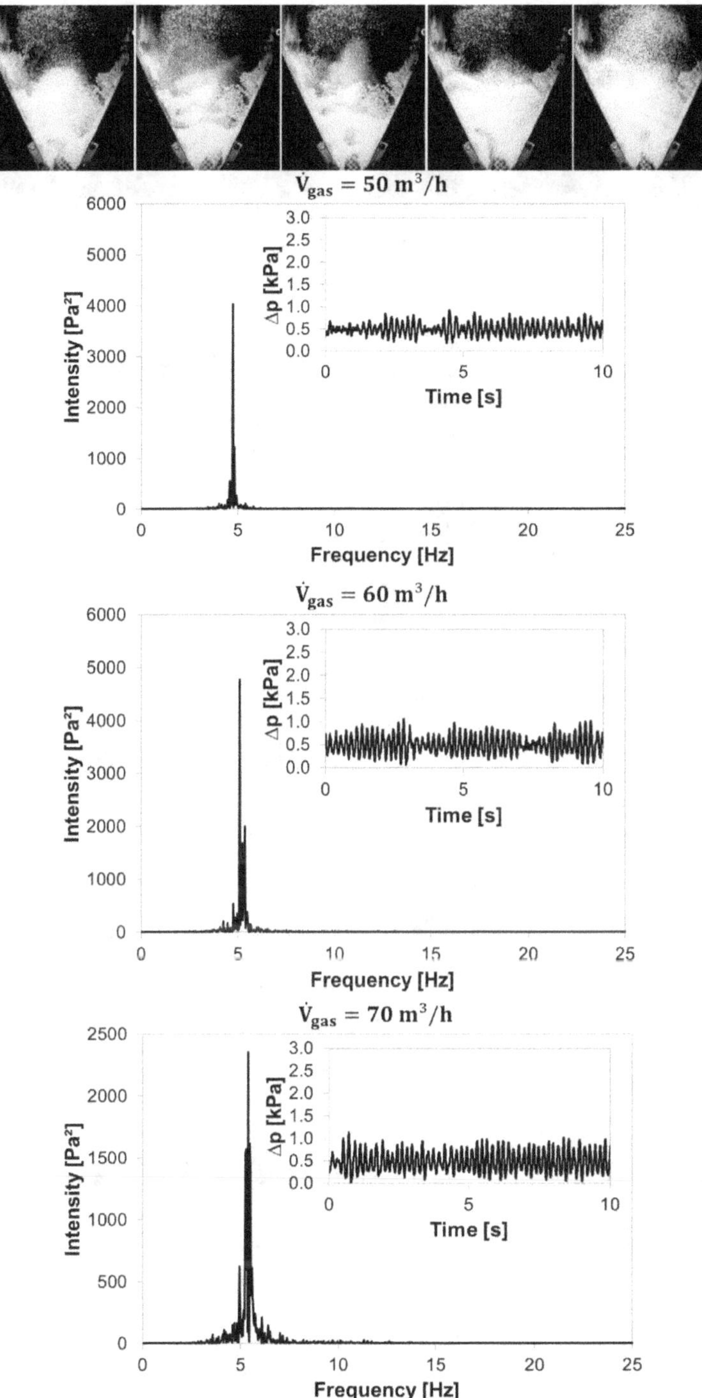

FIGURE 5.5: FFT power plots with measured pressure drop fluctuations for the stable regime with selected gas volume flow rates of a) 50 $m^3\,h^{-1}$, b) 60 $m^3\,h^{-1}$ and c) 70 $m^3\,h^{-1}$ in time interval of 0.1 s for 1 kg *Cellets® 500* particles. Examplarily, the recorded flow pattern is shown for 50 $m^3\,h^{-1}$.

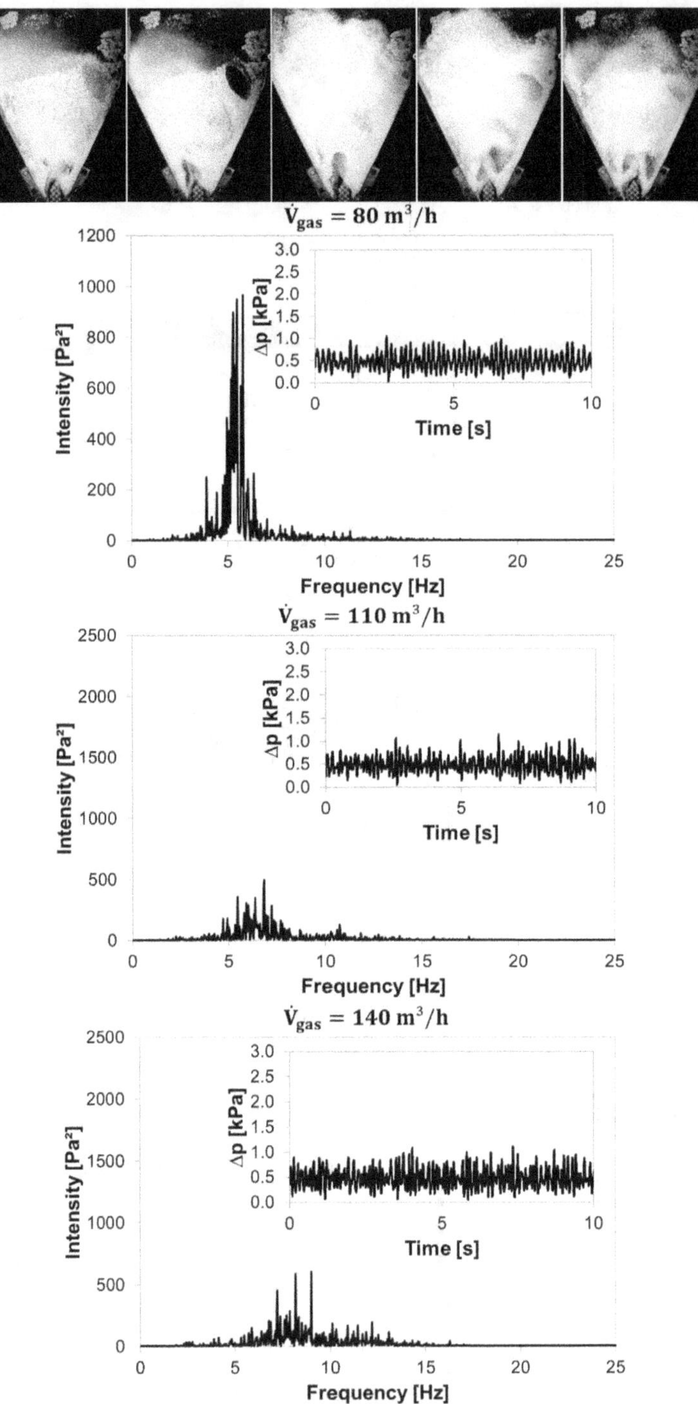

FIGURE 5.6: FFT power plots with measured pressure drop fluctuations for the instable regime with selected gas volume flow rates of a) 80 m^3 h^{-1}, b) 110 m^3 h^{-1} and c) 140 m^3 h^{-1} in time interval of 0.1 s for 1 kg *Cellets® 500* particles. Examplarily, the recorded flow pattern is shown for 80 m^3 h^{-1}.

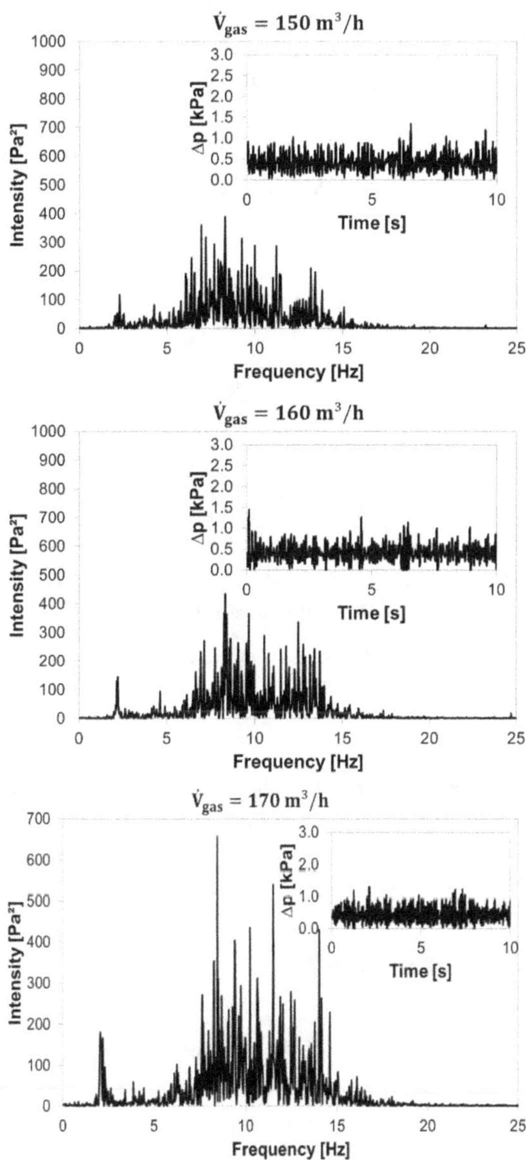

FIGURE 5.7: FFT power plots with measured pressure drop fluctuations for the instable regime with selected gas volume flow rates of a) 150 $\text{m}^3\,\text{h}^{-1}$, b) 160 $\text{m}^3\,\text{h}^{-1}$ and c) 170 $\text{m}^3\,\text{h}^{-1}$ in time interval of 0.1 s for 1 kg *Cellets® 500* particles.

of the different spouting regimes. Analogous to the evaluation of the experiments with
γ-Al2O3 particles, the standard deviation of the pressure time series is plotted against
the gas volume flow rate for identification of the regime ranges. This is exemplarily
shown in figure 5.8 for a bed mass of 2 kg. In the stable regime the amplitude is almost
constant, whereas instable spouting is marked by an increased standard deviation.

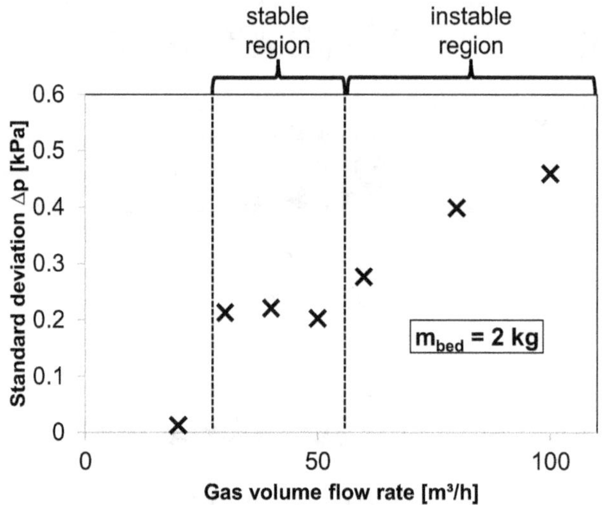

FIGURE 5.8: The standard deviation of the pressure time series as function of the gas
volume flow rate for a bed mass of 2 kg *Cellets*® *500* particles.

By evaluating the amplitudes of the pressure drop fluctuations for different bed fillings,
a regime map (figure 5.9) showing the dependence of the spouting stability on the bed
mass and the gas volume flow rate was obtained, which indicates a maximized stable
spouting region for a bed filling of around 1.25 kg (Kieckhefen et al., 2018).

5.3 Simulation conditions

After the experimental characterization of the laboratory spouted bed, the focus is now
placed on its numerical investigation. As all simulations in this thesis, the evaluation of
applicable models and simulation conditions was performed with γ-Al2O3 particles with
mean particle size of $d_{50,3} = 0.656$ mm.

5.3.1 Mesh independence

In order to ensure that the simulation mesh does not have an influence on the numerical
results, a mesh independence study was performed. The geometry of the *ProCell*® *5*

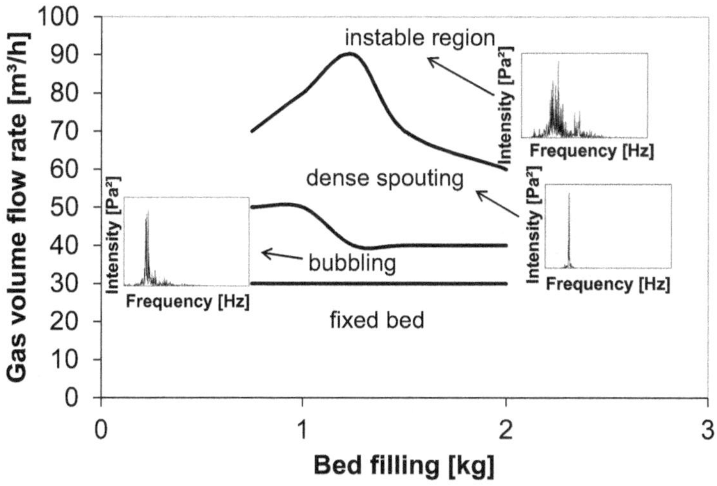

FIGURE 5.9: Regime map obtained by visual observations and analysis of pressure drop fluctuations (valid for *Cellets*® *500* particles in the *ProCell*® *5* apparatus (Glatt GmbH)).

process chamber was supplied by Glatt Ingenieurtechnik GmbH (Weimar, Germany) and constructed in CAD software *SolidWorks*. As described in section 3.3, the meshing was performed in *OpenFOAM* meshing tool *snappyHexMesh*. In order to validate the mesh independence of the flow on the grid cell size, five different refinement levels were chosen (0, 1, 2, 3 and 4) for pure CFD simulations. The resulting cell numbers and the simulation conditions are listed in table 5.5.

TABLE 5.5: Simulation conditions of CFD simulation for investigation of mesh independence.

Refinement level	0	1	2	3	4
Number of cells	2644	4339	6208	22915	64379
Cell diameter [mm]	40	20	10	5	2.5
Air volume flow rate [m³ h⁻¹]			125		
CFD time step [s]		2.5×10^{-4}		5×10^{-5}	2×10^{-5}
Turbulence model			realizable k-ε		

For quantification and comparison, the vertical velocity profiles were recorded at two different heights above the middle profile under steady state conditions as shown in figure 5.10. The two zones are supposed to be zones with intense particle-fluid contact. As can be concluded from the diagram, the velocity distributions above the width as well as the spout get narrower with increasing refinement level. Especially the increases from refinement level 2 to 3 and from 3 to 4, respectively show almost a doubling of the

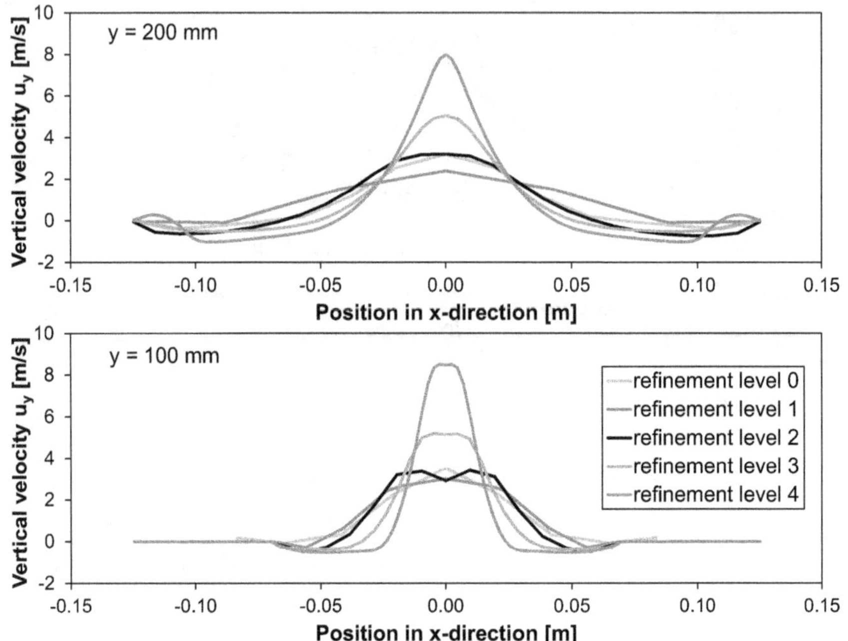

FIGURE 5.10: Vertical velocity profiles on two different heights (100 mm, 200 mm) for different refinement levels of a pure CFD simulation; gas volume flow rate: $125\ \mathrm{m^3\,h^{-1}}$.

maximum velocity. Coupled CFD-DEM simulations are not applicable with refinement levels of 3 or 4 as the numerical effort would be too high. Therefore, only levels below 3 were analyzed for evaluation of dependence of the results on the refinement with the conditions given in table 5.6. The resulting vertical particle velocity profiles are given in figure 5.11 for four different heights in order to cover the whole range of spouting behavior from spout to fountain region.

TABLE 5.6: Simulation conditions of CFD-DEM simulation for investigation of mesh independence.

Refinement level	0	1	2
Number of cells	2644	4339	6208
Cell diameter [mm]	40	20	10
Air volume flow rate $[\mathrm{m^3\,h^{-1}}]$		125	
CFD time step [s]		1.25×10^{-4}	
Turbulence model		realizable k-ε	
Mass of particles [kg]		1	
Scaling factor δ		4	
DEM time step [s]		1.25×10^{-6}	
Drag model		Koch-Hill	

The differences in the particle velocity profiles get bigger with increasing height. At the smallest height of 50 mm the refinement level of 2 results in a precise spout profile, whereas the profile is not that sharp for the lower refinement levels. At 300 mm only by using a refinement level of 2 particles are recorded. As they were detected in experiments at this height, a refinement level of 2 was chosen for all following simulations as it is the best compromise between a precise representation of the spout and an adequate simulation time.

5.3.2 Turbulence model

Based on a refinement level of 2, CFD-simulations with different turbulence models (laminar, realizable k-ε and k-ω-SST) were performed with the simulation parameters given in table 5.7. The resulting vertical velocity profiles for a height of 100 and 200 mm are shown in figure 5.12.

TABLE 5.7: Simulation conditions of CFD simulation for investigation of turbulence model.

Turbulence model	laminar	realizable k-ε	k-ω-SST
Refinement level		2	
Air volume flow rate [$\mathrm{m^3\,h^{-1}}$]		125	
CFD time step [s]	2×10^{-6}	2.5×10^{-4}	1.25×10^{-6}

As can be seen from the two plots, the curves are similar for the turbulence models k-ε and k-ω-SST. In contrast, the curves of the laminar model indicate a slimmer spout and higher velocities in the center of the spout and a split in the spout profile. The broader spout profiles from the k-ε and k-ω-SST models can be explained by the Eddy viscosity. Paradoxically, the laminar model showed the biggest problems in terms of convergence. For further investigations the realizable k-ε model was used.

5.3.3 Drag model

As mentioned in section 3.3 four different drag models have been evaluated regarding their influence on the gas-solid flow behavior: the drag model of (i) Gidaspow et al. (1991), (ii) Di Felice (1994), (iii) Koch and Hill (2001) and (iv) Beetstra et al. (2007). The drag model of Beetstra et al. (2007) had not been included in the used software version before but was implemented within this work. For comparison of the models and for validation with experimental data, the bed expansion and qualitative spouting

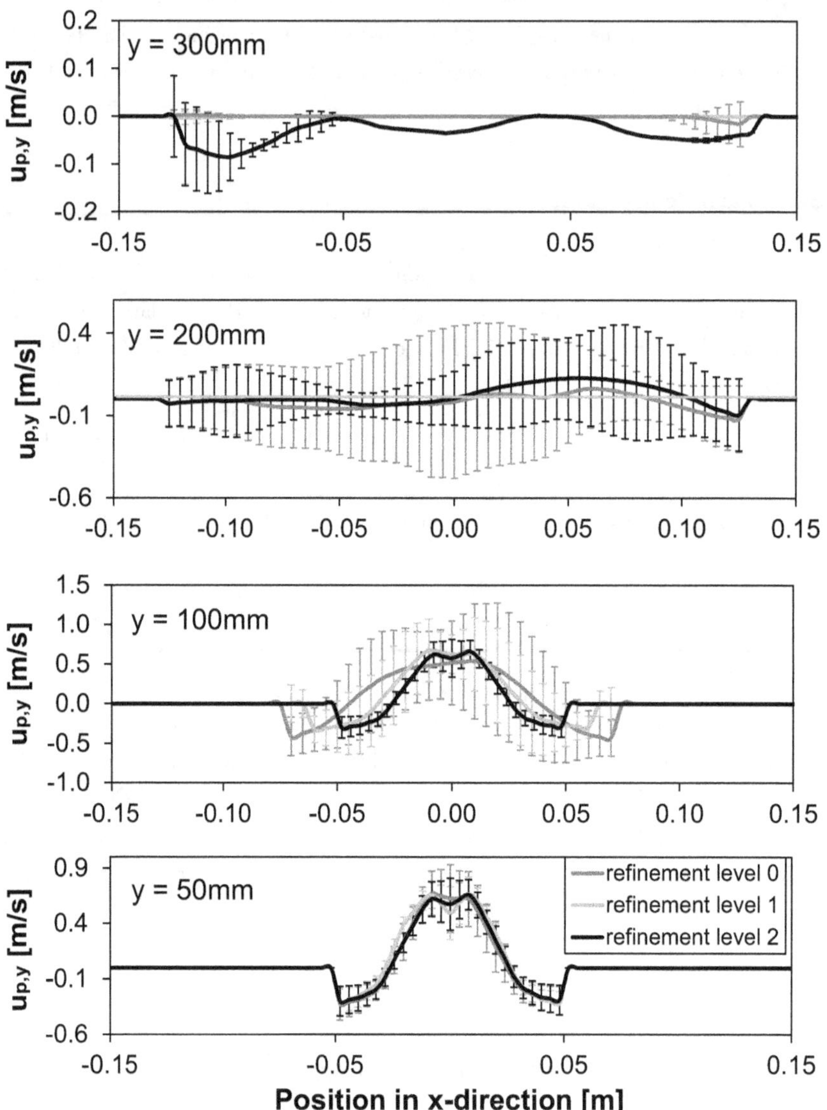

FIGURE 5.11: Vertical particle velocity profiles on four different heights (50 mm, 100 mm, 200 mm and 300 mm) for different refinement levels of a coupled CFD-DEM simulation; gas volume flow rate: $125 \, \mathrm{m^3 \, h^{-1}}$, 1 kg γ-Al2O3 particles, particle diameter: 656 µm.

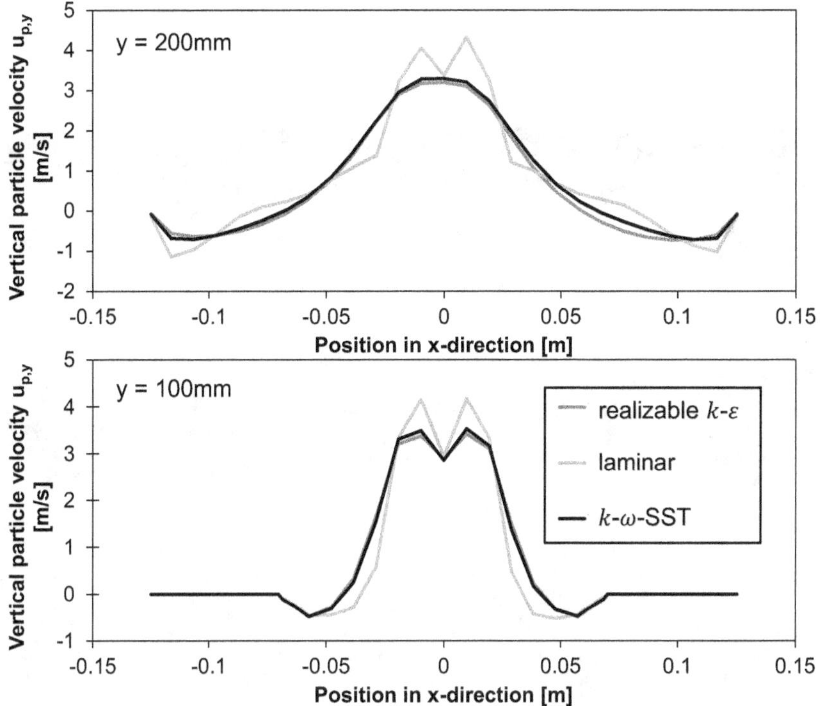

FIGURE 5.12: Comparison of the three different turbulence models by analysis of the vertical particle velocity profiles at two different heights; gas volume flow rate: $125 \mathrm{\ m^3\,h^{-1}}$.

behavior were used. Snapshots from simulation with a time interval of 0.2 s and the corresponding images from experiments are shown in figure 5.13.

Both drag models by Gidaspow et al. (1991) and Di Felice (1994) underestimate slightly the bed expansion height and show an elutriation of particles, which could not be observed in experiments. The spout profile is more stable and homogeneous compared to the deflections that can be seen in the snapshots from the laboratory process chamber. The drag models of Koch and Hill (2001) and Beetstra et al. (2007) show a higher physical consistence with the experiments as both bed expansion height and spout deflections are predicted in a similar way. Both Hill et al. (2001) and Beetstra et al. (2007) reported that the Ergun equation underpredicted the drag force in case of low Reynolds numbers. Hill et al. (2001) proposed as explanation that the particles used in the experiments of Ergun were not as homogeneous and monodisperse as those used in the simulations. Figure 5.14 shows the fluid void fractions α_f occurring in the process chamber. It can be seen that the fluid void fraction in the region of the spout is with values between

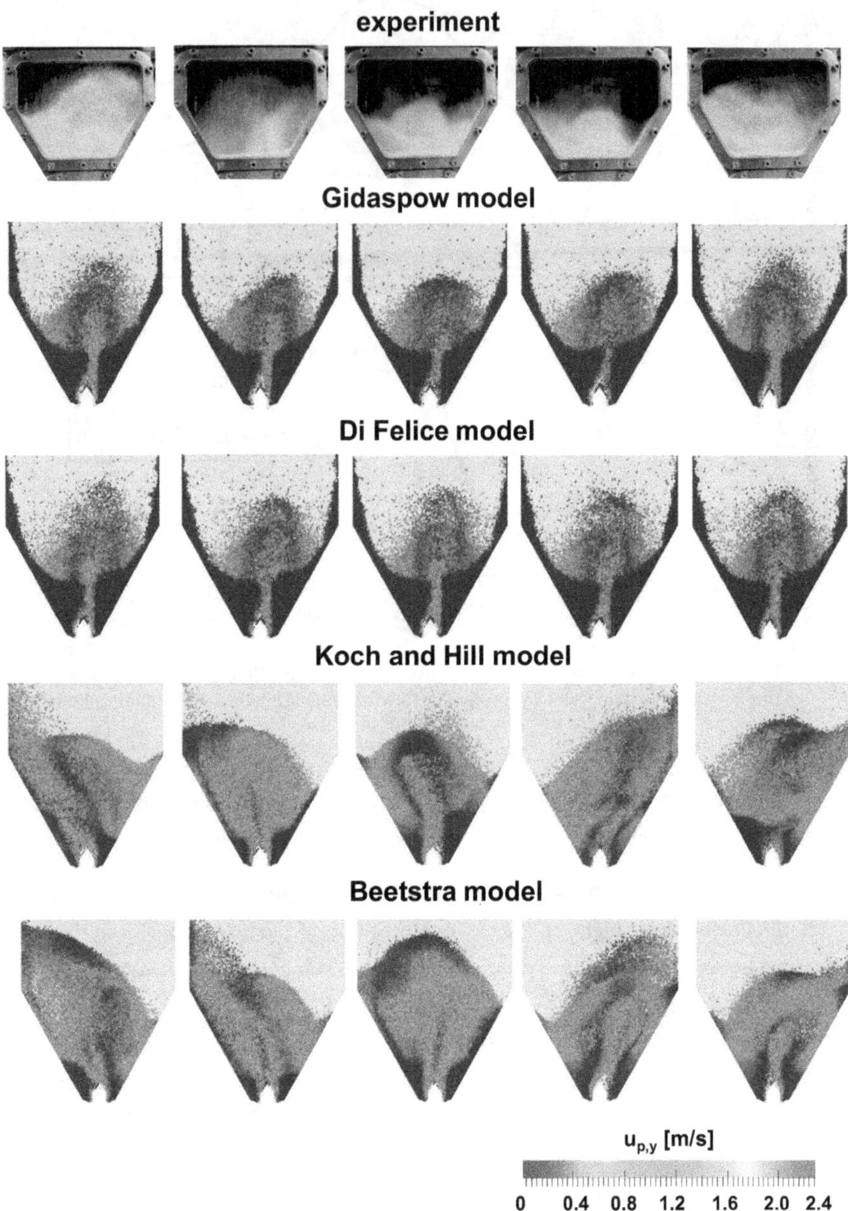

FIGURE 5.13: Comparison of flow regimes from experiment and simulations with different drag models; gas volume flow rate: 125 m³ h⁻¹, 1 kg γ-Al2O3-particles, particle diameter: 656 µm. The time interval between images is 0.2 s.

0.8 and 0.9 high. Only sometimes high particle void fractions as e.g. seen in the right pictures could be observed in the spout region.

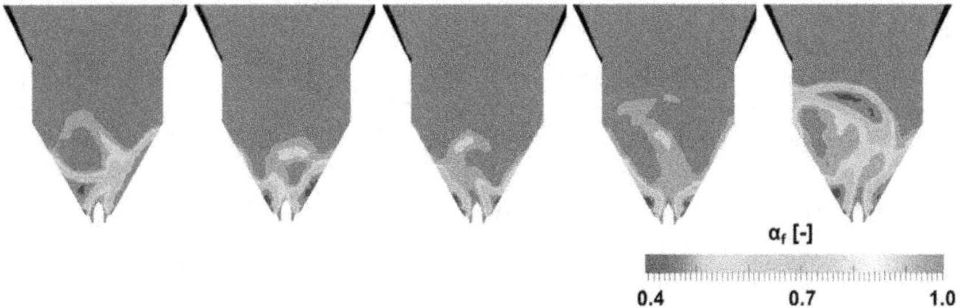

FIGURE 5.14: Instantaneous void fractions of fluid phase; gas volume flow rate: 125 m^3 h^{-1}, 1 kg γ-Al2O3-particles, particle diameter: 656 µm. The time interval between images is 0.1 s.

A comparison of the momentum exchange coefficients depending on the particle Reynolds numbers for a fluid void fraction of $\alpha_f = 0.85$ (figure 5.15) shows that this coefficient is much lower for the Gidaspow and Di Felice drag model than for the Koch and Hill respective Beetstra model. This might be the reason why the bed expansion in the spout is underestimated with the first two models. Due to the above shown results, the drag model of Beetstra et al. (2007) was chosen for further simulations.

5.4 Validation

In order to validate the numerical model, pressure data from simulations were compared with experimental high frequency pressure measurements recorded in the transparent replica. By means of the Fourier transform a comparison in the frequency domain is possible. As base case, a bed mass of 1 kg γ-Al2O3 particles (656 µm) at a gas volume flow rate of 100 m^3 h^{-1} was chosen. The pressure drop time series and the resulting power plots are shown in figure 5.16.

As can be seen from the power plots, the main frequencies fit well in experiment and simulation. Deviations occur in the measured amplitudes of the intensity. This can be explained by the different sampling frequencies in simulation and experiment and by variations in sampling time which encompassed 10 s in simulation but 30 s in experiment allowing more three-dimensional fluctuations. Higher amplitudes in simulations than in experiments were also observed by Salikov (2017). He explained the deviations by the different locations of the pressure measurement. In order to measure the pressure drop over the whole particle bed in the experiments, the high frequency pressure detector is

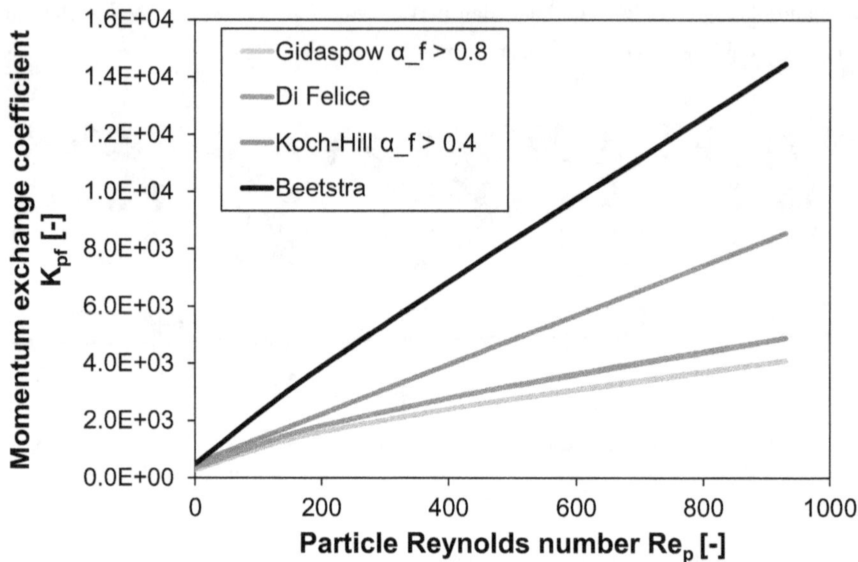

FIGURE 5.15: Dependency of momentum exchange coefficient K_{pf} from particle Reynolds number for different drag models for a fluid void fraction of α_f=0.85.

located above the particle bed as the plant is operated in under-pressure mode. The boundary conditions in simulations represent a pressure operation and the pressure drop was measured below the particle bed at the height of the gas inlet slits.

5.5 Insertion of draft plates

As mentioned by Salikov et al. (2015b) the installation of draft plates can increase the range of stable spouting. It has been reported that the spouting stability is very sensitive to the size and positioning of the draft plates, which have to be adjusted individually for a given type and bed inventory. In order to reduce the experimental effort and due to limitations in reconstruction applicability, both the geometry and the position were optimized in several simulations. Exemplarily, the test cases with the geometric conditions given in table 5.8 are presented, whereby the height of the plates, their distance to each other and the vertical position were varied. A sketch of the plates and their installation in the process chamber is shown in figure 5.17. As demonstration example the case with 1 kg γ-Al2O3-particles at a gas volume flow rate of 100 m^3 h^{-1} is used, which was already chosen before for the validation of the numerical model. As shown in section 5.4 the power plot of this gas volume flow rate is characterized

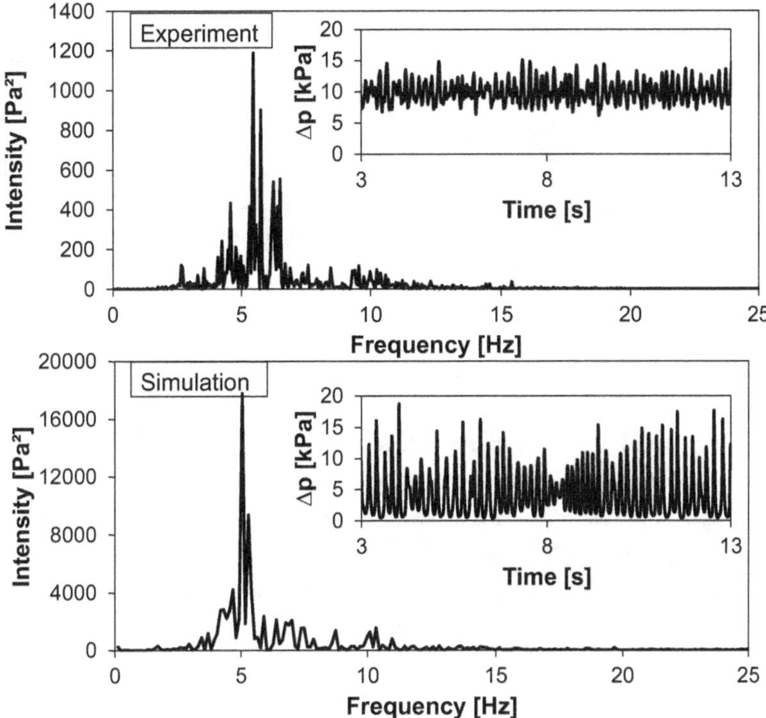

FIGURE 5.16: Comparison of pressure drop fluctuations and FFT plots from experiment (top, sampling frequency 400 Hz) and simulation (bottom, sampling frequency 1000 Hz); gas volume flow rate: 100 m³ h⁻¹, 1 kg γ-Al2O3-particles, particle diameter: 656 µm.

TABLE 5.8: Geometry and positions of draft plates that were used for simulations.

Name	Height [mm]	Width [mm]	Distance from middle profile [mm]
Case A	80	55	10
Case B	80	55	30
Case C	50	55	10
Case D	60	45	10

by a broad peak distribution indicating the instable spouting regime, which might be stabilized by the draft plates.

The horizontal distance of the plates was given by the maximum width of the gas inlet zone and was only varied from 55 to 45 mm. In figure 5.18 snapshots from the simulations are shown. It can be seen that with cases A, B, C and D the spout is more stable compared to the original process chamber. In the case without draft plates, the spout is deflected to the sides and deviations in bed expansion occur. In the chambers

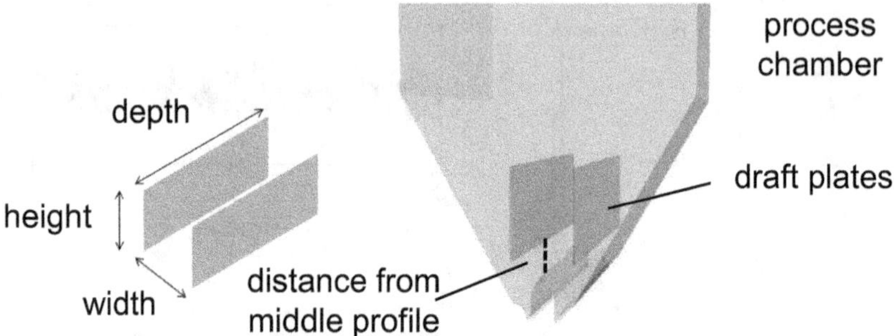

FIGURE 5.17: A sketch of the geometry of the draft plates and their installation in the process chamber of the *ProCell®* 5 apparatus.

with draft plates the bed expansion height is more homogeneous and less deviations are observable. Nevertheless, a big influence of the plates' geometry is detectable. A comparison of the cases A and B shows that the higher distance from the middle profile, as in case B, results in higher spout deflections, which might be explained by the higher degree of freedom that the spout has in the zone between the middle profile and the plates. Therefore, the distance of only 10 mm is favorable.

In case C the height of the plates is decreased compared to case A. It can be seen that in both variants the bed expansion height is almost constant. As the heat and mass transfer is affected by the plates, the smaller height is preferred for following investigations with liquid injection. By detailed analysis of the spout profiles in cases A and C, small pendular movements can be observed between the plates. In order to reduce this, the gap between the plates was decreased to 45 mm in case D. Again, the bed expansion is homogeneous and no deflections occur. Additionally, the velocity spout profile is more homogeneous and less particles move directly above the plates back into the annulus zone but follow the spout into the fountain height. As this seems promising for processes with liquid injection in order to allow a sufficient drying after passing the spray zone and before entering the annulus zone, the reduced gap size was chosen as optimized configuration.

For validation of the conclusion from visual analysis, the pressure drop fluctuations were recorded. The fluctuations are shown in figure 5.19 with the corresponding power plots. Again, it is obvious that case B with its spout deflections comes along with the highest instability. All other cases are defined by slim single peaks and therefore correspond to stable spouting. Due to the more homogeneous velocity distribution and the higher bed expansion, which seems promising for a high heat and mass transfer with a liquid phase, the configuration D was still found best and chosen for further investigations. It can be concluded that heights of the sheets of 60 mm, a gap of 45 mm between both

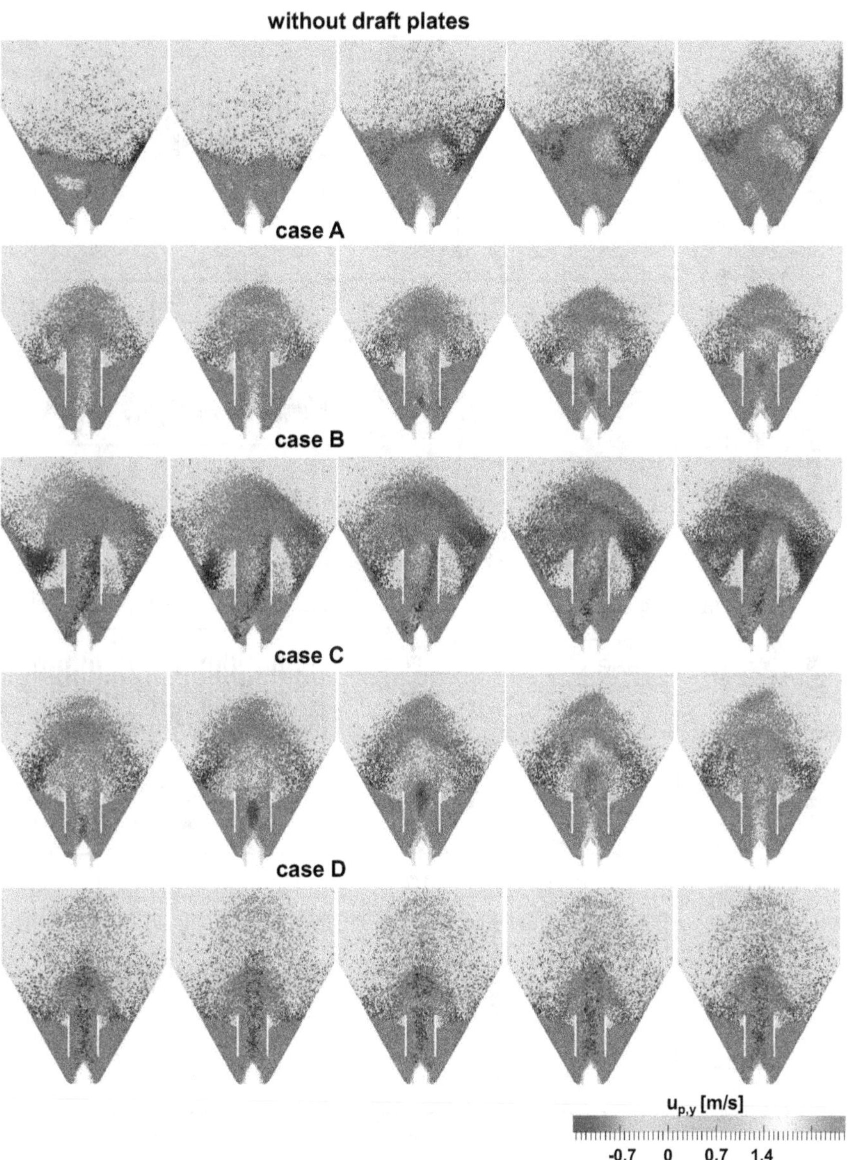

FIGURE 5.18: CFD-DEM simulation of instantaneous particle positions and velocity distributions in the original apparatus and in the geometry with inserted draft plates; gas volume flow rate: $100\ \mathrm{m^3\,h^{-1}}$, 1 kg γ-Al2O3-particles, particle diameter: 656 µm. The time interval between images is 0.1 s.

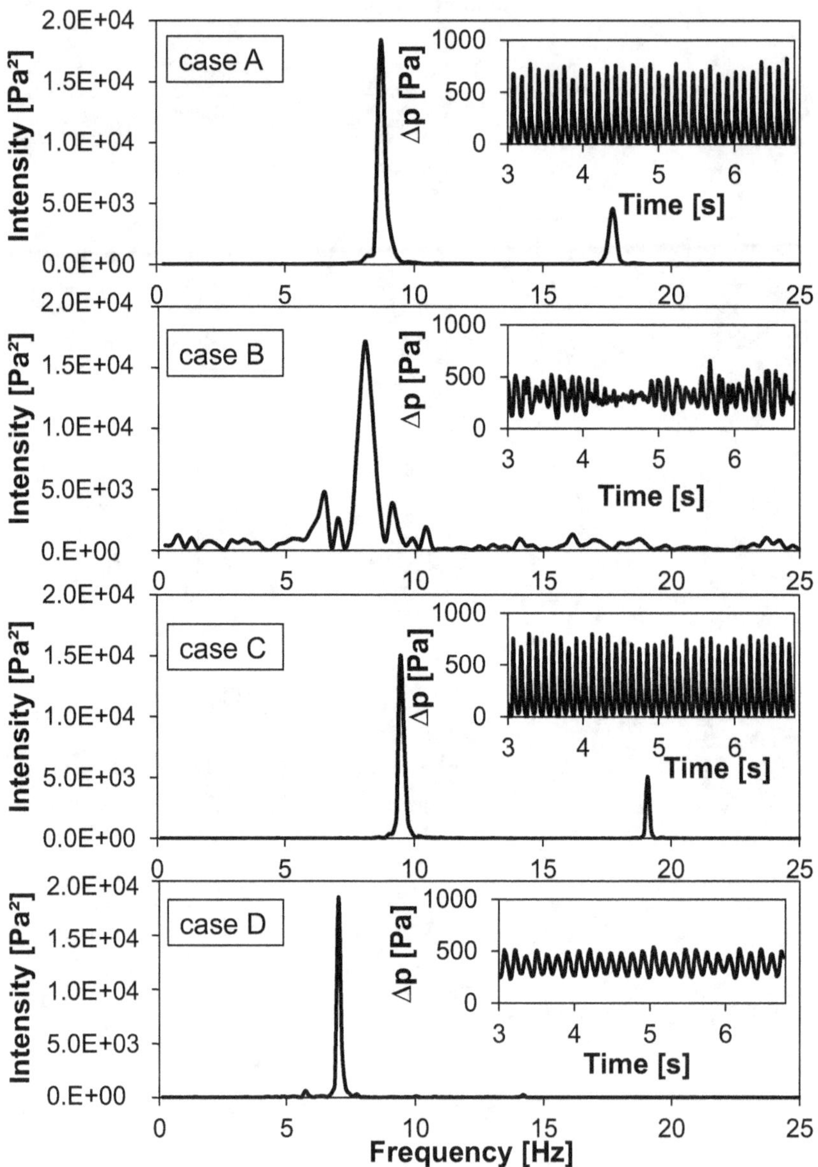

FIGURE 5.19: Pressure drop fluctuations and corresponding power plots of the chamber configurations with inserted draft plates; gas volume flow rate: $100 \ \mathrm{m^3 \, h^{-1}}$, 1 kg γ-Al2O3-particles, particle diameter: 656 µm. The time interval between images is 0.1 s.

parallel plates and a distance of each sheet from the middle profile in vertical direction of 10 mm were found to result in the highest spouting stability. The plates were produced and inserted into the original laboratory spouted bed. It can be seen in figure 5.20 for both the experiments and the corresponding simulations that the spouting behavior is stabilized by the draft plates (Pietsch et al., 2017).

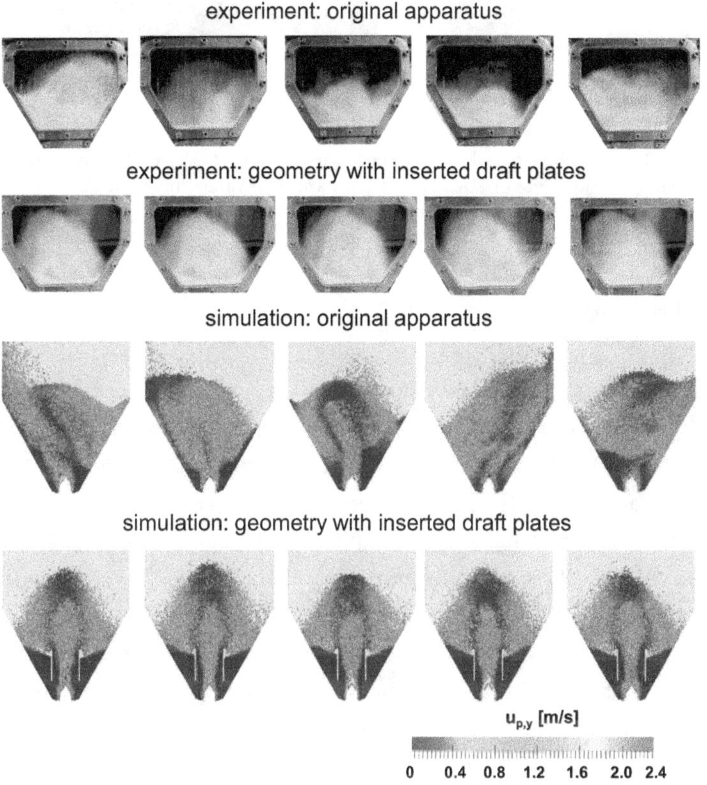

FIGURE 5.20: Experiments and CFD-DEM simulation of instantaneous particle positions and velocity distributions in the original apparatus and in geometries with different draft plate configurations; gas volume flow rate: 100 $m^3\,h^{-1}$, 1 kg γ-Al2O3-particles, particle diameter: 656 µm. The time interval between images is 0.2 s.

The optimized configuration will be further investigated in chapter 6 to evaluate the influence of the draft plates on the coating progress. Before, it was checked whether the draft plates affect the liquid injection. Therefore, the spouted bed was used for coating of 1 kg γ-Al2O3-particles with water containing methylene blue. After the experiment was stopped, no particles were sticking at the plates and no blue color was observable on them as shown in figure 5.21. It can be concluded that the draft plates do not impair the spray zone.

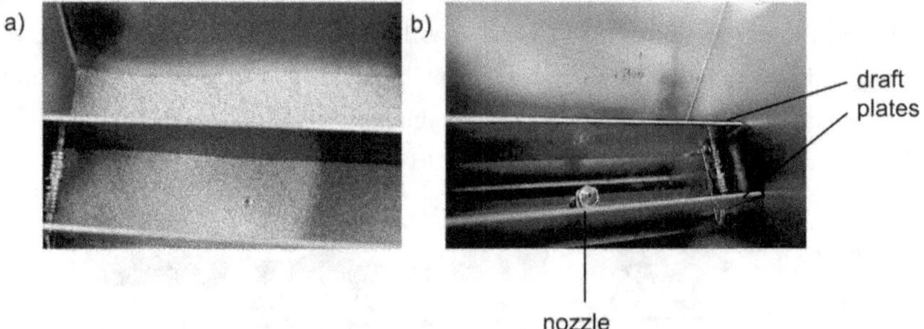

FIGURE 5.21: a) Particle bed in the apparatus after coating. b) Empty apparatus after coating. No droplets or sticking particles are detectable on the draft plates after coating of particle bed with methylene blue, 1 kg γ-Al2O3-particles, particle diameter: 656 µm.

5.6 Binary system

Previous numerical investigations were focused on the handling of monodisperse particle beds in the laboratory prismatic spouted bed. In order to evaluate the influence of the bed composition, simulations with γ-Al2O3-particles of two different sizes, 1.8 mm (white colored) and 3.0 mm (red colored) were performed analogous to the experimental work in section 5.2.1.2. Similar to the experimental results, segregation of particles can be observed from the snapshots shown in 5.22, where almost no small particles are detectable. The segregation might influence the droplet deposition as bigger particles seem to accumulate near the nozzle. This should influence the particle growth during granulation. As the experiments and simulations in this thesis were performed with almost monodisperse particles and the layer increase due to the coating was small, this influence was neglected for further investigations.

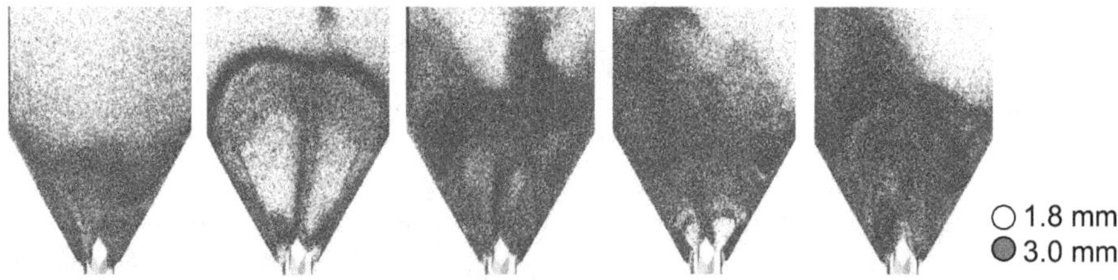

FIGURE 5.22: CFD-DEM simulation of instantaneous particle positions in the original *ProCell*® 5 apparatus; gas volume flow rate: 125 m³ h⁻¹, 1 kg γ-Al2O3-particles, 50 wt.-% 1.8 mm (white colored) and 50 wt.-% 3.0 mm (red colored). The time interval between images is 0.2 s.

6

Coating process

6.1 Introduction

The previous chapter was focused on stability analysis of the laboratory prismatic spouted bed. This chapter is dedicated to the efficiency of the apparatus for spray coating and the resulting coating quality. The presented results are referred and connected to the stability investigations in order to understand the link between the spouting behavior and the deposition behavior of droplets. The liquid injection was investigated with both numerical and experimental analysis. By numerical investigations the residence times of single particles in the spray zone and their time-dependent mean liquid surface coverage was determined. The application of the rCFD method allowed determination of the surface coverage for a duration of the real process. For experimental investigation, the digital image analysis algorithm introduced in chapter 4 was applied. Additionally, the coated particle fractions were analyzed off-line with the *CamSizer XT* device and microscopes. The quantitative results are compared to coating layer thicknesses measured with OCT method that was introduced in subsection 2.5.1.

6.2 Numerical investigations

All numerical investigations regarding spray coating were performed with 1 kg γ-Al$_2$O$_3$ particles (656 µm) as already used for stability analysis in chapter 5. Though the material contains open pores, the porosity was neglected in simulations and layer formation around the core particles without a penetration into them was assumed.

6.2.1 Droplet injection

As described in section 3.4, liquid droplets with a rate of 5 g min^{-1} were injected in simulations during post-processing. Gas volume flow rates of 70 m^3 h^{-1} (stable regime), 100 and 120 m^3 h^{-1} (instable regime) were chosen for comparison. Additionally, simulations with the optimized process chamber geometry with draft plates as found in section 5.5 were performed for a flow rate of 120 m^3 h^{-1}. By means of the post-processing liquid injection, the cumulative number distribution of surface coverage of the particles (Q_0) was determined every 0.05 s within a simulation time of 10 s. Exemplarily, this distribution is shown in figure 6.1 for a gas volume flow rate of 120 m^3 h^{-1} for selected time points. The function is shifted to the right hand side meaning to higher surface coverage with increasing simulation time. Additionally, a simulation snapshot showing the particles (black dots) and the droplets (colored dots) with their age after injection is shown in figure 6.1.

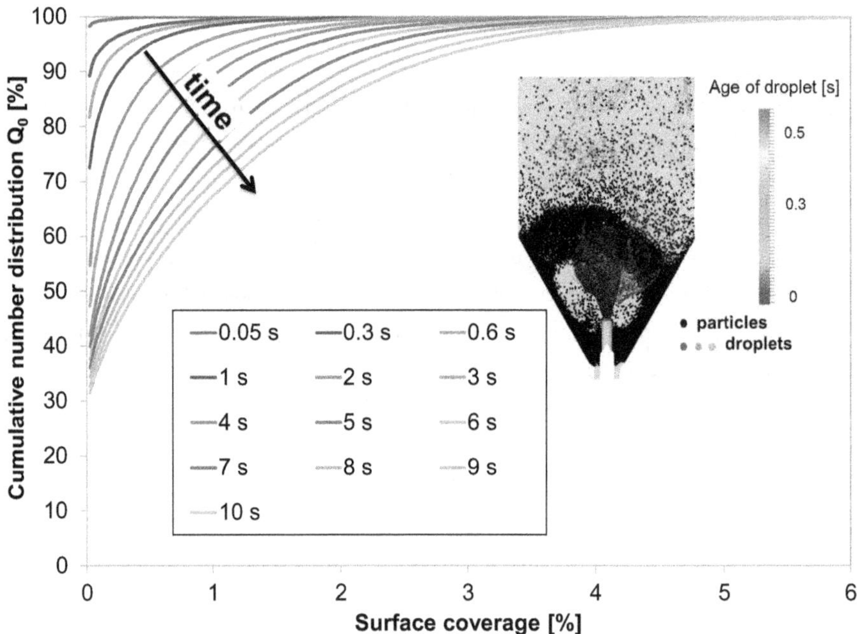

FIGURE 6.1: Time-dependent cumulative number distribution Q_0 of particle surface coverage; 1 kg γ-Al2O3 particles (656 µm), 120 m^3 h^{-1} with a snapshot of liquid injection in post-processing step.

To determine the deposition efficiency for the different gas volume flow rates, the corresponding rates are shown as moving average of ten values in figure 6.2 for a simulation interval of 1.5 s. It can be seen that the deposition rate is most homogeneous in case

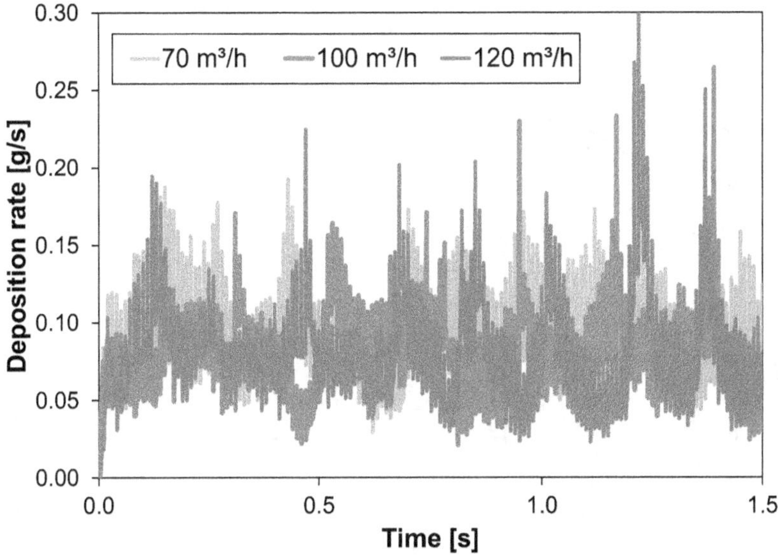

FIGURE 6.2: Liquid deposition rates during a simulation interval of 1.5 s; 1 kg γ-Al2O3 particles (656 µm), different gas volume flow rates, spray rate $= 5$ g min^{-1}.

of stable spouting $(70\text{m}^3\,\text{h}^{-1})$, which can be explained by the regular spouting behavior that benefits a homogeneous amount of particles in the spout zone without events of drop or sudden increase in bed expansion and resulting moments with low or high deposition rates. In case of irregular spouting (100 and 120 m$^3\,$h^{-1}), the deviations in deposition rates are higher and the deposition is more inhomogeneous probably caused by spout deflections and varying bed expansion heights.

To quantify the influence of the spouting stability and the corresponding droplet deposition homogeneity on the particle surface coverage, the respective distributions for a simulation time of 10 s are given in figure 6.3. A comparison for the original chamber geometry shows that in case of stable spouting $(70\text{m}^3\,\text{h}^{-1})$ around 50 % of the particles are uncoated after 10 s, while about 32 % are completely uncoated in instable regime (120 m$^3\,$h^{-1}). Nevertheless, the number of particles with a surface coverage of almost 6 % is comparable for both regimes. This means that the distribution of surface coverage is slimmer and the coverage more homogeneous in case of instable spouting. The curve of the optimized chamber geometry with draft plates is similar to that of the stable spouting, which again indicates the stabilizing effect of the draft plates. Similar to the stable regime, a lot of uncoated particles (around 56 %) remain after 10 s, which again shows the big distribution and thus inhomogeneity of coverage during stable spouting. It should be pointed out that the simulation time of 10 s is very short and that it does not allow the investigation of a real-time coating process, which needs more time for

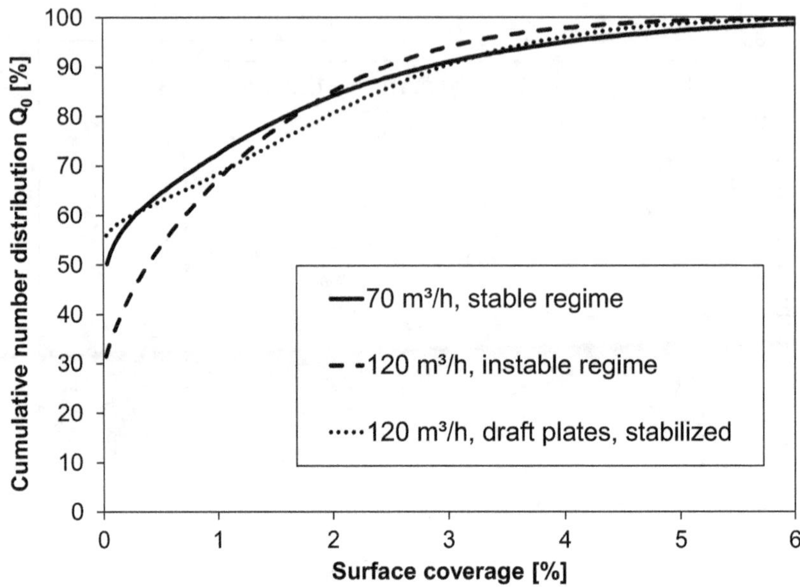

FIGURE 6.3: Cumulative number distribution Q_0 of particle surface coverage after 10 s; 1 kg γ-Al2O3 particles (656 µm); 70, 120 $\mathrm{m^3\,h^{-1}}$ and 120 $\mathrm{m^3\,h^{-1}}$ with draft plates.

the given bed filling and the spray rate. Considering the pressure drop fluctuations and their frequencies, it can be assumed that the circulation of particles is slower in stable regime. This would explain the broader distribution of surface coverage within the first seconds as the movement of particles is slower and therefore their probability of crossing the spray zone not at all in the first seconds is higher.

6.2.2   Circulation frequencies

In order to determine the movement of particles and thus the throughput through the spray zone, the circulation frequencies were calculated for three different cases (figure 6.4) as described in subsection 3.5.2. In case of stable spouting (70 $\mathrm{m^3\,h^{-1}}$) the main frequency is about 1 Hz. The distribution shows tailing of the respective peak up to around 7 Hz. In the instable regime (120 $\mathrm{m^3\,h^{-1}}$), the distribution is shifted to the right and it is markedly broader. The broad distribution indicates instable spouting due to inhomogeneous spouting events and is in agreement with visual observations and pressure measurements. The distribution of the optimized apparatus shows a high slim peak at a frequency of about 1.5 Hz, which is lower than in the original apparatus. The peak distribution is narrower compared to the original apparatus at 120 $\mathrm{m^3\,h^{-1}}$, which reaffirms the stabilizing effect of draft plates. Again, the curve of the optimized chamber is more similar to that one of the stable regime. As assumed, the circulation frequencies

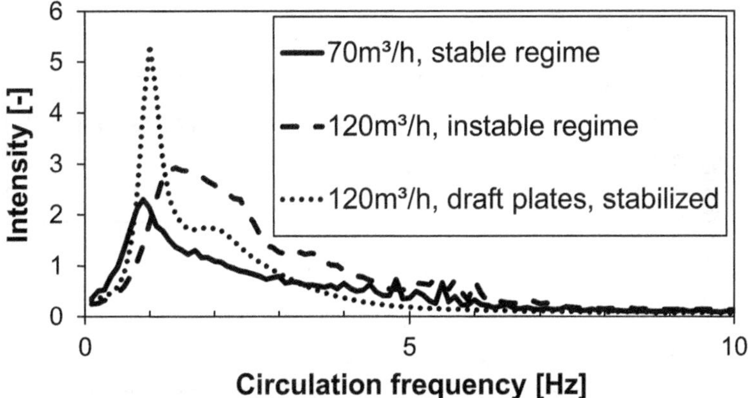

FIGURE 6.4: Intensity distribution plot of circulation frequencies; 1 kg γ-Al2O3 particles (656 µm); 70, 120 $\mathrm{m^3\,h^{-1}}$ and 120 $\mathrm{m^3\,h^{-1}}$ with draft plates.

are reduced in stable regime and in the stabilized system, which explains the higher number of uncoated particles in figure 6.3 as a lot of particles have not encountered the spray zone within the first ten seconds due to the slower movement. Nevertheless, a long-term investigation is necessary in order to validate whether the more homogeneous spouting results in a homogeneous liquid layer formation or whether this is benefited by instable spouting.

The distribution of the vertical particle velocities is shown in figure 6.5 for a gas volume flow rate of 120 $\mathrm{m^3\,h^{-1}}$ for the original and the modified process chamber. It can be seen that in the optimized chamber the particle velocity is homogenized and more particles have a velocity of around zero indicating more particles in the packed annulus region with slow downwards movements. The assumption that more particles reside in the unfluidized annulus region in the optimized chamber is also confirmed by the number density distribution of the relative spout residence times in figure 6.6, which gives the ratio between the residence time in the spout and the total residence time. This quantity is almost halved by the installation of draft plates. The relative residence time and the velocity distribution indicate that the reduced circulation frequency in the optimized chamber is caused by lower particle concentrations in the spout and by reduced velocities. The reduced vertical particle transport might occur due to the restricted flow pattern by the plates, which strictly separate the regions of up- and downflow.

As shown before, the draft plates come along with a homogenized velocity distribution and homogenized circulation frequencies regarding the entire particle bed but also with a broader coating distribution and reduced residence times in the spout. The latter

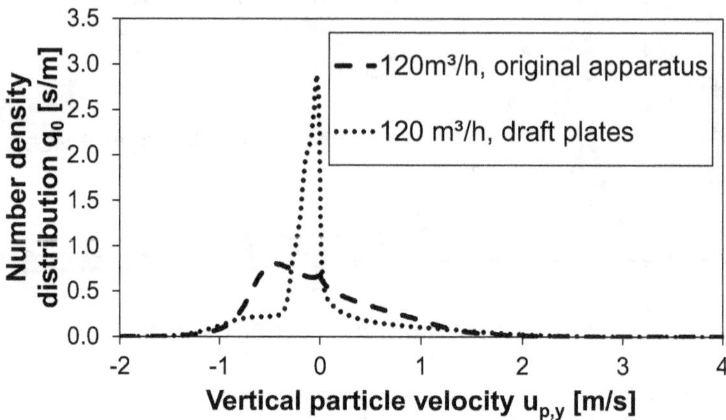

FIGURE 6.5: Number density distribution q_0 of vertical particle velocities after 10 s simulation time; 1 kg γ-Al2O3 particles (656 µm); 120 $m^3\,h^{-1}$ with and without draft plates.

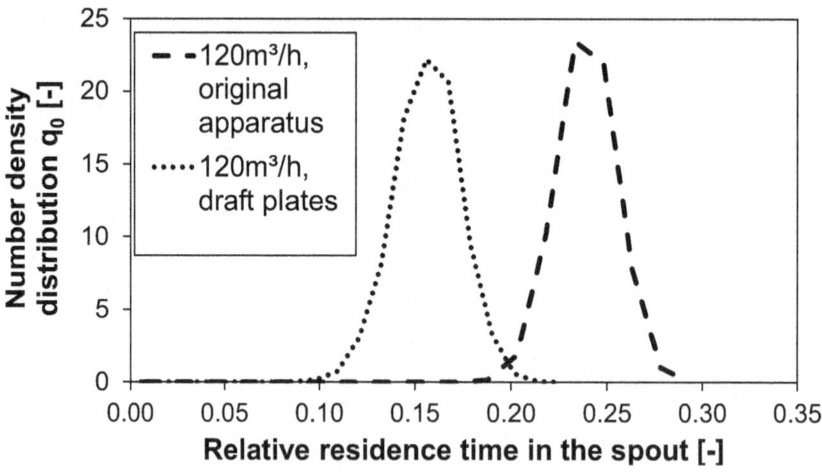

FIGURE 6.6: Number density distribution q_0 of relative spout residence time after 10 s simulation time; 1 kg γ-Al2O3 particles (656 µm); 120 $m^3\,h^{-1}$ with and without draft plates.

increases the risk of agglomeration as the highest packing and therefore the most particle-particle contacts occur in the annulus zone, which enables adhesion of wet particles. The particle contacts acting at a certain time step can be visualized by force chain networks, which are shown in figure 6.7 for the different spouting regimes. Extensive force chain networks appear during stable spouting in the annulus region and persist through the entirety of the process. During instable spouting (100 and 120 $m^3\,h^{-1}$) the bulk is frequently interrupted by lateral ejections reducing the risk of agglomeration. Again, the similarity of the stable spouting and the stabilized chamber with draft plates can be seen as extensive contact networks also occur in the optimized chamber. To evaluate the risk of agglomeration, liquid evaporation was modeled and the resulting liquid mass distribution is shown in figure 6.8 for a gas volume flow rate of 100 $m^3\,h^{-1}$. Only a miniscule particle population is wetted at a given point in time. Equilibrium is reached after a simulation time of 3 s with a total liquid water mass of $4.99 \cdot 10^{-5}$ mg. This indicates that particle drying takes place before entering the annulus zone and thus the risk of agglomeration can be excluded for the given particle type and the injection of pure water. The consistently low liquid content in the system validates the assumption of neglected liquid bridges.

By means of the surface coverage analysis it was shown that the coating process is slower and more inhomogeneous within the first ten seconds for the stable regime and the stabilized system compared to the instable regime. The reason for the slower progress was found in the circulation frequencies, which are lower in stable regime resulting in a slower movement and a slower throughput through the spray zone (Pietsch et al., 2018). Due to the higher relative residence time in the spout zone during instable spouting, the particles have longer contact times with the droplets, which seems promising for achieving a homogeneous coating layer on the particles of the entire bed. As the CFD-DEM simulations go along with high computational effort, it is not possible to simulate the duration of a real-time coating process. In order to investigate the long-term behavior, the performed CFD-DEM simulations were used to obtain a recurrence plot, which then allows the performance of an rCFD simulation as described in section 3.6.

6.2.3 Spray coating analysis with rCFD

The simulation conditions and the setup of the rCFD simulation are described in detail in the work of Kieckhefen et al. (2018). Here, just a short overview is given. In order to ensure the validity of the rCFD simulations and avoid overpacking, the intensity of the velocity fluctuations was calibrated. For this, simulations using different diffusion coefficients in the range of $0 \leq D_0 \leq 1 \times 10^{-2}$ $m^2\,s^{-1}$ were performed for a duration of 35 s. By means of the ability to reproduce the instantaneuous volume fractions at probe

a) 70 m³/h, stable

b) 100 m³/h, instable

c) 120 m³/h, instable

d) 120 m³/h, stabilized by draft plates

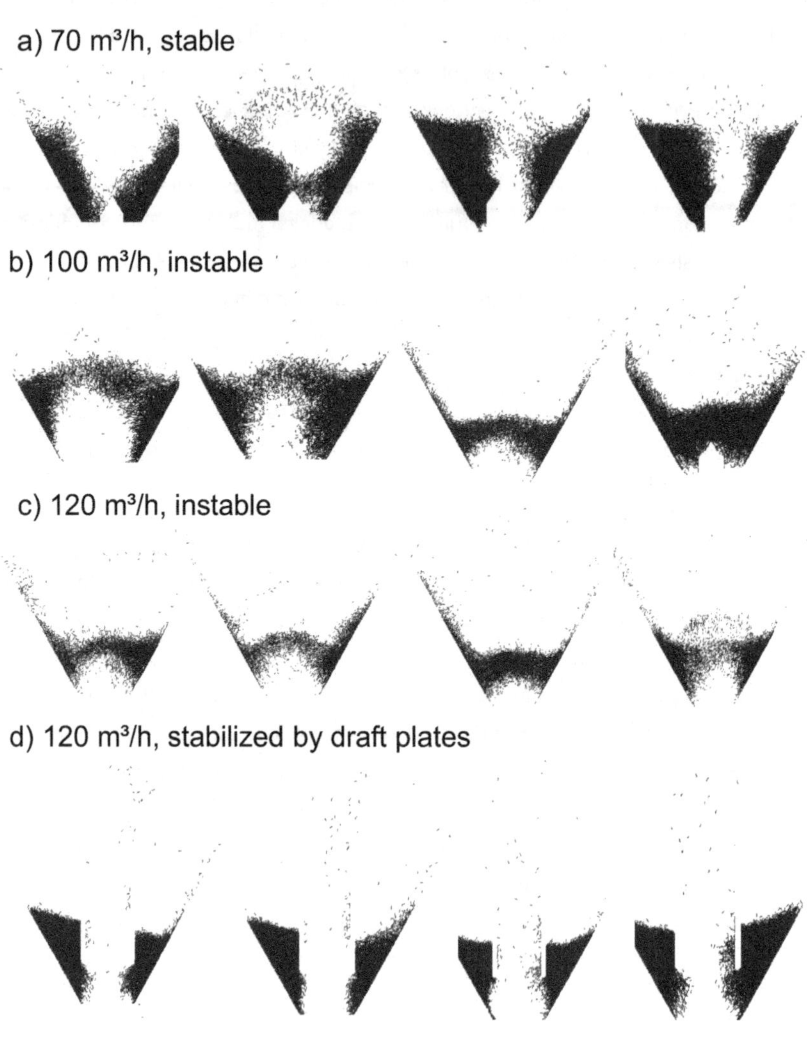

FIGURE 6.7: Simulation images of force chain networks for the different spouting regimes (a) stable, b) instable, c) instable, d) stabilized by draft plates); time interval between snapshots is 0.2 s; 1 kg γ-Al2O3 particles (656 µm).

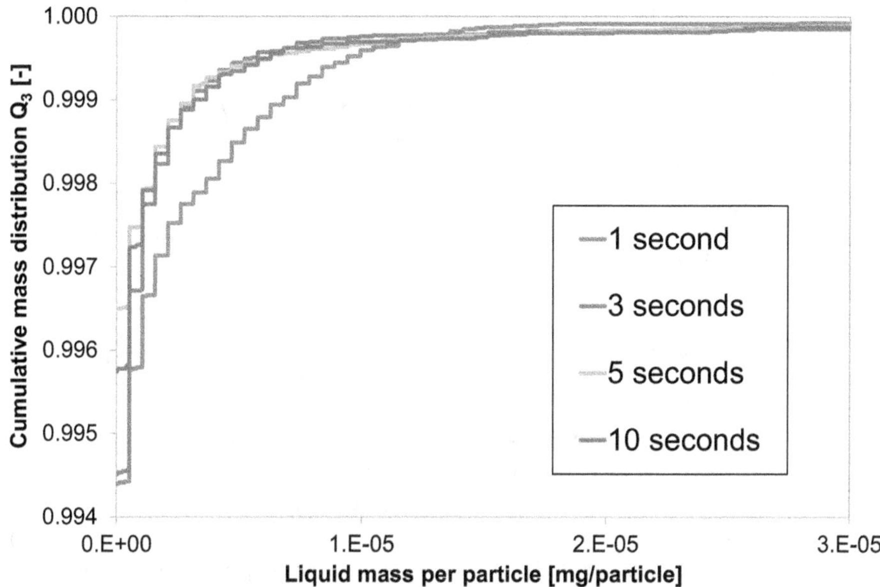

FIGURE 6.8: Cumulative mass distribution Q_3 of liquid mass deposited on single particles; 1 kg γ-Al2O3 particles (656 µm); 100 m^3 h^{-1}.

locations relative to the recurrence fields and the time-averaged volume fraction, as well as to predict accurately the residence time in the spray zone the method was validated. It was found that a diffusion coefficient of $D_0 = 5 \times 10^{-4}$ m^2 s^{-1} is the lowest viable one as lower coefficients result in high, unphysical tracer volume fractions near the walls and subsequently lower bed concentrations and expansions in the spout region. With the mentioned diffusion coefficient rCFD simulations of the previously described CFD-DEM cases of 120 m^3 h^{-1} with and without draft plates were performed. The time-dependent particles' surface coverage distribution, which is shown in figure 6.9, was again calculated according to Kariuki et al. (2013) as described in section 3.4.

Similar results to the analysis in figure 6.3 were obtained showing a broader distribution of the surface coverage in case of the inserted draft plates, meaning the stabilized systems. Thus, the results from section 6.2.1 are not attributed to start-up effects. In fact, the draft plates result in a broader surface coverage distribution even though the circulation pattern is homogenized. Therefore, not the stability of spouting but a high relative residence time in the spout zone near the nozzle (figure 6.6) seems advantageous for a homogeneous coating. As this zone is characterized by improved heat, mass and momentum transfer due to the flow pattern, a smaller relative residence time seems disadvantageous as the longer stay in the annulus zone with its high packing has no

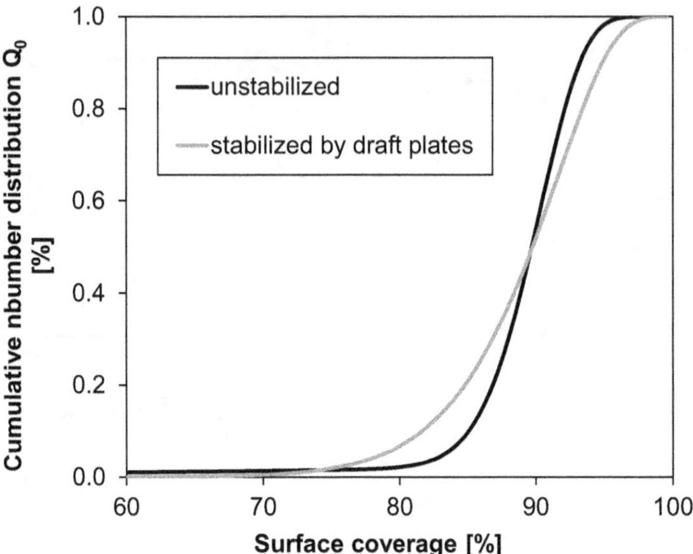

FIGURE 6.9: Cumulative number distribution of relative spout residence time after 3600 s simulation time with rCFD approach; 1 kg γ-Al2O3 particles (656 µm); 120 $\mathrm{m^3\,h^{-1}}$ with and without draft plates.

positive effect. Thus, for the given process conditions, the instable regime is recommended when conducting spray coating. Nevertheless, when handling sticky or cohesive materials, the lowered residence time in the spout and a reduced circulation frequency seem still promising as the wet and dry particles are physically separated reducing the risk of agglomeration. Under that circumstances, the slightly broader surface coverage distribution should be acceptable when avoiding unwanted agglomeration at the same time.

6.3   Experimental analysis of coating quality

In this section, the real-time coating process in the laboratory spouted bed *ProCell*® *5* is investigated. The analysis was performed with digital image analysis introduced in section 4.3. As this method allows the measurement of coating quality but not of quantity, additional investigations were performed with in-line optical coherence tomography (OCT) as well as off-line measurements with particle size and microscopic analyses in order to measure the coating thickness. As described in section 3.2 the alumina particles are characterized by open pores. As this would affect the coating behavior due to the penetration of liquid into the pores, all experiments were performed with *Cellets*® *500* particles. Due to their non-porous structure the coating is mainly characterized by layer build-up without diffusion of suspension into open pores.

6.3.1 Digital image analysis

The described image analysis algorithm from chapter 4 was used to monitor the coating progress in two exemplary experiments conducted in the *ProCell® 5* apparatus.

6.3.1.1 Experimental procedure

Experiments were performed with 1 kg particles. The gas volume flow rate was set to $120\,\mathrm{m^3\,h^{-1}}$, which yields, as described in subsection 5.2.2.1, instable spouting but intense particle-fluid interactions and homogeneous layer coverage. The operation conditions of the two experiments, named *Coating 1* and *Coating 2*, are summarized in table 6.1.

TABLE 6.1: Process conditions for the two conducted coating experiments *Coating 1* and *Coating 2*.

Parameter/setting	Coating 1	Coating 2
Gas volume flow rate $[\mathrm{m^3\,h^{-1}}]$	120	120
Nozzle pressure [kPa]	4600	4600
Nozzle air flow rate $[\mathrm{m^3\,h^{-1}}]$	4	4
Coating composition [wt.-%]	Water (98.3), methylene blue (1.7)	Water (71), PEG (13.65), titanium dioxide (13.65), methylene blue (1.7)
Temperature of suspension [°C]	21	40
Agitation of suspension	No agitation	Magnetic stirring
Liquid injection rate $[\mathrm{g\,min^{-1}}]$	5	5
Total amount of liquid injection [g]	500	50
Process duration [min]	100	10

One used coating suspension (*Coating 1*) consisted of water with 1.7 wt.-% methylene blue and a second one (*Coating 2*) of polyethylene glycol (PEG 6000) (13.65 wt.-%), titanium dioxide (13.65 wt.-%), water (71 wt.-%) and methylene blue (1.7 wt.-%). For production of *Coating 1*, the methylene blue was dissolved in distilled water during stirring and afterwards stored at room temperature ($T_{\mathrm{room}} = 21°\mathrm{C}$) without preheating and stirring. For production of the coating suspension with PEG, the pure water was heated up to a temperature of $T_{\mathrm{liq}} = 40°\mathrm{C}$. PEG, titanium dioxide and methylene blue were added consecutively during stirring. After suspending, the coating agent was directly used in the process, whereby it was stored under magnetic stirring at a temperature of 40°C in order to decrease its viscosity. In both cases, the suspensions were injected with a rate of around 5 g min^{-1} with a peristaltic pump (*Medorex TB*, Germany). The temperature in the process chamber was set to 50°C as it is limited by the melting point of PEG ($T_\mathrm{m} = 55 - 60$°C). For later digital image analysis the whole coating process was recorded by the high-speed video camera *IDT NX4 S2* (Imaging Solutions GmbH, Germany) with the same Sigma 50 mm f/2.8 macro lens used for particle tracking velocimetry and an installed global shutter, which exposes all pixels simultaneously. The resulting data was simultaneously saved on an external hard disk drive. The quality of the captured image data is critical to the following steps, because all errors that are introduced in the acquisition step can propagate up. To be able to evaluate the coating layer with good precision, a tradeoff between high resolution per particle and a high number of observed particles has to be made. The resolution per particle must be high enough to distinguish it from disturbances, like e.g. scratches or dirt, on the observation window. A high number of particle observations can be achieved by increasing the frame rate of the acquisition or by observing a larger area of the apparatus, which then comes along with a decreased resolution per particle. As good particle detection could be achieved in preliminary tests with a particle resolution of 30 px, the camera was positioned with the corresponding distance of the lens to the window and the frame rate was set to 2 Hz. The main factor on observing the coating quality is the particles visual appearance, i.e. its color and the distribution of the color on the surface. As the sensor of the used high-speed camera is a monochrome sensor only, a color filter was used. If a color filter is used in front of the sensor, the absorption of this specific color will be rendered as darker pixels in the acquired images, thus the contrast in the relevant range increases. If the color filter is chosen according to the coating color, the brightness of the particles can be used as indicator of the coating level. For the used methylene blue dye, a yellow – the complimentary color of blue – filter was used. The resulting raw data was characterized by a very high noise distribution. In order to extract usable information, a Kalman filter was implemented. Most parameters used to link the brightness of the particles to the coating quality are based on assumptions as mentioned in section 4.3. Therefore, both experiments have been evaluated using the same but arbitrary set of parameters. This means that the presented results give a qualitative interpretation of the actual state of particle coating fraction but do not contain quantitative information about the layer thickness. For quantification, calibration experiments for linking the brightness to the coating thickness have to be conducted for every coating agent used. This is in so far difficult as the same lighting conditions have to be achieved as those obtained by using the lights in front of the apparatus window. At the same time a method is needed to create defined layer thicknesses in μm-range on the particles.

6.3.1.2 Raw measurements

An estimation of the number of particles in the experiment is needed to reason about the distribution of coating levels in the set of particles. The *Cellets® 500* particles were in a diameter range of 500 to 710 μm. The mean of the particle diameter was determined experimentally to $d_{50,3} = 0.57$ mm.

$$N = \frac{m_{\text{bed}}}{\frac{\pi}{6}d_{\text{p}}^3\rho_{\text{p}}} \approx \frac{1kg}{\frac{\pi}{6} \cdot (0.57 \cdot 10^{-3}m)^3 \cdot 1515\frac{kg}{m^3}} \approx 6.8 \cdot 10^6 \tag{6.1}$$

As the total number of particles N is very large due to the small particle diameter, a reasonable assumption for the distribution of α_c is a normal distribution. Any image frame captured through the observation window of the *ProCell® 5* apparatus shows $\bar{n} \approx 220$ particles on average. This is a small amount when compared to the total number of particles in the system and explains the high noise distribution that was already mentioned and that is shown in figure 6.10a.

6.3.1.3 Statistical filtering

In order to estimate the coating fraction from the raw measurements and to handle the high noise, a Kalman filter was implemented. A Kalman filter is a solution to the discrete-data linear filtering problem (Welch and Bishop, 2006). For one-dimensional data, two parameters, the process variance PV and the measurement variance P, are needed. The measurement variance is a tuning parameter, which influences how fast the estimated signal responds to changes in measurement input. The Kalman filter will yield the least-squares optimal estimation of the actual coating fraction, assuming the measurement and process noise are guided by a normal distribution (Kalman and Bucy, 1961). For the coating experiments, the process variance was estimated based on the variance of the raw signal obtained after the liquid injection was stopped meaning that the color, i.e. brightness of the particles, should not change anymore. The resulting coating fraction distribution after application of the Kalman filter with the mentioned values is shown in figure 6.10b. The noise was markedly reduced and the coating process is well detectable with time.

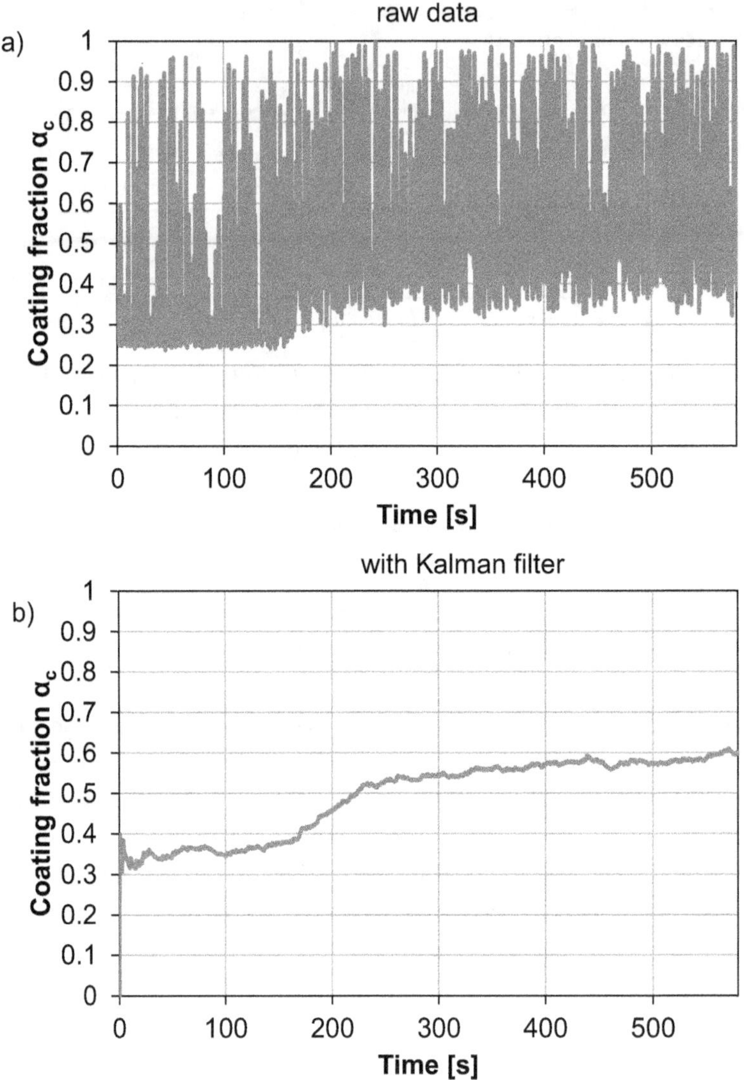

FIGURE 6.10: Effect of Kalman filter on raw measurement data. a) Due to the bad ratio of the simultaneously observed particles n and the total number of particles in the process chamber N, a high noise distribution is obtained in the time dependent analysis of coating fraction. b) By statistical filtering with Kalman filter with $PV = 1 \times 10^{-5}$ and $MV = 0.3^2$ the coating fraction can be estimated.

6.3.1.4 Coating experiments

During the experiment with water and methylene blue as coating agent, the increase of blue particles in the process chamber was observed. The resulting plot of the coating fraction in figure 6.11a shows a rather linear raise of the coating fraction with time within the first hour. The corresponding plot of the coating uniformity u_c shows a very slow decrease as presented in figure 6.11b. Afterwards, the coating fraction and the uniformity are only slightly increasing and decreasing, respectively. This indicates that the color change happens not linearly but gets slower the more color is already deposited on the particles. This goes along with the fact that the increase in coating layer thickness is also nonlinear as the particle diameter and therefore the spheres' surface is increasing over time and more coating has to be added to achieve the same increase in diameter as for smaller spheres. After switching off the nozzle, the coating fraction and uniformity remain constant as expected. In total the blue intensity of the coated particles was not as strong as the color of the dyed water solution. This is due to the fact that the solution consisted mostly of water that was evaporated during coating. Therefore the layer formed around the particles had a little solids concentration resulting in small layer thicknesses. In order to obtain a thicker layer with higher color intensity, the experiment *Coating 2* with a higher solids concentration due to the PEG and the titanium dioxide was performed.

The observed progress in color change during the injection of coating suspension with PEG, titanium dioxide, water and methylene blue was much faster than in the experiment before though the weight concentration of methylene blue in the suspensions was the same. The different behavior is based on the fact that the increased solids content in the suspension of *Coating 2* allows a better application of the dye on the particles. A higher solids content at the same flow rate results in a bigger layer around the core particles, which then shows a higher color intensity. After around five minutes, the flow rate decreased from the adjusted $5\,\mathrm{g\,min^{-1}}$ to less than $1\,\mathrm{g\,min^{-1}}$ indicating a blockage of the nozzle. After the experiment, the particles were collected from the process chamber and the blockage of the nozzle could be observed in reality. The plot of the coating fraction over time is shown in 6.12a. It can be seen that the change in coating fraction is slow during the first minute. After around 60 s a quick increase was observed, where the coating fraction starts to increase in a linear manner. It is assumed that the quick increase occurred due to a temporary blockage of the nozzle, which could be loosened but again occurred. After 240 s, the increase comes to a stop, which correlates with the observed decrease in liquid injection due to the assumed blockage of the nozzle. Due to the blockage, the injection needed to be stopped after around 400 s. The injection was stopped by switching off the pump. In order to avoid ingress of particles into the

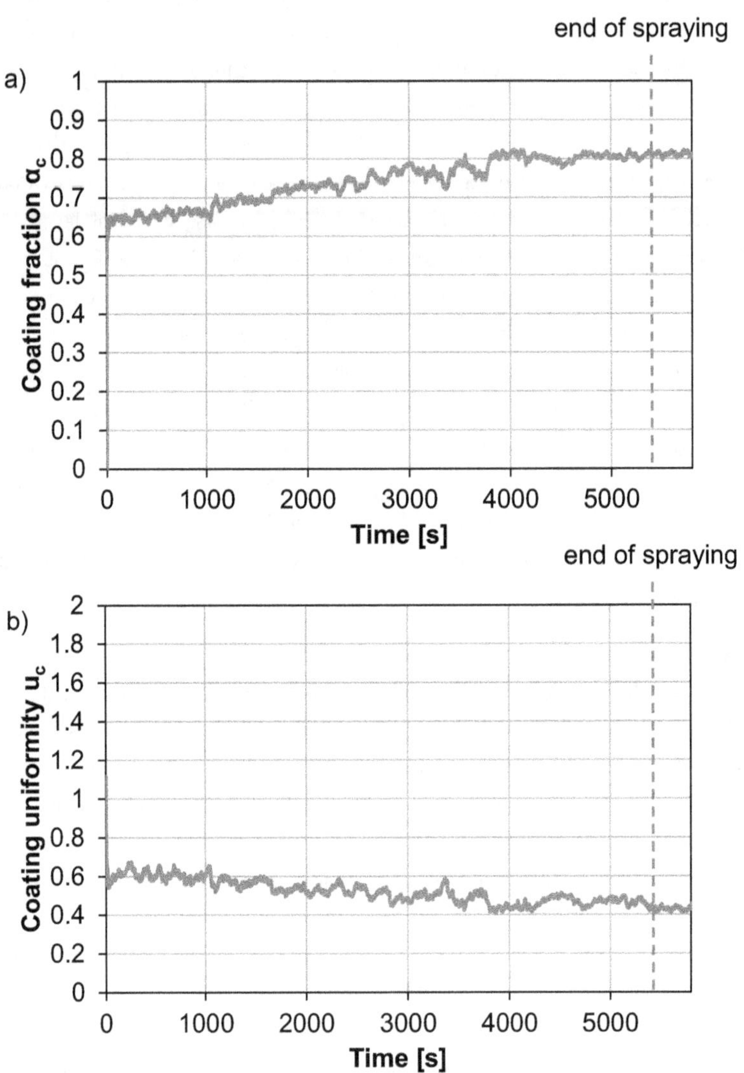

FIGURE 6.11: Experimental results for the coating experiment with methylene blue in water (*Coating 1*) using digital image analysis. a) Time-dependent coating fraction. b) Time-dependent coating uniformity.

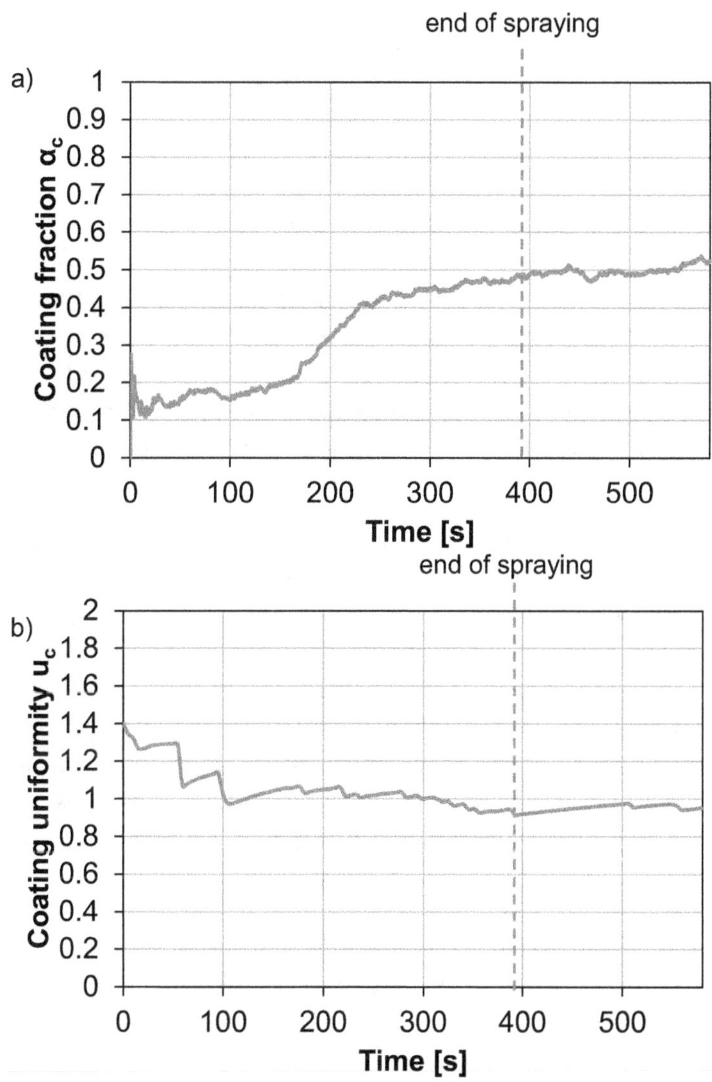

FIGURE 6.12: Experimental results for the coating experiment with suspension of PEG, titanium dioxide, water and methylene blue (*Coating 2*) using digital image analysis. The blockage of the nozzle after around 240 s can be seen by the stop in the diagrams. a) Time-dependent coating fraction. b) Time-dependent coating uniformity.

nozzle tip, the nozzle air was not stopped during the following four minutes needed to cool the process before opening the chamber. Due to the ongoing under-pressure in the nozzle and the compared to pure water higher viscosity and reduced flowability, a small amount of coating was still injected though the pump was turned off. This can be seen by the small increase in coating fraction and the decrease in coating uniformity after the end of spraying. The increase and decrease, respectively gets smaller over time as the liquid holdup in the tube is limited. Around 200 s after the end of spraying the coating fraction and uniformity are constant indicating a dry running of the pump.

From the plot of the coating uniformity it is obvious that the coating fraction seems to be connected to the uniformity of the coating of the particles in the apparatus. The sudden increase in coating fraction after 60 s is associated with a sharp increase in the plot of coating uniformity. This seems logical, as an intense burst of spraying would color a small badge of particles very intensely, while leaving the remaining particles uncoated. If the spraying process is slow and more homogeneous as afterwards during the linear increase of coating fraction, all particles build up a coating layer more consistently with smaller coefficients of variations.

The main focus of the application of digital image analysis to spouted bed coating was the determination of coating quality. As no calibration regarding the coating fraction and the layer thickness was possible with the tested experimental setup, as e.g. coating of cellulose plates in the spin coater SPIN150 (SPS-Europe B.V., the Netherlands), the values of α_c and u_c just give qualitative information. The method is applicable but suitable calibration experiments for the certain material and coating suspension need to be found in order to obtain quantitative information about the coating layer thickness. In order to get information about the layer thickness and structure, additional methods were applied in this thesis, which include OCT, particle size measurements and microscopic analyses that are described in the following subsections.

6.4 Experimental analysis of coating quantity

The previously described image analysis based method allows the time-dependent tracking of the coating quality. By means of that the minimum process duration for a complete coating of all particles in a charge can be found or problems, as e.g. blocking of the nozzle or partial spraying of one part of the bed, can be determined. Nevertheless, a measurement of the layer thickness and its deviation needs intense calibration work, which has to be conducted every time the core material, the coating suspension or the exposure is changed. In this section, the optical coherence tomography (OCT) is applied in order to measure the layer thickness by in-line monitoring as described in section 2.5.1. For validation purposes, off-line measurements were performed and a theoretic growth model was applied.

6.4.1 Optical coherence tomography

The optical coherence tomography (OCT) is a widely applied method for medical purposes but has found application in process engineering as described in 2.5.1. In this thesis, the general applicability for monitoring the coating layer thickness in a spouted bed is evaluated by one exemplary presented experiment. Within the first trials of using the OCT sensor for the spouted bed apparatus problems occurred during image capturing due to particles sticking to the window or droplets polluting the glass. Again, $Cellets^{®} 500$ were used as core particles. The coating suspension consisted of PEG (28 wt.-%) in water (72 wt.-%). No titanium dioxide was used as this would negatively affect the measurement of the refraction. Additionally, no dye was needed as the method is not based on optical analysis. As the coating suspension was assumed to produce a sticky layer, the draft plates, as described in section 5.5, were installed in order to reduce the circulation frequency and to physically separate the wetted particles from dry ones. The experiment was conducted until the observation window was too dirty for analysis, which was equal to a total injection of 2300 g coating suspension. The experimental setup of the experiment is shown in figure 6.13.

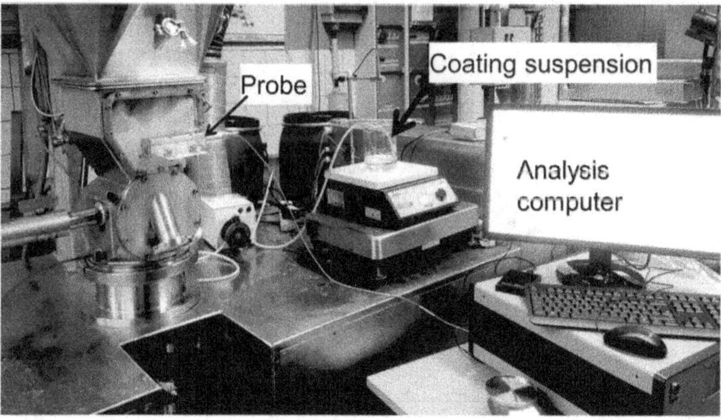

FIGURE 6.13: Experimental setup of in-line coating layer measurement by OCT in the laboratory spouted bed $ProCell^{®} 5$.

6.4.1.1 Validation

During in-line OCT measurements, the displayed coating layers showed a high noise. Due to the different particle velocities, particles appeared in varying sizes in the images. Especially for small appearing particles, the ellipsoidal shape was not suitable for layer shape representation, which resulted in a lot of wrongly determined layer thicknesses. Therefore, the data was reevaluated by applying a filter in order to stabilize the analysis system. By means of that the time-dependent coating layer thicknesses from the in-line data were determined.

The layer thickness measurement itself was manually validated by image analysis tool *ImageJ*. This validation is demonstrated here with one exemplary picture: The image shown in figure 6.14 was found to be positive by the OCT system. It can be seen that the coating layer, which is marked by the green ellipse, was detected correctly. The thickness was measured by the internal OCT algorithm to 36.68 µm. The analysis with measuring tool *ImageJ* gave a value of 37.63 µm, which is equal to a deviation of less than 3 %. Discrepancies might be caused by the ellipsoid shape of the mark by OCT, which seemed not sufficient to represent the coating layer in detail. Nevertheless, it can be assumed that the distance measurement is conducted correctly by the OCT system.

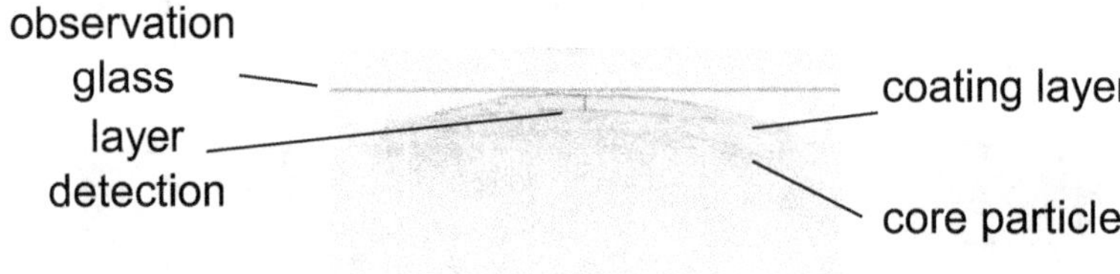

FIGURE 6.14: Exemplary coating layer detection performed by in-line OCT analysis.

6.4.1.2 In-line measurements

The OCT method gives reliable results from coating layer thicknesses of at least 20 µm. Therefore, the data sampling was started after the minimum necessary layer thickness was achieved for most of the particles in the bed. The resulting plot showing the increase of layer thickness with time is shown in figure 6.15. From the plot an increase in coating layer thickness with time can be determined, which is characterized by a high deviation. At the end of the experiment, layer thicknesses between 30 and 105 µm were measured.

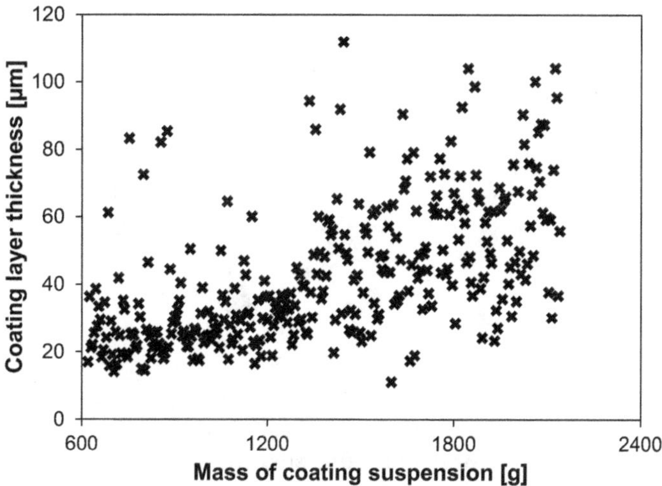

FIGURE 6.15: Increase of coating layer thickness determined by analysis of previously filtered in-line data with optical coherence tomography (OCT).

6.4.1.3 Off-line measurements

Representative samples were extracted from the process and analyzed on the rotary plate after the injection of 900, 1300, 1700 and 2100 g. The measured thicknesses are plotted in figure 6.16. The data agree well with corresponding points from in-line measurement indicating the in-line applicability of the OCT method with the sensor. The off-line data are in general a bit lower than the in-line measurement values. This might be caused by the extraction process as the device for particle sampling is positioned at the top of the process chamber promoting the output of smaller particles as they are usually higher fluidized.

6.4.2 Theoretical growth model

The particle growth or the layer thickness, respectively, were predicted with a theoretical growth model presented in section 2.5.3 analogous to the calculations in the work of Markl et al. (2014). The time-dependent coating thickness can be calculated according to equation 2.37 to:

$$s_c(t) = r_{core}\left(\left(\chi\frac{\dot{m}_c \cdot x}{m_p^{bed}}\frac{\rho_{core}}{\rho_c} + 1\right)^{\frac{1}{3}} - 1\right) =$$

$$285\ \mu\text{m}\left(\left(0.95\frac{9\frac{g}{min}0.28 \cdot 308\text{min}}{1150g} \cdot \frac{1515}{1232} + 1\right)^{\frac{1}{3}} - 1\right) = 60.5\ \mu\text{m}. \tag{6.2}$$

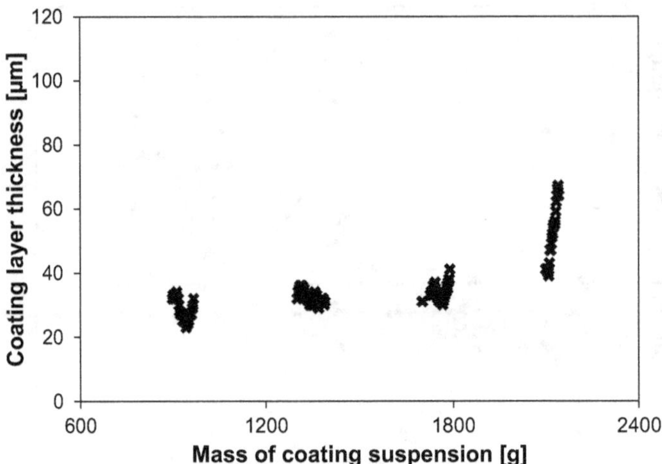

FIGURE 6.16: Increase of coating layer thickness determined by off-line optical coherence tomography (OCT) as described in section 2.5.1.

The theoretical coating layer thickness for the presented OCT experiment was determined according to equation 6.2, whereby the suspension mass deposited on the particle bed was assumed as 95 %. The theoretical coating layer is smaller than those values determined with OCT. This is logical as the model assumes a homogeneous layer around the particles and a spherical shape. But as seen from OCT data, the particles are characterized by surface irregularities, which results in spots with thicker layers that might be detected by the OCT as well. Additionally, the model assumes a constant bed mass during the whole spray coating process but in the conducted experiment, part of the bed material (in total about 200 g) was removed for off-line analysis, which again results in a higher coating layer in practice especially at the end of the experiment.

6.4.3 Light microscope

As additional validation method, some representative particles were sliced and its inner cross-section and structure were analyzed with light microscope *BX51* (Olympus, Germany). Two exemplary cuts are shown in figure 6.17 indicating on the one hand the increase in particle size and on the other hand the increasing surface inhomogeneities due to different layer thicknesses on one particle with time.

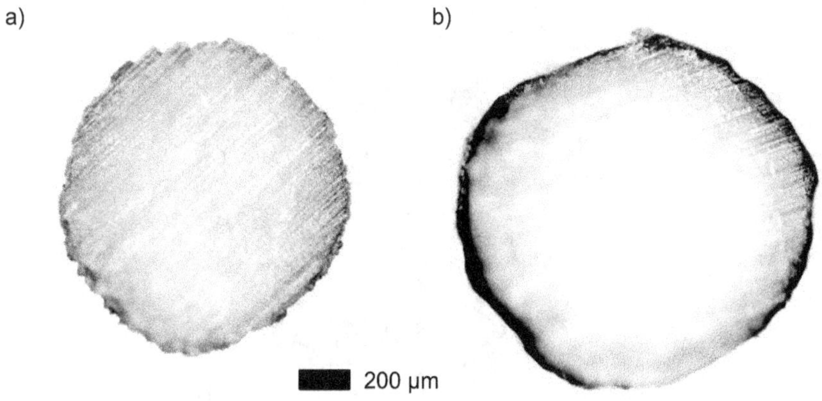

FIGURE 6.17: Results from cross-section analysis of sliced *Cellets® 500* particles, total injection of a) 115 g and b) 690 g coating suspension per batch.

6.4.4 X-ray microtomography

For micro-CT analysis, particles from the end point of the process were chosen. In total, 21 representative particles were investigated, whereby 20 of them were analyzed as collective and the other one was measured separately in order to judge the coating homogeneity on one single particle. The layer thickness was determined by analyzing the particle diameter in *ImageJ*. Therefore, one slice from the middle of the particles showing the cross-sectional area was selected from the data. In order to enhance the contrast between the core particle and the coating layer, the contrast was increased by 5 % and a binary image was produced afterwards. Then, the diameter was measured randomly meaning that a stochastic line was plotted through the cross-section and the distance was measured. This is exemplarily shown for one particle from the collective in figure 6.18.

By applying the random diameter measurement to all the particles shown in the picture, the plot given in figure 6.19 was obtained. From the plot, a high deviation can be observed, which is in accordance with the deviations measured with OCT. Even though the particles are extracted at the same time and in the same way from the process, the measured thicknesses vary significantly by more than factor 2 when referring to the smallest measured layer. The variation was previously explained by the surface inhomogeneities of the particles and the resulting variations in coating layer thickness on single particles and on particles of the same batch. In order to corroborate this hypothesis, the thickness on one single particle at ten random positions was evaluated based on the increase in

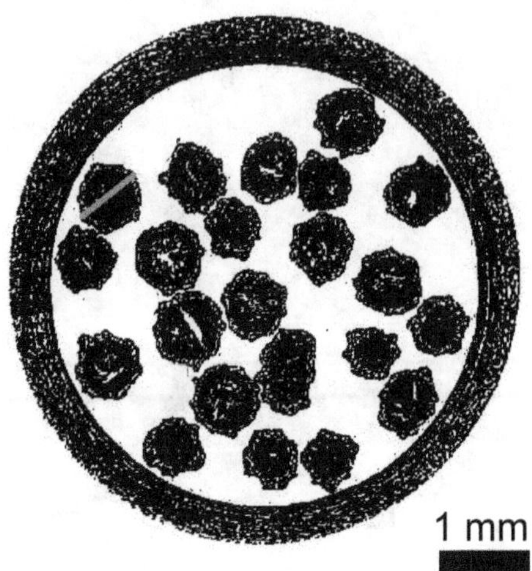

FIGURE 6.18: Exemplary determined diameter by analyzing the cross-sectional area of the particle from the micro-CT data. The image was binarized and its contrast enhanced for visualization purposes. The core particle is almost completely dark, whereas the coating layer appears brighter.

mean particle diameter as shown in figure 6.20. It can be seen that the coating layer thickness depends on the point where the measurement was conducted. The thickness measurement via the determination of the particle size includes two coating layer thicknesses. It has to be mentioned that this results in deviations from the true thicknesses but this method was found to be less sensitive to errors than the measurement of the coating layer itself as this includes only some pixels. Again, high deviations can be seen which emphasizes the inhomogeneuos layer formation on single particle scale and the resulting high deviations in the measurements.

6.4.5 Particle size analysis

Samples were taken at different time points during the process and analyzed with *CamSizer XT*. The coating layer thickness was determined as the difference between the mean particle diameter $d_{50,3}$ of the raw material and that of the coated particles. The resulting layer thickness increase referred to the injected coating suspension after every 500 g and at the end of the process is shown in figure 6.21. It can be seen from figure 6.21 that the increase ascends steeply and almost linear at the beginning. As the volume of the sphere is increasing, the amount required for a total layering of the surface is also increasing and therefore the reduced growth rate with time is as expected. Even though particles are extracted from the process for off-line analysis, the particle growth rate is

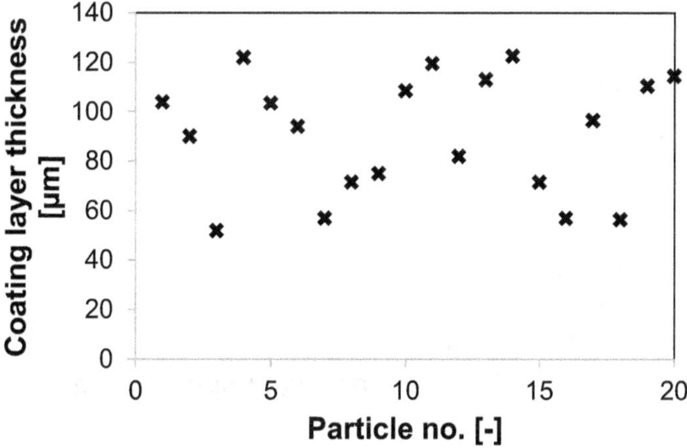

FIGURE 6.19: Coating layer thicknesses determined by off-line analysis with X-ray microtomography. Analyzed were particles from the end of the process ($m_{\text{suspension}}$=2300 g).

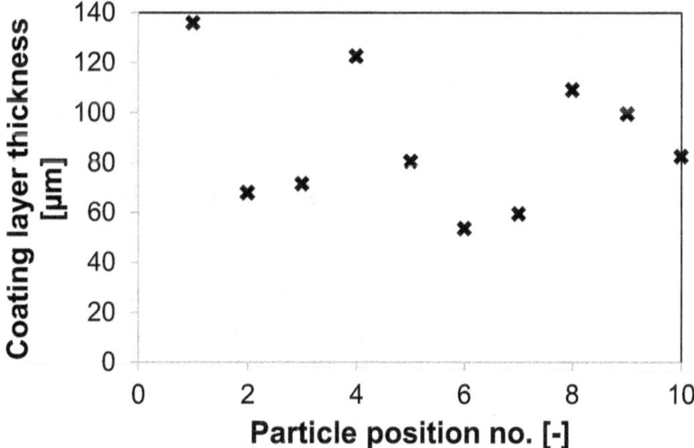

FIGURE 6.20: Coating layer thicknesses determined by off-line analysis with X-ray microtomography at different positions on one single particle. Analyzed was one representative particle from the end of the process ($m_{\text{suspension}}$=2300 g).

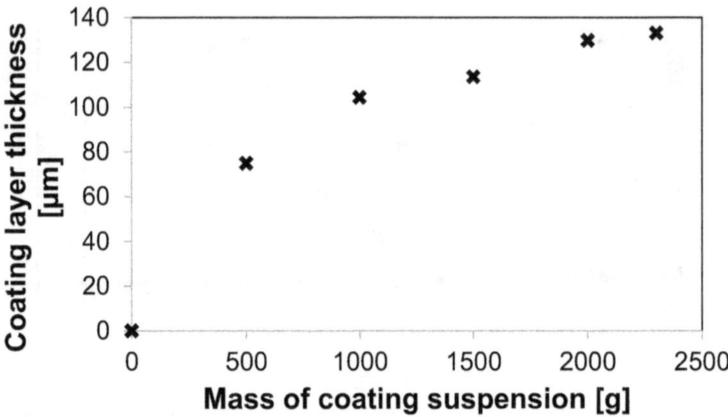

FIGURE 6.21: Coating layer thicknesses determined by off-line analysis with particle size distribution measurement device *CamSizer XT*.

decreasing with time. In total, the measured values are in the range of the data obtained by OCT. With OCT, a higher scattering was observed especially with increasing time. This is probably caused by the uneven layer formation and the resulting structure inhomogeneity on the scale of single particles. As with *CamSizer XT* the x_{area} was calculated, which is equivalent to the diameter of the area equivalent circle, every time the whole particle with its high unevenness is analyzed. Therefore, all spots with high or low coating fraction are taken into account resulting in a more homogenized average layer thickness. Additionally, the measurement of the whole particle results in average in a higher calculated layer thickness as with OCT randomly spots with thick or thin layer are measured, which gives then smaller values. Nevertheless, with regard to the variation, the values are in the same range as determined from OCT, validate the applicability of the measurement method.

Last but not least, it can be concluded that the OCT approach can be used for monitoring in-line the layer thickness in the spouted bed apparatus. The detected layer thicknesses were measured correctly and the in-line data was validated by off-line OCT analysis, particle size measurement and microscopic analyses. The detection algorithm operates reliably with layer sizes of at least 20 µm. Therefore, it seems more promising for granulation of multilayer-components than for coating processes as the granulation comes along with higher target layer thicknesses. Additionally, the shape of layer detection needs to be improved for future work in order to model the uneven and not homogeneous shape of the layer. Nevertheless, the method has a high potential for in-line measurements as it gives not only qualitative but also quantitative information.

7

Continuous process in pilot scale spouted bed

7.1 Introduction

After investigation and characterization of the laboratory scale prismatic spouted bed in the previous chapters, the focus is now set on the pilot scale apparatus, namely *ProCell® 25*. In the first section 7.2, the novel method for production of tracer particles, as already introduced in section 2.4.1, is discussed and validated regarding the tracers' suitability. In the following section, experimental residence time measurements under different process conditions and with different transfer geometries in the plates are presented and compared with each other. As the residence time distribution itself and also the characterization with the dimensionless Bodenstein number offered no precise information about the back-mixing in the system, additional experimental work in batch operation was performed, which is presented in section 7.4. In a first step the rotary valve was included in the investigations, whereas in a second step (section 7.5) the valve was closed in order to fulfill the requirements of a closed-closed system without particle flow via the in- or outlet, which is necessary when applying Fick's laws.

7.2 Tracer characterization

As described in subsection 2.4.1 the tracer particles were produced by coating the bed material, namely *Cellets® 500* particles, with a magnetizable paint in the laboratory prismatic spouted bed *ProCell® 5*.

Despite the small size of the particles, they can be easily separated from the uncoated particles by applying a magnet. A small-scale demonstration in a Petri dish is shown in figure 7.1. All coated particles stick to the magnet and are separated completely. When handling bigger sample sizes, as e.g. the 1 kg samples from residence time measurements, a bigger magnet needs to be applied. Thus, a magnetic rod *MTN 25/200 N* (Sollau s.r.o., Czech Republic) was used with which the sample could be separated in one iteration (figure 7.2). In order to determine the minimum coating amount necessary for adhering of the particle bed to the magnetic rod, samples were taken from the coating process every two minutes. All particles of a sample adhered to the magnetic rod after 50 minutes, which is equal to a liquid injection of 250 g coating agent. Under the assumption

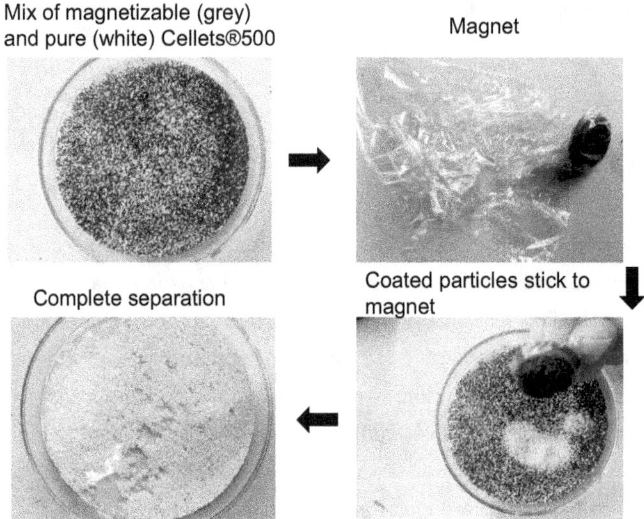

FIGURE 7.1: Separation of magnetizable tracer particles from small scale mixed sample with uncoated *Cellets® 500* particles. Separation by a pinboard magnet.

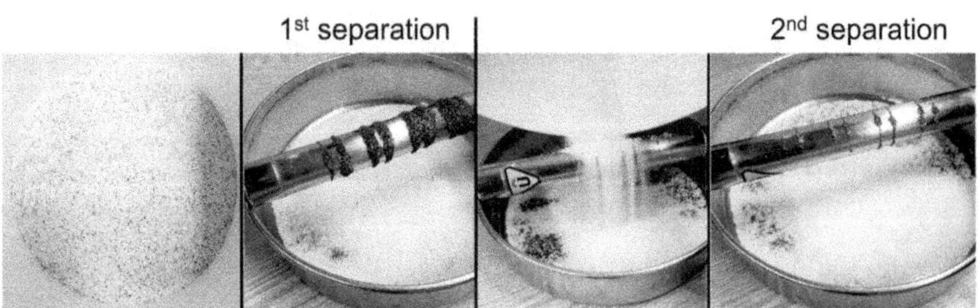

FIGURE 7.2: Principle of tracer separation from bed material in a mixed sample by a magnetic rod.

of non-porous *Cellets® 500*, this led to an increase in particle mean diameter of 23 µm to $d_{50,3,\text{coated}} = 612$ µm. The comparison of the particle size distribution of uncoated and coated particles is shown in figure 7.3. The deviation of both distributions is with mean values below 5 % small. Thus, it is assumed that the variation in particle size does not influence the fluidization behavior of tracer particles, which could result in segregation during the process. Size variations are not observable under the light microscope and even uncoated *Cellets® 500* deviate from the ideal spherical shape. The sphericity, as determined using the *CamSizer XT*, decreased from 0.956 to 0.936 during the coating process.

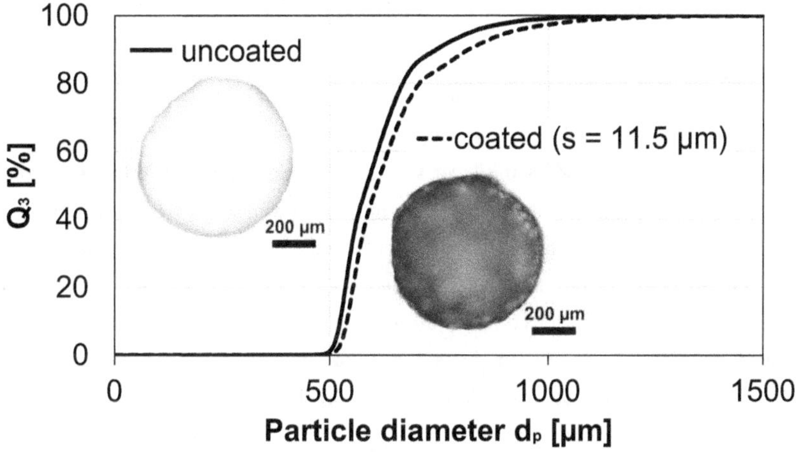

FIGURE 7.3: Cumulative particle mass size distribution for uncoated *Cellets® 500* and *Cellets® 500* with a coating layer thickness of 11.5 µm and light microscope image showing the comparison of coated (right) and uncoated (left) *Cellets® 500* (magnification 10 x).

In figure 7.4 the particle densities of uncoated particles and particles with the minimum required thickness of 11.5 µm are compared. The standard deviation from triple determination is in the range of 1.5 $\mathrm{kg\,m^{-3}}$ and therefore almost not visible in the plot. Densities were measured using helium pycnometry to 1455 and 1623 $\mathrm{kg\,m^{-3}}$, respectively. To evaluate whether the density increase of 11.5 % causes segregation effects in fluidization behavior, a 50:50-mixture (wt.-%) was fluidized in the *GF3* insert of the laboratory fluidized bed system *ProCell® 5* for 30 min. Visual observation showed a homogeneous mixture of particles without clustering or segregation effects. Thus, it is concluded that the particle density difference is uncritical for the flow behavior and the tracer criterion is fulfilled regarding this property.

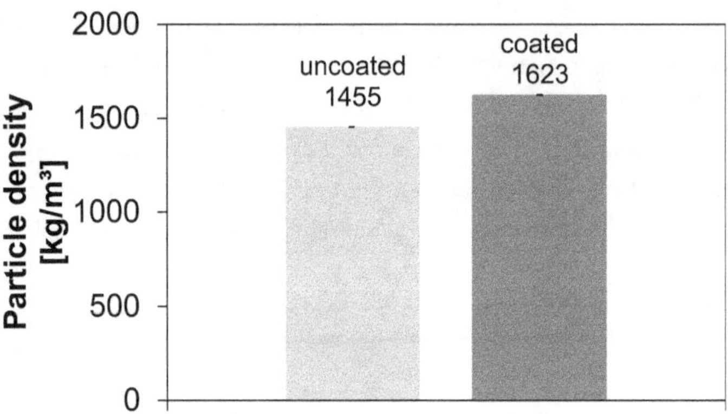

FIGURE 7.4: Particle density of uncoated *Cellets*® *500* and *Cellets*® *500* with a coating layer thickness of 11.5 µm.

For characterization of the coating layer texture and consistency, scanning electron microscope (SEM) images were taken from the coated tracer particles. From figure 7.5 it can be seen that the whole particle surface is covered with magnetizable paint. The surface roughness is increased in contrast to the smooth surface of uncoated *Cellets*® *500*, which is accompanied by the reduced sphericity. Small variations are assumed to cause negligible differences in fluidization behavior. In order to validate if the increased roughness is associated with dust production due to abrasion, tracer particles were fluidized for five hours in the laboratory fluidized bed *GF3*. After the experiment, no dust was found in the installed filter cartridges and all particles were still magnetizable indicating that stress due to particle-particle or particle-wall collisions does not affect the coating layer and its functionality. Thus, it is assumed that the tracer is re-usable for several RTD experiments.

FIGURE 7.5: SEM pictures of coated *Cellets*® *500* with a coating layer thickness of 11.5 µm (left: magnification 100 x, electronic high tension 5 kV; right: magnification 1000 x, electronic high voltage 5kV).

As a developed method should ideally be applicable for a wide range of applications other bed material particles were also investigated. Coating of γ-Al2O3 particles resulted in an even smoother surface (figure 7.6) due to the higher porosity of the material. Coated glass particles could also be used for RTD measurements but showed some abrasion during experiments. An additional coating with a protection layer of shellac successfully prevented the loss of magnetizable material. The density increase of 2 % compared to 1.6 % for regular coating is negligible and did not show changes in fluidization behavior or induced segregation.

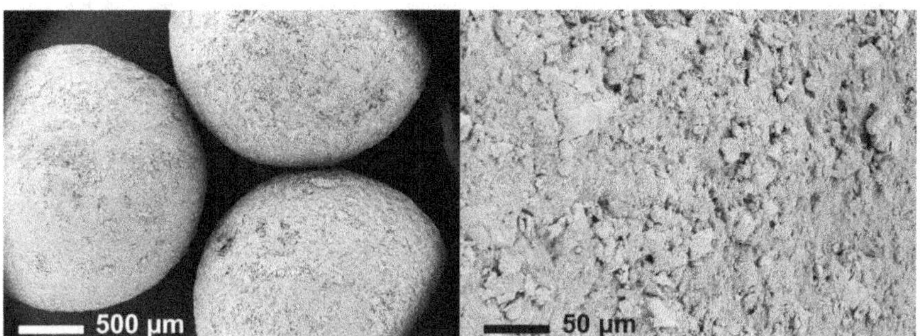

FIGURE 7.6: SEM pictures of coated γ-Al2O3 particles of $d_{50,3} = 1.8$ mm size (left: magnification 100 x, electronic high voltage 5 kV; right: magnification 1000 x, electronic high voltage 5kV).

7.3   Residence time measurements

As described in section 2.4.2 residence time distributions were measured during continuous operation of *ProCell*® *25* with a bed mass of 10 kg *Cellets*® *500* particles and additional 3 kg in the rotary valve. The original configuration of unseparated chambers was compared with the results of chambers separated by plates with defined transfer geometries. In total, four additional configurations were tested: (i) an inclined plane, (ii) the geometry of (i) in a meandering pattern, (iii) a centered hole with 2 cm diameter (iv) and a hole with 1 cm diameter. The geometry (i) was constructed based on results from simulations, which showed lowest back-mixing for this geometry. As its detailed geometry cannot be mentioned due industrial secrecy reasons, it is named *geometry (i)* in the following. Each separation plate consisted of two of the planes, one on the right and one on the left side. In case of the meandering pattern, one side was closed by sticking plasticine into the opening.

During investigation of the transfer geometries, in a first step, the separation plates were inserted only in the region of the process chamber. By means of discontinuous operation of the spouted bed, it was found that particles move from one chamber to another one even though the holes or inclined planes were closed. It was concluded that the particles move above the plates via the freeboard zone into the other chambers. Therefore, the height of the plates was increased resulting in a complete separation of the chambers from the bottom to the top. For handling reasons the plates were inserted in form of three pieces: The lowest part (1) had the prismatic form and contained the hole and geometry (i), the second rectangular plates (2) ranged from the process to the expansion chamber and the third and biggest plates (3) were positioned at the top of the expansion chamber in the broadest part (see figure 7.7). The following discontinuous experiment showed a reduced particle transport through the basically closed plates but nevertheless some particles moved into the next chambers. It was concluded that the particles were transported through small slits between the plates and the apparatus. On the one hand small spaces existed between the plates and the apparatus walls due to manufacturing reasons and on the other hand particles could move under the lowest plate slightly above the movable cylinders. Thus, in a next step, the entire slits were sealed using plasticine. The resulting validation experiment showed no particle transport between the chambers. Therefore, every time the plant was operated in the spouted bed configuration with plates, the plates needed to be sealed with the plasticine in order to force the particles to move only through the designated transfer geometry.

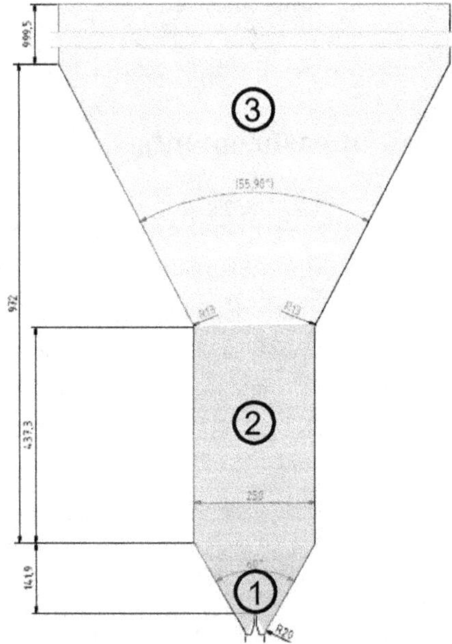

FIGURE 7.7: Plates for separation of chambers consisting of three pieces. The lowest part (1) consisted of the certain transfer geometry.

During experiments 1 kg *Cellets*® *500* particles were fed into the process every minute and 1 kg was extracted at the outlet via the rotary valve. Thus, hydrodynamic residence times of 13 min were expected due to the 10 kg bed mass in the process chamber and additional 3 kg in the rotary valve. At a defined time point, $t = 0$, the feed of this minute consisted of 500 g pure *Cellets*® *500* particles and 500 g tracer particles. All experiments were conducted for 23 min. The conditions of the performed experiments are listed in table 7.1 together with the indeed measured mean residence times. It can be seen that the exact hydrodynamic residence time was not obtained. The deviations from the hydrodynamic residence time in the cases *open*, *geometry (i)* and *hole d* = 2 cm are small and probably caused by measurement mistakes and by the data extrapolation process. The deviations in the two other cases indicate that material accumulated in part of the apparatus, which inhibited the particle transport.

TABLE 7.1: Process conditions for the performed residence time measurements in cotinuously operated pilot scale spouted bed *ProCell*® *25* and measured mean residence times.

Configuration	Total bed mass [kg]	$\dot{V}$ [m³ h⁻¹]	$\bar{t}$ [min]
Open	13	125	13.75
Geometry (i)	13	125	12.98
Geometry (i) meandering pattern	13	125	15.30
Hole d = 2 cm	13	125	13.75
Hole d = 1 cm	13	125	14.87

To evaluate the influence of the transfer geometries, first of all an experiment without plates, termed as *open*, was performed. The resulting residence time density distribution with extrapolation is shown in figure 7.8. In the experiment about 80 % of the tracer particles were found in the outlet after the experiments which gave the need for extrapolation that was performed with the Weibull scheme as described in section 2.4.3. Deviations from an ideal shape occur as ups and downs are detectable especially at subsequent time points. Nevertheless, a similarity to the density distribution from a continuous stirred tank reactor is obvious, which is validated by the corresponding dimensionless plot shown in figure 7.9. In contrast to the CSTR model a slight shift to the right hand side is observable, which can be explained by the undefined flow pattern in the rotary valve resulting in a delayed outflow. The flow behavior in the rotary valve is in-between the plug flow and the CSTR as especially near the walls good mixing was observed, whereas in the center a tunnel flow was detected. Nevertheless, the rotary valve cannot be stated as an additional stirred tank reactor as otherwise the similarity with a cascade with 2 tanks would be higher.

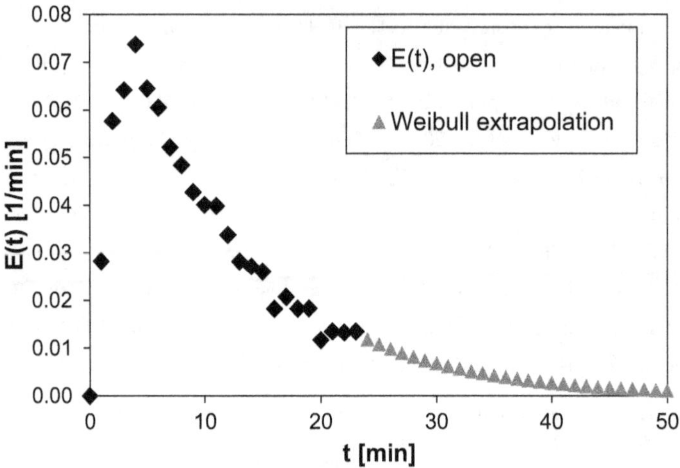

FIGURE 7.8: Residence time distribution measured with magnetizable tracer particles in the original chamber configuration of continuously operated *ProCell*® *25* and corresponding Weibull extrapolation of experimental data; $\dot{V}_{\mathrm{gas}} = 125$ m^3 h^{-1}, $\dot{m}_{\mathrm{p}} = 1$ kg min^{-1}.

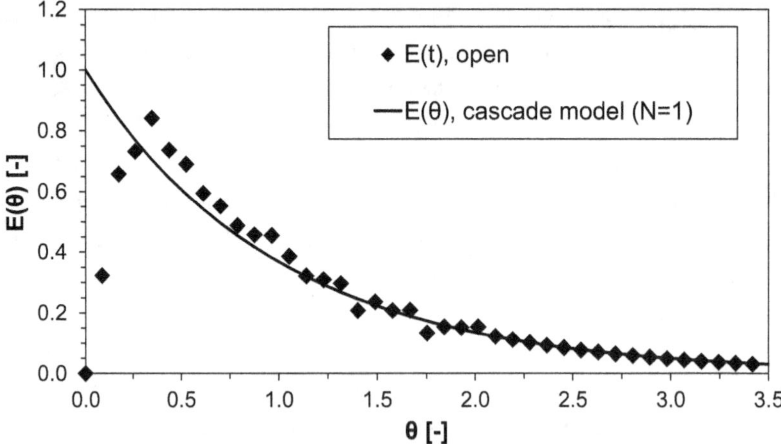

FIGURE 7.9: Dimensionless residence time distribution of the original chamber configuration in comparison with the cascade model with one CSTR: $\dot{V}_{\mathrm{gas}} = 125$ m^3 h^{-1}, $\dot{m}_{\mathrm{p}} = 1$ kg min^{-1}.

The residence time distributions of the two configurations with geometry (i) are shown in figure 7.10. As the *geometry (i)* had shown most promising in terms of back-mixing during simulations, this configuration was chosen for proving the repeatability and reproducibility and was performed three times. It can be seen that the standard deviation is at every time point below 12 %, which allows the assumption of reproducibility of all experiments. Within the first minutes, the measured values are coincident and in comparison to the open configuration almost no tracer material is detectable at the outlet within the first two minutes. This is advantageous as no particles should leave the process chamber directly after insertion as this would increase the risk of uncoated material or insufficient drying. When comparing the distributions of the two planes with each other, the *geometry (i)* configuration results in a narrower distribution, which equates to a homogeneous product. Nevertheless, when comparing the Bodenstein numbers given in table 7.2 the meandering pattern seems advantageous in terms of back-mixing as a higher value and therefore a lower axial dispersion is obtained with the meandering configuration. On the other hand, when remembering the mean residence times, it was assumed that material accumulated in the chamber, which would make this configuration not useful. The flow through the meandering pattern is definitely slowed in comparison to two openings on each plate. Nevertheless, the constant outflow of 1 kg min^{-1} could be maintained during the experiment. The bed distribution after the experiment is shown in figure 7.11. It is obvious that the particle mass in the fourth chamber is the smallest, which confirms the assumption that a long-term operation of the meandering pattern is not possible as the transport is slowed by the closed side resulting in an unwanted accumulation in the first chambers.

In figure 7.12 the residence time distributions with their extrapolations for the two hole configurations are shown. Again, the outflow of particles within the first two minutes is minimized compared to the configuration *open*. When looking at the shape of the two curves a narrower one can be detected for the hole with the bigger diameter (*hole $d = 2$ cm*). No quantitative comparison via the Bodenstein number is possible as they are in the same range (table 7.2). During process operation in the configuration *hole $d = 1$ cm*, the time interval of the outflow needed to be extended as otherwise the flow rate could not be maintained anymore. This indicates that the opening diameter is too small for the desired flow rate. This assumption is confirmed by the bed mass distribution after the experiment that shows a strong material accumulation in the first chamber and almost no material in the fourth chamber (figure 7.13). Thus, the smaller hole size is not suitable for the desired process conditions.

In summary, both the geometry (i) and the hole configurations reduce back-mixing, which was confirmed by the longer time interval without tracer outflow at the beginning of the experiment and the higher Bodenstein numbers. With the smaller hole and the

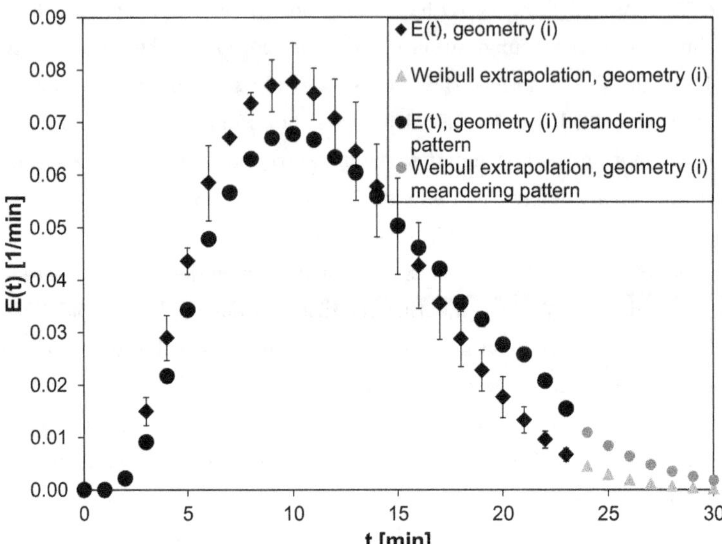

FIGURE 7.10: Residence time distribution measured with magnetizable tracer particles in the configurations *geometry (i)* and *geometry (i) meandering pattern* of continuously operated *ProCell® 25* and corresponding Weibull extrapolation of experimental data; $\dot{V}_{\mathrm{gas}} = 125 \ \mathrm{m^3\,h^{-1}}$, $\dot{m}_{\mathrm{p}} = 1 \ \mathrm{kg\,min^{-1}}$.

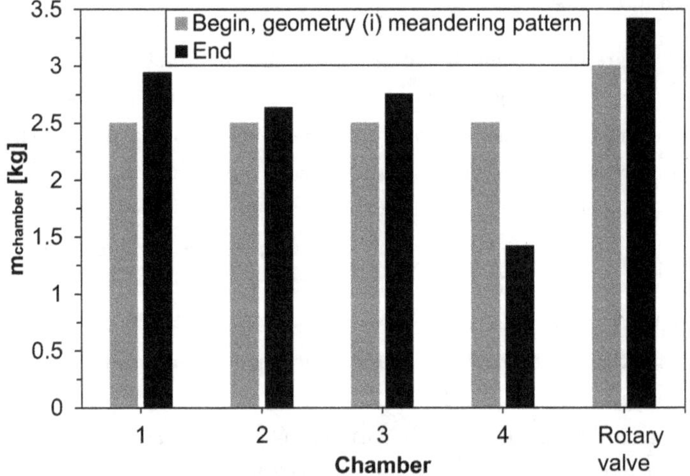

FIGURE 7.11: Bed mass distribution at the beginning and the end of continuous operation of *ProCell® 25* with configuration *geometry (i) meandering pattern*; $\dot{V}_{\mathrm{gas}} = 125 \ \mathrm{m^3\,h^{-1}}$, $\dot{m}_{\mathrm{p}} = 1 \ \mathrm{kg\,min^{-1}}$.

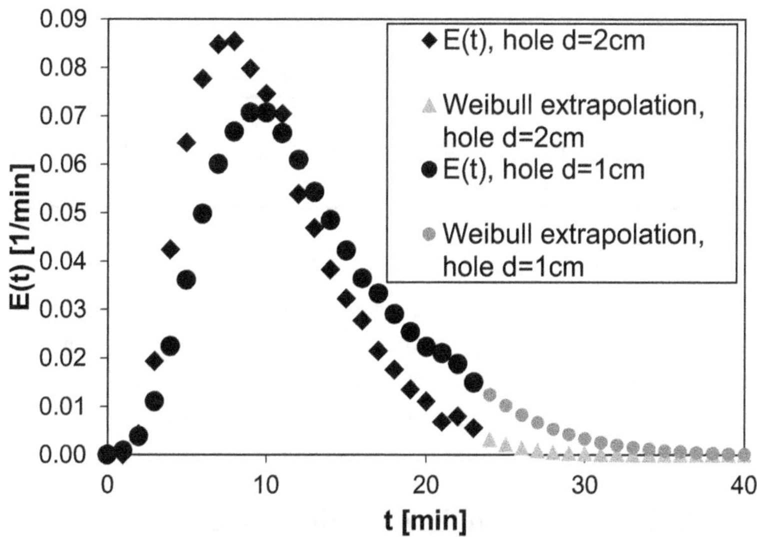

FIGURE 7.12: Residence time distribution measured with magnetizable tracer particles in the configurations *hole* $d = 2$ cm and hole $d = 1$ cm of continuously operated *ProCell® 25* and corresponding Weibull extrapolation of experimental data; $\dot{V}_{gasp} = 125 \ \mathrm{m^3 \, h^{-1}}$, $\dot{m}_p = 1 \ \mathrm{kg \, min^{-1}}$.

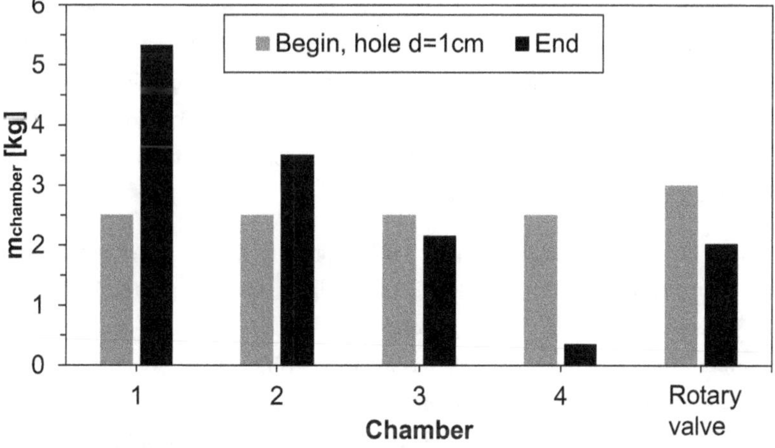

FIGURE 7.13: Bed mass distribution at the beginning and the end of continuous operation of *ProCell® 25* with configuration *hole* $d = 1$cm; $\dot{V}_{gas} = 125 \ \mathrm{m^3 \, h^{-1}}$, $\dot{m}_p = 1 \ \mathrm{kg \, min^{-1}}$.

TABLE 7.2: Charactersitic values obtained from residence time measurements in continuously operated pilot scale spouted bed *ProCell® 25*.

Parameter	Open	Geometry (i)	Geometry (i) meandering pattern	Hole d=2cm	Hole d=1cm
$t_{\min}$ [min]	1	2	2	2	1
$E_{\max}(t)$ [1/min]	0.074	0.08	0.067	0.085	0.071
Bo	0.36	3.92	6.82	4.4	4.77

meandering pattern of geometry (i) the desired flow rate could not be maintained during long-term operation making these options not suitable. Thus, they are not further investigated in this thesis. In contrast, the bigger hole and the geometry (i) could maintain the desired flow rate. As the Bodenstein numbers are in the same range a further quantification of back-mixing was necessary as explained in the next section.

7.4   Back-mixing: qualitative description

In order to describe and compare the axial mixing behavior and to evaluate the risk of back-mixing from one chamber into the previous one, discontinuous experiments without in- and outlet flow were performed. As the *open* configuration comes along without a chamber separation, no comparison experiments could be performed. Instead, the following results act as comparison of the different transfer geometries *geometry (i)* and *hole d* = 2 cm. For qualitative description, the rotary valves and the four chambers were filled with the partial amount of bed material (3 kg in the rotary valve and 2.5 kg in each chamber), whereby the bed mass of the third chamber contained 500 g tracer particles as sketched in figure 7.14. The process was started up and conducted for two minutes. After shutdown, the bed masses of each chamber and the rotary valve were extracted and the tracer amount was measured.

The tracer concentrations x_T in the chambers and the rotary valve after the experiments with the *geometry (i)* and the *hole d* = 2 cm configurations are plotted in figure 7.15 for the two transfer configurations. A comparison of the tracer concentration in the first chamber shows that in case of the *geometry (i)* configuration almost no tracer is detectable, which is advantageous in terms of back-mixing. The tracer concentration is higher with the *hole d* = 2 cm in all chambers (except in chamber 3) and the rotary valve indicating a more random particle flow in both directions also without convective flow. In both cases tracer was detected in the rotary valve, which shows that the chambers cannot be seen as a closed system. For both configurations the bed mass distribution was measured after the experiment (figure 7.16). Obviously, the bed mass is almost constant

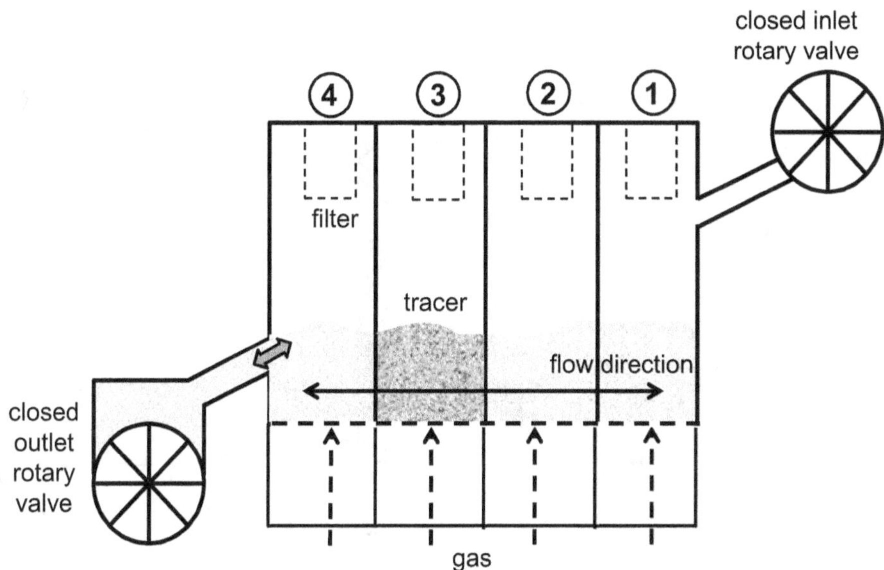

FIGURE 7.14: Experimental setup for qualitative analysis of the axial mixing behavior in *ProCell® 25* apparatus. All chambers and the rotary valve were filled with *Cellets® 500* particles, whereby a defined amount of tracer was added in the third chamber. The process was started up and stopped after 2 min. $\dot{V}_{\text{gas}} = 125 \text{ m}^3 \text{ h}^{-1}$.

when using the *hole* $d = 2$ cm configuration. With the *geometry (i)* configuration a preferred transport into the forward direction is observable. This indicates that the particle transport into the direction of the outlet is enhanced by the configuration of the inclined plane even though no convective flow is applied. After this qualitative description of back-mixing and of the direction of particle transport, a quantitative comparison is pursued in the next subsection. In order to find a quantitative value for the back-mixing, namely the dispersion coefficient, similar experiments were performed but without the rotary valve involved.

7.5 Back-mixing: quantitative description

For quantitative description by means of the dispersion coefficient, the experimental setup was changed as shown in figure 7.17. From figure 7.15 it was observed that the particle flow between the chambers and the valve influences the tracer concentration. As the flow behavior in the rotary valve is not predictable, the valve was closed. Another difference compared to the former experiments is that the process was started up and the tracer was injected afterwards into the fourth chamber. Again, the process

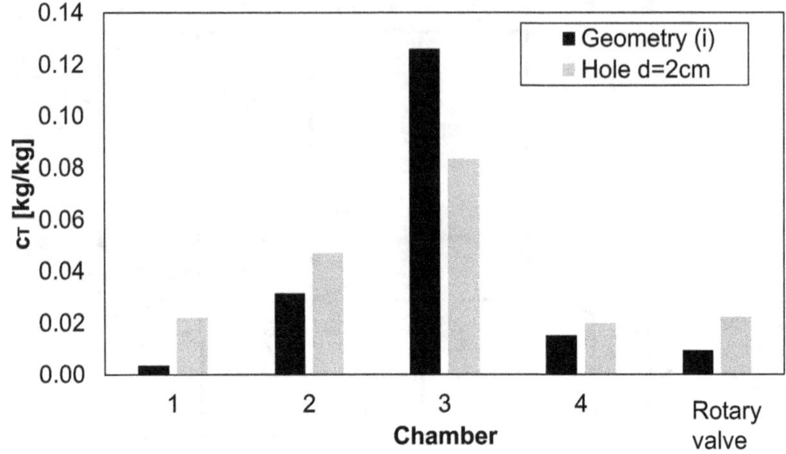

FIGURE 7.15: Tracer concentration after discontinuous operation of *ProCell*® *25* with the configurations *geometry (i)* and *hole d* = 2cm; $\dot{V}_{gas}$ = 125 m³ h⁻¹, $t_{process}$ =2 min.

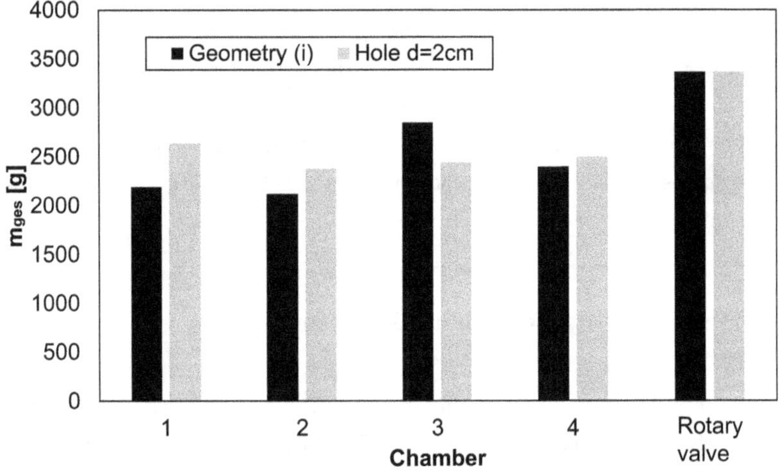

FIGURE 7.16: Bed mass distribution after discontinuous operation of *ProCell*® *25* with the configurations *geometry (i)* and *hole d* = 2cm; $\dot{V}_{gas}$ = 125 m³ h⁻¹, $t_{process}$ =2 min.

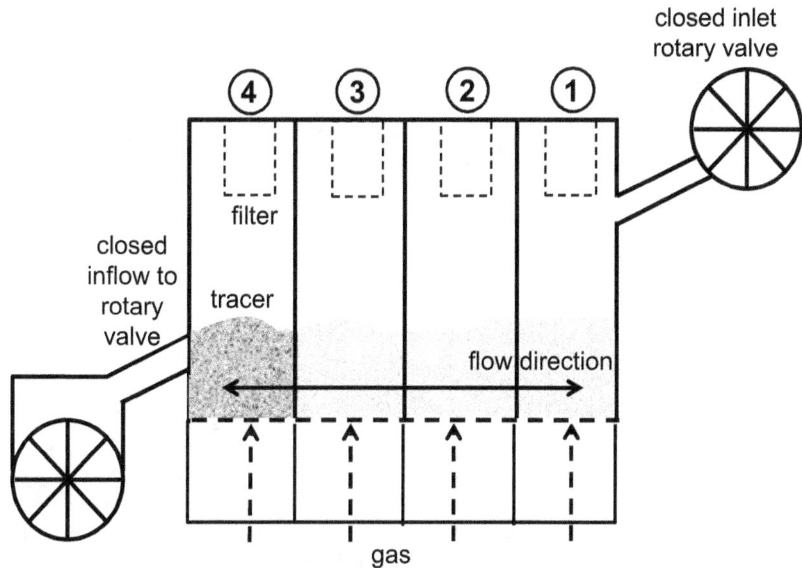

FIGURE 7.17: Experimental setup for quantitative analysis of axial mixing behavior in *ProCell®25* apparatus. All chambers were filled with *Cellets®500* particles, whereby a defined amount of tracer was added in the fourth chamber after start-up. The rotary valve was closed, t_{process} =2 min, $\dot{V}_{\text{gas}} = 125$ m^3 h^{-1}.

was conducted for two minutes and the tracer distribution was determined afterwards. Analogous to the explanations in section 2.4.4.3 initial conditions are defined according to the setup:

$$t = 0, 0 \leq x \leq L_1; C = 1 \qquad t = 0, L_1 \leq x \leq L_{\text{bed}}; C = 0, \tag{7.1}$$

with L_1 the length of the fourth chamber and L_{bed} the length of the whole spouted bed. The dimensionless concentration is determined by correlating the tracer mass concentration to the concentration at the beginning of the experiment:

$$C = \frac{c_{\text{T}}}{c_{\text{T,0}}}. \tag{7.2}$$

As mentioned before, the dispersion coefficient is obtained by means of the least square method meaning that the residual sum of squares of the experimental data and the objective function is minimized. The obtained experimental data of dimensionless tracer concentration and the fitted curves with the corresponding dispersion coefficients are shown in figures 7.18 and 7.19.

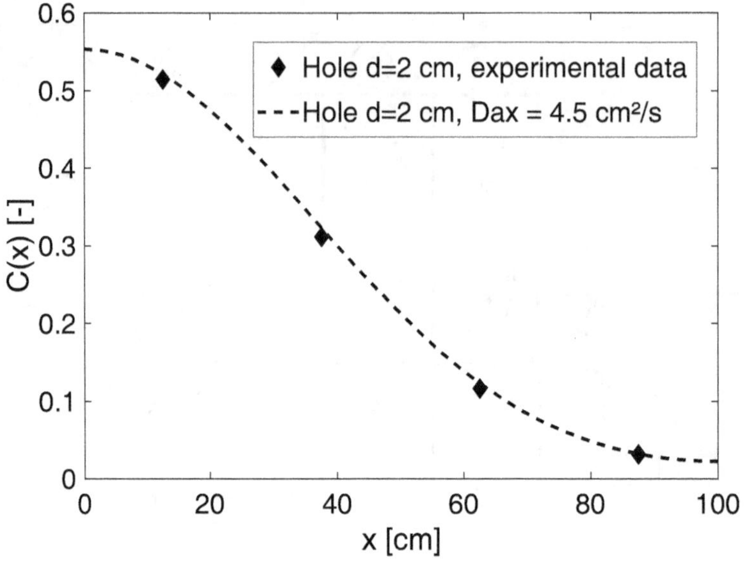

FIGURE 7.18: Fitting of experimental data to the equation of dispersion for the configuration *hole*, $d = 2$ cm.

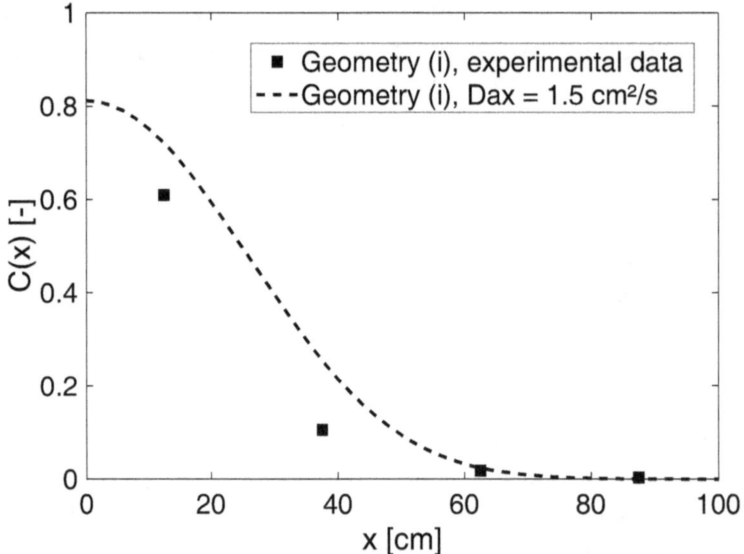

FIGURE 7.19: Fitting of experimental data to the equation of dispersion for the configuration *geometry (i)*.

The coefficients are in the range of the values obtained by Shi and Fan (1985) for sand particles with a mean diameter of 491 µm in a fluidized bed without separation plates. Also Bachmann and Tsotsas (2015) found similar values for a continuously operated fluidized bed. Thus, it can be concluded that the diffusion, here termed as dispersion, model is also applicable for spouted beds and the parameter is accessible by discontinuous operation of the plant. Obviously, the highest axial dispersion occurs with the configuration *hole, $d = 2$* cm as the dispersion coefficient is more than doubled compared to the *geometry (i)* configuration. From the diagram referring to the *geometry (i)* configuration, it is obvious that the fits show only low agreement. The fitting of the curve for the *hole* configuration shows higher consistence. A reason for the low fitting might be the directed configuration of the inclined planes, which is discussed in the following.

Besides a low back-mixing, here characterized by the tracer distribution, the distribution of the bed mass is a characteristic of the process configuration. In figure 7.16 the bed mass distribution after the discontinuous experiment was shown. It was concluded that the configuration *geometry (i)* enhances the particle transport toward the outlet. As no convective transport by particle feed or output was given, the directed transport is attributed to the inclination of the planes. The transport reduces dispersion in backwards direction and is therefore beneficial regarding the back-mixing but on the other hand, the bed mass is not homogeneously distributed over the whole bed length, which dissents the assumptions of the diffusion model and causes the bad fitting results. In addition, the process chamber contains three transfer geometries making a quantification of the entire dispersion coefficient difficult. Nevertheless, the obtained values can be seen as comparable parameter.

Besides the chosen standard condition of 125 m^3 h^{-1} ($u - u_{\mathrm{mf}} = 0.59$ m s^{-1}) two other gas volume flow rates, namely 90 ($u - u_{\mathrm{mf}} = 0.42$ m s^{-1}) and 160 m^3 h^{-1} ($u - u_{\mathrm{mf}} = 0.75$ m s^{-1}) were tested regarding the influence of the gas velocity on the back-mixing. The resulting plots with the dispersion coefficient curves are shown in figure 7.20 for both configurations, *hole, $d = 2$* cm and *geometry (i)*. It can be seen that the dispersion is increased with increased gas volume flow rate, which meets the expectations as the increased fluidization results in a higher transfer probability due to an increased mobility. The dependence is almost linear. This trend was also found by Kato et al. (1985) and Shi and Fan (1985) for fluidized beds.

7.6 Conclusions

It can be concluded that the *geometry (i)* configuration shows the lowest back-mixing as the particle transport into the forward direction is forced by the slant of the planes.

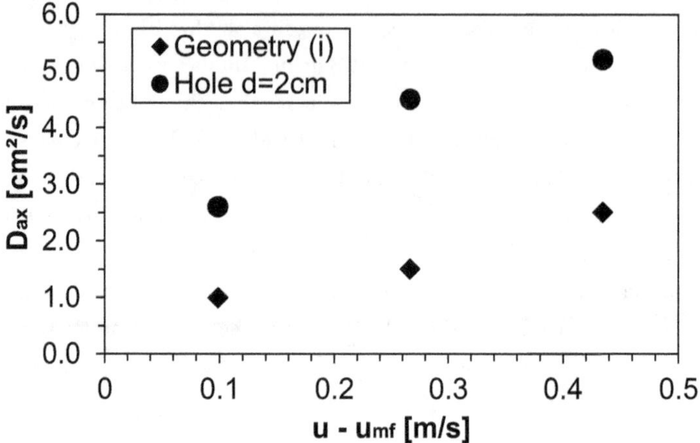

FIGURE 7.20: Experimentally determined dispersion coefficient for continuously operated *ProCell® 25* apparatus with the transfer geometries *geometry (i)* and *hole d = 2* cm in dependence on the gas velocity.

The meandering pattern showed no advantage in terms of back-mixing. Additionally, problems during long-term operation occurred as the maintenance of the mass flow rate was not possible due to material accumulation. The *hole* configurations show no desired transport direction and therefore a more constant bed mass distribution during experiments. Nevertheless, a strong axial dispersion and back-mixing were observed. Back-mixing was reduced by a smaller diameter of the *hole* but then the desired particle transport could not be maintained, which makes the geometry not suitable. In total, the *geometry (i)* showed best results in terms of a reduced back-mixing and good applicability for continuous operation. The results were quantified using the dispersion model. Nevertheless, the obtained values can only be seen as estimations as the regarded entire apparatus is characterized by three transfer geometries making it difficult to define an overall dispersion coefficient. The found influencing shape of the transfer geometry and the cross-section are not included in the underlying theory of Fick's law. Thus, the correlation can be used for a quantitative comparison but the results cannot be correlated to the physical theory.

8

Conclusions

In this thesis prismatic spouted beds were investigated both experimentally and numerically. Besides the batch operated laboratory scale apparatus *ProCell® 5* and a transparent replica of that kind the pilot scale plant *ProCell® 25* was used for continuous experiments. On laboratory scale the coating quality was investigated and pilot scale experiments were focused on measuring of residence time distributions with the aim of back-mixing minimization.

The laboratory scale apparatus was investigated by means of high frequency pressure drop measurements and following Fourier transform in the transparent replica. For two Geldart B particle systems the range of stable and instable spouting was determined. The stability interval was increased by installing two parallel draft plates into the chamber. The fluidization behavior was simulated by means of the coupled CFD-DEM approach and a coarse-graining method for handling high numbers of particles was applied. The draft plates enforced a more homogeneous circulation frequency distribution and a reduced main frequency. The residence time in the spout zone was found to be smaller in the chamber geometry with plates. CFD-DEM simulation predicted a broader surface coverage distribution with installed draft plates. This was validated for a real process time of 60 min by recurrence CFD (rCFD) simulations. The broader liquid distribution in the stable regime was hypothesized to occur due to the lower residence times in both spout and spray zone, which results in an inhomogeneous exposure of the particles as the mixing in the depth of the apparatus is reduced. Nevertheless, the increased residence time outside of the spray zone seems promising for coating experiments in which a sufficient drying is inevitable in order to prevent agglomeration. For further investigations the installation of several nozzles in the process chamber with draft plates might be promising as thereby the probability of crossing the spray zone could be increased for all particles in the bed.

The investigation of the coating process was the main application of the prismatic spouted bed in this thesis. In order to validate the coating quality, a digital image analysis algorithm was implemented. By analyzing high-speed camera images with the algorithm, the change of particles' brightness over time was recorded. With that approach the coating fraction and uniformity could be determined and the blockage of the nozzle during the experiment was detected. For measurement of the coating layer thickness a calibration method is needed to link the color or brightness with the layer thickness. In this work the coating layer thickness was monitored in-line with optical coherence tomography (OCT). The applicability of the method was validated by external microscopic and particle size analyses.

In this thesis a novel method for experimental quantification of residence time distributions was developed in which part of the bed material is coated by a magnetizable paint allowing a fast separation of this tracer material from the samples after passing the process. The magnetizable coating is abrasion resistant and can also be used for processes with higher humidity. Residence time distributions were measured in the *ProCell® 25* apparatus with additional investigation of the influence of separation plates with different transfer geometries between the four chambers. By means of discontinuous experiments, the back-mixing was quantified via the dispersion coefficient. It was found that the dispersion and therefore the unwanted back-mixing is lowest with two inclined surfaces in the plates making this configuration promising for industrial scale applications in order to obtain a high throughput with constant product quality. When performing continuously operated experiments it was shown that not only the back-mixing is a quality criterion but the desired particle flow rate must be feasible for a long time. If the transfer geometry is too small for the flow rate, bed material accumulates in some of the chambers which causes a collapse of the fluidization after a while.

Especially when performing granulation experiments, the influence of the particle size distribution on the flow behavior and the liquid deposition needs to be taken into account in future work. Thus, processes with higher liquid injection as needed for granulation purposes should be investigated with focus on the possible accumulation of bigger particles in the spray zone and the resulting risk of defluidization due to an excessive growth of the coarse particle fraction. In addition, the influence of non-spherical particle shapes needs to be determined as in industry often non-spherical products are handled, which might influence the fluidization behavior and the process stability.

Appendix A

Specifications of used equipment

A.1 Components of laboratory *ProCell®5*

Air ventilator:

Elektror Hochdruckventilator HRD 60 FU – 105/4,0

Air heater:

Leister Lufterhitzer Typ 40 000, 3x 400 V, 11.2 kW elektrische Leistung

Air filter:

Mahle Entstaubungselement (conical shape) Type 852 903 TI 07/1 – 0.5 + DRG V4A
FRV

Two-fluid nozzle:

970.0/0-S4 Schlick

Temperature sensor:

Rössel Messtechnik Mantel-Widerstandsthermometer (PT 100), Ø 3 mm

Peristaltic pump:

Medorex TBE / 200 84 – 1 – 8 – 4.8 x 1.6

Balance:

Kern DS, 30 kg $\pm$ 0.1 g

A.2 Components of transparent replica

Air ventilator:

Elektror Hochdruckventilator HRD 60 FU – 105/4,0

High frequency pressure sensor:

Type PD-23/8666.1, Keller

A.3   Components of pilot scale *ProCell*® *25*

Rotary valve:

Type ZRD 150-630 with drive, coperion

Flowmeter:

COMBIMASS basic, AL IP, BINDER

Two-fluid nozzle:

GKWZ 2.10, Schlick

Appendix B

Behavior of the empty transparent replica

As all presented experiments were performed with the maximum slit height of 3.5 mm, only the pressure drop dependence from the gas volume flow rate for this slit height is presented here (figure B.1 and table B.1).

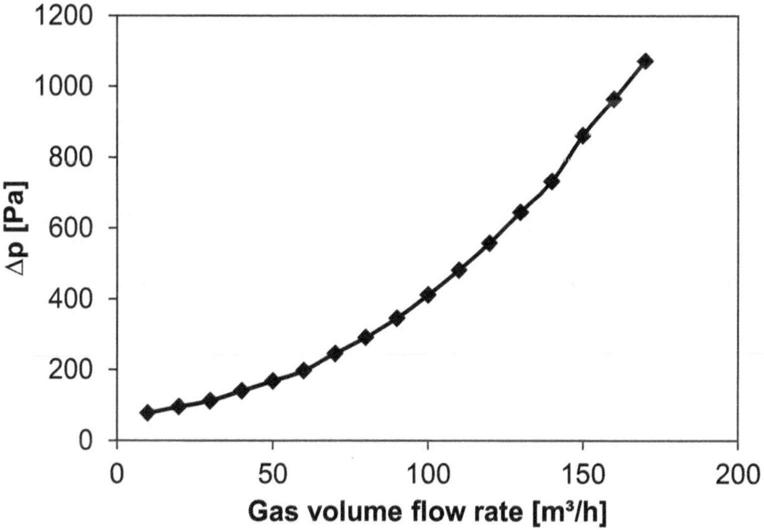

FIGURE B.1: Pressure drop of the empty transparent replica of laboratory *ProCell*® *5* with a slit height of $h = 3.5$ mm.

TABLE B.1: Pressure drop and and pressure loss coefficients for different gas volume flow rates measured in the empty transparent replica of laboratory spouted bed *ProCell®* 5.

Volume flow rate $[\mathrm{m^3\,h^{-1}}]$	Velocity $[\mathrm{m\,s^{-1}}]$	Pressure drop $[\mathrm{Pa}]$	Pressure loss coefficient [-]
10	0.87	77.38	170.56
20	1.74	94.93	52.32
30	2.60	112.43	27.54
40	3.47	140.12	19.30
50	4.34	167.64	14.78
60	5.21	196.89	12.06
70	6.08	245.42	11.04
80	6.94	291.12	10.03
90	7.81	345.52	9.40
100	8.68	411.43	9.07
110	9.55	481.56	8.77
120	10.42	557.46	8.53
130	11.28	644.94	8.41
140	12.15	732.96	8.24
150	13.02	861.55	8.44
160	13.89	964.58	8.31
170	14.76	1071.68	8.17

Appendix C

Liquid injection in CFD-DEM simulations

Calculation of the wet bulb temperature (T_{wb}) as mentioned in section 3.4. The enthalpy of the moist air is calculated as:

$$h_{1+x}(Y, T) = c_{\mathrm{pf}}(T - T_{ref}) + Y\left(c_{\mathrm{pv}}(T - T_{ref}) + \Delta h^{\mathrm{lv}}\right), \qquad (C.1)$$

with Y the water loading of air, T_{ref} the reference temperature 273.15 K, c_{pf} the specific heat of constant pressure of air (1004 $\mathrm{J\,kg^{-1}\,K^{-1}}$), c_{pv} the specific heat of constant pressure of water vapor (1900 $\mathrm{J\,kg^{-1}\,K^{-1}}$) at 273.15 K and the vaporization enthalpy of water ($\Delta h^{LV} = 2500$ kJ $\mathrm{kg^{-1}}$ K). The enthalpy of the air bulk $h_{1+x}(Y, T)$ is set to be equal to the enthalpy of fully saturated air $h_{1+x}(Y_{\mathrm{sat,wb}}, T_{wb})$, which surrounds the particles liquid layer. h_{1+x} is calculated iteratively to yield the wet bulb temperature. The saturation loading is calculated according to:

$$Y_{\mathrm{sat,wb}} = \frac{0.622}{\frac{p}{p_{\mathrm{sat}}(T_{\mathrm{wb}})} - 1}, \qquad (C.2)$$

where p_{sat} is the saturation pressure. The saturation pressure is calculated with the Antoine equation and the parameters of A, B and C given in (Stull, 1947):

$$p_{\mathrm{sat}} = 10^5 Pa \cdot 10^{\left(4.6543 - \frac{1435.364}{T - 64.848}\right)}. \qquad (C.3)$$

To eliminate the effort of iteration, a 2D Taylor series was fitted to the data with the following equation:

$$T_{\mathrm{wb}} = \alpha_0 + \alpha_{01}T + \alpha_{10}Y + \alpha_{11}YT + \alpha_{21}Y^2T + \alpha_{12}YT^2 + \alpha_{22}Y^2T^2 + \alpha_{20}^2 + \alpha_{02}T^2, \quad (C.4)$$

with $\alpha_0 = -31.66$, $\alpha_{01} = 1.675$, $\alpha_{10} = 1198$, $\alpha_{11} = -61.44$, $\alpha_{02} = -0.00209$, $\alpha_{12} = 0.08229$, $\alpha_{22} = -1.087$, $\alpha_{21} = 796.7$ and $\alpha_{20} = -150000$. The fitting is shown in figures C.1 and C.2.

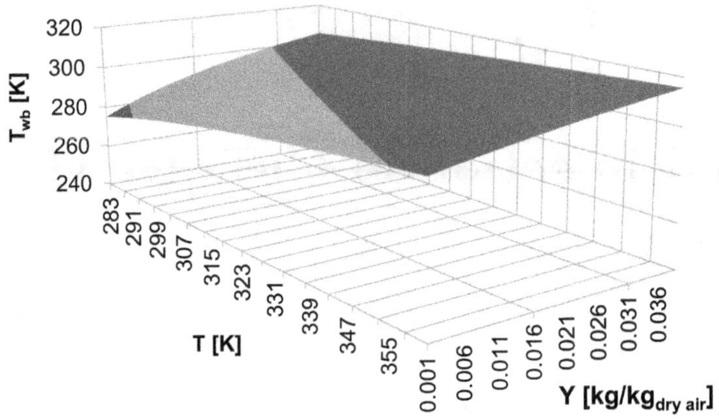

FIGURE C.1: Dependence of temperature T, the wet bulb temperature T_{wb} and the water loading of air Y.

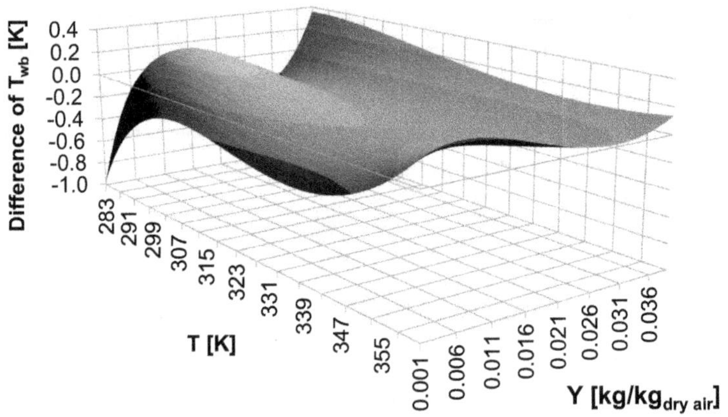

FIGURE C.2: Fitting of a 2D Taylor series in order to determine T_{wb}.

Appendix D

Algorithms used for PTV

```
1   def attraction_step(u, u_aux, S, T, alpha=0.8):
2       neighbors_su = (S + u).nearest_neighbor_to(S + u_aux)
3       neighbors_t = (T).nearest_neighbor_to(S + u_aux)
4
5       return alpha * u_aux \
6           + (1 - alpha) / 2 * (neighbors_t - S) \
7           + (1 - alpha) / 2 * (neighbors_su - S)
```

LISTING D.1: Attraction step towards minimizing E_I.

```
1   def global_smoothing(u, S, alpha=0.9):
2       avg_u = np.zeros(np.shape(u))
3       for i, particle in enumerate(S):
4           neighbors, dist = (S).get_n_nearest_neighbors(particle, n=3)
5           for k in range(len(neighbors)):
6               avg_u[i] += 1 / dist[k] * matching_u(neighbors[k], u)
7
8       return alpha * u + (1 - alpha) * avg_u
```

LISTING D.2: Global regularization step towards minimizing E_{II}.

Bibliography

Altzibar, H., Lopez, G., Aguado, R., Alvarez, S., San Jose, M. J., and Olazar, M. (2009). Hydrodynamics of conical spouted beds using different types of internal devices. *Chemical Engineering & Technology*, 32(3):463–469.

Altzibar, H., Lopez, G., Alvarez, S., José, M. S., Barona, A., and Olazar, M. (2008). A draft-tube conical spouted bed for drying fine particles. *Drying Technology*, 26(3):308–314.

Andersson, B., Andersson, R., Hakansson, L., Mortensen, M., Sudiyo, R., and van Wachem, B. (2011). *Computational Fluid Dynamics for Engineers*. Cambridge University Press, Cambridge.

Andersson, M., Folestad, S., Gottfries, J., Johansson, M. O., Josefson, M., and Wahlund, K.-G. (2000). Quantitative analysis of film coating in a fluidized bed process by in-line NIR spectrometry and multivariate batch calibration. *Analytical Chemistry*, 72(9):2099–2108.

Antonyuk, S. (2006). *Deformations-und Bruchverhalten von kugelförmigen Granulaten bei Druck-und Stoßbeanspruchung*. PhD thesis, Germany: Otto von Guericke University of Magdeburg, Docupoint Verlag, Barleben.

Antonyuk, S., Heinrich, S., Deen, N., and Kuipers, H. (2009). Influence of liquid layers on energy absorption during particle impact. *Particuology*, 7(4):245–259.

Atkins, P. and de Paula, J. (2011). *Physical chemistry for the life sciences*. Oxford University Press, USA.

Bachmann, P., Bück, A., and Tsotsas, E. (2016). Investigation of the residence time behavior of particulate products and correlation for the Bodenstein number in horizontal fluidized beds. *Powder Technology*, 301:1067–1076.

Bachmann, P. and Tsotsas, E. (2015). Analysis of residence time distribution data in horizontal fluidized beds. *Procedia Engineering*, 102:790–798.

Baerns, M. (2013). *Technische Chemie*. Wiley-VCH, 2nd edition.

Bao, X., Du, W., and Xu, J. (2013). An overview on the recent advances in computational fluid dynamics simulation of spouted beds. *The Canadian Journal of Chemical Engineering*, 91(11):1822–1836.

Barimani, S. and Kleinebudde, P. (2018). Monitoring of tablet coating processes with colored coatings. *Talanta*, 178(Supplement C):686–697.

Basu, P. and Fraser, S. A. (1991). *Circulating fluidized bed boilers*. Springer.

Beetstra, R., van der Hoef, M. A., and Kuipers, J. A. M. (2007). Drag force of intermediate Reynolds number flow past mono- and bidisperse arrays of spheres. *AIChE Journal*, 53(2):489–501.

Bierwisch, C., Kraft, T., Riedel, H., and Moseler, M. (2009). Three-dimensional discrete element models for the granular statics and dynamics of powders in cavity filling. *Journal of the Mechanics and Physics of Solids*, 57(1):10–31.

Brandt, K., Wolff, M. F. H., Salikov, V., Heinrich, S., and Schneider, G. A. (2013). A novel method for a multi-level hierarchical composite with brick-and-mortar structure. *Scientific reports*, 3(2322):1–8.

Buck, B., Tang, Y., Heinrich, S., Deen, N. G., and Kuipers, J. A. M. (2017). Collision dynamics of wet solids: Rebound and rotation. *Powder Technology*, 316:218–224.

Cahyadi, C., Karande, A. D., Chan, L. W., and Heng, P. W. S. (2010). Comparative study of non-destructive methods to quantify thickness of tablet coatings. *International Journal of Pharmaceutics*, 398(1):39–49.

Chen, Z., Lim, C. J., and Grace, J. R. (2008). Hydrodynamics of slot-rectangular spouted beds: Effect of slot configuration on the local flow structure. *The Canadian Journal of Chemical Engineering*, 86(3):598–604.

Cohen, L. D. (1996). Auxiliary variables and two-step iterative algorithms in computer vision problems. *Journal of Mathematical Imaging and Vision*, 6(1):59–83.

Crüger, B., Heinrich, S., Antonyuk, S., Deen, N. G., and Kuipers, J. A. M. (2016a). Experimental study of oblique impact of particles on wet surfaces. *Chemical Engineering Research and Design*, 110:209–219.

Crüger, B., Salikov, V., Heinrich, S., Antonyuk, S., Sutkar, V. S., Deen, N. G., and Kuipers, J. (2016b). Coefficient of restitution for particles impacting on wet surfaces: An improved experimental approach. *Particuology*, 25:1–9.

Cundall, P. A. and Strack, O. D. L. (1979). A discrete numerical model for granular assemblies. *Géotechnique*, 29(1):47–65.

Danckwerts, P. V. (1953). Continuous flow systems: Distribution of residence times. *Chemical Engineering Science*, 2(1):1–13.

Di Felice, R. (1994). The voidage function for fluid-particle interaction systems. *International Journal of Multiphase Flow*, 20(1):153–159.

DIN German Institute for Standardization (2012). Representation of results of particle size analysis.

DIN German Institute for Standardization (2016a). Paints and varnishes - Determination of density - Part 1: Pycnometer method.

DIN German Institute for Standardization (2016b). Solid biofuels - Determination of particle density of pellets and briquettes.

Duarte, C. R., Olazar, M., Murata, V. V., and Barrozo, M. A. (2009). Numerical simulation and experimental study of fluid–particle flows in a spouted bed. *Powder Technology*, 188(3):195–205.

Eckmann, J.-P., Kamphorst, S. O., and Ruelle, D. (1987). Recurrence plots of dynamical systems. *EPL (Europhysics Letters)*, 4(9):973–977.

Eichner, E., Salikov, V., Bassen, P., Heinrich, S., and Schneider, G. A. (2017). Using dilute spouting for fabrication of highly filled metal-polymer composite materials. *Powder Technology*, 316:426–433.

Elsevier B.V. (2018). Scopus.

Epstein, N. and Grace, J. R., editors (2011). *Spouted and spout-fluid beds: Fundamentals and applications: Introduction.* Cambridge University Press, Cambridge and New York.

Ergun, S. and Orning, A. A. (1949). Fluid flow through randomly packed columns and fluidized beds. *Industrial & Engineering Chemistry*, 41(6):1179–1184.

Ernest, G. P. and Mathur, K. B. (1957). Method of contacting solid particles with fluids.

Fabritius, T., Alarousu, E., Prykäri, T., Hast, J., and Myllylä, R. (2006). Characterisation of optically cleared paper by optical coherence tomography. *Quantum Electronics*, 36(2):181–187.

Fercher, A. F. (2010). Optical coherence tomography – development, principles, applications. *Zeitschrift für Medizinische Physik*, 20(4):251–276.

Freitas, L. A. P., Dogan, O. M., Lim, C. J., Grace, J. R., and Bai, D. (2004). Identification of flow regimes in slot-rectangular spouted beds using pressure fluctuations. *The Canadian Journal of Chemical Engineering*, 82(1):60–73.

Fries, L., Antonyuk, S., Heinrich, S., Dopfer, D., and Palzer, S. (2013). Collision dynamics in fluidised bed granulators: A DEM-CFD study. *Chemical Engineering Science*, 86:108–123.

Fries, L., Antonyuk, S., Heinrich, S., and Palzer, S. (2011). DEM–CFD modeling of a fluidized bed spray granulator. *Chemical Engineering Science*, 66(11):2340–2355.

Geldart, D. (1973). Types of gas fluidization. *Powder Technology*, 7(5):285–292.

Gendre, C., Boiret, M., Genty, M., Chaminade, P., and Pean, J. M. (2011). Real-time predictions of drug release and end point detection of a coating operation by in-line near infrared measurements. *International Journal of Pharmaceutics*, 421(2):237–243.

Gibson, J. J. (1950). *The perception of the visual world.* The perception of the visual world. Houghton Mifflin, Oxford, England.

Gidaspow, D., Bezburuah, R., and Ding, J. (1991). Hydrodynamics of circulating fluidized beds: Kinetic theory approach. *Conference: 7th international conference on fluidization.*

Glatt Ingenieurtechnik GmbH (2006). Innovative technologies for granules and pellets. *Company brochure.*

Gnielinski, V. (1978). Equations for calculating the heat and mass transfer in packed beds of spheres at medium and large Peclet numbers. *Verfahrenstechnik*, 12(6):363–366.

Goldschmidt, M. J. V., Weijers, G. G. C., Boerefijn, R., and Kuipers, J. A. M. (2003). Discrete element modelling of fluidised bed spray granulation. *Powder Technology*, 138(1):39–45.

Goniva, C., Kloss, C., Deen, N. G., Kuipers, J. A., and Pirker, S. (2012). Influence of rolling friction on single spout fluidized bed simulation. *Particuology*, 10(5):582–591.

Gonzalez, R. C. and Woods, R. E. (2007). Digital Image Processing. Ed III.

Gryczka, O. (2009). *Untersuchung und Modellierung der Fluiddynamik in prismatischen Strahlschichtapparaten.* PhD thesis, Germany: Otto von Guericke University of Magdeburg.

Gryczka, O., Heinrich, S., Deen, N. G., van Sint Annaland, M., Kuipers, J., Jacob, M., and Mörl, L. (2009). Characterization and CFD-modeling of the hydrodynamics of a prismatic spouted bed apparatus. *Chemical Engineering Science*, 64(14):3352–3375.

Hagemeier, T., Bück, A., and Tsotsas, E. (2015a). Estimation of particle rotation in fluidized beds by means of PTV. *Procedia Engineering*, 102:841–849.

Hagemeier, T., Roloff, C., Bück, A., and Tsotsas, E. (2015b). Estimation of particle dynamics in 2-D fluidized beds using particle tracking velocimetry. *Particuology*, 22:39–51.

Hager, A., Kloss, C., Pirker, S., and Goniva, C. (2014). Parallel Resolved Open Source CFD-DEM: Method, Validation and Application. *The Journal of Computational Multiphase Flows*, 6(1):13–27.

Hazewinkel, M. (1995). *Encyclopaedia of mathematics*. Kluwer Academic Publishers, Dordrecht and Boston and Londres.

He, Y.-L., Lim, C. J., Grace, J. R., Zhu, J.-X., and Qzn, S.-Z. (1994). Measurements of voidage profiles in spouted beds. *The Canadian Journal of Chemical Engineering*, 72(2):229–234.

Heinrich, S., Dosta, M., and Antonyuk, S. (2015). Chapter two - Multiscale analysis of a coating process in a Wurster fluidized bed apparatus. *Advances in Chemical Engineering*, 46:83–135.

Hertz, H. (1882). Ueber die Berührung fester elastischer Körper. *Journal für die reine und angewandte Mathematik*, 92:156–171.

Hill, R. J., Koch, D. L., and Ladd, A. J. C. (2001). Moderate-Reynolds-number flows in ordered and random arrays of spheres. *Journal of Fluid Mechanics*, 448.

Horn, B. K. P. and Schunck, B. G. (1981). Determining optical flow. *Artificial intelligence*, 17(1-3):185–203.

Hull, R. L. and von Rosenberg, A. E. (1960). Radiochemical tracing of fluid catalyst flow. *Industrial and Engineering Chemistry (US) Formerly J. Ind. Eng. Chcm. Superseded by Chem. Technol.*, 52.

Idakiev, V. and Mörl, L. (2013). Study of residence time of disperse materials in continuously operating fluidized bed apparatus. *Journal of Chemical Technology and Metallurgy*, 48(5):451–456.

Itseez (2017). Open Source Computer Vision Library.

Jacob, M. (2009). ProCell technology: Modelling and application. *Powder Technology*, 189(2):332–342.

Jacob, M. (2010). *Experimentelle Untersuchung sowie Beiträge zur Modellierung von Prozessen in Wirbelschichtrinnen am Beispiel der Sprühgranulation*. Universitätsbibliothek, Magdeburg.

Jasak, H. (1996). *Error analysis and estimation for finite volume method with applications to fluid flow*. PhD thesis, University of London.

Kalman, R. E. and Bucy, R. S. (1961). New results in linear filtering and prediction theory. *Journal of Basic Engineering*, 83(1):95–108.

Kariuki, W. I., Freireich, B., Smith, R. M., Rhodes, M., and Hapgood, K. P. (2013). Distribution nucleation: Quantifying liquid distribution on the particle surface using the dimensionless particle coating number. *Chemical Engineering Science*, 92:134–145.

Kato, K., Sato, Y., Taneda, D., and Sugawa, T. (1985). Lateral solid mixing in the fluidized bed with multi-tubes internals. *Journal of chemical engineering of Japan*, 18(3):254–261.

Kieckhefen, P., Pietsch, S., Höfert, M., Schönherr, M., Heinrich, S., and Jäger, F. K. (2018). Influence of gas inflow modelling on CFD-DEM simulations of three-dimensional prismatic spouted beds. *Powder Technology*, 329:167–180.

Kloss, C., Goniva, C., Hager, A., Amberger, S., and Pirker, S. (2012). Models, algorithms and validation for opensource DEM and CFD-DEM. *Progress in Computational Fluid Dynamics, An International Journal*, 12(2/3):140–152.

Klukkert, M., Wu, J. X., Rantanen, J., Rehder, S., Carstensen, J. M., Rades, T., and Leopold, C. S. (2016). Rapid assessment of tablet film coating quality by multispectral UV imaging. *AAPS PharmSciTech*, 17(4):958–967.

Knop, K. and Kleinebudde, P. (2013). PAT-tools for process control in pharmaceutical film coating applications. *International Journal of Pharmaceutics*, 457(2):527–536.

Koch, D. L. and Hill, R. J. (2001). Inertial effects in suspension and porous-media flows. *Annual Review of Fluid Mechanics*, 33(1):619–647.

Koller, D. M., Hannesschläger, G., Leitner, M., and Khinast, J. G. (2011). Non-destructive analysis of tablet coatings with optical coherence tomography. *European Journal of Pharmaceutical Sciences*, 44(1-2):142–148.

Launder, B. E. and Sharma, B. I. (1974). Application of the energy-dissipation model of turbulence to the calculation of flow near a spinning disc. *Letters in heat and mass transfer*, 1(2):131–137.

Lee, M.-J., Seo, D.-Y., Lee, H.-E., Wang, I.-C., Kim, W.-S., Jeong, M.-Y., and Choi, G. J. (2011). In line NIR quantification of film thickness on pharmaceutical pellets during a fluid bed coating process. *International Journal of Pharmaceutics*, 403(1):66–72.

Levenspiel, O. (1999). *Chemical reaction engineering*. Wiley, Hoboken, NJ, 3rd edition.

Li, S., Xin, F., and Li, L. (2017). *Reaction Engineering*. Elsevier Science.

Li, Z., Kind, M., and Gruenewald, G. (2011). Modeling the growth kinetics of fluidized–bed spray granulation. *Chemical Engineering & Technology*, 34(7):1067–1075.

Lichtenegger, T., Peters, E., Kuipers, J., and Pirker, S. (2017). A recurrence CFD study of heat transfer in a fluidized bed. *Chemical Engineering Science*, 172:310–322.

Lichtenegger, T. and Pirker, S. (2016). Recurrence CFD – A novel approach to simulate multiphase flows with strongly separated time scales. *Chemical Engineering Science*, 153:394–410.

Link, J. M. (2006). *PhD thesis: Development and validation of a discrete particle model of a spout-fluid bed granulator*. PhD thesis, University of Twente, Enschede.

Link, J. M., Godlieb, W., Deen, N. G., and Kuipers, J. (2007). Discrete element study of granulation in a spout-fluidized bed. *Chemical Engineering Science*, 62(1-2):195–207.

Liu, G.-Q., Li, S.-Q., Zhao, X.-L., and Yao, Q. (2008). Experimental studies of particle flow dynamics in a two-dimensional spouted bed. *Chemical Engineering Science*, 63(4):1131–1141.

Liu, M., Wen, Y., Liu, R., Liu, B., and Shao, Y. (2015). Investigation of fluidization behavior of high density particle in spouted bed using CFD–DEM coupling method. *Powder Technology*, 280:72–82.

Lu, L., Yoo, K., and Benyahia, S. (2016). Coarse-grained-particle method for simulation of liquid–solids reacting flows. *Industrial & Engineering Chemistry Research*, 55(39):10477–10491.

Lundberg, J. and Halvorsen, B. M. (2008). A review of some exsisting drag models describing the interaction between phases in a bubbling fluidized bed. *Proc. Scand. Conf. Simulation and Modeling, Oslo University College, Oslo, Norway*, 2008(49):7–8.

Luo, B., Lim, C. J., Freitas, L. A. P., and Grace, J. R. (2004). Flow characteristics in slot-rectangular spouted beds with draft plates. *The Canadian Journal of Chemical Engineering*, 82(1):83–88.

MacMullin, R. B. and Weber, M. (1935). The theory of short-circuiting in continuous-flow mixing vessels in series and the kinetics of chemical reactions in such systems. *Trans. Am. Inst. Chem. Eng*, 31(2):409–458.

Markl, D., Hannesschläger, G., Sacher, S., Leitner, M., Buchsbaum, A., Pescod, R., Baele, T., and Khinast, J. G. (2015a). In-line monitoring of a pharmaceutical pan coating process by optical coherence tomography. *Journal of Pharmaceutical Sciences*, 104(8):2531–2540.

Markl, D., Hannesschläger, G., Sacher, S., Leitner, M., and Khinast, J. G. (2014). Optical coherence tomography as a novel tool for in-line monitoring of a pharmaceutical film-coating process. *European Journal of Pharmaceutical Sciences*, 55:58–67.

Markl, D., Zettl, M., Hannesschläger, G., Sacher, S., Leitner, M., Buchsbaum, A., and Khinast, J. G. (2015b). Calibration-free in-line monitoring of pellet coating processes via optical coherence tomography. *Chemical Engineering Science*, 125:200–208.

Mathur, K. B. and Epstein, N. (1974). *Spouted beds*. Academic press, New York.

Mathur, K. B. and Gishler, P. E. (1955). A technique for contacting gases with coarse solid particles. *AIChE Journal*, 1(2):157–164.

May, R. K., Evans, M. J., Zhong, S., Warr, I., Gladden, L. F., Shen, Y., and Zeitler, J. A. (2011). Terahertz in-line sensor for direct coating thickness measurement of individual tablets during film coating in real-time. *Journal of Pharmaceutical Sciences*, 100(4):1535–1544.

Mitev, D. T. (1979). Theoretische und experimentelle Untersuchung der Hydrodynamik, des Wärme-und Stoffüberganges in Strahlschichtapparaten.(russ.). *Habilitation, LTI Leningrad.*

Mörl, L., Heinrich, S., and Peglow, M. (2007). Chapter 2 Fluidized bed spray granulation. In A.D. Salman, M.J. Hounslow, and J.P.K. Seville, editors, *Granulation*, volume 11 of *Handbook of Powder Technology*, pages 21–188. Elsevier Science B.V.

Mörl, L., Krüger, G., Heinrich, S., Ihlow, M., and Jordanova, E. (2001). Steuerbare Gasanströmeinrichtung für Strahlschichtapparate. *Deutsche Patentanmeldung*, 10004939.

Nilsson, L. and Wimmerstedt, R. (1988). Residence time distribution and particle dispersion in a longitudinal-flow fluidized bed. *Chemical Engineering Science*, 43(5):1153–1160.

Olazar, M., San Jose, M. J., Aguayo, A. T., Arandes, J. M., and Bilbao, J. (1992). Stable operation conditions for gas-solid contact regimes in conical spouted beds. *Industrial & Engineering Chemistry Research*, 31(7):1784–1792.

Olazar, M., San José, M. J., Alvarez, S., Morales, A., and Bilbao, J. (1998). Measurement of particle velocities in conical spouted beds using an optical fiber probe. *Industrial & Engineering Chemistry Research*, 37(11):4520–4527.

Ozarkar, S. S., Yan, X., Wang, S., Milioli, C. C., Milioli, F. E., and Sundaresan, S. (2015). Validation of filtered two-fluid models for gas–particle flows against experimental data from bubbling fluidized bed. *Powder Technology*, 284:159–169.

Ozel, A., Kolehmainen, J., Radl, S., and Sundaresan, S. (2016). Fluid and particle coarsening of drag force for discrete-parcel approach. *Chemical Engineering Science*, 155:258–267.

Pedersen, S. J. K. (2007). Circular hough transform. *Aalborg University, Vision, Graphics, and Interactive Systems*, 123:1–6.

Pietsch, S., Heinrich, S., Karpinski, K., Müller, M., Schönherr, M., and Kleine Jäger, F. (2017). CFD-DEM modeling of a three-dimensional prismatic spouted bed. *Powder Technology*, 316:245–255.

Pietsch, S., Kieckhefen, P., Heinrich, S., Müller, M., Schönherr, M., and Jäger, F. K. (2018). CFD-DEM modelling of circulation frequencies and residence times in a prismatic spouted bed. *Chemical Engineering Research and Design*, 132:1105–1116.

Piskova, E. and Mörl, L. (2008). Characterization of spouted bed regimes using pressure fluctuation signals. *Chemical Engineering Science*, 63(9):2307–2316.

Radl, S., Radeke, C., Khinast, J. G., and Sundaresan, S. (2011). Parcel-based approach for the simulation of gas-particle flows. In *8th International Conference on CFD in Oil & Gas, Metallurgical and Process Industries, Trondheim*.

Retsch Technology (2018). CamSizer - Dynamische Bildanalyse zur Bestimmung von Partikelgröße und Partikelform. *Company brochure*, 2018:1–20.

Richardson, J. F. and Zaki, W. N. (1997). Sedimentation and fluidisation: Part I. *Chemical Engineering Research and Design*, 75:S82–S100.

Risken, H. (1996). *The Fokker-Planck equation: Methods of solution and applications*, volume 18 of *Springer Series in Synergetics*. Springer Berlin Heidelberg, Berlin, Heidelberg, 2nd edition.

Rocha, S. C. S., Taranto, O. P., and Ayub, G. E. (1995). Aerodynamics and heat transfer during coating of tablets in two-dimensional spouted bed. *The Canadian Journal of Chemical Engineering*, 73(3):308–312.

Romero-Torres, S., Pérez-Ramos, J. D., Morris, K. R., and Grant, E. R. (2006). Raman spectroscopy for tablet coating thickness quantification and coating characterization in the presence of strong fluorescent interference. *Journal of Pharmaceutical and Biomedical Analysis*, 41(3):811–819.

Rong, L.-W., Zhan, J.-M., and Rong, L.-W. (2010). Improved DEM-CFD model and validation: A conical-base spouted bed simulation study. *Journal of Hydrodynamics, Ser. B*, 22(3):351–359.

Ruhnau, P. (2006). *Variational fluid motion estimation with physical priors*. PhD thesis, Universität Mannheim.

Ruhnau, P., Guetter, C., Putze, T., and Schnörr, C. (2005). A variational approach for particle tracking velocimetry. *Measurement Science and Technology*, 16(7):1449.

Salami, E. (1968). *Einfluss verschiedener Parameter auf die Verweilzeitverteilung in einem Strömungsrohr*. PhD thesis, ETH Zurich.

Salikov, V. (2017). *Charakterisierung der Fluiddynamik und Diskrete-Elemente-Modellierung eines neuartigen Strahlschichtapparates*, volume 11 of *SPE-Schriftenreihe*. Cuvillier Verlag, Göttingen.

Salikov, V., Antonyuk, S., and Heinrich, S. (2012). Using DPM on the Way to Tailored Prismatic Spouted Beds. *Chemie Ingenieur Technik*, 84(3):388–394.

Salikov, V., Antonyuk, S., Heinrich, S., Sutkar, V. S., Deen, N. G., and Kuipers, J. (2015a). Characterization and CFD-DEM modelling of a prismatic spouted bed. *Powder Technology*, 270:622–636.

Salikov, V., Heinrich, S., Antonyuk, S., Sutkar, V. S., Deen, N. G., and Kuipers, J. (2015b). Investigations on the spouting stability in a prismatic spouted bed and apparatus optimization. *Advanced Powder Technology*, 26(3):718–733.

Satija, S. and Zucker, I. L. (1986). Hydrodynamics of vibro-fluidized beds. *Drying Technology*, 4(1):19–43.

Schulze, D. (2008). *Powders and bulk solids: Behavior, characterization, storage and flow*. Springer, Berlin and New York.

Serrels, K. A., Renner, M. K., and Reid, D. T. (2010). Optical coherence tomography for non-destructive investigation of silicon integrated-circuits. *Microelectronic Engineering*, 87(9):1785–1791.

Shi, Y.-F. and Fan, L. T. (1985). Lateral mixing of solids in gas—solid fluidized beds with continuous flow of solids. *Powder Technology*, 41(1):23–28.

Shih, T.-H., Liou, W. W., Shabbir, A., Yang, Z., and Zhu, J. (1995). A new k-epsilon eddy viscosity model for high reynolds number turbulent flows. *Computers & Fluids*, 24(3):227–238.

Sinclair, J. L. and Jackson, R. (1989). Gas-particle flow in a vertical pipe with particle-particle interactions. *AIChE Journal*, 35(9):1473–1486.

Stifter, D. (2007). Beyond biomedicine: A review of alternative applications and developments for optical coherence tomography. *Applied Physics B*, 88(3):337–357.

Stifter, D., Wiesauer, K., Wurm, M., Schlotthauer, E., Kastner, J., Pircher, M., Götzinger, E., and Hitzenberger, C. K. (2008). Investigation of polymer and polymer/-fibre composite materials with optical coherence tomography. *Measurement Science and Technology*, 19(7):074011.

Stull, D. R. (1947). Vapor pressure of pure substances. organic and inorganic compounds. *Industrial & Engineering Chemistry*, 39(4):517–540.

Sutkar, V. S., Deen, N. G., Patil, A. V., Salikov, V., Antonyuk, S., Heinrich, S., and Kuipers, J. (2016). CFD–DEM model for coupled heat and mass transfer in a spout fluidized bed with liquid injection. *Chemical Engineering Journal*, 288:185–197.

Toole, G. and Toole, S. (2008). *Essential AS biology for OCR*. Nelson Thornes, Cheltenham, 6th edition.

van Buijtenen, M. S., van Dijk, W.-J., Deen, N. G., Kuipers, J. A., Leadbeater, T., and Parker, D. J. (2011). Numerical and experimental study on multiple-spout fluidized beds. *Chemical Engineering Science*, 66(11):2368–2376.

van den Bleek, C. M. and Schouten, J. C. (1993). Deterministic chaos: A new tool in fluidized bed design and operation. *The Chemical Engineering Journal and the Biochemical Engineering Journal*, 53(1):75–87.

van Kampen, A., Hitzmann, B., and Kohlus, R. (2015). Assessment of coating quality by use of dissolution kinetics. *Powder Technology*, 286:325–331.

Versteeg, H. K. and Malalasekera, W. (2007). *An introduction to computational fluid dynamics: The finite volume method*. Pearson Education Ltd, Harlow, England and New York, 2nd ed. edition.

Welch, G. and Bishop, G. (2006). An introduction to the Kalman filter. *Proc. Siggraph Course*, 8.

Weller, H. G., Tabor, G., Jasak, H., and Fureby, C. (1998). A tensorial approach to computational continuum mechanics using object-oriented techniques. *Computers in physics*, 12(6):620–631.

Wen, C. Y. and Yu, Y. H. (1966). Mechanics of fluidization. *The Chemical Engineering Progress Symposium Series*, 162(162):100–111.

Werther, J. (1999). Measurement techniques in fluidized beds. *Powder Technology*, 102(1):15–36.

Wojtkowski, M. (2010). High-speed optical coherence tomography: Basics and applications. *Applied optics*, 49(16):D30–D61.

Wolff, M., Salikov, V., Antonyuk, S., Heinrich, S., and Schneider, G. A. (2014). Novel, highly-filled ceramic–polymer composites synthesized by a spouted bed spray granulation process. *Composites Science and Technology*, 90:154–159.

Yang, S., Luo, K., Fang, M., and Fan, J. (2014). CFD-DEM simulation of the spout-annulus interaction in a 3D spouted bed with a conical base. *The Canadian Journal of Chemical Engineering*, 92(6):1130–1138.

Yoo, J.-C. and Han, T. H. (2009). Fast normalized cross-correlation. *Circuits, Systems and Signal Processing*, 28(6):819.

Curriculum vitae

Personal information

Name	Swantje Pietsch
Born	29.03.1990 in Bremerhaven

Education

1996 - 2000	Alfred-Delp-Schule Bremerhaven
2000 - 2006	Edith-Stein-Schule Bremerhaven
2006 - 2009	Lloyd Gymnasium Bremerhaven
2009	Abitur

Academic history

10/2009 - 09/2012	Study of Bioprocess Engineering (B.Sc.), Hamburg University of Technology, grade 1.4
10/2012 - 11/2014	Study of Bioprocess Engineering (M.Sc.), Hamburg University of Technology, grade 1.4
Since 01/2015	Scientific researcher and PhD student at the Institute of Solids Process Engineering and Particle Technology, Hamburg University of Technology. Supervisor: Prof. Dr.-Ing. habil. Dr. h.c. Stefan Heinrich

Internships

04/2014 - 09/2014	BASF SE, Düsseldorf